James Alder and the Magic

James's disappearance

Once upon a time, this story began in a small town in England, it was about a boy who was very clever and a good student throughout the school. Many envied him because of this, since he was the first in everything, won prizes, went to competitions and won almost everything he could. His parents were very proud of their son, who was of course already a high school student. James family was not very rich, they just about got by, but they were not sad because they knew that one day their fate would change for the better. One fine autumn morning, when James was getting ready for school, he was very excited because he could meet the girl he was very much in love with, but she was someone else's girlfriend. He had two good friends, one called Oliver and the other Evelin.

"James, dark brown hair and green eyes."

- Evelin has blonde hair and brown eyes.

- Oliver has red hair and blue eyes.

Evelin was secretly in love with James, she didn't really show her feelings to anyone, and she didn't tell anyone about it. Oliver is crazy but funny at the same time.

The three of them were almost always together. The road to school led through a forest, which was a ten minute walk, James and his best friends always went to and from school together.

1

They were on their way home from school when they were attacked by the school's bullies who entered the school on bikes.

Kain: Hello, bed bedwetter's, didn't you get lost in the forest? And they had a good laugh at them, as there was size of them against the three. They dropped their bikes and approached them, threatening to beat them up just for fun. You crapped yourself?!: - He looked at her frighteningly.

Bob: - Oh, mommy's little son, he's shitting eggs in his pants!: - He laughed at him.

Kain: You think you can win anything you want, you little bastard! Cristine is my girlfriend, don't think that she'll end up with someone as unfortunate as you, you're a nobody to her, she doesn't even notice that you go to school there at all, you little slob!:- He growled at her angrily. all six had a good laugh at them. James didn't even regain consciousness when Kain pushed him with a powerful movement and he fell backwards in the grass, which was full of tiny little mushrooms. As soon as he fell between them, two small mushrooms suddenly crawled into his ears, which James did not even realize. These mushrooms have special powers, they weren't there by chance, they were just waiting for James to fall into the grass so they could crawl into his ear. Two of James' good friends started yelling at the six bullies and threatened them to tell the teachers everything about what happened. The six pink boys continued to ride with mocking laughter, looked behind them a few more times and had a good laugh at them. Oliver approached his good friend and helped him up from the ground, dusted off the dirt and asked him.

Oliver: - Are you okay my friend? Did you hurt yourself?: - He asked in despair.

Evelin: - Is everything okay? He asked her in horror.

James: -Yes, everything is fine, let's go home and forget about all this, and see you at school tomorrow. But thank you guys for helping out, but I think we didn't go far against them.: - He said with a groan. With that, they parted ways, and everyone went home safely. James arrived home and immediately rushed to the bathroom so that his parents would not notice his dirty clothes and bruises.

Kimberly: - Baby, dinner!!!! He woke up.

James: - I'll go right away!: - He answered. He went into his room and changed his clothes, but all the while his mind was on how he could avenge this. He hurried down to the dining room and took a seat at the table, he had a slightly sad and worried face as if he wasn't there. While they were having dinner, his mother immediately noticed that something was wrong with James.

Kimberly: "Son, is something wrong?" – She asked curiously.

James: - No mom, there's nothing wrong, I was just thinking about my homework that was given at school today, thank you for the dinner. with that he went up to his room. He laid down on the bed and kept thinking about what he should do to prevent this from happening again. He did his homework in the middle of a lot of thinking, but as time passed, he felt more and more strange, he was tired, depressed, dizzy, he thought it better to go to bed and see if it would go away by morning. So the morning came and this time his mother woke him up because she didn't hear the alarm clock ringing.

Kimberly: - Good morning my son, get up you have to go to school soon!: - She woke him up.

James: "Okay, I'm getting up!" He said sleepily. As soon as his mother left the room, a strange feeling came over him, as if he was physically stronger than ever before, full of energy and self-confidence. So he went down to breakfast and his parents noticed his behaviour, but they didn't say anything to James because they didn't know how it would end. He said goodbye to his parents, left school and met his friends at the usual place on the road leading to the forest by a big, huge tree, where they always waited for each other.

Oliver: - Hello guys, how was James at home yesterday?: - he asked inquisitively.

James: - You won't believe what happened to me, I've never felt this before, yesterday when I went home... and told his friends. They arrive at school, and they are already laughing at them from afar, as Kain has already informed everyone about yesterday's incident, but of course he didn't present it as it actually happened, but he wanted to make it look better in the eyes of the others and, of course, in the eyes of Cristine. Cristine gave James a kind look, which told James a lot, she didn't even seem so happy, the girl only seemed to hide the reality, or so James's thought. As soon as he noticed this, James suddenly couldn't place this feeling, he still felt strange, but he didn't understand why. Everyone went to class, they wrote the paper in English, which plays an important role for the children's future. During the break, they met Kain again in the hallway, he bumped into James with his shoulder, and he fell towards the lockers.

Kain: - What are you jumping about, you don't see me coming, get out of my way, otherwise I'll trample you like a cockroach: - He instructed James with a laugh. At this reaction, James seemed to have changed, he was not at all afraid of him like before, he stood in front of him, looked deeply into him eyes and told him.

James: - Then pay close attention, you clever one, if you touch me even with a finger one more time, you will regret it very much: - He said seriously. The others standing behind Kain burst into loud laughter, including Kain of course.

Kain: - What's up my little brother, what a big man you've suddenly become, you didn't train all night, on the ant-shot muscle of yours, just to show your strength today, you "SUPERMAN": - He said sarcastically! At this, the little mushrooms started their powers in James' ears and started whispering these lines:

- Close your eyes!

- See, your strength will save you,

- If your heart is beating

- You won't be in trouble anymore.

During this, James completely changed (internally), he looked deeply into Kain's eyes and just beamed the anger and the desire for revenge from it. Kain soon noticed this and suddenly couldn't put it down, he had never seen James like this before. They stood there facing each other and the air around them almost froze, you could even hear the buzzing of the fly, everyone who was there and surrounded them suddenly became quiet, curiously waiting to see what the outcome of this would be. During this time, the mushrooms kept whispering their little verses in James's ear, thereby giving him a magic power that helped James. James felt strange, he felt stronger and unstoppable, which was actually true. Kain suddenly raised his fist to hit James, but at that moment James hit Kain with such force that he fell to the onlookers. As he sprawled on the ground, everyone looked at James in surprise, as no one expected this. Someone spoke from the background.

Student: - It was nice James! Give it to him!: - He encouraged him with a smile. And with that, everyone started cheering for James and they didn't even bother with Kain. As soon as Kain regained his senses, he stood up from the ground, and Kain punched James so hard that he fell into the closet and with that momentum the door closed on him. The teachers rushed there to put an end to the trouble.

Teacher: - What is going on here? Everyone disperse! Don't you have lessons?: - He looked at the children. The children were dispersed, everyone went about their business, but somehow, they all forgot about James. As he lay face down in the closet, the wall opened, on the other side, a huge winding staircase led down in the dark, rough rock walls surrounded the stairs, little fireflies were flying back and forth as if they were just waiting for the James to come down that way. on the stairs. As soon as James regained consciousness, he opened his eyes and noticed that the wall had disappeared into the closet and was not there. He was scared, he didn't know how he got there, what this place actually was. A strange voice began to lure him inside.

Strange voice: - Come with courage! I'm waiting for you down here! Feel free to come! James noticed this strange sound and started down the stairs. He started following the sound, the strange rock walls that were surrounding him were quite terrifying, mysterious pairs of eyes peered at him from the cracks, but the small fireflies showed the way to James. In the second bend of steps, a strange being stood in James' way.

Strange being: - Where are you in such a hurry? What wind brought you here?: - He asked in a deep spiritual voice. James was a little scared by the strange being, but the strength he felt inside him did not allow him to back down.

James: - What kind of being are you? What place am I in? Where does this staircase lead?: - He kept asking.

Strange monk: - You ask too many questions, stranger, I could ask you the same thing! He moved closer and closer to James. James started to back away from the scary looking creature, but he plucked up the courage to face him. He climbed into the monster's shell and spoke.

James: - Look here! I don't know what this place is, and I don't know how I got here, but I know that for some reason I have to go down these stairs now and I'll find the answer I'm looking for, so don't stand in my way if you want good!: - He growled. at him maturely. At this, the strange being suddenly transformed into an angelic girl and said like this.

Angelic girl: - Welcome, James, on the path of the powers, you passed the first test that was imposed on you, go ahead and make your way, there are many more surprises waiting for you on this path, and with that she disappeared. James didn't even realize what was happening to him, he thought it was just a dream. But he soon realized that he was wrong, as soon as he continued down the stairs in front of him the stairs disappeared, only the great emptiness gaped in front of him, as soon as he turned to go back, the stairs behind him disappeared as well. It's a strange mystery, he thought to himself, what exactly is this supposed to be, he didn't really understand the meaning of it, he only knew that his heart was pounding in his throat from fear, his feet were rooted to the ground, and he couldn't move. As he stood there wondering how to proceed while trembling with fear, he looked down again to see if he had misjudged the disappearance of the steps, but he was wrong, the steps really weren't there. As soon as he was looking around, he looked down for some reason and only saw that the steps had completely disappeared in front of his feet. As soon as he realized this, he was almost on the verge of fainting when monsters with the body of a snake and the head of a man crawled out of the cracks in the wall and came closer and closer to James.

They kept whispering: - Where to next! There is no way out, give up, you will be nothing but a loser. His legs were shaking so much from fear that the power that the mushrooms radiated to him was spread back to real life, which means that he feels as much power in himself as ever. He immediately grabbed his backpack and began to attack these disgusting creatures. At one point he looked into the eyes of one of the abominations and spoke.

James: - Well listen, you disgusting monster, know that I'm not afraid of you at all, come here if you dare! James's eyes glowed with rage as soon as the monster approached him, James caught him in one move and twisted his neck. As soon as he finishes with the penultimate monster, the last one immediately transformed into a beautiful angelic girl whom he had already met before.

Angelic girl: - Welcome, James, you have passed the second test of courage on the path of strength, there is only one test left and you will know the next step.: - She said to James. James wanted to ask her something, but the angelic girl disappeared. The stairs became visible again, so now he continued his way down more calmly. The little fireflies gave him the light and followed him down the stairs in the dark. He reached a part where the steps were missing, he stopped to think about how to proceed. He sat down on the step and looked with his foot to see if the next step was there, but there was nothing. He sat on the steps in despair and thinking about how to go on now, or rather turn back? But if you've come this far, he should go further, since you were driven by curiosity? He became aware of strange noises, he looked back but did not see anything, nor could he really see because it was dark, only the fireflies lit up for him. He took one of the books out of his bag and dropped it to find out how deep it was underneath. He slowly counted to 30 and only then did he hear that the book hit the ground, which terrified him because the next step was far enough away from him that he would not have been able to jump over to it. As soon as he sat there on the steps, he heard that strange noise again and got closer and closer to him. He got up from the stairs and walked back to see what the strange noise was. He walked back towards it very carefully and noticed a shadow, at that moment he stopped and began to observe. He also heard shuffling and footsteps, but he didn't notice anything, even though he was paying close attention. As soon as something touched his shoulder, James immediately turned to see what it was, but saw nothing. James became more and more terrified; his palms began to sweat from fear.

James: - Who's there? Show yourself? Why are you hiding, you're not afraid of me?: - He asked in a trembling voice.

James: - Come forward if you dare?: - He asked more and more bravely now. A cold air touched his face with such force that it blew his hair aside. James turned around to see what it was but saw only a dark shadow. He didn't have to stand there for long because that dark shadow attacked again, and of course from different directions, so that James couldn't see him every time, James just rolled after him to catch him, but of course he didn't succeed.

James: - That's all you know? Don't you dare stand in front of my eyes? Show yourself, or maybe you're such a coward?: - He asked more and more bravely.

James: - Come stand in front of me and tell me what you want from me?: - He asked in a commanding manner. The shadow rubbed against James more and more, but James couldn't catch it because it's impossible to catch a shadow. As soon as he tried to catch the shadow, he only noticed that the light of the fireflies went out and everything became dark, which made James's job much more difficult. Then James gathered all his courage and closed his eyes, stood still and didn't move, he started paying attention to the noises, concentrating with all his might. In the middle of the great silence, he heard the approach of the shadow, but he didn't move, he waited patiently until he got close enough to it. When the shadow had fully reached James, it stopped in front of him, then James opened his eyes and looked into the shadow's eyes, the shadow did not expect this, and because James looked into the shadow's eyes, the shadow was destroyed. James passed the third test successfully, so that beautiful angelic girl appeared to him again.

Angelic girl: - James! You successfully passed the third test, I can already see that you are the chosen one to save, so the tests are over here, you can continue on your way. With that, the angelic girl disappeared, the fireflies once again shed their light on James and the steps returned to their place. James sighed, picked up his bag and continued his way down the stairs, which was a lot of going down. In the end, he made it down successfully, but he found himself in a place where he again had to think about his next step.

Teacher: - You! Just come here! Tell me, what the hell is going on here? Why were there so many students here? Who was Kain fighting with?: - He suddenly asked a lot of questions.

Student: - Please, sir! All I saw was that the Kain hit James!: - He replied scared.

Teacher: So far so good, but where is James? Has anyone seen James?:- Ask this while shouting. Everyone looked at each other and couldn't answer him because no one saw where he had gone.

Teacher: - Kain! You will appear in the principal's office after class! Everyone go back to their classes, there's nothing to see here!: - He glared at them angrily.

Bob: - Kain, what are you going to do now? You hit James and now he's gone!: - He asked worriedly.

Kain: I'll think of something, don't worry! Let's go to class now!: - He replied calmly.

Cristine: Cain! I don't know what this was good for, but this is not the way to solve it! If something goes wrong with James, you will be solely responsible for it, you know that, right? There are plenty of witnesses to the fact that you hit him, and the cameras recorded the incident, you won't be able to explain it. You have to tell the truth, otherwise you'll get into even more trouble if you lie!: - He warned with good advice.

Cain: - Fuck! Shit! To hell with this whole thing! It was all because I'm jealous of James! Is that okay now?: - He looked at her nervously.

Cristine: - Cain!! When did I ever give you reason to be jealous? You can't beat everyone who lays eyes on me, you know that too! James means nothing to me! If he did, I wouldn't be with you but with him, I think that's clear!: - He replied seriously.

Kain: - Cristina! Please forgive me for being so blinded by your beauty, but unfortunately, it's already happened, and I can't undo it. I don't know how I'm going to get out of this.: - He replied in despair.

Cristine: - It will be best if you tell the truth because everyone will appreciate it, trust me.: - She reassured her. They went back to class, but everyone was staring at Kain and talking behind his back. Kain felt pretty bad for him now, but it was too late. The lesson ended, everyone tried to go home, but Kain had to stay after the lesson because he had to answer for his actions.

Mrs. Hildred: - Hello Kain! Take a seat, please! Here with me is Mr. Miller who was there at the end of the incident and of course your parents too. Well, Kain, I would like you to tell me what happened between you and James?: - He asked curiously. Everyone in the room, including his parents, watched Kain with suspicious eyes, wondering what he would answer.

Kain: - First of all, I want to apologize for what I did. It happened out of sudden excitement, I confess that there is no excuse for what I did because it had already happened, but I did it all out of jealousy, that's the truth.: - He confessed honestly.

Mrs. Hildred: - I appreciate your honesty Kain, the only problem is that James disappeared in the middle of the fight, and no one knows where he went, the parents have already called here but I didn't tell them what happened here because first we wanted to clarify this with you. If James doesn't appear, you're unfortunately in big trouble, I hope you're aware of that! Well, if that's all that happened, then everyone can go and wait for tomorrow, maybe he just ran off somewhere where he wants to be alone, that will be revealed tomorrow. Thank you for coming here, and let this be a lesson for you Kain!: - He finished what he had to say.

Kain's father: Thank you, Headmistress! Of course, we will also talk to Kai at home, and we are sorry that he did such a thing. See you later.: - He expressed his apology. Kain and his parents left the principal's office.

Mr. Miller: - Mrs. Mildred! Have James' parents really called yet?: - He asked in surprise.

Mrs. Mildred: - Of course they didn't call, I only said this so that Kain would learn a lesson, since this is not the first time that the students have complained against him.

Mr. Miller: I see, but what about James? Shouldn't you call his parents?: - He asked.

Mrs. Hildred: - We don't have to call them yet, since he's sixteen years old, twenty-four hours haven't passed yet, it could also be that she's hanging out with her friends somewhere and will go home later, let's give the case time.: - Se answered calmly.

Mr. Miller: - It's okay! If something happens and you need help, you know my phone number, feel free to call me anytime! See you later, Mrs. Hildred!: - Goodbye.

Oliver's blue stone….

Oliver is paying attention to maths class, but Evelin is paying less attention, his mind is constantly wondering where James might be. That's why he sent a message to Oliver with the caption: - how can you sit on your ass so calmly when we don't know anything about James, we have to do something...!!!! He brought it to his friend and he read it, signalling to him that there would be a short break and then they would talk. Kain also noticed these movements and reacted immediately.

Kain: - Teacher, Oliver is sending letters with his girlfriend in class! - He said mockingly. Of course, the teacher immediately questioned Oliver.

Teacher: - Is what Kain claims true? If it's true, please send me the little piece of paper!: - He said sternly. Oliver glanced at Evelin just when the bell rang, so he missed whether he had to give the note. Everyone quickly ran out of the class, Oliver and Evelin discussed in a small corner that they had to do something for James, because something is not right here, he doesn't normally just disappear. Oliver: - Lets think where we last saw James before we went to class, he and Kain were fighting around there, and if I remember correctly they was at the lockers, then he disappeared, but where did he go?: - He asked curiously.

Evelin: - Listen! Let's go home and collect some things and come back here later when no one is here, then we can search more easily.: - She said firmly.

Oliver: - It's okay, maybe you're right, there's just a little problem!: - He said thoughtfully.

Evelin: What? Come to think of it, James' parents will be worried, and they will question our parents, and then what we will say about him, because we don't know either! That's why we have to hurry!: - She said worriedly.

Oliver: - Then let's hurry to see if we can find out something, we'll meet in the back garden of the school at nine in the evening.: - He said firmly.

Evelin: - Okay, evening then!: - She said goodbye to Oliver. When he got home, Oliver ate quickly, while he put away some of his friend's food, since he disappeared, he must have been hungry since then, he thought to himself. He went upstairs to his room and took out his large wooden chest in his closet and took out the flash-light, blanket, rope, matches, as he was looking in the chest something shone very brightly, so it stood out, he reached there and a sea blue stone bloomed from the chest, he carefully took out the stone and he started turning it around to look, even though he examined it, he didn't remember that he had this kind of stone. Of course, he didn't remember it, since it was a magical stone, it was hidden by the little magical mushrooms. He liked it so much that he took it with him, put it in his pocket, he thought it would be in a good place. At this time, Evelin didn't hesitate either, she ate quickly, of course, as a precaution, she also put some food away for James, she also prepared her survivor's pack and headed to the meeting place.

Evelin: - Hello Oliver!: - She said excitedly.

Oliver: - Yo, did you pack everything?: - He asked excitedly.

Evelin: - Well, of course, I even packed food for James because he's been hungry since then!: - He replied.

Oliver: - That's good, because I also packed it for him! Well, it seems we thought of the same thing.: - He said with a smile.
Evelin: - Well, if everything is done, then we should sneak into school now!: - She said enthusiastically. Oliver: - Well, let's go through the gym, no one will notice us there.: - He said cautiously. Well, they set off cautiously but sneaked so that no one would notice them, but with a little difficulty they made it into the gymnasium. They carefully got out of the room and continued through the hallway, heading to where they had last seen James, at those certain cabinets. Since the cleaner was just cleaning the hallway, it was a little more difficult to get there on time, as they

would have liked. The trouble seems to be quieting down, but as they got closer to the cabinets, a strange sound was heard in their vicinity. They stopped and began to listen to where the sound was coming from.

Evelin: - Listen, I think this sound is coming from your pants pocket, what's in your pocket?:- She wondered.

Oliver: - Really, you're right! Imagine I found this in my chest while I was looking for the equipment, I don't know how it got there but I put it away, I thought it would be good for something, and I see that it started to light up for some reason, maybe it wants to show something, let's continue along the cabinets and it will become clear what it wants:- He said curiously. As soon as they were about to leave, someone grabbed Oliver's shoulder. Oliver was so scared that he almost fainted. He turned and it was the cleaner.

Cleaner: - What were you doing here?: - He asked them. Oliver watched the cleaner with a horrified face and answered him!

Oliver: - You know, we forgot something in my closet here, and we came to get it now because it is important for tomorrow's paper.: - He answered in horror. The cleaner looked at the two students, then looked deeply into Oliver's eyes, as if he wanted to draw the truth out of them. He let go of the boy's shoulders and spoke like this. Cleaner: - Hurry up, because I'm about to finish cleaning and I have to close the school. He said them firmly.

Oliver: - OK, we will hurry and we'll be gone!: - He replied a bit relieved. Of course, the cleaner knew why they were there, he just pretended to let them go. They started slowly and waited for the cleaner to disappear so that they could safely continue what they had started. The small blue stone was getting brighter and brighter as they approached the cupboard where James had fallen. As soon as they got there, the cupboard popped open, as if it knew that they were going there for a reason. As soon as the cupboard popped open, the two good friends were scared!

Oliver: - What was that?: - He asked in horror. They started to look at the cupboard to see what caused it to pop out suddenly, since they didn't even touch it, and then they realized that the small blue stone was so brightly lit that they took it for the fact that they had arrived at their destination. Oliver opened the door a little shyly, looked in and saw nothing but books and pamphlets scattered everywhere, he didn't notice anything out of the ordinary. In the meantime, Evelin was watching the cleaner to come back, but in the meantime, she heard some noise and wanted to warn Oliver. She accidentally pushed Oliver and he also fell through the door, but this all happened without Evelin noticing, because she was watching the movements with her back turned, and during that time Oliver also disappeared. Evelin turned back and even then, Oliver was not there. Evelin was very scared, she didn't know what to do suddenly, now two of her good friends were lost. The cleaner came up behind her and asked.

Cleaner: - Tell me, where did your friend go? he was here before, wasn't he?: - He wondered. Evelin:- But yes, he was here, he just had to run to the toilet, he'll be right back.: - Evelin answered. Cleaner: - Look here, girl! Maybe I'm just a cleaner, but I wasn't born yesterday, I just came out of the men's room and there was no one there! Well, shouldn't you tell me something I should know about?: - He questioned. Well, Evelin was terrified, she didn't know what to answer, so she had to think carefully about what to answer, because her life might depend on it, she remembered everything, what would happen if..., and thought of all possible variations of what would be well a, plausible and believable story. The cleaner looked deep into Evelin's eyes and saw the fear in her, the uncertainty, the desperation and the fact that she didn't know what to answer in such a case, to which the cleaner spoke before Evelin could say anything.

Cleaner: - Look! I know what's going on here, I've been working at this school for 25 years, I've seen a lot of things and experienced certain things, I know every nook and cranny of the school, if something strange happens, I know for sure, because I'm everywhere, this is my home, I've lived here for years. Now I'll tell you a secret, this school was cursed, very long ago the story started about 150 years ago, it's a true story that has now become a legend, not everyone knows this story because they keep it a secret because they fear the good reputation of the school few people know about it. I'm telling you this secret because I see the fear in your eyes that I felt when I was a child when I came to this school. Upon hearing this, Evelin looked at the cleaner in surprise and said something like that in a bit of horror.

Evelin: - Tell me, please, why are you telling me all this, since you don't even know me, how can you trust me, a stranger!:- She was amazed.

Cleaner: - Well, if you hear the story, you will understand why I am telling you these things. He was just about to start the story when someone or something interrupted them, the cleaner said.

Cleaner: - Wait here, I'll be right back. But Evelin didn't wait and jumped into the closet with that movement and disappeared into the depths. Evelin was also inside, but on the other side of the closet, she almost bumped into Oliver, they immediately greeted each other.

Evelin: - Is that it? How is that possible? What is this place? She was amazed.

Oliver: - Well, I'm also trying to figure this out, but I haven't figured it out yet.: - He answered surprised. During this time, the cleaner was about to leave to see what, or who, interrupted them

conversation. As soon as he got to the end of the corridor, he noticed that the cursed cat that always sneaks into the school was lurking by the cupboards, looking for some leftover food. The mystery solved, he started back to Evelin, but as soon as he turned onto the hallway, she wasn't there, she was absorbed, she disappeared. The cleaner was in doubt and started looking for the children, shouting at them, looking everywhere but nothing. Already very worried, he gave them an hour's respite to see if they would come back by then. He calmly continued cleaning, thinking that he would get to it anyway. During this time, Oliver and Evelin looked at the place where they were in amazement, both of them started shouting after James, but it fell on deaf ears. They looked around to see what kind of place they ended up in, it looked quite eerie, it was surrounded by harsh, damp jutting rocks, only the fireflies provided lighting, although the light did not come from anywhere. The winding stairs led down as if they seemed endless, it was endlessly long. As they looked at this place in awe, they slowly made their way down the stairs, shouting James's name more and more. The cleaner became more and more nervous, even though the hour had already passed and there was no sign of the young people. Of course, he didn't leave it at that, he went to his little house to look at a certain book about how to find James. You have to know that that particular book is not just any book, it belongs to the school for 150 years, in this book it is described in detail how to lift the curse. James' parents were already starting to worry, as it was very late and their son was nowhere to be found. This is not typical for him, they started making thousands of phone calls to his friends to see if they could possibly find out more. The three good friends had another classmate, who kept wanting to sit next to them as the fourth, but somehow this always failed. The boy's name was Gabriel, a bit of a strange child, because he farts all the time and, as is well known, not everyone liked this kind of expression. But you should also know that he is very good with computers, almost a bit of a genius, but when there is a problem, he is the first to be consulted. The parents have already called everyone, and there is no result in getting the children, so the other parents also started to worry, only Gabriel was left. They called Gabriel's parents, but they didn't have much success either, as they didn't know where the children were. At school, while the cleaner arrived in his house, he started looking for the book, which he soon found. He opened the book, surprised by all the dust and cobwebs, he started to turn the pages of the old magic book, as he flips through the pages he realizes that certain pages are missing, he looks more closely and someone tore out these pages a long time ago, as if he wanted to prevent the curse from being lifted, someone wants to prevent this. Now it's just a matter of figuring out when the pages were ripped out and who did the dastardly thing. Since the cleaner had no luck, with this he quickly hurried back to the school to the principal's office to inform the principal about all this. He dialled the principal and answered the phone.

Mrs. Hildred: - Hello, good evening this is Mrs Hildred Dewdney, how can I help you?

Cleaner: - Good evening, Principal Hildred, the cleaner is talking about a very important matter, I'm looking for you, please.

Mrs. Hildred: - Yes, I'm listening: - She interjected curiously.

Cleaner: - Well, there is a bigger problem here, which no one else can solve except you.: - He answered in a broken voice.

Mrs. Hildred: - Well, please continue, I would like to know what is the big problem that caused you to call me so late: - She replied a little embarrassed. The cleaner told them what had happened and that the book would not help them. When Mrs. Hildred heard this, she suddenly did not know what to answer. She thought for a while about what the cleaner had told him,

Mrs. Hildred: - Sir! We are in big trouble, those children have disappeared and now, how are we going to tell the parents, they will think I'm crazy. I have to come up with an effective story, because otherwise I'm playing with my job. Do you have any ideas?: - She asked in despair.

Cleaner: - Ma'am! We'll figure something out together and everything will be fine, don't worry. What happened to the children is a sign that the time has come for James Alder to save the world he is in now. His friends followed James because the children are curious, and I think that the three of them should not leave each other since they are good friends.: - He finished what he had to say. Both the cleaner and the headmistress went back to the school, once again looked around the whole school to see where they could have disappeared, but they didn't have much success. They went back to the headmistress's office and Mrs. Hildred wrote a note about the incident and informed the police because this is her duty, by the time she finished the report to the police, the parents had already called the headmistress when she hung up the phone.

Mrs. Hildred: - Listen here! This is a very serious matter, I also informed the police about it, but as you can see, the parents also called. Now how am I supposed to tell them that their children have disappeared in another world, 'please don't worry, they will be found!' We have to do something, you know that!: - She said firmly.

Cleaner: - Yes, I know! For now, all we can do is buy time until we know something for sure.: - He answered seriously.

Mrs. Hildred: - It's okay! When the police get here, they will comb the whole school, but soon the parents will also get here and ask questions, but somehow, we will solve it.: - She said nervously.

A mysterious person

Desperate parents called the headmistress, but they couldn't find her at home, so they went looking for the children. Oliver and Evelin walked slowly down the stairs, shouting James's name incessantly, but unfortunately, they didn't hear anything back. This whole place was quite scary for them, but they didn't give up the search, they knew that James could be here somewhere, that's why they continued on the stairs. James reached the end of the stairs, as soon as he stepped off the last step, he found himself in a strange place, there were windows carved into the jutting rocks, behind which were various human figures, both male and female. They looked quite terrifying, but there were not only windows in the rocks, but also three doors, one opening to the south, the other to the north and the third to the west. Behind these doors was a mysterious room. These strange figures were once magicians, fortune tellers, seers, but there is a reason why they are locked up there (five men and five women in total), these strange people only knew the certain secret needed to lift the curse. The clock had already struck midnight and the children still could not be found, the parents and the headmistress had just begun to hold a meeting. While everyone was trying to say something at the same time, of which no one understood anything, as there was a lot of confusion, the cleaner was overcome by a strange feeling, as if someone or something was luring him out of the room. While everyone was talking at the same time, in the great noise, something big boomed out in the back garden. Suddenly, everyone fell silent, they looked at each other and, like good children, quietly started to go out of the room and then out of the building to find out what the huge bang was. As soon as they got to the back garden, a beautiful, coloured light shone at the place of the explosion. They were getting closer and closer towards the light (it was a trap after all), suddenly they were so blinded by the light that they had to close their eyes, and then it disappeared. Everyone who was there couldn't even imagine what it could be and what to make of this light-like phenomenon, they immediately thought that it must have been just some mischievous kids, because they heard laughter outside the fence. Evelin and Oliver kept going lower and lower in the cave and shouted out to James, but to no avail. James stood in front of the doors at a loss, unable to decide which way to go.

Close your eyes.

Your heart will guide you.

If you're on the right track

The force always accompanies me.

James closed his eyes and the strange voice that penetrated his heart finally made a decision and started towards the west door. He carefully placed his hand on the doorknob and began to press it, while behind him the strange people watched James' every move with suspicious eyes. As soon as he started to press the doorknob, one of the magicians spoke: - think carefully about which doorknob you press, because one of the rooms leads to eternal darkness from which there is no way out. James flinched and released the doorknob with that movement. The little mushrooms rang in his ears,

- Close your eyes

- See, your strength will save you,

-If your heart is beating

-You won't be in trouble anymore.

This strange voice that he constantly hears in his head gives James newfound strength. He stood there in front of the three doors and closed his eyes, in his imagination he began to spin around in that small room, the strange power that always helped him out of trouble came to his aid and stopped at the north door, knowing that this was the right direction... The mages watched the boy with suspicious eyes to see how he would decide, because if he opened the wrong door, they would all be done for. The mages had a lot of faith in the boy and his judgment, since they are not mages for nothing, so they know what others don't. Well, James made up his mind and went to the north door. He went to the door and pressed the handle....... As soon as he pressed the handle, the door opened, and the light pierced through the gap and no one knew what was waiting for James over on the other side. As soon as the door opened wider, the sudden bright light blinded James, but James just moved forward, crossed the threshold, put his hand in front of his eyes because of the blinding light, and when he took his hand away from his eyes, a shop full of books was revealed, with people behaving strangely inside, some of them speaking in a completely different language, as if they were not of this world. This bookstore had three floors, full to the brim with books, James just stood there, staring, turning around, marvelling at what he saw there, he felt as if he had fallen into a fairy tale world. The bookseller spotted James right away, as he was quite striking in the world in which he found himself. The salesman was surprised, put his hand on his shoulder and spoke.

Salesman: - 'Good morning, stranger, what flight are you on here?': - James suddenly didn't know what to say, but he finally came to his senses and answered.

James: - 'Good morning, sir.' 'I came from a small town in England, tell me please, what is this place? Where am I? Well, young man, do you really want to know?': - 'Yes, I would like to': - answered excitedly. I would like to show you something, please come with me. Surprised, James started after the man, as soon as they went through the labyrinth-like hallway, they stopped in front of a door that was locked. The stranger reached into his pocket and took out a large bunch of keys, among the many keys he grabbed a larger rusty key and inserted it into the lock. You could also see from here that it was not used many times, so something exciting will happen. The creaking of the also rusty door was eerie, he opened the door and walked into the room full of cobwebs, suddenly mice came running back and forth. In the middle of the strange room stood a round table and on the table, there was an old book with a very thick dusty cobweb on display, it was of course closed.

The strange man closed the door and looked at James.: - Well, here we are in this room, it may be a bit strange for you, but for us this book is a mystery and a treasure at the same time. Please go and open the book. A little shyly, James went to the book, looked at it for a long time, then he blew off the dust and cobwebs, revealing a small bunch of mushrooms, the colour of which was breathtakingly beautiful. He grabbed the book to open it, but he couldn't. At this moment, he looked behind him and asked the stranger.

James: - why can't I open the book?

The bookseller replied: - Well, only you know the answer to this, the book has a special power that can be opened with a certain inner key that lies in your heart. With that, the stranger left the room and left James there. During this time, the parents stood bewildered in the school hall, desperately waiting for the police to call. The cleaner looked around the garden for the mischiefs to teach them to behave well. As he was stumbling through the trees with the flashlight in his hand, something suddenly moved in the bushes, it shone, and a hooded stranger was standing in front of him.

Hooded stranger: - What are you doing here in the school yard so late at night, are you okay, aren't you hurt?: - asked the cleaner.

With this momentum, the hooded man raised his hand and took the cleaner with him with a sudden movement. The hooded stranger came here to reveal to the people again, because their world is in danger, and he sent those little mushrooms to James's path for help, because he is the only one who can help them. The cleaner suddenly found himself in his own cubicle, a little startled and scared. He looked at the hooded stranger and as the light illuminated his face, he immediately recognized who he really was. Meanwhile, the police arrived at the school and started questioning the parents about the case. The stranger was none other than the emissary of the world where James was, the world called BOLETUS. The name of the city where James arrived is Moltius.

James stood in front of the book confused, he didn't know what the stranger was talking about, what kind of special power is there to open the book!!! He put it back in place and headed for the exit. He was about to take the doorknob when the book spoke to him.

Book: - James open me…., the voice whispered. He immediately turned back and went over to the book. He began to turn around to see where the sound was coming from, but he couldn't see anyone. Well, he put it back in place when he addressed James again. James looked at the book and was amazed that the book was talking to him.

Book: - Open me..., - the book whispered again, to which James asked him.

James: - But I don't know how to open you, I tried and it didn't work!: - James said a little surprised. Book: - Only you can open me: - said the book, only you can save this world, and only you can do that. James tried to open the book again but couldn't, he folded it back and forth but couldn't figure out how to open it.

The book told him: - Don't spin me around, you don't have to open me in a traditional way, but an inner voice whispers the opening of the secret, your "heart", and you hold this certain key in your heart. James put the book back in its place.

James: - I will come back when I'll understands this certain mysterious key, because I cannot do it for now. With that he went out the door and went back to the stranger who led him there. Oliver and Evelin wanted to turn back, but the same thing that happened to them, like James, the stairs disappeared around them. They were very frightened by this, suddenly closed their eyes and started screaming. As soon as they stopped screaming, a voice rang out: - come on, what is this great terror! You didn't get scared, did you? Suddenly they opened their eyes and there was an Angelic girl standing in front of them who also appeared to James. The two good friends looked at each other and almost at the same time they asked: - who are you? And how did you get here? The Angelic girl then asked: - You're looking for James, aren't you? The two good friends answered at the same time: - Yes, we are looking for him, but we can't find him anywhere: - they answered in despair.

Angelic girl: - No problem, you went to the right place, your friend also went there, just follow the road down and you'll find him: - answered the fairy and disappeared with that momentum. Evelin and Oliver looked down in a bit of a fright when the stairs came back and became visible to them again. They sighed and started down deeper. They didn't know what was waiting for them, how they could have known, since they went to the great unknown, feeling fear, but they didn't give up the hope that they would find their friend. It was cold in the cave, it was dim, they heard strange sounds, but they walked closely together, trusting that nothing would happen to them until they got down. The industrious little fireflies kept shining a light on them, showing them the way down so they wouldn't be so afraid in the dark. The pieces of rock protruding from the walls took interesting shapes in the darkness, strange shapes looked back at them, which made the hair on their backs stand on end from fear. After not much time, they reached the bottom of the cave, where three doors opened in front of them. The magicians watched the children with suspicious eyes to see which door to open, because if I open the wrong door, it's all over, they'll never find James. Oliver looked at Evelin and then at the magicians, the light of help radiated from his eyes, he stood in despair and could not decide which door to open. Of course, the magicians immediately saw that they were in trouble, and one of the magicians just called out to them: - children, listen to your hearts and then you will make the right decision..., with that, the room became gravely silent. Oliver took Evelin's hand and spoke.

Oliver: - Together we can go further, and we can decide better. They closed their eyes and started walking towards the doors. They approached the doors slowly, stopped for a moment and headed towards the west door, before they got there, suddenly Evelin stopped and led Oliver towards the north door. They rushed to the door and pressed the handle at the same time, the door opened, and a flood of light blinded the room, and with that they burst through the door. As soon as they got through, they found themselves in a huge library that had at least three floors. Winding stairs led up to the upper floor. They were just turning around, staring in amazement at the room they were in, suddenly someone jumps there and welcomes them with great joy.

James: - Hello, my dear friends: - greeted them. They suddenly looked at each other, and the good friends began to cheer.

Oliver: – Hi James, we finally found you!:– they said happily,:– how did you get here?:– what is this place?:– but what is going on here? Tell me what this is all about?: – asked happily. They kept asking James their questions. James explained roughly what this place was and how the people here were counting on him to save them from a certain curse that plagued the place. The good friends listened in shock to James as he told them this story, the librarian asked them.

Librarian: - Children, is there a place for you to sleep tonight?: - Actually, we don't have anywhere to sleep, but we'll figure it out somehow!: - All three answered, almost at once.

Don't worry, feel free to come and sleep in my home, I'd be happy to see you and my wife would be happy for you too. The good friends were very grateful for the offer, and they gladly accepted. They went out of the store to look around a bit, the shopkeeper told them not to go far because he would finish his work soon, and then they would go home. They took note, they didn't want to get into trouble again. They looked in amazement at this strange place, the buildings were also different, they looked as if they were built all over the place, they were absolutely not symmetrical. They thought they discovered something interesting about the numbering of the houses, there were two different colours associated with the family's name. For example, if the name of the family is Mr. Jones, the colours above the numbering are blue and red. A total of six different types of family surnames lived in this strange place. The curious little ones asked what these colours meant, they tried to get to know this mysterious place. There was a rather narrow road between the houses and the sidewalks were also narrow, of course there were no cars, people travelled mostly on foot or by bicycle and horse-drawn carriage. The entire street was covered with cobblestone roads, strange looking streetlamps, even the houses were lit by candles, only the bigger shops had lighting, this was the custom here. As soon as they walked the streets, they noticed a strange side street, the buildings almost touched each other, the place was so narrow, there was no sidewalk there, because there was no need for one. The good friends looked at each other and started making their way down the narrow path smiling. They reached the edge of the building and of course they had to go on one by one, to let the curious little ones discover the new place. And so, they set off, Evelin went in front, followed by Oliver and finally James. As soon as James reached the corner of the building, he looked behind him, he knew that he shouldn't let this happen now, he should tell them not to go any further, and as soon as he looked around, the world behind him disappeared. Even if he had wanted to speak, it would have been useless anyway because there was nothing behind them. James: - 'STOP': - exclaimed James!!! At this, the others suddenly stopped and asked in horror: Oliver: - What happened James?

James: - Listen! - said James, something went wrong, because the city disappeared, and we can't go back, it's not there anymore. They all stood there terrified and looked to see that there really was nothing behind them, they tried to go back, but it was impossible.

Oliver: - Well all of us are in big trouble now: - said surprised.: - And now, how to proceed? - Evelin asked . A voice suddenly spoke, behind them: - come children, don't be afraid, come here.: - Suddenly they looked there, and there was an old lady standing in front of them. She seemed nice, and so they went there. The aunt led them to into her house, offered them warm food, the inside of the house was a huge two-story building, and only the little old aunt lived in it, it was a bit striking to them. After they had dinner, the old aunt led them into a large room, where there was a huge fireplace, a room paved with old style stones, candles everywhere, the windows were placed high up like in a castle. They sat around the fireplace and started talking. James stood up and looked around the room, there were old painted pictures hanging on the wall but there was nothing holding them there, they just hung in the air, this scared him a little, the candles were also just hanging in the air, this was strange to James, he looked at them, so that the others could see this strange phenomenon, but the others were talking, not paying attention to James. The cabinets were also quite interesting, there were strange objects in them that he had never seen in his life. However, there was a closed cupboard in the room, which was very worn and covered in cobwebs, as if no one had ever opened it. James sat back next to the others, trying to watch the old lady, but he didn't succeed, half of the closet kept turning, as if a voice was calling him there. Well, children: - said the old lady, it's quite late, it's time to go to bed. With that, he led them to the rooms where they could relax as they were very tired.

Everyone was comfortably relaxing in their beds, but they were just about to sleep when a noise was heard in Evelin's room. The wall opened, Evelin spoke in terror: - who is there, what do you want!

It's just me, James said softly.

I found a secret passage, come with me, I want to find out something: - said James quietly.

Evelin sighed, "God, I was scared, but what do you want to find out?" Evelin asked.

There is a very old cupboard in the great hall, and I don't think it has ever been opened, I would like to take a closer look: - said James.

Okay then, well let's go: - answered Evelin. They set off through the secret hallway, which led them right into the great hall. They carefully opened the wall and slipped through it, so that the old lady wouldn't hear them, but luckily for them there was no one there. And so, they quietly entered the room. There were only a few candles burning, and so the room wasn't so bright, but the light of the moon illuminated a part of the room. They crept up to the closet, looking at it from both the right and the left, but it was locked, they couldn't open it, of course there was no key anywhere. They began to think about where the key to this cupboard could be, they searched to see if it was there somewhere.

During the great search, Evelin accidentally knocked down a candle from the table, it was very loud since the candle holder was covered with cast iron and elaborate stones. 'Carefully, Evelin, we're going to fall, pay attention': - said James in horror.

'Sorry, it was an accident': - replied Evelin. No one heard the noise, and so they decided to go up to the old aunt's room. They went upstairs in the room, but the door was locked, they could not enter. Now they were in big trouble, they went back to James's room to discuss what to do next, when they opened the door there was a figure in a long black cloak standing in front of the window looking outside, the young people were scared of course, they backed away, but the stranger spoke,: - there's no need to be scared, come on in. Both of them stepped through the door of the room at the same time, they were quite terrified, they just rushed into the room, finally they stopped at the edge of the bed, they didn't dare to go closer to him. The stranger turned around, looked at them and said: - I came to help you, the key you were looking for is in a chest in the basement, in order for you to get a hold of the key, you have to go down to get the key, but it won't be as easy as you think. : - the stranger finished the sentence.

Anyway, how did you get into my room?: – James asked, surprised.

Who are you?: – Evelin asked.

The stranger only said: - Be careful! With that he disappeared from the room. The two good friends looked at each other in surprise, the door suddenly opened, Oliver stomped in and said: - I've been looking everywhere for you all, but where did you go!: - Why aren't you in your room?: - What the hell are you doing here?: - Surprised Oliver asked at them. Sshhh quieter, come here, you need to know this too: - called Evelin. With that, they also told him what had happened, and set off in the basement to look for the chest in which the key was. They reached the cellar door,

James put his hand on the handle to open the door, he was about to press the handle when someone grabbed his shoulder, James was so scared that he screamed. When he looked behind him, the old aunt was standing behind him, he asked them: - Well, you children, where are you going? - The old aunt asked. All three of them stood frozen in front of the cellar door, unable to speak.

Maybe you just didn't want to go to the cellar?: - The old lady asked suspiciously.

Aaaa…., not only….: - said James scared.

But yes, we just wanted to go down to the cellar, because the delicious pickles, cheese, and sausages are down here, we were a little hungry,: - replied Oliver quickly.

'Oh, children, why didn't you start with this, go to the great hall, I'll bring you all half of the delicacies right away.': - the old lady assured them. The three good friends turned the corner and hurried into the room. On the way, they discussed that somehow, they should just go down to the basement to get the key, while when they got to the hall, they discussed what the next step should be. They arrived in the hall and politely waited for the old lady with the encore dinner. They didn't have to wait long; the old lady soon reached them.

'Come on, kids, there's delicious food here': - The old lady said.

They got to eating right away, quietly, they ate the food, but after a while James spoke up: - dear aunt, tell me, how long have you been living here alone in this big house?: - He asked inquisitively!

You know, children, I've been living here alone for a long time, I don't even know how long it's been,: - answered the old lady patiently.

You know, many people used to live here, not just me alone, I had a husband who unfortunately died a long time ago. I also had children who, of course, moved away from me a long time ago, they live their own lives, I also have grandchildren,: - said the old lady sadly, we all lived together once, but something changed, something happened, something very terrible. No one knows where this terrible thing came from, which pushes everyone away from each other.: - The old lady says sadly. Good friends watch the old lady without batting an eye. That something made people feel that life here was no longer the same as it used to be. Magic reigns everywhere, it is rumoured that someone can break this magic, and then everything will return to the old situation, as it was a long time ago,: - the old lady continued her conversation, but no one knows who that person is, or when this person will arrive.

Hearing this, James got up from his seat and said: - Auntie, I will be honest with you now,: - said James determinedly, I just need to know if you can be trusted:- James finished the sentence.

Of course, my child: - answered the old aunt, a little embarrassed,: - continue what you started, if I can, I will help: - continued the old aunt.

Well, okay then!!! The truth is that we got here by accident.... and with that James told the old aunt everything.

Old aunt: - 'My dear children', the old aunt said in an excited voice, 'come with me', and with that they started to make their way down to the cellar. The old aunt opened the door for them and wished them good luck and to be careful, and with that they started down the stairs, each holding a torch, as there was no light down there either. A new adventure has begun for them, they didn't know what would be waiting for them there, they were very careful, everyone warned them about that. They got further and further into the basement, wet walls, rats running everywhere, strange noises, coming from the dark, but they encouraged each other and continued. They reached a section where there was a lot of water, they had to go into it, as there was no other way to go any further, but none of them dared to walk into it because they didn't know how deep it was. They just looked around and picked up a stone from the ground and threw it in, but unfortunately from this they didn't find out what kind of water it was. They sacrificed one of the torches for this purpose, since they had to go further. Oliver started to put the torch in the water, he just put it in the water, the torch itself was one meter long, so they knew what to expect. When he only saw a centimetre of the torch rod, they started to get scared, but finally the torch hit the bottom.

Well, who volunteers to go into the water first?: – Evelin asked.

I'll go first,: - said Oliver, With this momentum, he was already in the water, moving forward in a section of approximately two meters. James looked at Evelin and he also climbed in, started after Oliver. Of course, Evelin also followed them, as she didn't want to stay there alone. Slowly and surely, they made their way to the other end to finally get out of the water, as it was quite cold. They were about halfway there when a rat jumped into the water, they were so scared that they started screaming and quickly ran to the other side. They climbed out of the cold water, drenched and cold, they continued to look for that particular chest. While shivering they were looking for the chest, which was not far from them, a little light glimmered in the darkness, they noticed it and went there. At last, they found the chest, they hurried there very happily, and sat there waiting to finally open it. James was about to open the top, but the chest was closed, they couldn't open it. This made them realize that they are not having any luck at the moment, but they did not give up hope, they just need a tool, and it will open. Evelin said: - I have a hair clip, if that helps!!! They sighed and tried to see if they could open it or not. James poked it until it opened, and inside it was the key they went there for. Evelin put it in her pocket, there were many other scraps left inside. Many newspapers, letters, invoices, photographs, various documents, there was also a battered and worn parchment-like letter, but it was yellowed, Evelin took it in her hands, which she opened to see what was written in it. The guys were looking at the pictures of the elderly aunt and her entire family. Meanwhile Evelin read the letter, she swallowed hard and looked at the two guys and began to tremble. What was in that letter also took her breath away, she didn't expect that, she didn't know how to address her two friends, she just shoved it in front of James's nose and looked away when James took the letter. James started to read the letter, but Oliver also noticed and wanted to go to see too, but Evelin took his hand and stopped him. Oliver looked at Evelin in shock, but Evelin quietly said only this: - 'wait...'

James finally read the letter, looked up and said: - 'Guys, we have to get out of here as fast as possible.' Of course, Oliver didn't understand why they had to disappear from there quickly, he didn't know because he didn't know what was written in the letter.

James put the letter in his pocket, everything else was put back in the chest. However, they needed a plan on how to get out of there, after all, they couldn't go back. Oliver: - Wait!! I'm not going anywhere until you tell me what's in that letter! I think I should know this too, since we are here together, or not?

James: - 'Yes, Oliver, we really came here together, we got into trouble together, I'll give it to you to read, because I can't bear to read it again.' Oliver also began to read the letter, but he also began to tremble after what he read in the letter:

Dear James!

Now that you have received the letter, I think you know that you cannot go back to the house, because if you go back, you will all die.

The old aunt home is cursed, she didn't tell you because it was erased from her mind so she couldn't remember it. You have to choose other ways to get out of the house if you want to get out.

Regards,

Stranger.

Evelin: - well, guys, what's the plan? Well, let's find a window we can climb out of!: – said James.

Because this basement is huge, full of labyrinths, it takes an age's to get out of there.

The protective shield

In the small town in the Boloteus world, where James and his friends arrived, the town's name was Molthius. The bookseller was nervously looking for the children, as he knew they were missing. Mr. Monghur! Mr. Monghur!: – His colleague Mr. Tregas called for him. Please wait! Come quickly in the hall, you must see this: - said Mr. Tregas excitedly.

(After the Mr. Monghur family name, the colour is green and yellow, after the Mr. Tregas family name, the colour is purple and pink.)

They quickly went to the room, as soon as they opened the door, they saw that the book was covered by a protective shield. Since Mr. Monghur was the senior elder and scholar in this town, he knew all about this book, he knew that the boy was in trouble. 'The boy is in trouble!': – said Mr. Monghur a little thoughtfully. In the hall, three elderly scholar wizards, who only worked here in the bookstore, burst into view. Mr. Monghur was the most experienced among them, he said: - 'My dear friends, we need to get the council together, we have something important to discuss. The council chamber was located on the lowest level of the building in the basement room, behind a secret wall. They were all in the room, which means that six scientists were standing at the round table, in the middle of which was a big book that had special powers. Only scientists could open this book, only if there was a problem, which had not happened often so far.

I welcome you, my dear friends!: – Said Mr. Monghur, continuing his speech.: - Well, we have gathered here because James and his friends are in trouble, which the book told us in the room. We need to find out where they got into trouble. Where are they now? After all, they have disappeared, and we have to help them.: - Mr. Monghur finished what he had to say.

The name of the third scientist and magician: - Mr. Onthasy, after the family name, his colour is orange and brown.

The name of the fourth scientist and mage: - Mr. Zathen, after his family name, his colour is yellow and light green.

The name of the fifth scientist and magician: - Mr. Vinthus, after the family name, his colour is white and black.

The name of the sixth scientist and magician: - Mr. Ambeth, after the name of his family, his colour is indigo and grey.

Please, gentlemen, let's all take a seat and open the book: - Mr. Ambeth said. All six mages took out their necklaces and placed them on the table, in its proper place. When they were all placed them inside, a large, combined light shot up to the ceiling and back straight to the book that opened it. After the book was opened, a hologram of an ancient mage stood there with living needles and said: - I welcome you, mages! I saw this day coming, I know that James is in trouble, he has been transferred to the world where the evil witch cursed our world.

Your task is to create a protective shield around them, which will lead them safely to the appointed place "to the evil witch", their mission will not be easy, but only the James can defeat this evil witch.

All we can do is help pave his way and give him protection.

Hologram: - As where he is, we can't go there now.: - The hologram of the ancient magician finished what he had to say.

I think there is something we can send to them; it can be of help if we can't go to them.: - Said Mr. Zathen.

We can really send them help over there, which will surely come in handy for them!: – Said the ancient magician of the hologram. Gentlemen, turn the necklaces around and I will send them some help, the rest will be your jobs to deliver.: - The ancient great mage finished what he had to say. The six magicians turned the necklaces that were in the joint on the table, suddenly a great light flooded the room, the book closed and above the book a huge dragon began flying around. The mages took the necklaces out of their places, put them back around their necks, got up from the table and started muttering a magic spell that sent this dragon through the world where the three good friends were. The dragon came to where the three good friends were, lurking in front of the house to free them.

'Did you guys hear that?': - Evelin said. In the meantime, they found the window they could have climbed out of, but it was barred. The dragon went to the window and pulled the bar out of the wall. Needless to say, both of them were very scared, only James stood and looked into the dragon's eyes. There was a special contact between them that he didn't understand yet, but he would soon find out. They escaped from there, Evelin and Oliver were afraid of the dragon, but James went towards it like someone who is enchanted, he stretched out his hand and the dragon bent down to bring him, James knew that he had to get on it and get away as soon as possible. They got on the dragon's back, held on, and with that the dragon flew away. They enjoyed the flight, the view from up there was beautiful, they suddenly forgot what trouble they were in, they were overwhelmed with happiness. They arrived above a huge forest, it seemed endless, the dragon just flew purposefully, the good friends silently watched where they were going. Finally, the dragon landed in a clearing behind a huge mountain where there was an old house, they went to the house and knocked on the door. The creaking door opened, an old man in a hood who was blind stood in the doorway,: - hello children! – The old uncle greeted them.: - I was waiting for you, the old man continued the sentence. The good friends looked at each other and wondered how the old man knew who they really were.: -Please come in kids, you don't need to be afraid, come inside in the warmth, it's cold outside: - the old man invited them in. The children entered the house, greeted each other politely, and stopped in front of the fireplace to warm themselves.

Well, I heard what happened to you, the old wizards told me, I'm glad you managed to get out of that house in time, that house is cursed anyway, if you had stayed there, you would have been swallowed by the darkness of the curse. The dragon you came here with was sent to your aid by the old wizards to save you, that dragon is your protective shield and will only appear next time when you are in trouble. Come and sit at the table, you must be hungry from the journey.: - The old man kindly finished the sentence. After the children had warmed up and had their fill, they asked the old uncle where they were and where they needed to go to find the evil witch. The old man told them that they had to wait until midnight because then a secret train would come and take them to the place where they would find the evil witch. This train only appears once every night, exactly at midnight, and there is only one stop, so you can't miss the stop. After a long conversation, they had to leave because the secret train had arrived. Before they left for the train, the old man gave small bottle in James's hand: - open this bottle only when it starts to glow, and you can defeat the evil witch with it:- the old man whispered in James's ear. Well, they said their goodbyes and boarded the train. The train started immediately, the children started looking for a seat, there were many interesting and strange people traveling on the train, finally they found an empty compartment and sat down.: - This train is very strange! And people too! Where did we end up?: – Oliver asked, surprised and a little scared.: – Take it easy, it's a good little adventure! It's not boring, that's for sure: - replied Evelin, smiling and excited. Besides, what did that old man James give you! And what did he whisper in your ear?: - Oliver wondered. Well, a bottle! There is some kind of liquid in it, he said that!: - James suddenly stopped the sentence, because a strange tall woman stood in front of their door and just stood and stared through the door, not taking her eyes off of James. James's blood froze in his veins, his heart pounded in his throat, he literally froze. There was something strange about that woman's gaze, hauntingly harsh, mystical, yet charming and soothing. Evelin looked at James and her gaze was glassy, her eyeballs were white, she was not herself. That strange woman tried to get into his thoughts to find out who they were and what they were doing here. Of course, Evelin was very scared, she started pulling James to come to his senses, she started shouting for help, but of course no one heard this, because this strange woman was, well, a witch, she did what she wanted because no one could stop her. Yes, but Oliver didn't hesitate either, he took the bottle from James' pocket, as soon as the witch saw this, she immediately let go of James and disappeared from there as if the earth had swallowed her. When James regained consciousness, he immediately asked what had happened. Both

Oliver and Evelin started to tell what happened at the same time, only problem was that James didn't understand anything.: - Stop, James interjected! I don't understand anything from that, you are talking at the same time, only one of you tell me!: - said James a little understated. But since Evelin was the fastest, she told James what happened.: - I felt strange, it was as if she had taken me to another world where this evil witch is, maybe she wanted to show the way, maybe she wanted to help: - said James thoughtfully.: - We have to find that strange woman, I have to talk to her! With that, he got up to go look for her, but both Oliver and Evelin held him so that he wouldn't go anywhere and stay in the booth with them. What if she is evil and wants to get that little bottle for herself, and then this was all for nothing, we might be stuck here forever: - Oliver said firmly. 'Even then, we have to find her, I sensed that she wasn't evil, she just wanted to help: - answered James. The young people pondered and finally decided together to find that strange woman. They left the booth, James and Evelin started in one direction; Oliver went in the other direction. They went from booth to booth, but so far not with much success. Oliver started walking towards the front of the train, James and Evelin started towards to the back of the train, Oliver was a little afraid because there were quite strange people sitting on the train and people standing and talking on the hallways. But there was only one wagon left that Oliver needed look at, he opened the passage doors and went into the last wagon, there were open seats and no booths, he slowly started to look around, but his heart was beating faster and faster as he was moving forward, suddenly someone patted his shoulder, Oliver was so scared that he suddenly cried out. He turned around and James and Evelin were standing behind him.: - Oh my goodness! You nearly made me shit myself!: – Oliver said scared.: – Well, we didn't succeed, let's go on together,: - said James. They went on together, but for some reason they did not succeed together either. They went back to their booth and sat down a little disappointed on how she could

41

have disappeared so quickly. Since they were not successful, they talked, laughed, told each other jokes, tried to pass the time. Since they were very tired, they soon quietened down, they lay on each other's shoulders and fell asleep. As they slept, the strange woman came back and crawled into James' head again. James stood up like a robot and walked out of the booth. Oliver and Evelin didn't hear anything, as they were in a deep sleep. James disappeared from the train. Evelin woke up after a while, opened her eyes, vaguely, sleepily, began to stretch when she realized that James was not there. She suddenly jumped up and shouted to Oliver: "Oliver, wake up!" James is gone! Oliver jumped up, suddenly he didn't even know which world he was in!: - What happened?:- Where is James?: - Oliver asked, surprised and scared. - Come, we have to find James, right now: - Evelin said firmly. But now they parted ways again on the train, they set off to find James. They went all the way through the train, but he was nowhere to be found. They started back in the cab and James was sitting there, looking thoughtfully out the window as if nothing had happened. Oliver and Evelin looked at each other and did not understand what was going on.: – James! We were worried to death about you, you disappeared, what happened to you?: - We looked everywhere and we couldn't find you anywhere!: - Oliver and Evelin asked in despair. They sat next to him, Evelin took James's hand, looked into his eyes and saw emptiness. She took his face and asked him: - Where were you James?: - Where did that woman take you?: - Please answer!: - Say something: - Evelin asked quietly.: - James didn't disappear! He was with me the whole time, there's no need to be scared, I'm not hurting your friends, I want to help him.: -The strange woman suddenly answered. With that, she walked into the booth with them and sat down between them. Both Oliver and Evelin looked at the strange woman in shock.: - allow me to introduce myself. My name is Hanna, I was born here in this world, this is my home, my friends and family members are here. I guess it wasn't hard for you to decipher that I'm not an average person, yes, I'm a witch, but I'm not evil. Our family has been good witches for thousands of years. My mother has a sister, when she was born, the storm was raging outside, there was great poverty at that time, there were no nurses like now, at that time experienced women helped the newborns into the world. The storm was huge, thundering, lightning, lightning struck many places. On the night when my mother's brother was born, a black raven flew over her bed, then landed on the baby's head, flapped its wings and put its beak in her ear, and placed something inside, then flew away. Of course, they tried to push it away, but they couldn't, because that raven had a lot of power. It was bewitched by an evil witch to put that thing in the baby's ear for sure. This is how evil passed on its power. It should be known that the previous evil witch lost her life when one of her spells went wrong and because of this she died. But she thought of everything, she was prepared for every possible mistake, if something didn't come together the way she wanted, she bewitched one of her ravens so that she could pass on that certain great power to the right person. So that her evil may live on. This is how an innocent child became an evil witch, this world is cursed, and we have to help defeat the evil witch without hurting her just to get that something out of her ear! Then my mother and her sister can be together again. Hearing all of this, surprised they were watching Hanna, they couldn't believe what she had just told them. James: - what you have told us up until now is a very shocking story, what happened to your mother's sister is very sad. The only thing I don't understand, how do I come into the picture and how did you know that I was going to be on this train? – Why exactly are you telling all these important things to us, how on earth can we help you? Hanna: - Like I have already said, I am a witch and I know who arrives at this world, we have been waiting for you a while now. So as soon as I found out that you have arrived, I came as fast as I could so I could meet you. As you are the only one that can help us, I had to find you as fast as possible. Hanna replied kindly. James: - I understand! All this information I will still have to process, as everyone expects redemption from me. But I don't really understand why I have to save everybody, what do I know that the wizards and which are unable to solve? James said surprised. Hanna: - James, I know you guys are really tired I think we should go to sleep and with a fresh mind, I will thoroughly explain everything. She replied smiling.

There was silence in the booth, everyone was lost in their own thoughts. Since a lot had happened to them during the day, they were also tired, and soon they were all asleep. James had a dream, the little mushrooms that were in his ears tried to guide him to the right path, because of this they helped him make the right decision in his dreams. The train went without stopping, since this train actually only had one stop, both there and back. They have a long way to go, and it's better if they rest.

In James's dream, his path leads him through an enchanted forest, swampy, creepers, strange looking birds, strange plants, strange-looking trees. In this forest, there were two types of paths, the "good path" and the "bad path", but you can only really know which path is which if you make good decisions along the way. This means that the good path will glow golden yellow, and the bad path will glow dark green. If you don't make the right decisions, you won't see the paths at all, and you'll get lost in the everything. This information was suggested by the little mushrooms to help James, but the rest was up to him to do his job. The young friends have been well rested, the sales lady knocked at their door: - good morning, sleepy heads! - The sales lady spoke up.: - What can I give you?

- There is coffee, tea, cocoa, carbonated and non-carbonated soft drinks, baked goods, sweets, hazelnut sorts, the specialities are magic capsules, no one knows what's in them, and to this she had a good laugh. Everyone chose the right breakfast for themselves, of course Oliver the curious chose for himself from the magic capsules. Everyone started to eat breakfast, but in the meantime, they were watching Oliver. Oliver took nothing of this, swallowed one of the capsules and waited for its effect. He didn't have to wait long; the first capsule was a muffin: - Hmm this is very delicious: -said Oliver happily. The others just smiled at him; he had two capsules left. He took the next capsule: - I'm sure this will be a tasty treat; I can feel it: - Oliver grinned.

As soon as he said it, his eyes widened, red smoke came out of his ears and nose, he jumped up from the chair and quickly held his mouth: - 'Aaa this is spicy, aaaa this is a spicy, water, give me water', and meanwhile he was jumping up and down.

The others burst out laughing, they couldn't give him water, they were laughing so hard. Finally, he got water and rinsed his throat. He took the third capsule with a bit of trepidation, but in the end, it was a delicious chocolate drop. Oliver: - Guys! How long is this train journey going to take? - asked excitedly.

Hanna: - we will stop soon at a huge station and everyone there will know where to go, you can't get lost.: - She answered. James was thinking, he remembered his parents, he missed them a lot. I wonder what will happen to us when the train stops! How are we going to save this world! These were the thoughts that crossed James's mind.

Of course, the parents were still looking for the children, the police also issued a warrant for the disappearance of the children.

The train arrived at the station, everyone left the train, after all, this was its final station.

There was a huge big station in front of them, everyone went into the building, there were a lot of people in there, it was 3rd floors, shops everywhere, playhouses for the little ones, a bowling alley, an air surfing alley, a ghost room, a monster room, a roller coaster room that travelled between bubbles, a journey on clouds room, flying in the breeze room, potion making room, storyteller, story book room, snow room, rain room, sunny beach room, forest room. Actually, these were the rooms where people chose a suitable exit for themselves. James remembered that he had to continue his journey in the forest room, so he went to where the forest room was. The others followed him, knowing that James knew what he was doing. Oliver: - James! Do you know where we should go? Are you sure we're halfway there? He asked a little scared.

James: I think I know, Oliver, something tells me that I should take the forest room. He answered calmly. They reached the entrance of the room, stopped in front of it, looked at each other and finally stepped inside. As soon as they entered the room, they found themselves in a huge area of forest, they were greeted by an endless sight, they looked behind from where they entered and the exit road to the station disappeared, that is, it closed behind them. And before they took a single step, they marked a tree so that they would know that the exit would be there, as it would be helpful to know. They set off on the golden path that led east, there were huge trees everywhere, strange birds, strange bugs, strange creepers and strange sounds could be heard. They got deeper into the forest, the sun started to go down, it will soon be dark. Oliver was walking behind everyone, but he had marked the trees for some reason, that's why he was a little behind the others. But as soon as it got dark, he tried to catch up to the rest. Something fell on his head; he was so scared that he started screaming and brushing off the thing that fell on his head. Upon hearing this, everyone stopped, turned back and made their way to Oliver.

Hanna: - What is it? What happened? She asked surprised.

Oliver: - Something fell on my head, it's on my head! Take it down! He said scared. They started to see what had fallen on his head, finally they found him, he was down on the ground, a little elf, he was the guardian of the trees. He had been following them for quite some time, but accidentally fell down and directly on Oliver's head. They picked him up from the ground, he was a little dazed from the blow, but he soon recovered.

Elf: - Who are you? What were you doing here in this dangerous forest? He asked surprised.

James: - Hi little elf! He greeted him politely! I would like to introduce myself, I'm James okay here my friends. He answered the elf patiently. He introduced his friends to the little elf.

James: - Why did you say that this forest was dangerous earlier? He asked curiously.

Elf: - Don't you know what kind of forest this is? He asked them. Almost simultaneously they answered 'No'.

James: - All we know is that…. And he was about to answer the elf when Oliver suddenly interrupted: "The evil witch is here!" The elf suddenly turned towards Oliver with one movement and covered his mouth while looking quickly around. Elf: - Quietly, not so loudly, don't say it because she has eyes and ears everywhere, come with me, I'll take you to a safe place, it's getting dark anyway.

The elf answered a little nervously. Of course, Oliver's blood froze with fear, he didn't dare to say anything anymore. The elf led them to a tree with a huge trunk and stopped in front of it. He muttered something to himself, and the door opened at the trunk of the tree, letting everyone in. They went inside the tree, then the elevator took them down to the city of fairies, there were a lot of elves, life among them suddenly stopped when they saw the strangers in their home. The little elf spoke in his language, and everyone continued to do their work.

Elf: - Follow me, I will take you to the big boss and he will give you guidance. The inside of this tree was beautiful, it was huge, it seemed as if it reached up to the sky. Different branches led everywhere, it was full of small houses, it was decorated with beautiful roads, bridges, small lanterns, and of course there were labyrinth like roads everywhere. They arrived at the area of the great boss, it was on a large clearing, more and more beautiful flowers and flying elves surrounded the big boss, watching his every wish. As soon as they got there, the flying elves made their way, a beautiful girl elf, with long blonde hair, blue eyes and a beautiful green dress, sat in a chair full of flowers. Elf: - Welcome, big boss! I brought these people before you, I found them in the forest. She introduced them to the big boss properly. And with that the elf left.

Big Boss: - Welcome to our place, come closer and take a seat. He accepted them.

They went closer and sat down at the table that the other elves had laid out for them, filled with food and drink so that they could eat and drink as much as they could. They duly accepted, and ate as much as they needed, then continued the conversation.

Big Boss: - Let me introduce myself too! My name is Casandra. I know why you're here, it won't be easy to overcome it, as it very powerful, but like everyone has a weak point, you have to find out what it is. You can only find this out from a close relative. But as I see, there is someone with you who can definitely help you with this. He looked at Hanna, as she is also a wizard. You can stay tonight, but tomorrow you have to leave this place, you have to go on, you can't stay here for long. She ended her speech kindly. Casandra was the keeper of the trees.

The little diligent flying elves led them where they could rest until the next day; beautiful huge rooms were waiting for them where they could relax. They went to rest and soon enough they fell asleep, as they were very tired. The next day, when they awoke, they found themselves in a clearing, sleeping on beds of flowers and soft leaves, each of them having a satchel full of food and water, with which they could set out to find the evil witch.

Evelin: - James! Shouldn't we ask Hanna what Casandra meant! She asked curiously.

James: - I already thought about asking but at the right time, because if we want to defeat the evil witch, then it's good to know what's the easiest way. He answered thoughtfully. They went on to more and more beautiful places, through clearings, they even reached the shore of a stream, there were small fish swimming, they were jumping out of the water, water gliders also swam in it, the kids path led to the other side of the shore. They had to cross a small bridge, after reaching the bridge, they stopped to look at the stream, the small fish, the interestingly shaped stones, everything looked so peaceful, but it wasn't peaceful at all, it was just the appearance. It is an enchanted forest, made so by the evil witch to trap intruders who wish to harm her. Unsuspectingly, they were looking at the gently trickling stream, meanwhile a cold breeze came up from behind them out of nowhere, they all looked back and a huge wave was heading towards them. They broke into a fast run across the bridge and on to the path to the road that continued their journey. They were saved, of course, but that was only the beginning, much worse is coming for them, which they have no idea about. The evil witch knows they are there and will do anything to destroy them. Panting, they tried to continue on their way, but James sensed that it would not be an easy task to get to the evil witch. Someone was following them, but they didn't know this, because she was following them very quietly and unnoticed. Hanna feels that something is wrong, but at the same time James also feels that something is wrong, the silence is too much to bear, and this won't end well. James stops and looks behind him, as if sensing that someone is following them. The others also stopped and asked James what was wrong, can he see anything? But both James and Hanna looked around to spot the person following them. Oliver walked up to a tree and looked around, as he had many a surprise from there, while he walked carefully and slowly around the tree. He stood on something that made a loud crack, of course he was scared, and the others suddenly looked at Oliver.

Everyone continued to scan, Oliver looked at James and then he noticed that someone was sneaking up on him, and with careful steps he went close to James and threw himself at his feet to catch him. James jumped up, seeing this,

Oliver: - Sorry James, but I think I caught that thing that was circling at your feet.: - He said this with a satisfied face. He gets up from the ground, carefully opens his hand and a tiny hand reached out, says: - 'Okay, you won, you caught me, now let me out of here, I can't breathe!' Oliver opened his hand, and they were facing another little elf.

James: 'Why are you following us?' He asked her. 'Wouldn't it have been easier if you just addressed us?' He asked the elf.

Elf: - 'don't be angry, but I had to follow you, I had to see if you were enemies or not. This forest is cursed, and interesting things happen around here, no one is completely safe here. I have to take you to the big boss so he can find out why you're here.

Oliver: - 'Well, it starts again!': - He muttered, while rolling his eyes. The little elf looked around, took 3 steps to the west, 5 steps to the east, 2 steps to the south and hit the ground twice, after which a door opened from the ground and stairs led down. She quickly ushered them down and the door immediately closed and disappeared.

Oliver: - 'Oh wow! It's funny, it's well thought out, these elves

are really damn smart! They can really tell us how they do this….
Hmm!': – He said loudly.

Evelin: - 'What are you mumbling, Oliver? You are always talking to yourself, is everything okay?': – She asked sarcastically and with a smile.

Oliver: - 'But honestly! These elves are something else huh'…….
He stopped what he was saying when he saw what kind of underground town they had arrived in, Oliver's breath stopped, Evelin also looked there, and she also froze at the sight.

Evelin: - 'Oh wow! Oh my god, where are we? It's beautiful!'
She said surprised. The hurried little elves stopped yet again and all looked at the youngsters, they didn't dare to move, but the little elf who took them there spoke to them in their language and then they continued where they had left off.

Elf: - 'Come, follow me, we'll get to the big boss soon.' She said to them. They were greeted by a beautiful sight as if from a fairy tale, they just marvelled and stared, the beautifully crafted country cottages had columns in front of each house, hand-carved figurines, hand-carved decorations on the houses, more beautiful flowers, carved Thuya and bushes. They entered a large room, it was like the interior of a palace, more beautiful flowers, carved figurines, a beautiful fountain, and of course the lighting under the ground, that was done so by shining mushrooms.

Elf: - 'Welcome Big Boss!': - The little elf bowed to him.' Let me introduce you to these people who are here to….' The little elf finished what she had to say. After all, the big boss interrupted her.

Big Boss: - 'Welcome underground! come closer." The Big Boss was a beautiful lady elf with beautiful long black hair, green eyes, and orange and light green clothes. The elves also watched her every move and wish. The Big Boss's elves gave her the name "Big Boss" because she holds a power which the other elves do not have. They are the only elves who can keep their existence and whereabouts a secret from the evil witch. But this special power only works on elves. So, because of this, for now they can only give helpful advice.

Big Boss: - 'Let me introduce myself, my name is Kleopatra. I know why you are here, but I think you also know that I can't help you any more than my sister could, I can only provide you with information. I'm not going to tell you anything new, but the solution is here between you, only a family member can defeat the evil witch, but there's something you don't know, I'm not authorized to tell you, because if I do, I'll break our invisibility and we're all going to be in trouble here. You can stay here tonight, but you have to leave in the morning.'- With that she finished what she was saying, waved and the little elves led them out of the room. Kleopatra was the guardian of the earth. Everyone got a room, just like at the elves previously.

James: - 'something doesn't smell right to me!'

Oliver: - 'Sorry, it wasn't me!' he interjected.

James: - 'No, Oliver, I know it wasn't you, that's not what I'm talking about. I'm talking about something being wrong here!' He said a little confused. Hanna got up and started walking up and down; she knew something but didn't dare to say it. Evelin had been watching Hanna for some time, she was watching her now again, she didn't like something about her.

James: - 'Somehow, we need to find out what is going on here, what is this all about? Everyone just says that only a family member can defeat the evil witch. Well, if I put the puzzle together correctly, it should only be Hanna, not me. He finished his sentence thoughtfully. Hanna couldn't take it anymore and left the room. James fell into thinking, he didn't say a word, he just thought about this whole thing.

Evelin didn't hesitate either, she went after Hanna to find out what was going on here.

Evelin: - 'Hanna, wait!' She addressed her hastily. Hanna turned and looked at Evelin, and with almost pleading eyes, she said: - 'Evelin, please go back to the others, don't come after me.': - She said in despair. Evelin: - 'wait, wait, just for a minute, what's going on here? You know something! Why do not you tell me? Are you hiding something? I knew you couldn't be trusted, you're just taking advantage of us, to get rid of us?': - She snapped at her angrily.

Hanna: - 'No Evelin, you are wrong! It's not the way you think.': - She tried to explain.

Evelin: - 'Is it not as, I think? Well then how is it then? She replied angrily.

James: - 'Wow, wow, girls! There's no need to fight, I know what Hanna doesn't want to say and I also know what the elves don't want to say, we'll talk about it tomorrow when we're out, ok!?' He interjected in the fight. Both of them looked at James in surprise, then at each other, they didn't understand what this meant, but they accepted James' statement.

Everyone went back to their own room, of course Evelin looked at Hanna with bloodthirsty eyes before moving aside. Hanna sat on the bed, and stared in front of her, she knew that James had finally figured out the truth and the time had finally come for them to solve this task.

When they woke up the next morning, they found themselves in a beautiful little clearing, lying on beautiful flower beds, and of course, again everyone had fresh supplies for their journey. Hanna woke up first, looked around and James wasn't there. Sensing that he was nearby, she started walking towards him they met on the way.

James: - 'Oh, good morning, Hanna': - He greeted her kindly. 'Are you prepared for the long journey that lies ahead?': - He asked with a smile.

Hanna: - 'Oh, good morning, James, yes, I'm ready, we can get in the middle of it if you want': - She replied smiling. Together they headed back to the others who were already awake and looking for them.

Evelin: - 'Where have you been? You're driving us nuts! You can't just walk away!' Meanwhile, her voice softened. After all, she fell in love with James and she doesn't know how long she can hold it in herself, sooner or later she will tell him, she is waiting for the right time. James: - 'Good morning, everyone, I hope we won't be in danger again like last time, I found out something that I can't tell you, but only when the time comes. But now we have to go further.

Ancestry of James

They continued their journey in the mystical forest, on muddy, slushy, dark, foggy roads, they walked in places where even the sun did not shine, they were surrounded by terrifying voices, they had to go through rocky places, on paths that where so narrow only one person could fit, so they followed each other in a line as they went along. The power of magic began to come to James more and more, because of this, he began to hallucinate, at least he thought it was a hallucination, but these were the memories that slowly came to the surface to wake him up to reality. In order for this to happen, Hanna will need her help, but she doesn't know that yet. Suddenly, James had to fall asleep, he started to feel dizzy, his memories came back, and he felt strange. Evelin tries to get there, saying.

Evelin: - James! Are you okay? What's wrong? Are you not feeling well? She suddenly asked a bunch of questions in desperation.

James: - I'm fine, I'm just a little dizzy, that's all, nothing will pass, we don't have to stop, we can keep going. He reassured Evelin and the others also continued their journey. They reached a cave, but it was getting dark, and they had to stop somewhere for the night. When they entered the cave, they looked carefully to see if it was safe or not. They found torches, which they lit, so they had lighting. On the surface, the cave seemed safe at first however, it was everything but. They lit a fire to warm themselves; Hanna brought two rabbits for dinner, which they put on a skewer to roast. They sat peacefully by the fire, talking while they slowly turned the rabbits over the skewer, they were laughing, but suddenly it was as if someone had passed them by. Of course, only Oliver noticed this, since he gets scared by everything. He looked around, but he didn't see anything. Someone walked past again, which Oliver noticed again, the others were laughing and talking, but Oliver started to get a little bothered by this situation, he stood up and looked around, Hanna noticed Oliver's strange behaviour and started watching Oliver. Since Oliver didn't see anyone again, he sat back down and started looking around to see if someone was there or if he was just imagining things. That someone passed by them again, Oliver saw it, but he couldn't make out the shape of that thing, because it was very fast. He suddenly jumped up from his seat and called out loudly: - 'Someone is here! Or something! I don't know exactly what it is, but there is someone here besides us.' He finished the sentence, horrified. Hanna: 'Yes, I saw it too, but I can't say what it was.' Suddenly there was silence, everyone started to look around, they spun around, stood up to look around,

55

and they realized that Evelin had disappeared, she was simply not there. Everyone shouted Evelin's name in desperation, they took torches in their hands to look for her, they looked around the cave. The cave was not too big, it had another room that led through a small gap and that was it, it was a small cave, but Evelin was nowhere to be found, she simply disappeared. They stood there in the other room, trying to find a clue to find Evelin. They looked at the walls, protruding pieces of rock, to see if something caught their eye. Hanna and James started to feel something, and they both went to the same place. They both made their way to a small drop-in part of the cave, as if something had led them there. I got there and there was an inscription on the wall: -

"IF YOU WANT GOOD, THEN TURN BACK!"

'BLOOD CANNOT BE WIPED AWAY!

THE AGE OF LIGHT IS OVER!

THE POWER OF DARKNESS HAS COME!

This was written on the wall, they read it out loud at the same time, Oliver also went there to see. They didn't know what it meant, but they didn't give up, they tried to think about it, maybe a message just needs to be deciphered and then they'll find Evelin.

Hanna: - 'You know James, I have to tell you something, I think now is the time for this to come to light,: - she said a little sadly.

James: - 'I know what you want to say, that we are siblings... James wanted to continue what he was saying when Hanna took his hand, looked into his eyes and spoke.

Hanna: - No James, you are not my sibling, but my cousin, the son of the evil witch.: - replied sadly. When James heard this, he suddenly became weak, memories came to the surface, thousands of memories broke to the surface in his mind, which was incredible to him, because it's not what he expected. His parents, who raised him, aren't they, his parents? How is it possible? When did I come to my foster parents? Such questions were constantly in his head. Confused, he walked back and forth like the flying Dutchman. He stepped aside to be alone with his thoughts. Oliver and Hanna tried to figure out what this writing on the wall could mean, they went their separate ways to find some clues on how to find Evelin.

The evil witch kept Evelin locked in a cell, where it was dark, there was a very small, barred window on the wall so that she couldn't look out, a little light came in from there just so she could see. Evelin shouted for help, but of course no one answered her, after all, apart from the witch, only her subordinates were there who kept an eye on Evelin. Evelin went and started to bang on the door: - 'Let me out! You can't hold me here! I have to go back to my friends! Let me out!': – Evelin shouted in despair.

Evelin heard footsteps approaching her.

Wicked witch: - 'Open the door! She said to her people firmly! The guards opened the door and the evil witch stepped into the cell.

Wicked witch: - 'Good morning my child! I hear you want to get out of here! Humph. The Evil Witch expressed! 'Well, it won't be easy. As you won't be going anywhere, you will stay here until James gets here.' As I hear, he is getting closer, and he wants to destroy me! HAHAHAHAHAHHA!' The evil witch laughed. You can't just destroy me that easily, my power has no bounds, there is no chance against me, AHAHAHHAHAHA. The evil witch laughed like all evil witch laugh. With that she left the cell, and the guards closed the door.

Evelin: – 'Oh yes! he will destroy you, because he is much

stronger than you are!' She shouted back at her crying. The witch hearing this, started laughing even more while she walked up the stairs, leaving the basement. She went into her secret room and closed the door behind her and went to her magical ball.

Evil Witch: – OSTENDE MIHI FACIEM MAGICAE PILA JAMES ALDER (In Latin) The magical ball started floating in the air, and started to look for James Alder, it didn't much time as it had found him. He was sat on a rock in deep thought, mumbling to himself.

James: – 'This isn't possible. No this isn't possible. Suddenly he stopped talking and looked up, directly into the eyes of the Evil Witch, he looked deeply and penetratingly at her with tearful eyes, because he could feel that in this moment he is being watched by the Evil Witch. The Evil Witch was taken aback by this and immediately took two steps back, the ball turned off and went back to its original position, the Witch suddenly put her hands on her chest and sat on the floor, like something had clicked inside her but she didn't know where to put this feeling. She was sat there for a good while, this weird feeling that she had was stirring inside her, sparked began to break out inside her, very faint sparks of memories but this wasn't enough to bring her back from her evil plan. James went back to his friends after an hour feeling relieved, he joined them in the search like nothing had happened. Hanna looked at James with a smirk and she also continued the search. James could feel the power inside of him that was passed down to him by his mother, as this memory that broke through brought everything to the surface, even when he was born and how he got to his current parents. The Evil Witch when she was young fell in love, and she was very happy with her partner who was a prince, but in that world the prince couldn't be married to a peasant girl, and so because of this they were together as much as they could be. But with time they were both really in love with each other. This love arrived in the ears of the king which he of course did not like, he did not allow his son to leave the palace again. His every move was followed forever. Meanwhile, the evil witch became pregnant with the prince's son. The prince didn't know anything about this, since he couldn't leave the palace anymore. The Evil Witch had enough that her prince would not come to the usual meeting place no matter how much she waited. Because of this she sent a white dove with a message to the prince. Message:

My dear!

I don't know what happened to make you not come to me anymore! But I have a hunch, I think the king found out that the two of us are together.

My dear! I want you to know, I love you very much and I will always love you, I'm going to sneak into the palace because I have an important news to deliver to you personally.

See you soon.

Your dear Miriam!

'The Prince name is Gilbert'. Gilbert became very excited after reading the message, waiting every minute to see his love again. He didn't have to wait long, after a couple of days he realized that his love is serving them food. Gilbert became very happy; he almost blossomed, from his previous sadness. The king immediately noticed how happy the prince suddenly became, which of course made him very happy that his son finally got over it and moved on. The love continued secretly between the two lovers.

Gilbert: - 'My sweet love! I'm very excited, now you can tell me what you wanted to tell me, I haven't been able to sleep from my curiosity.' He expressed himself happily. Gilbert waited two months to ask this question because something always came up and they couldn't discuss it. Yes, but the king wasn't exactly ignorant either, he soon realized that his son was happy because the girl he loved was here in the palace. The king had informers and there was a wizard there. The informants, of course, confirmed to the king that she was indeed in the palace and that she was with the prince. The king became so angry that he went to his wizard and asked him to make a magic potion that would make him forget his memories and he would no longer know his secret love. This will make it easier for the king to pass on the kingdom to his son. The sorcerer prepared the magic potions and handed them to the king. The king was very happy that he could finally get rid of the girl who did not belong to his son. His trusted people planned a romantic dinner for the king in one of the most beautiful places in the garden. Beautifully decorated, the king created a cozy atmosphere, of course the king had all this done and arranged so that everything was the prince's idea. After all, the king had the tools and the men. The prince was influenced, and they led him by the nose, it was easy to create this because he was endlessly in love. The prince was very happy about this, because it was planned in such a way that it seemed it was entirely the prince's idea. That day the king also left the palace on some pretext to make the plan work perfectly. The couple in love were very happy that they could finally spend their day together in calm conditions without being revealed. The certain dinner time came, they sat down at the table to eat and drink. There was a welcome drink beforehand, after which they were served dinner. After they had dined, the prince immediately asked for a bottle of champagne to celebrate. Well, when they toasted and drank the champagne, the magic potion that was already in the glass worked at that moment, both of them suddenly stood facing each other and did not know who was and how they got to where they are now. The prince was amazed at what he was doing here with this girl, Miriam also looked wide-eyed as to what she was doing in this place, they apologized to each other, and everyone went back to their work. Miriam left the palace, as she did not belong there and did not work there, she only went there for the time to see the prince and to be with him. Since the magic potion had taken effect, Miriam also went back to her home. Flashback to the conversation between Gilbert and Miriam, when Gilbert asked Miriam if she could tell him what she wanted to say.

Miriam: - 'My love, I am pregnant with your child, the fruit of our love!: – she finally said happily. Glibert: - 'My goodness! This is amazing! My love, is this really true?: – asked back happily. They fell in love with each other, and they were very happy. They were just planning how to run away together, when the certain last dinner together in the palace, at least for them, didn't happen and from then on, they didn't know who the other person was, why they were there together, at a cozy dinner table. But the wizard didn't count on a certain thing because he didn't know that Miriam was pregnant, that was the cause of the trouble. After Miriam went home, but didn't remember anything, except that one day she felt the child in her belly, suddenly she held her belly and the little baby started kicking and fiddling. Her memory began to break, the magic potion did not have as much of an effect on her as it did on Gilbert, this is due to the fact that she was pregnant, it only worked for a short while on Miriam. All Miriam's memories came back, she became very sad, sobbing that the king had tricked them like that, unfortunately she couldn't help the prince just by going back to the palace. But she couldn't do that because her belly was getting bigger and bigger and would have been noticeable to everyone. The big day came when her son was born, and she named him James. She worked out a spell that opened the gate to another world, when it was ready, she recited the spell and took James to the other world, placing him at the door of the Alder family who raised him. Miriam after thinking long and hard about this did so, because she gifted her son with something that he would find Miriam and bring back when needed and he would be able to save Miriam from what she was about to do. Miriam took an evil revenge against the king, she vowed that if her love could not be Her's, so he couldn't be anyone's. She went to her secret room and took out the darkest and most evil spells, this book was kept in a hidden place not to be seen by anyone. She worked for years on the evil spells because it had to be perfect. During this time, she built a huge palace in a place that is very difficult to access. She conjured soldiers from various animals into human form, and she held nature in her grip. She cursed the thousands of hectares surrounding the palace, she also cursed the animals, and everything surrendered by her. Not a single race could be brought under the mercy of her, those were the little elves, because they lived under the earth in a place where her magic could not reach. She left her own family there a long time ago, she didn't want to be with them anymore, because they didn't stand by her. They kept telling her to forget about the prince, to move on and they would raise the little boy together. But she was not willing to accept this and continue to live like this, not to be with the one she loves.

After many years, she had the perfect revenge to strike the king. After many years, unfortunately, Gilbert got married a princess, who gave birth to two beautiful children, a boy and a girl. They were very happy together; of course, it was thanks to the magic potion, since Gilbert didn't remember anything. The king secretly gave a great reward to the wizard, who made the magic potion and also paid for his silence. The years passed as if nothing had happened, they were happy, especially the king, that they finally got rid of that peasant girl. The king had no idea what was going to happen next, because no one knew. Nobody else knew that Miriam was pregnant when they were separated, only Gilbert. Well, certain news arrived at the king that a huge palace has been built somewhere, which is surrounded by darkness and vultures fly over the palace. People called the palace 'The Palace of Darkness '. After all, rumours spread quickly, as the king found out, of course. He wanted to find out about the nature of this palace and who owns it, why the news reached him so late, when he needs to know about everything! He sent a couple of soldiers there to explore and to bring news back to the king. When the soldiers reached the border of the magic line, of course there was no way to know, since it was invisible, Miriam immediately knew that someone had crossed her border. She sent four ravens to scout, and until then she watched the events from her magic sphere. When the ravens got there, Miriam immediately saw that the king's military scouts were the ones who crossed the border of the magical forest. Seeing this, she had a good laugh, she couldn't wait for them to venture closer to the palace. She watched their every footstep, because the ravens never lost sight of them for a minute. The soldiers wandered in the cursed place, which was very cold and scary, the place was mostly covered in fog, it was a slimy damp place full of chills. The soldiers didn't continue their journey on their horses, but on foot and took the reins of the horses.

Edmond (soldier): - 'Shouldn't we turn back? I don't like this place! We'll come up with something for the king!': – He asked his comrades nervously.

Rick: - 'Let's continue the search, soldier!': – He answered firmly and decisively.

Edmond: - 'Yes, I understood, commander.': – He answered somewhat indecisively. Miriam was amused by this sight, and in the meantime, she was chanting a spell against them. The elves tried to warn them not to go further into the forest, and to turn back, but it was all in vain, the commander didn't care, he didn't even want to hear about them turning back, he threatened them that they would be killed if they turned back. They were very close to the palace, they could see the top of it, as the vultures circled above it.

Rick: - 'Well, gentlemen, we're not that far! It won't be long before we get there and find out who owns the palace. We are going to camp now, the horses also need to rest, we will spend the night here, we will continue tomorrow morning.': - He stated firmly. They camped, had dinner, and then went to rest. The night was very long, full of strange sounds, Edmond didn't like the whole place, but unfortunately, he had no choice. The next morning came, the soldiers woke up, collected their belongings and moved on. They arrived at the palace in the evening, but they couldn't get in, it was standing on a rock that was surrounded by water, and the crocodiles were swimming in the water, it was impossible to get into the palace.

A strange witch's laugh was heard from the palace, which had a huge sound range. The soldiers also shuddered at the sound.

Rick (commander): - 'Gentlemen! We need a war plan, we have to get into that palace, so we will!' The commander declared. The soldiers got off their horses and gathered to discuss further steps. Suddenly, hundreds of vultures flew in circles around soldiers' heads, which was not a good sign. In the middle of the big meeting, one of the soldiers looked up and froze.

Soldier: - 'Commander, I'm reporting that vultures are flying over our heads...' He couldn't finish the sentence because the vultures attacked them. They drew their swords, and the fight began. Many vultures were executed, and many soldiers were injured. The commander blew a retreat, and so they fled from the palace and retreated into the forest. As soon as they entered the forest, they saw a dense, large black spot in the distance, as if it was approaching them. The soldiers were trying to help their wounded comrades when they realized that this black cloud was approaching them, they warned each other again, quickly jumped on their horses and started galloping home as fast as they could.

They arrived back at the royal court broken and with many wounded, the commander presented himself to the king.

Rick: - 'My dear king sir! I regret to inform you that our mission failed, we were not successful, we were attacked by forest animals controlled by that evil witch. There were many wounded, so we retreated, your Majesty!'

King: - 'Hmmm…. Commander you can leave!' - The king declared.

King: - Immediately call in the king's hand! – The king said sternly. They brought the king's advisor there to discuss further steps. The king's advisor was a wizard, but no one knew about this except the king. The king vacated the room because this conversation was strictly confidential.

King: -'Well, my dear friend! I would like to ask for your help in this matter, as you heard the mission against the evil witch was unsuccessful. I am asking you to find out how to get into that palace and how to catch the witch. Then let me know about the developments, but don't take too long because the witch is brewing something bad!': – The king asked the wizard.

Advisor: - 'Yes, Your Highness, you will not be disappointed in me, sir! He bowed respectfully to the king and left. The wizard hurried home to please the king, he entered his house, closed the door behind himself and went to work. The sun was well up when the wizard finished his work, he immediately went to the king, because what he found was very important. The king received the wizard in a separate room.

Advisor: - 'Good morning, my lord, I have come with extraordinary news, this is the only chance we have to defeat the evil witch.': - The wizard said a little nervously.

King: 'Greetings, my dear friend! Tell me the news! I'm curious!': - Said the king excitedly.

Advisor: - 'Your Majesty! I worked all night, using every bit of my magical power to find out how…….'

King: - 'Get to the point, my friend, don't beat around the bush, tell me right away what needs to be done and I will do it!': - The king interrupted impatiently.

Advisor: - 'Only one boy can help us and humanity, whose name is James Alder! Sir.': – The wizard finished the sentence. The king got up from his chair, held his chin, thought about what the wizard had told him, walked to the window, looked at the life outside, all the while the only thing running through his mind was what the wizard had told him.

King: - 'Where is this boy? James A….'

Advisor: - 'James Alder, sir!'

King: - 'Yes! James Alder?'

Advisor: - 'Sir, this boy is on his way to the palace, he wants to eliminate the evil witch.

King: - 'That's great, then we don't have to do anything, just wait to see if he succeeds! Then I will reward him abundantly!' Said the king joyfully.

Advisor: - 'Yes, Your Majesty! This is indeed great news, but it will not be easy for him to get into the palace either, so far no one has succeeded.' - The wizard said.

King: - 'Come on! Don't be so hopeless! If the spell says that only he will succeed in defeating the witch, then it will be so.': - The king laughed happily.

Advisor: - 'Yes, Your Majesty!' He bowed to the king.

King: - 'Nice job my dear friend.' He finished the sentence with satisfaction.

James: - 'Hanna! If the wicked witch is my mom, who was my

dad?'

Hanna: - 'James! It was never revealed who your father was, as your mother made sure that nobody would ever find out. I can't explain the reason why she did it, but I think she had a good reason for it. No matter what magic spell you try to use, you won't succeed, as I have already tried, my mom tried too, but we didn't succeed. In our opinion, its someone who is an influential person can be very famous or very poor, and these are just guesses that will not surface any time soon. I'm sorry, James.': - She said exasperated.

James: - 'But these memories that came up in me contain a lot of information that is not entirely clear, but I know that the king has something to do with it, and I can't say for now, but if these memories came back, I think this will also be revealed soon.' They went to bed and James, with all the information in his mind that started coming to him, slowly returned like an open book. This magic that his mother gave him when he was a baby began to dissolve in his memories, precisely when he was in deep sleep it was projected back to him like a movie when it is shown from beginning to end. In his dream, everything was revealed, including who his real father was and that king was his grandfather. How she tore them apart and why the evil witch is plotting an evil revenge against the king. In the meantime, it was morning and James suddenly woke up as if he had a terrible nightmare. Everyone woke up to his loud wake-up call and tried to go to James to see if everything was okay.

Hanna: - 'James, is everything alright? You had a bad nightmare, didn't you?'- She asked scared.

James: - 'Oh my god! My goodness! I can't believe this; it was a nightmare! But at the same time, it's a good dream, I'm confused.'

Hanna: - 'I know, you got too much information during the night, don't worry, everything will be fine, you'll see it soon.'- She tried to calm James down. James began to think about whether he should tell them who his real father is, or should he keep it a secret, because as Hanna had said that night, that his mother had deliberately not let the others know who his real father was, so he decided not to tell anyone for the time being because she doesn't know why her mother hid this from everyone.

Evelin and the wicked witch!

The Evil Witch was constantly keeping an eye on the events. It was a beautiful starry night, the palace was silent, Evelin sat sadly in her cell and stared outside as much as she could, listening to the crickets chirping and crying softly.

Evelin: - 'James! Wherever you are, I hope your plan succeeds and you come for me!': – She whispered bitterly. The morning dawned, nature began to wake up, the birds chirped in the far distance because the screeching of the vultures drowned out the beautiful song of the birds.

Evil witch: - 'Well, well, well! What a morning we woke up to! Isn't it wonderful? Well, my child, I have decided that from today you will have a special room, from which you will not be able to escape, unless you want to be the crocodiles' lunch... haha-haha.': – She laughed mockingly.

My guards will escort you to your room, there will be a change of clothes, you can wash up, then you can join us in the great hall for breakfast, my dear. We'll continue chatting there. The witch left, her guards took care of the rest of the work, they escorted Evelin to her room, closed the door and kept guard. After Evelin entered the room, which was huge, her room was decorated with many windows, many beautiful flowers, her fangs were prepared, her clothes were ready to be worn. There was also a large closet in the room filled with more and more beautiful clothes. When she opened the closet, she was very surprised to see how many beautiful clothes were in it. She got dressed and went down the great hall with guards accompanying her, to have breakfast with the wicked witch. That room was huge, like everything in this palace, it was beautifully decorated with flowers, the whole palace was cozy from the inside, only the outside of the palace had a harsh appearance.

Evil Witch: - 'Good morning my child! Take a seat at the table, feel free to eat whatever your heart desires.' The Evil Witch said with a smile. Evelin couldn't explain this sudden kindness, but she didn't ponder on it too much, as she was very hungry.

Evil witch: - 'Tell me, my child! James knows he won't be able to get in here without my permission! Haha-haha….' The wicked witch laughed as she looked out the window.

Evelin: 'How do you know that James is coming here?' Evelin asked, surprised. 'If James wants to enter the palace, he will, he doesn't need your permission.' Evelin said angrily.

Evil witch: - 'Come on my child, anger will not protect you, my power is unsurpassed, no one wins…….'

Evelin: 'Yes! Everyone is beatable! And you, too, evil bitch! You know everyone has weak points, and you do too'……. She jumped up from the table and yelled at the witch. The witch looked at Evelin in surprise, thought for a while and let out a good laugh. Evelin ran out of the room, the guards wanted to run after her, but the witch waved them off, she let her go where she wanted, since there is no way out of the palace, she calmly looked out the window and laughed at what Evelin said. The witch thought it was a joke; she was so amused by it. After all, she

69

doesn't think that she can be defeated. The thing in her ear is only focused on keeping the evil plan alive in her. But she also has a weak point, as Evelin said, she just doesn't know that her mind is clouded. Evelin ran up to her room, slammed the door behind her, threw herself on the bed, buried her head in the pillow and cried herself out. During this time, James and his friends came out of the cave, sketched the drawings that were on the wall, and moved aside to the stream to collect their thoughts. Meanwhile, the little mushrooms were constantly trying to send information to James, his head was buzzing. James walked over to the stream, crouched down and bent over towards the water, he looked into the water and didn't see his own reflection, but the face of his real mother and father appeared on the water. He suddenly jumped when he saw this, he was scared for a while, but he was driven by curiosity, so he bent back over the water again. But there was no image of his real parents there anymore, only his own, he dipped his hands in the stream and began to wash his face with it in order to refresh himself and regain his senses. As soon as he washed his face, a special fish swam in front of James, it partially came out of the water and spoke.

Fish: - 'James the wicked witch is already waiting for you! There is only one way you can get into the palace, the little bottle you got from the wizard will help you, but only you and no one else can get in.' With that, the fish swam away before James could ask him anything.

Oliver: - 'Is everything alright my friend?' Oliver was interested.

James: - 'Yes Oliver, everything is fine. I'll be right back; I just need to think about the next steps.' He continued to stare at the water hoping to see his real parents again, suddenly some huge animal from the water pulled James into the water and disappeared with it. The others waited for James to return and let him be alone with his thoughts for a while. An hour passed, but James still did not return. The others began to worry and both of them went back to the stream to look for James. When they got there, the James wasn't there. Hanna was surprised, Oliver was scared as to where his friend could be. Oliver was about to shout out after James when Hanna shut his mouth...: - Hanna: - 'Tssssh! Do not shout! You won't bring James's back, I'll try to find him, but don't make noise because then we'll become an easy target.' She reassured Oliver. Hanna let go of Oliver, they looked at each other, the fear had left Oliver's face, but he trusted Hanna, so he didn't shout so that he wouldn't disappear like the rest of his friends.

Hanna: - 'Listen Oliver! We need you to help us find James, we need to collect some plants for a special potion, with the help of that we will find James!' Oliver – 'Okay!' He said soothingly.

Oliver: - 'I'll help! Of course! Just tell me what needs to be collected and I'll do it.' He answered somewhat relieved. They started to collect the plants, it took a while since they were not all in one place, but they collected them and went back to the cave where they could brew the potion. It was evening when the concoction was ready.

James was kidnapped by a huge underwater fish; he was taken to an underwater palace where the guardian of the waters lived. They led James to the guardian of the waters, a beautiful mermaid.

Mermaid: - 'Welcome James! First of all, I'm sorry about your trip. I had no other choice and no other means to solve bringing you here, I hope you didn't get hurt?' She asked politely.

James: - 'Welcome Your Highness! (James bowed to her) Of course, I'm not hurt, I'm just scared. If I may know, Your Majesty! Why did you bring me here?' He asked curiously.

Mermaid: - 'Since everyone knows why you are here James, to save us from the terrible evil witch, I feel it is my duty to help you in whatever way I can. I know where you're going, I know the place where the palace is very well, the water surrounds the palace and the water is full of crocodiles, it's impossible to get in there because the crocodiles don't even have to be charmed to prevent them from destroying anyone who ventures into the water. I brought you here to give you something that will help you get past the crocodiles.'

James: - 'I don't want to interrupt Your Highness! But when I was at the water, a little fish told me that my bottle........' James wanted to continue the sentence when the Mermaid interrupted: - Mermaid: - 'Yes, I know about it James, because I know everything about what happens in the water, I know. That little fish was the work of the evil witch, she wants you to be unable to defeat her and she will do anything to stop you. It would have been a trap to use your vial and then you can't defeat the witch. You only need to take out your bottle and use it when you are directly in front of the witch. Well, now I suggest that you rest for the night, you will be my guest, they will escort you to your room and I will let you go on your way tomorrow.' They started towards James's room, the view of the road leading there was impressive, finally they reached the room, James entered and looked around in amazement because the view was beautiful.

Hanna finished the concoction, scooped out a portion from the pot and drank it, Oliver waited curiously for its effect, he didn't have to wait long because Hanna had already seen where James was. Falling to her knees, she raised her head, fixed her gaze on the sky and sobbed.

Hanna: - 'JAMES IS SAFE!

HE'S RELAXING IN THE UNDERWATER WORLD

JAMES IS SAFE!

With that, her vision ended, she stood up and calmly turned to Oliver, grabbed his shoulder, she looked in his eyes and said.

Hanna: - 'Oliver! James is fine, He's not hurt, he's in a place where the evil witch's power can't reach, we'll meet James again tomorrow, let's rest in the meantime.' Finished the sentence.

Oliver: - 'That's good! I'm glad that he's fine and that he's not hurt, but I think there's a little problem. When you went into a trance you told me where James was. I don't know if this means good or not, if the evil witch can see and hear everything, then she had to have heard and seen this too, and it does not mean good.' He answered in despair.

Hanna: - 'I appreciate your concern, but the evil witch can't hear us here, that's why we came back to the cave. But if she did hear it, we're all in trouble.' She answered a little thoughtfully. Unable to sleep, Evelin lay there in front of the window, staring out at the moon and the stars, thinking about how to get out of there. She sat down on the bed thoughtfully and sadly, remembering the adventures she and her friends had been through together. At the same time, she also remembered her family, because of course she missed them very much. As soon as she thought about what had happened, she reached into the inside pocket of her jacket and found the key she had put in her pocket in the basement. She took it out and started to look at it, rotating it and wondered where this key is good for? Why did she put it away, if they are not in that house anyway? Thoughts and thoughts followed each other in her head, she put it back in her pocket, it felt safe there. Something drew her to the closet, she opened it but it was full of clothes, there was nothing interesting in that closet. She started to pull them aside, she started looking at the clothes one by one, she couldn't sleep anyway so she diverted her thoughts, there were some clothes that she took out of the closet so she could see them more easily. There was a door in the right inner part of the cupboard, but it had no handle, just a keyhole, nothing more, but Evelin doesn't know this yet, because she didn't get to look inside, since the cupboard was quite big. She was only halfway through looking at the clothes when something hit the window, which made a loud noise. Evelin got very scared and stopped looking. She went to the window to check what hit it; it was a little bird who was lying passed out from the impact on the window ledge. She opened the window, and she began to stroke it so that the bird would hopefully wake up, the little bird slowly woke up and Evelin let it go. She decided to lie down to sleep because it was very late, she needed to be fresh the next morning. The next morning came, Evelin woke up, jumped out of bed excitedly as if she had a feeling that something good would happen to her today. She washed up, got dressed and went to breakfast in the great hall. She is entering the great hall, and the Evil Witch greeted her.

Evil Witch: - 'Good morning, my child, I heard you stayed up for a long time, you weren't looking for something right?. Hahaha…. but my child, you can't get out of here, no matter how much you want to, you have no chance, because remember, I see and hear everything here in the palace, and not only in here but also outside. I hear your friend James is getting help to get in here, it's very interesting and fascinating, but there's just one problem, he won't be able to get in here with any help at all, as I made sure he can't get anywhere near the palace HAHAHAH.'

Evelin: - 'You are really very evil!' She looked deeply into the Evil Witches eyes. 'I know that you also have a heart, you are not as evil as you show yourself to be, because then your palace would not be so beautifully decorated on the inside, but its appearance would be harsh, gloomy and depressing as you hold yourself to be.' She answered calmly. When the witch heard this, she raised her hand and gave Evelin a big slap, who flew away from the blow and fainted. The guards took Evelin back to her room and laid her down in the bed. When Evelin regained consciousness, she opened her eyes but saw dimly, her clear vision slowly returned, but what she saw was not a good sight. All the beautiful flowers and decorations disappeared from her room, her room was plunged into darkness, there were torn black shades in front of the windows, instead of flowers, there were spiky cacti, there were cobwebs everywhere and of course spiders, but besides that, there were also mice who were now Evelins new room-mates. The sight of the room was creepy, Evelin was a little scared, she sat up in bed and looked around, the sight saddened her, but actually she expected that, but not this harshly. She regretted what she said to the witch, but it was too late, she couldn't undo it, she set about removing the cobwebs and cleaning the room because it looked disgusting, not to mention the mice. Since she hadn't eaten breakfast a tray of dry bread and a glass of water were left there for her, of course, the guards left it on the ground for her because this was the witch's order, which the mice grabbed and quickly ate it on her behalf. After finishing cleaning, she went to the closet and opened it again, but for some reason the clothes were still inside. She was surprised by this, because if she changed the whole palace, why didn't she take out the clothes and change them? This question was running through her mind. She closed all the blinds and blocked all the holes so that there would be no uninvited guests in the room. Only the candles lit the room, of which there were a total of seven, she took one to the closet, placed it in front of herself and continued looking through the clothes. It is true that she had not seen such beautiful clothes, since people do not make such clothes in her world; because of this she began to look through them and admired each piece because one was more beautiful than the other. Hours passed in picking out the clothes and admiring them, she got closer and closer to the right side of the closet, now only one piece of clothing separated her from reaching the hidden door inside the closet. She wanted to take the clothing off the it's hanger, that is she takes out of the closet then she will notice the secret room, but at that moment the door of the room opened, so she couldn't take out the dress, instead closed the closet door quickly. The guards burst into the room to escort Evelin to the

Evil Witch.

Evil Witch: - 'Hahaha...., well, my child, I hope you are satisfied with the appearance of the palace! Now you can see what I am really like, how wonderful my world is, and no one will change that! Neither you! Nor anyone else. Hahaha..., well Evelin, I hope you like your new room, because from now on it will stay like this, and no one will change it. Hahahaha.'

Evelin: - 'Yes, I like my new room, and thank you for your kindness, I'm sure I'll have a good time.' She replied with a smile.

Evil Witch: - 'Get this bastard out of my sight! I don't want to see you anymore, stay in your room forever! Hahahaha.'

They took Evelin back to her room, slammed the door on her and locked it, but during this time her door was replaced, and they also took her to the boss so that they could complete this. The door they replaced it with, was like it they brought it from a prison, you don't have to open it to get food, you just have to slide it in. Evelin ran to her bed, laid down and started to cry, blaming herself for everything, that she had ruined everything and that there was no way out of this. She fell asleep crying a lot, in her dream she was at home with her loved ones, they were grilling the most delicious meats outside in the yard, drinking soft drinks, playing football, laughing, her friends were there, and they were having a good time. But in her dream, the laughter suddenly ended, the evil witch appeared in front of her and laughed at them, and then Evelin suddenly woke up, sweaty and scared. She sat up in the bed and stared blankly into the distance. Two days have passed since then, and in those two days James returned to the others who had been waiting for him.

Hanna: - 'Thank God that you are well and that you are not in any pain, we were very worried about you.' She welcomed James. Oliver also went there and hugged his friend.

Oliver: - 'Welcome, friend!'

James: 'I'm fine! No problem, I was in the right place, with lovely underwater fairies. There is a little problem though, while I was there, Hanna, you went into a trance, which you shouldn't have done. I know you were worried, it's only natural, but unfortunately the evil Witch found out and now she made it difficult for me to get into the palace. We will have come up with something together so that no one can stop us.

Hanna: - 'I'm very sorry, but you disappeared, and I had to do something to see if you were okay. We went into the cave to be safe, but apparently it wasn't.'

James: - 'No problem! But it doesn't matter anyway, we redo it, it's a thing of the past, but we have to figure something out because our way there won't be safe. From now on, we have to find a place where she can't hear or see us. The most important thing is not to say anything out loud, we will communicate in a different way from now on, I will tell you how this will happen. They went back to the cave, sat around next to a big fire, and James began to write a message on the stone wall, the message was: - FROM NOW ON IF WE HAVE ANYTHING TO SAY TO EACH OTHER, WE WILL WRITE IT DOWN, AND WE WILL WRITE IT SO THAT NOBODY WILL SEE IT ONLY THE TITLED PERSON. With this, he quickly wiped it off so that no one could see it. They walked out of the cave, when they reached the exit, they hit an invisible wall that blocked the exit.

James: - 'Well, here is the first obstacle, the evil witch closed it with a spell so that we could not get out. However, we can fix this, we can dissolve this spell, I hope.'

Hanna: - 'James, please give me your hand, the magic is in you, no one can take it away from you, because you also feel its power, if the two of us work together, we will succeed.' With that, they took each other's hands and started saying the counter spell to break the witch's spell. This challenge went easily, they broke the spell, the invisible wall disappeared, and they got out of the cave. They set off towards the palace. They followed the path that only James's saw, but the evil witch set a trap for them again. The trees suddenly started to move, just like when there is a big wind and the trees sway back and forth, but here there was no wind, the trees started swaying on their own. All three of them stopped because they knew that this was not normal, something was going to happen. They stood back-to-back and began to look from side to side to see where this surprise was coming from. But they didn't see anything; they cautiously moved on, they could only go forward a hundred meters, as soon as they crossed the hundred meters, at that moment, a bolt of lightning struck and the ground opened up, where a trap prepared in advance welcomed them. All three of them fell into it; there was a big whole full of slippery creepy critters, spiders and rats. They were scared and looked around to see what had happened, and then they realized that they had fallen into a huge hole, they were standing close to each other, and they were trying to think of something to get out of there. Suddenly they heard a great roar from above; all three of them looked up and saw riders circling at the edge of the hole.

James: - 'Help! Help! Help us out of here.' He shouted at them. They heard a loud thud, someone dismounted from the horse, went to the edge of the rim and looked inside. There was a wraith who looked down in the hole and said to them: - 'I advise you not to come close to the palace, otherwise we will skewer you for dinner.' He spoke down to them in a very deep voice. With that they galloped away. James began to think about what to do and how to get out of there, because the hole was so deep that it seemed impossible to get out. All three of them started thinking about how they could climb out of this hole. James closed his eyes and shut off the outside noises from his thoughts, silence took over, and now he was able to find a solution easier. The mushrooms again sent information to their master suggesting: -

IF YOU'RE IN TROUBLE, USE YOUR POWER!

THE POWER IN YOUR STRENGTH WILL HELP YOU OUT!

ACT WISELY!

STRENGTH AND LOVE WILL LEAD YOU OUT.

James opened his eyes, and they were swarmed by crawlers, spiders, and rats. The magical power inherent in him began to take over him; it broke to the surface like never before. The magic coming from the heart had formed inside him; what he saw in front of him was not creepers or spiders and rats, but flowers, tendrils and different butterflies that showed them the way out. He had to see this with his heart, because love is stronger than hate, love conquers everything, he said the spell out loud, and the many creepers and other animals disappeared, and what replaced it was what James's saw, the many beautiful flowers, the tendrils, and butterflies grew in their place. And the butterflies showed the way out of the hole.

Hanna: - 'I knew you had the magic power in you, and it didn't let you down, I'm very proud, James.'

Oliver: - 'Wow. James! How did you do that dude! You were amazing! I didn't think a wizard was my friend.' He smiled to himself.

James: - 'You know! So far, I haven't told anyone what's really happening to me. I feel that now is the time to share this with you. The flowers suddenly began to grow, the tendrils also, and the butterflies became more and more numerous to provide safety to the three in trouble while he shared this important information with them.

James: - 'This happened to me at home on the first day of school on the way to school. Oliver, you must remember when we were attacked, I fell off my bike onto the grass, there were small mushrooms in the grass that crawled into my ears, that's when I changed, I had these small mushrooms in my ears. They guided me to this point, they whisper to me what is the right thing to do, and I also get strength from them. I don't really know what that means, why they crawled right into my ear, because then I wasn't the only one who fell off my bike, but the mushrooms chose me anyway. Well, this is my secret, now you know. He said with a smile.'

Hanna: - 'I'm glad that you shared this with us, although it's not strange, because I also have small mushrooms in my ears, which means that when the mushrooms found you, it happened because it was time for you to help us. Since there was a lot of trouble here, since you also saw, that's why mushrooms searched for you. That fight didn't happen by accident; it had to happen to lead you here. Our meeting on the train wasn't a coincidence either, I knew you'd be there on the train, that is precisely why I looked for you, but you know the rest.'

Oliver: - 'And how did we come into the picture? Do I have mushrooms too? And if there are, are they in my ears? Why can't I hear them? Maybe they will communicate with me later?' He suddenly asked a lot of questions.

James: - 'No, you idiot! Hahahaha…. Mushrooms are a family heirloom; they are only placed in the ears of our family members and no one else. They also put something in the evil witch's ear and when she was a baby, a black raven flew over her bed when she was a baby; she put that something in the baby's ear. But we still don't know what was put in her ear.'

Hanna: - 'That's right! The thing that the raven put in his ear made her an Evil Witch from that moment on; of course, this only became clear when my aunt could speak.' They finished the conversation and started walking out of the hole. They managed to reach the surface, rested and continued their journey. In the evening, they rested in a safe place, built a fire to warm themselves and prepared their dinner. They sat by the fire and talked quietly; James watched the dancing of the fire while falling into deep though. He wandered off to his foster parents' home to see what happened to them! The fire poured out its flames beautifully, as if there were dancing couples in it, it was almost enchanting. James was so engrossed in the sight that he didn't hear the others talking. Oliver went to get firewood, Hanna stayed with James. An unrecognizable being emerged from the fire and said in a creepy voice: - 'James! If you want to see Evelin, you'd better not go into the palace, you won't be able to defeat the evil witch anyway!' With that, the strange creature disappeared. James and Hanna looked at each other, not knowing what to think of this phenomenon, they were about to speak when Oliver came back with the firewood and said: - 'That! What the friggity finky funk was that? I was so scared I almost shat myself. This thingy was seriously talking, are you serious? I think we should invent something else to defeat evil....' Oliver couldn't finish the sentence, because James jumped there and covered his mouth with one quick movement.

James: - 'Tsh, tsh, don't talk! Something or someone is around us.' He whispered in Oliver's ear. 'Don't say anything, just listen.' With that, they listened in silence, looking around to see who might be there with them because they felt that they were not alone. They heard wood creaking, from different directions, as if someone was trying to scare them. Oliver was very afraid of what would happen to them now. The crackling sounds in the trees did not go away, the crackling sounds continued to get closer and closer. James closed his eyes and began to concentrate; he shut out the noises and tried to find whatever that was around them. Suddenly, all the noise stopped, only great silence reined around

James, the mushrooms were constantly sending him power and information. But this something that was around them was not visible to the naked eye. James discovers a shadow, a ghost. This spirit was the guardian of the fire, he appeared to warn them. The ghost stood in front of James and said: - 'James! Your path up to now was not very easy, and it won't be any easier after this point, getting into the palace will be easy for you, but your companions won't get anywhere near it. I have a message for you to share with your friends. Because their journey ends here, they can't go any further with you; it will be too dangerous for them and Hanna as well. She doesn't have as much magic power as you, so she won't be able to protect herself or your friend. Your magic power won't be able to protect them because the Evil Witch took care of it.' With that he finished the message and disappeared. James regained consciousness, and suddenly fell into deep thought for a while. Hanna and Oliver approached James and began to ask him about what he saw, what did he hear?

James: - 'Guys! Today is our last night together, tomorrow morning only I will go on, you can't come with me, it will be too dangerous.'

Hanna: - 'You're kidding me now! If we have come this far together, we will continue our journey together; we will not leave you alone.'

Oliver: - 'Dude! What will happen to you without me? Who will protect you? Well, of course, I'll go with you.' Both of them decided on James' side and did not want to let him go.

James: - 'You guys are very nice, but I have to continue the rest of the journey alone, I won't be able to protect you. The way there will be dangerous, you go back to the cave, and we'll meet there.

Oliver: - 'no god-damn way! I'm going with you, I won't leave you alone, come what may, I'll be there for you.' He pulled himself out proudly.

Hanna: - 'Tell me who you just saw? And what did he say to you that made you change your mind so quickly? This is why you don't want to go with us anymore, is that right?'

James: - 'The person I met earlier gave me a message to warn you of further dangers on the road, where you might not survive, and I don't want you to get into any trouble.

Hanna: 'I understand! Well then, I suggest we vote. If you want to go further with James, raise your hand.' Both Oliver and Hanna raised their hands. Hanna knew that this was the only way she could stay with James for the rest of the journey ahead.

James: - 'It's very kind of you to call out for me like that, but I've already decided, I'll continue the journey to the palace alone tomorrow.' He smiled to himself. Everyone went to sleep, to rest for tomorrow's journey as the road ahead of them was long and dangerous. But when they were all asleep, James carefully left so they wouldn't notice. He continued on his way alone in the middle of the night, he did not want to endanger the lives of his companions. It was dawn; Hanna opened her eyes and realized that James had left them there. She immediately jumped up and started to wake Oliver up. She didn't have to try very hard as he immediately jumped up and was ready to go. They set off in pursuit of James.

Parents unite!

Back home, the parents feel helpless, they are in despair, but don't give up hope, they are constantly looking for the children; they are doing everything they can to find the children. One afternoon, the parents whose children had disappeared had a meeting. The gathering was held at James' house. When everyone had arrived, they sat down over a cup of tea and suggestions were put on the table. Oliver's father suggested: - 'I think at night, when everyone is sleeping, we should sneak into the school and thoroughly look around, because that is where they were last seen. We bring all the necessary tools, flashlights, and search the entire school. Today is Friday anyway, school is closed tomorrow, perfect timing to do something, we can't wait for the police to do something.' Evelin's dad: 'I'm in, I'll collect the right tools and we'll meet at the back entrance of the school at midnight.'

James's father: - 'I'm in too, we really can't wait with folded hands, so everyone gathers what we need, we'll meet at midnight.' Everyone went home and collected the necessary tools. They were very excited because they didn't know what to expect. The long-awaited time had come, everyone was ready for the invasion. They jumped over the fence and started towards the entrance. Of course, the door was locked, and it had to be opened with a key, which was an obstacle for them.

James's dad: - 'Do any of you know how to open this door?'

Evelin's father: 'I'll try!' He took the appropriate tools from his bag to open the lock. He once worked for the secret agency, but no one knows about that, of course. The others just listened and suddenly did not speak.

Oliver's father: 'How the hell do you know how to open this lock?'

Evelin's father: - 'It's a long story, I won't explain it now if possible.' They managed to open the door, so they continued to the front of the school.

Evelin's father: - 'Listen! We have to split up so we can find something faster, than if we stay together. Do you have the CB radio?'

Dads answered at the same time: - 'Yes, we got it.' Their paths diverged in the search for the children. Evelin's father went east, Oliver's father went west, James' father went south. Wherever James's father went, there were children's lockers. The canteen was where Oliver's father went. Where Evelin's father went, there were large gyms and showers. James's father looked into each classroom, while in the hallway were all the lockers which he had walked past. Evelin's father looked through every single corner of the large hall, he went into the showers, he also looked carefully at everything there, he also went past the cupboards, but he didn't notice anything unusual so far. Oliver's father also got to where the canteens were, he looked around carefully, but he didn't find anything unusual either. The only one left is James' father, who might find something. They called out to him on the CB radio: - 'John! Receiving! Over!'

John: - 'I'm here on the long hallway where the lockers are! Over!'

Oliver's father - Kev: - 'We will be there immediately! Over!' They both made their way there when they heard someone walking along the hallway not far from them. It was the cleaner who lived at the garden at the back of the school, he used to check the school to see if everything was in order. They even hid from him so that he wouldn't notice them. But no one can hide from the old man, because he knew they were there, he was waiting for them. He walked straight towards them.

Cleaner: 'Good evening, gentlemen! How can I help? What are you doing here at such a late hour?

Evelin's father - Timber: - 'Good evening, sir! Sorry to break in like that, but we can't sit at home on our backside when our children are missing, we have to do something, we came here to school because this is where they were last seen, right?'

Cleaner: - 'Please, gentlemen, follow me!' He led them to where James' father was. When James' father saw that they had arrived there with the cleaner, he suddenly got scared and thought that they were in big trouble.

Kev: - 'He found us and brought us here; he is the cleaner of the school, and he came to check the hallways at night.

John: - 'We apologize for the….' He wanted to continue the sentence, but the cleaner stopped him.

Cleaner: - 'Gentlemen, please, if possible, let's move aside to another place where we can talk safely. Just follow me please' The cleaner led them out to his residence so that they could have dinner in a calm environment.

Cleaner: - 'Here we are, please come in.' He invited them in. They go into his house, which was pretty neat on the inside considering he lived there alone.

Timber: - 'Please sir! Why did we have to come here, since there is not much to discuss. Am I wrong?' And he looked at Kev for approval.

Cleaner: - 'Please pay attention! What I am about to say is very important, it cannot leak out of here, that why I brought all of you here. Maybe what I'm about to say will sound strange, but every word is true. Well, yes! The last time your children were seen was at school, but they did not disappear, at least not as you or others think. They are at the school until they complete their mission.

Timber: - 'What the hell did he just say?' He wanted to punch the cleaner, but Kev and John stopped him because they wanted to hear what the cleaner knew.

Kev: - 'Calm down! Hitting him won't help anyone; let him tell us what he knows maybe he can help us.

John: - 'Let him tell us what he knows, okay.?' So, he restrained himself and sat down on the chair.

Cleaner: - 'Your children are safe and alive I can assure you. But where there are reasons, adults cannot go there at the moment, I'm sorry.' John suddenly fell into thinking and was seized with a feeling that he knew where they were but did not want to believe it. He got up from the couch and walked towards the window. The cleaner noticed this immediately and knew that John knew where the children were. After all, when James was left in front of his door as a baby, a letter was left with him in his little cradle, in which was written his name, his origin, his mother's name and why he had to be left there and why he had to raise him. In the meantime, the cleaner explained everything he knew and only asks the parents to wait patiently because it will soon be over.

John: - 'I have something to say too! I didn't think this would happen.' Hearing this, Kev and Timber slowly got up from their seats and fixed their eyes on John. They went closer to him and couldn't believe their ears.

John: - 'I have to ask you to come over now, I have to show you something.' With that, they thanked the cleaner for the kind welcome and the story and left for John's house.

John led them to the shed where he used to tinker and craft, that shed was huge. They all went in, turned on the light and stood around the crafting table. John brought the safely kept letter, which he did not show to James because he felt that the time for it had not yet come, but apparently, he was wrong. He gave it to Timber to read the letter, which he had fearfully looked after for a very long time. After reading it, they looked at each other and waited for an explanation from John. John lowered his head and gave him the best explanation he could in a sad voice.

John: - 'My dear neighbours and friends! I know this doesn't help much now, but I didn't think that the time would come when I have to explain this to my neighbours, that my son is not my real son, that someone, and not just anyone, left him at my doorstep. Why right in front of my door? Well, I think my descendants were wizards a long, long time ago, but it was a long time ago, several decades ago, as far as I know, they had to hide in order to survive and each time they had to settle somewhere else with a different identity in order to survive, but I know that they did no harm to anyone in fact, from then on, they gave up magic and did it for the benefit of everyone. Because of this, this whole magic thing was forgotten, but after many years it was only remembered as a fairy tale. Maybe it has something to do with it, of course I'm the only one who thinks so, but I can't give a precise explanation, so I have to look it up, which I'm going to do, are you with me?'

Timber: - 'Okay! But when it comes to honesty, I also owe an explanation. I worked for the secret service, I can't say which one, but I think this will be enough. I know how to open any door and more. But this can't be revealed in any way shape or form of what we're talking about here, because then that's it for all for us.'

Kev: - 'All right, guys! These are very rough things, but we must end together.......' suddenly an owl flew in out of nowhere with a sealed letter in its beak, it flew over to their table and placed the letter in front of John. They all watched in surprise because all the doors and windows were closed, it was impossible to get in there, they suddenly looked around to see where it had flown in from, but they couldn't find a gap anywhere.

Timber: - 'That's interesting! How did it get here? How did it get here so suddenly? Open the letter, John.' John opened the letter, clicked the seal open and a huge light emanated from the letter. Due to the bright light, he dropped the letter from his hand and a hologram appeared in front of them from the bright light, this someone was from the world where the children were, the librarian said to the parents.

Message: - 'Greetings! You don't know me, but I know you, I had to send this message because I felt you should know what's going on here. Your children are fine (he showed them holographic pictures of the children so they don't have to worry) as you can see, I know you tried to find them, but I can assure you that it's an unnecessary effort and you won't be able to get in here, please wait patiently.' The message ended and the hologram disappeared.

Kev: - 'I don't understand this! Something stinks here, I don't like it, I don't know about you, but I can't wait patiently.'

Timber: - 'I agree! I don't know how, but we have to do something.' They both looked at John.

John: - 'Well fine then. I also agree with this, we will meet here exactly tomorrow and figure something out because I can't wait until this is over, I think we should also help, so we will help.' All at the same time: - 'Yes! That's what I'm talking about, off to fight.' Everyone went home and got ready for the next day. John couldn't sleep, so he went down to the living room and turned on the computer. He went to the search engine and typed in their family name, which brought up a lot of options, he went to one where there was a description saying 'magicians'. He clicked on the page and found what he was looking for; he started reading, which contained a lot of interesting information. He also learned a lot about how to get to where the children are. But that description was written in a dead language, because of this he printed it out. The next morning, they met in the cafe as they had agreed. 'Good morning, everyone' they greeted each other.

Kev: - 'Well, is everyone ready?'

Timber, John: - 'Yes.'

John: - 'I couldn't sleep last night, so I went on the internet and started researching all of this and I also managed to find how to get to where the children are.'

Timber, Kev: - 'Well that's great news! Well then, let's get into it.'

John: - 'There's a little problem! That part is written in a dead language, in order to decipher it, we need to take this description to someone who is reliable and knows about these things. So, this means that we have to take it to a person who is experienced in this and knows the story, otherwise all our efforts are pointless.'

Timber: - 'I have a very good and reliable friend, we used to work together so he can help us with this.'

John: - 'Then that's great, I'll see you at the snack bar in an hour.' Everyone went home and prepared all the necessary equipment needed to embark on the journey. After an hour, they met in the snack bar, ordered coffee and something to eat, so that nothing would be an obstacle later.

Kev: - 'Well, did you manage to arrange something Tim?'

Tim: - (Starting with a big sigh) 'Well yes, if we really get into this, we have to tell our wives what we are up to because it will be an adventurous journey.'

John: - 'Get to the point!!!'

Tim: - 'Okay! We have to travel to America, they can only help us from there, they don't have the equipment we will need here. That's why I said that we have to tell our wives in because America is not next door.' All three of them agreed to this and told their partners all this and of course that they support them, since it is about their children. The next morning, they left for the airport to travel to America. Everything went smoothly, but they were sitting on the plane on their way to America, New York to be exact, six hours of travel ahead of them, so they made themselves comfortable.

John: 'Listen Tim! Who are we going to meet anyway? Is that someone trustworthy? Because this can be a big scandal if we turn to the wrong person.'

Tim: - 'Calm down! Relax and leave this matter to me, it's about our children, I know what I'm doing.' They arrived in New York, a beautiful city, huge buildings, lots of people, cars, everyone was very busy.

Kev: - 'Well here we are! And now we're going to take a taxi to the hotel and make arrangements from there.' They got into the taxi and enjoyed the city on the way to the hotel, as they don't get to see that every day. Tim didn't show much interest in the city, since he already lived here and even worked here the most. Tim, who knows everything about this city, has booked a very elegant hotel. When they arrived, they were blinking like there wasn't tomorrow, they checked in at the reception, everyone got their room, which of course was next to each other. And that day they met the certain someone who would help them in this mission.

The meeting took place in a small cafe, of course the three of them got there before the person they were meeting. They didn't have to wait long, the long-awaited help arrived. Of course, it's about a pretty lady named Abby. They greeted each other, sat down at the table and got straight to the point, because time passes quickly, and they were in a hurry. Timber gave a quick initiation, and of course the others also contributed as well. Well, Abby nodded that she would help them, she gave them an address where they would have to go because that's the only place, she could translate for them. Everyone agreed and went their separate ways. The next morning, they got into a taxi again and went to the address that Abby had given them. They went to an old warehouse where Abby worked. They all met, went into a closed office and started work. The translation took ten minutes. Well, the translation read: -

Only a wizard can enter the realm of magic!

For a man who is not a wizard, the realm of magic cannot be seen.

To enter, a magic potion will be needed!

The ingredients for which can be found in Mexico.

There is a city where you can find all the ingredients in one place.

You have to look for a certain woman called Naiara!!

She alone can make the magic potion ATTENTION!

If you find Naiara, you can rest assured that you will enter the magical world.

Through this gate leads you one way, you must choose a different way back.

When you are ready with these and have decided for sure that you want to go, you cannot take anything with you, you must only go empty-handed.

Good luck!

John: - 'Thank you very much for your help, Abby!'

Abby: - 'You're welcome! Good luck to you, it was a pleasure to meet you again Timber and to be able to help you. Can I help with anything else gentlemen?'

Timber: - 'Thanks Abby! You have helped us a lot with this, our eternal gratitude. But if I will need your help, I know your number.' He Is smiling at Abby. They said goodbye to each other and went to a restaurant for lunch. While they were having lunch, each of them called their wives on the phone to tell them the happenings and, of course, that they have to travel to the old sorceress in Mexico who will help them prepare the certain drink they will need for the trip. They went back to the hotel, collected their things, got into a taxi again and went to the airport. They had to wait for the right time to board the plane that would take them to Mexico. They arrived in Mexico, and someone was waiting for them with their names written on a board. They were very happy about this because it will make their journey easier. Timber smiled to himself because he knows that Abby just arranged this for them to make their journey easier.

The stranger: - 'Welcome, gentlemen! He spoke to them with a Mexican accent. Please follow me, he invited them to a medieval looking car waiting outside.'

John: - 'Greetings to you too! Tell me, how do you know our name? Tell me…….' He wanted to continue his question but Timber pushed him and signalled him not to continue because he realized how he knew their names, he happened to be receiving a message from Abby that someone would be waiting for them at the airport and the old man would take them there to an old sorceress. He showed the message to John and pulled his mouth away with a smile, then just said: - 'That's what Abby's like!' - Timber continued. They got into the car and drove to the old sorceress. It took an hour of travel until they reached a small village, there was a lot of poverty but still everyone was happy, it was strange to see this but still good. They turned into a small shabby house where the car stopped.

The stranger: - 'We have arrived! Now you can get out, see you later!' They got out of the car, looked around and armed men appeared out of nowhere. After seeing this, they were very scared, of course Timber was less scared because he had experienced something like this before and calmed the rest of them down so that they wouldn't panic. The door opened and an old lady stood there.

Naiara: - 'Welcome my dear children! I've been waiting for you, come inside, don't be afraid, because they won't shoot me, they're just looking after me. Come on, come on in.' They entered the house and just stared in amazement, suddenly they didn't even know where to look, the inside of the house was by no means ugly, it was as if they had fallen into a huge castle, they couldn't believe their eyes. There were candles, torches, lots of books, experimental flasks, owls, crows, black cats, rats, ferrets, toads, and many other animals, which of course were locked in appropriate cages, except for the cats, owls, and crows. In the meantime, they followed Naiara, who entered a large room, with strange looking books and, above all, spider webs hanging all over the place. A special book shone in the dimness, they were heading towards it, Naiara pushed the book on the shelf and the whole shelf moved, a secret passage opened in front of them, they went through the door and came to a place with a dilapidated, full of cobwebs that resembled a laboratory. The door closed behind them, Naiara began to brew the potion, on a snow-covered table, on each side was grass, and there were many bottles of different colours and drinks with strange things in them. While Naiara was in working, they looked around the room, there was always something to look at, and the floor was full of strange scraps, at least to them they were. John was restless about all of this; he did not join the others but stayed with Naiara and assisted.

John: - 'Sorry Naiara! But how did you know we were coming here?'

Naiara: - 'Come on John! After all, you're a wizard too, you know the answer to that too.' She smiled to herself.

John: - 'But I'm not a wizard! All I know is that my ancient descendants were, but that was a long time ago, and since then it has long since died out. Naiara just smiled, then said: - 'Dear John! If your descendants were wizards, how would it die out? It's in the blood, the lineage carries it on from newborn to newborn, it will never die out.' She said seriously. Well, she started muttering the incantations to the potion, stirring it over a fire and not stopping muttering the incantations. John just watched and concentrated, the knowledge that Naiara was talking about came out more and more in him. A big grey cloud rolled into the room; the magic potion was finally ready.

Naiara: - 'Well John! Are you ready for the trip? Remember, this drink will only be enough for one way, you have to find a different way back, you will solve it from there, I trust you.'

John: - 'Thank you Naiara! I'm very grateful that you helped us, I hope we made the right decision and I'll make it there.'

Kev: - 'John! Save them, bring them home safely.'

Timber: - 'Dude! It will be fine! I know you can do it.' They all shook hands and said goodbye to John. John raised the drink to his mouth, looked his companions in the eyes and drank it. As soon as he drank the potion, a portal opened in one half of the room, into which he had to jump. Before he jumped in, he looked backed one more time and then jumped in. The portal immediately absorbed him and closed, Kev and Timber looked at each other and could hardly believe what they saw.

Kev: - 'Whaaat! My goodness! This is incredible! It worked, he got through the portal, absolutely mental! I never thought I would ever see something like this in my life and it happened right here in front of me.' He said, excited and paralysed.

Timber: - 'Well! Here, our mission is complete! It's time to go home my dear friend.' He spoke calmly.

Timber: - 'Naiara! Thank you for your help, we are very grateful for everything.'

Naiara: - 'I'm glad I could help, all the best, gentlemen!' With that, they said goodbye to each other and travelled back to England.

The witch's trap.

John successfully crossed over to the Boletus world to the city of Moltius, the magic potion was successful, the only big question is how he will find his son. The Evil Witch has planned the best evil that can possibly be done. She asked for Evelin to come to the great hall, after all, the real part of the evil begins now. Evelin was brought before the Witch.

Evil Witch: - 'Well, well, my child! You seem very down my dear. Come closer, let me take a closer look.' The Guards ushered her because she wouldn't move. She stood there in front of the Witch, broken, sad and in despair.

Evil Witch: - 'Well, my dear! Seeing how much losing your friends is hurting you, I decided to let you go back to your friends. But only on one condition, you sit down at the table and eat one last dinner with me, then you are free to go.' Evelin couldn't believe her ears; she thought she was just dreaming, it wasn't reality. Suddenly, she didn't know whether to laugh or cry.

Evelin: - 'Oh, Oh! I really don't even know what to say! What you just said has shocked me, but I say yes to finally being let go, thank you very much.'

Evil Witch: - 'Well, my child! Then there is nothing else to do, let's sit down at the table and enjoy this magnificent dinner.' The Witch took care of everything, including her favourite food on the table and her favourite drink, to make sure that she eats and drinks everything placed in front of her. This plan worked, Evelin ate and drank everything, of course she was very hungry because she had hardly eaten anything for days, since the mice had eaten most of the food. She ate her food very quickly to get out of there as soon as possible. The evil Witch sat calmly and watched her eat; she knew that she would not have to wait long.

Evil Witch: - 'Was the dinner delicious my dear?' She asked calmly.

Evelin: - 'Yes! It was delicious! Thanks for the dinner.' She said firmly, lowering her head over her plate. Evelin slowly raised her head and looked at the Evil Witch. Her glassy gaze was almost terrifying; she had completely changed, as if she were no longer Evelin, but a robot. The Evil Witch looked at Evelin with satisfaction that her evil plan had succeeded; now she can let her go back to her friends.

Evil Witch: - 'My child Evelin! You know what you have to do! When you are ready, you are free to leave.' She said to her calmly.

Evelin: - 'Yes! I know what I'm doing! Eliminate James Alder.' She replied viciously.

Evil Witch: - 'Right! I see you know what you have to do, now you are free to go. Hahahaha.' She laughed with satisfaction. Evelin got up from the table and walked out of the palace. The evil witch mixed an extraordinary potion for Evelin, this potion is designed to trap her best friend wherever the evil witch wants, and she has to obey her until James is in the palace of the Evil Witch. But that's not enough, the Evil Witch is cautious so she mixed up another potion specifically for James so that there would be no problem with transporting him there. This bottle was hidden in Evelin's coat pocket. She successfully got out of the palace and set out to find James. She found him after a whole day's walking, but she was successful in finding him. James was washing his clothes at the stream, when he was ready, he looked up and suddenly he didn't know whether to yell or just jump in joy.

James: - 'Oh my god! Evelyn! Is it really you? Isn't it a daydream? My God, Evelin, I can't believe you're here. I'm so happy for you, I have so many questions. Just tell me…….' He wanted to continue the questions, but Evelin surprised him and hugged him tightly.

Evelin: - 'Hi James! I'm finally here with you. I missed you so much and so did everyone else. Where are they?

James: - 'They are close by, as they followed me until now, they didn't want me to be alone in this, but come on, let's go to them, I'm sure they'll be very happy for you.' They started to meet Hanna and Oliver, when they reached their camp, Hanna noticed Evelin, her eyes lit up immediately and she greeted her.

Hanna: 'Hi Evelin!': - She shouted there from far away as soon as she saw her. Oliver immediately wondered what Hanna was shouting, since Evelin wasn't even here. When he realized it, he immediately ran in front of them.

Oliver: - 'Hi Evelin! Good to see you! I can't believe you're actually here! But how come you are here? Did you run away?': - He asked a lot of questions. Evelin just smiled and reacted normally, so that the others wouldn't notice that she was under the influence of the Evil Witch.

Evelin: - 'Hello guys! I missed you all very much, but I couldn't stand it any longer, I thought I was going to go mad.

Oliver: - 'But how did you manage to come? You can't just get rid of the Evil Witch.

Evelin: 'Yes, Oliver! This is indeed a good question. I don't even know what finally made her let me go, because she called me yesterday morning and said she would let me go. She doesn't hold me captive anymore because she doesn't see the point anymore, so she let me go.

Hanna: - 'This is strange! She kidnaps her and then lets her go. What has she been doing there with you until now?'

Evelin: - 'At first, I was locked in a musty basement where there was only a small window in the upper part of the wall, it was cruel to exist there, I thought that the end is near. But one day she took me upstairs to the great hall, where there was a large table full of food, of course I was hungry, and I ate without thinking. After that, I got a room that was very beautiful, full of beautiful clothes and flowers, I was satisfied, but I was still sad that I couldn't be here with you. As I already said, a day ago, for some reason she changed her mind and let me go. That's my story, she didn't treat me badly, in fact I was completely surprised.' Evelin smiled. Of course, she didn't tell the whole truth because she couldn't and of course she doesn't remember it because of the magic potion, so she just tells them what they want to hear. She performed perfectly because they believed her, so she didn't have to worry about failing.

Oliver: - 'Well, for that, we have to celebrate Evelin's return and then we can continue our journey towards to the finish line.'

James: - 'I agree, let's celebrate it, but only carefully, you never know what the Evil witch is up to against us.' Evelin just smouldered but didn't say anything. Everyone did their job, Oliver gathered wood, James went fishing, Hanna went hunting. and Evelin went separately to collect branches and twigs, they were not far from each other. Evelin's constantly watched Oliver to see how he would react to this news, but as she could see, he was happy about her return, he happily picked the tree branches, there was no problem with him. After a little while, everyone returned with some kind of loot, they all sought to prepare the food, they skewered the fish and made stew out of the rabbits.

Evelin: - 'Guys! Do we have drinking water here? I think we're all out, I'll go down to the creek and get some, okay?'

Hanna: - 'Okay! It's a good idea because we have really run out and we'll need it, thanks Evelin.' Evelin went to the stream to get water, filled the can with water, but all the while she was watching to see if anyone was watching her or not, because she had just put the magic potion that the Evil Witch had made for Hanna and James into the can. It didn't matter to Oliver, since he is not a wizard and poses no danger to anyone. She successfully mixed the concoction into the water and headed back to others.

Part of it was poured into the food, the rest of the water was slowly consumed. The Evil Witch was successful, she achieved what she wanted, she took away the magic power from Hanna and James so that they could not harm her. Without realizing it, James and Hanna ate the food and drank the water, which completely rid them of their magical powers. They sat by the campfire and talked, they enjoyed that they were all together again. The witch's ravens watched the events throughout to make sure everything went smoothly. After this took place and the plan was successful, the ravens immediately delivered the new to the Evil Witch. They flew through the window straight to the Evil Witch. The Evil Witch put her hand on the raven and what the raven saw, the Witch also saw and heard, she was able to watch the whole process as Evelin solved the task entrusted to her. Seeing this, she began to laugh so viciously that even the birds flew away from the vicinity of the palace. They were so engrossed in the big conversation that they forgot the passage of time that it was getting dark on them. They felt very good that Evelin was with them again. They gathered firewood again, caught a few fish and had dinner. But it was very late, so they went to sleep. The witch was only waiting for this moment for them to fall asleep, but the wraiths were waiting nearby so that she could carry out the plan that the witch had been waiting for a long time. They abducted James and, in addition to that, they also sprayed them with dream powder so that they wouldn't wake up. Finally, James was in the Evil Witches palace in the basement, of course everything he once had was confiscated, his pockets were emptied and his bag was taken, he had nothing left. The next morning came, they slowly started to wake up, Oliver woke up first, when he opened his eyes, he looked around to see if everyone was there, but James was missing. He jumped up and took a closer look around the area to make sure. In the meantime, Both Hanna and Evelin woke up and watched what Oliver was doing.

Hanna: - 'What are you looking for, Oliver?': - She asked him inquisitively.

Oliver: - 'Well, well, well... James!!': - He replied in despair.

Hanna: - 'Come on Oliver! You know that James always has to get up before us and goes down to the stream to wash himself. You don't have to worry, he'll be back soon, don't worry.'- She answered calmly to Oliver, and she lay back down for a bit to stretch and be lazy.

Oliver: - 'Oh, that's right, I thought that he was also kidnapped by the Evil Witch. But she can't kidnap him because he's a wizard, hahahaha, it's funny, but if she did, then we're in big trouble, no, it can't be, because if he's a wizard, the wretch can't harm him, right?' He said these things out loud to himself. Evelin heard all this and just smiled to herself, as she doesn't know what she's doing, she's not conscious because of the magic potion which the Evil Witch mixed in her drink, and it only stops when the Evil Witch dissolves the spell.

The king heard the news that the Evil Witch had released Evelin from her captivity. This news made the king think, he didn't let it rest, he called his advisor to him.

Advisor: - 'My king!' He bowed to him.

King: - 'I ask you, what is all this? Something is not clear here! Why did that wretch let that girl go?': - The king asked the councillor quite angrily.

Advisor: - 'My King! I will answer these questions soon. With your permission, you're Majesty.' With that he left the palace. The king was terribly angry, as he knew that this did not mean anything good, he could not calm down he walked up and down the hall. The prince stormed through the door as he had something to announce, only to see that the king was very upset and angry.

Gilbert: - 'My king! Dad! What upset you so much?'

King: - 'Oh nothing! Just the usual stuff, nothing to worry about.' The king said hurriedly.

Gilbert: - 'Your Majesty! I would like to remind you about tomorrow, which is a very important day for the whole family. It is my daughter's 13th birthday; I want it to be unforgettable in my daughter's life. And so, I came here to tell you that we've already sent the invitations throughout the city.' With that he bowed to the king and left. The king was so angry that he almost did not take into account what his son told him. He doesn't even know what he was talking about; he didn't even pay much attention to the whole conversation. It was a long day and to take his mind off of things he went out hunting from the castle. The Evil Witch was prepared for everything, since the ravens brought her information about everything, but meanwhile the magic ball also showed her the events to come. That's why she knew things in advance, including what the king was going to do, so she was prepared for everything. Even preparing so that the advisor wouldn't find out what the king was wondering about but would only bring the king news he wanted to hear. Now, for once, the Evil Witch stands to win, and so she is enjoying this whole situation, that she has everyone in her grip.

Hanna finally pulled herself together and went to the stream to get fresh water, but when she got there, no one was there. She looked around thinking maybe she lost sight of James, or they just avoided each other! She dunked the water bottle while thinking about how it was that they avoided each other when this never happened before. Maybe he went back the other way, or he's just hunting something for breakfast. These thoughts kept coming to her mind.

Hanna's thought: 'We probably avoided each other! It's okay, I'm just imagining things! What if Oliver is right? Oh, Hanna, stop it, it can't be, James will save us, it can't happen, he's probably just hunting, there's nothing wrong.' She calmed himself with these thoughts. The small camp returned to their place, Oliver and Evelin were there, but James was nowhere to be found.

Hanna: 'Hello guys! Did you see James? Because he wasn't down by the stream. Maybe he went hunting?'

Evelin: - 'I haven't seen him since we got up, maybe he really went hunting.'

Oliver: - 'I told you; I told you!! He must have been kidnapped by the Evil Witch!!'

Hanna: - 'Oliver! Calm down, let's spread out, let's go find him, I'll meet you here in 2 hours, okay?'

Oliver, Evelin: - 'Okay, we'll meet here in 2 hours.' Well, the three of them parted ways and set out to find him. Evelin didn't pay much attention to this whole thing, since she knew where James was, she pretended to be looking for him too, until Hanna and Oliver disappeared from the horizon, when she didn't see them, she calmly turned back to the camp and made himself some tea, which she drank calmly. While Hanna and Oliver were frantically looking for James, the Evil Witch laughed at this, because it was very funny to her. James finally woke up too, but where he found himself surprised him, he suddenly jumped up

103

and looked around, he didn't understand how he got here and what this place is? He looked up and there was the certain small window that Evelin had told them about when she returned to them. He already knew where he was, but he didn't understand how he got here! He doesn't remember anything, that's what worried him more. Well, he began to think about the whole meeting with Evelin, what had escaped his attention. He collected all the ideas and could not figure it out. He closed his eyes and fell into deep thought, in this case, when he falls into thought, the mushrooms always give him good advice, which did not happen this time. This was strange to him, 'Something is not right here', he thought to himself. But he knew that he shouldn't say anything out loud, because then the Evil Witch would find out, he was playing the events over and over in his head and trying to find a solution. The witch saw that he had just woken up and sent him breakfast and a letter. The guards slid James's breakfast and the letter as well. James went to the door to see what the guards slid through to him. He saw both the breakfast and the letter on the tray, he took the letter first to read it, it said: -

Dear James!

I thought I'd write you a few lines about where you are and how you got here. Well, the answer is very simple, bringing you here was very simple and easy to do, it's all thanks to Evelin. (When he read that, he looked up and it all started to make sense to him, but he didn't understand what Evelin had to do with all this.) I know you don't understand the whole thing, but I'll explain, I gave Evelin a magic potion that makes her do what I order her to do, and the rest went smoothly, problem-free. The effect of the magic potion only wears off if she drinks the antidote, which only I can give her. As for you, haha haha, you can't do anything about it, since she also made you drink a magic potion that makes you lose your magic power, just like Hanna doesn't have any more magic power, funny isn't it?

With that the letter closed, flew out of his hand and burned. When James came to the realisation, he was so devastated that he suddenly sat down on the ground, losing all his strength, hope and faith for which they had come here, everything seemed to be lost, it falls into small pieces, hope begins to dissipate like fog, their whole journey was in vain. James's thoughts also began to scatter, he lay on the ground and tears ran down his face, the knowledge that he couldn't help, that everything was over, there was no way out of this.

After two hours, Hanna and Oliver returned to their camp, of course they found Evelin there apparently waiting for them.

Evelin: - 'Oh, you finally came back, I was waiting for you.'- She said in seeming despair. 'While we were away, I was walking up the road when a raven dropped me a letter, but you won't like what it says.'

Hanna: - 'What letter?'

Oliver: - 'Yes, what letter? Who sent it?' Hanna took the letter and began to read aloud: -

'My dears!

Don't look for James, he is safe here with me, he's enjoying my kind hospitality, admit that you have lost, and no one has power against me, haha, haha.

Kindest regards! Evil Witch.'

With that, the letter flew out of Hanna's hand and burned along with a loud laugh. Hanna fell to the ground and didn't understand how the Evil Witch could kidnap James. Thoughts ran through her mind about what to do now. Oliver couldn't believe his ears; he was so shocked by the news that he couldn't even speak. When he came to his senses, Oliver said: -

'I told you that evil bastard kidnapped him! I told you so! I can't believe this happened! This is incredible.' Evelin started to cry because during the time that Hanna and Oliver were there, the Evil Witch released Evelin from under the spell, but unfortunately, she doesn't remember anything. Only the last dinner and the moment when she read the letter as she was waiting for her friends return.

Evelin: - 'Guys, I have to tell you something! Something strange happened to me, and I can't explain it, please help me.': - She said sadly.

Oliver: - 'Well of course Evelin! We will help you with anything we can.': - he said while ready to help.

Hanna: - 'What's wrong Evelin?'- She asked in despair.

Evelin: - 'When I was there at the Evil Witch, I remember the last dinner, but the next image is when I receive this letter that Hanna just read and that I am out here with you. But I don't remember anything else, it's very strange.'- She shook her head, sad and in despair. They sat down by the fire, all of them looked in despair

106

and thought about this whole incident. Hanna was absorbed in looking at the fire where she tried to collect her thoughts.

Hanna: - 'Evelin! I think the reason you don't remember is because the Evil Witch gave you a magic potion so you couldn't remember anything, she used you to trap James. I know of only one solution for this, I have to use my magic power so that we can get into the palace somehow. We have to save James from there.'- She said firmly.

Oliver: - 'What are you saying Hanna! This is really an Evil Witch! But now how do we get into the palace? Only James could have got in there alone, and well he bloody well did.'- He fell into thinking.

Hanna asked both of them to collect plants for the magic potion; she described to them what they had to collect. Unfortunately, Hanna didn't know that she doesn't have magical powers either, so collecting the plants was pointless. They diligently picked the plants, but of course it took time, since not all ingredients are in one place, they had to find those plants. During the great search, they heard a dog barking nearby. They looked at each other and stopped looking, they didn't know what to think of the dog's barking. It was the king and his men as they were just hunting. They soon met and greeted each other respectfully. All three of the, bowed before the king accordingly.

King: - 'Welcome, my children! What are you doing around here? Maybe you got lost?' The King asked curiously.

Hanna: - 'Greetings, my king! We're not lost, we're just collecting important plants.'- She answered politely.

King: - 'What kind of important plants are you picking here in the middle of the forest?'

Hanna: - 'I need them for an important brew, Your Majesty.'

King: - 'For an important brew?? For what kind of important brew? Is it not for a magic potion? What are your names, my children?'- The king asked curiously.

Hanna: - 'Your Majesty! My name is Hanna, the names of my other two friends are Evelin and Oliver.'- She answered politely.

When the king heard their names, he immediately jumped off his horse and went to Hanna.

King: - 'Did you just say Evelin......?'- He asked back, surprised.

Hanna: - 'Yes, Your Majesty...' she wanted to continue, but the king waved her off. 'Bring James before me!' the king ordered.

Hanna: - 'Your Majesty! With your permission, I would like to announce that James has been kidnapped by the Evil Witch and is being held captive in the palace': - With that she bowed politely to the king. When the king heard this, he almost collapsed and was caught by the soldiers.

King: - 'My dear! What an honour it was to meet you, thank you for the information, I will see what I can do for this. Peace be with you.'- With that the king said goodbye and they went back to the palace. Hanna, Evelin, and Oliver continued to collect the plants, when they had everything, they needed, they went back to the camp and put the cauldron over the fire, into which slowly all the plants needed for the magic potion were added. She began to stir the potion and say aloud the spell they needed. The spell: -

Amirante magratusz!

Sahrim ventis!

Maherit verrium!

Atredis peccolium!

She shouted these incantations loudly over the potion as she stirred it, but nothing happened. Since nothing happened, she suddenly stopped stirring and looked into the potion and nothing happened inside of it.

Hanna: - 'This is very strange! I must have said something wrong! I'll try again!'- She said to the others a little nervously. Spell: -

Amirante magratusz!

Sahrim ventis!

Maherit verrium!

Atredis peccolium!

She said this spell with much more clarity than ever before, because she knew that James' life was at stake, and she did everything very precisely. But unfortunately, that didn't help either, no matter how hard she tried, the magic spell didn't work. When she saw this, she collapsed to the ground in despair and then realized that her magic power had also been removed so that she could not help James. Both Evelin and Oliver rushed over to Hanna and sat next to her on the ground, they tried to talk to her, but the words didn't reach her ears, it was as if all sounds had stopped around her due to the sudden panic that she couldn't help James. They sat on the ground for quite a while, Hanna was completely surrounded by silence due to the shock, Evelin and Oliver looked helplessly at the collapsing Hanna, which was not a heartwarming sight. The witch knew that the king had an adviser who was not only an adviser but also a wizard, because of this she rid the power of the entire country's wizards without them even knowing. After the king returned to his palace, he immediately summoned his adviser to tell him what had happened.

King: - 'My dear friend! Something really bad happened! The evil witch kidnapped James, i would really appreciate it if you could come up with something quickly because no stone will be left unturned here if the witch gets the upper hand.'- He finished his statement angrily and firmly.

Advisor: - 'Yes, Your Majesty! I will do my best Your Highness!' He humbly replied and left with that. The king could not find his place, he walked up and down the palace and thought about how to stop the witch. The prince's son was just walking by and saw that something was wrong with the king, and he had never seen his father like this before.

Gilbert: - 'Father, is something wrong? What happened while you were away? Are you injured?' - He asked worriedly.

King: - 'Oh, no, my son, nothing happened to me, I'm fine! Only this, this, this evil witch really worries me, she's up to something and it won't turn out well, and I feel helpless because of her.': - The king replied brokenly.

Gilbert: - 'My father!': - He put his hand on his shoulder to calm his father down. 'Do not worry! We will find a solution for this as well as everything before, and everything will be fine.'- He tried to calm the king.

King: - 'Of course my son, of course it will be like that.'- He said uncertainly. Son, I'm going to rest now, don't disturb me.'- He said firmly.

Gilbert: - 'father it will be so, sir, it will be like that.'- He said a little relieved. With that the king left. The prince watched him leave, but he really didn't like his father's behaviour. The prince went to the library to look for the book in which it is written about the evil witch, he wants to know the story of it, which the king worries about so much. After a while, he found the book in a place where there were unimportant and useless books, it was put there so that it wouldn't accidentally be found by someone who shouldn't, because if he finds it, the truth about the witch will be revealed. Unfortunately, the king accidentally left it there because he was reading that very book before him and forgot to hide it in its original place. The prince started reading the book and couldn't believe what was written in that book. After all, the king's scribe documents everything that happens in the palace. Looking up from the book, he looked towards the window, thinking about what he had read, and he just stared out the window, he didn't come to believe what he read, he just sat there, and he was constantly thinking, but no matter how he thought about it, nothing came to his memory. He closed the book, put it back in its place and went to the window. He looked outside for a long time, but he didn't notice that there was a black raven outside on the windowsill, watching the prince. When the raven suddenly flew up, the prince was suddenly scared because it hit him unexpectedly. The prince looked into the eyes of the raven, and the raven looked into the prince's eyes, and with that the raven flew away. The Evil Witch watched all of this, and her eyes filled with tears for a moment, because he was his great love, with whom they had a son together and because of the king he was born a bastard. The prince left the library and headed straight for the king's suite. He went to the king and said: -

Gilbert: - 'Father! I don't know how you'll get out of this mess, but I hope you know what you're doing!' - With that he finished what he said and left the room. The king looked at his son surprised because of the way he told him this, as he had not seen his son like this for a long time, only when he was together with the witch. The king knew that he had to act very quickly, because if he didn't, it would be a big problem. The king quickly ran after his son, he left his room and went straight after his son, only to find that his son had disappeared from sight. So, he made his way towards his room, he knocked on the door which he opened straight away but he found only the princess sleeping there. He closed the door back carefully so as not to wake the sleeping princess and continued through the palace to find his son. He looked everywhere in the palace except in one place. The king was in great despair, he started to go to the library because he didn't go in there to look as he left it last. He went in there too, but he couldn't find him there either, only now did he really start to worry, because he had an inkling of where he might have gone, but the cold shook him even from the thought. He had no other choice, so he asked for his soldiers to bring him his horse so he could go after his son. During this time, the prince had already walked far in the enchanted forest, the light of the moon illuminated his path, he just galloped in the darkness without thinking, because he wanted to know the truth at all costs, he galloped a thousand gallops as fast as the wind. The witch was very happy because she got what she wanted again and helped the prince on his way to the palace. A raven accompanied him on his way to the. The king and the soldiers galloped as fast as they could, but despite their great haste, the forest in which they galloped was enchanted and they did not get far, the witch made sure that they did not reach their desired destination. They got stuck in a place full of tendrils, which blocked their way, no matter how they tried, it was impossible to get through. The king was extremely angry because he was forced to return to the palace, he had to give up the search for his son.

King: - 'Soldiers! Take out your swords and cut a way through the tendrils!' - The king issued an order. The soldiers did everything they could, but it was all in vain, as soon as they cut the tendrils, more grew back in its place with that momentum, it was all completely unnecessary.

King: - 'Soldiers! We are going back to the palace!' - The king said firmly! He saw that there was no point in all this, and they went back to the palace. The king called all the magicians of the area before him and announced that whoever brings his son back will receive a huge reward. All the magicians of the area appeared on hearing this news and they all stood before the king.

King: - 'With an immediate decree, I declare that whoever can bring my son back from the evil witch, I will pay him a cartload of gold and he can live happily ever after.' When the magicians heard this, they immediately left the palace, and everyone rushed home to get to work as soon as possible. The king was so nervous that he couldn't sleep all night. Gilbert successfully arrived at the palace, where he entered because the witch wanted him to. As soon as he entered the palace, the witch's guards caught the prince immediately and threw him into a cell. Gilbert tried to defend himself, but he had no chance against the guards. In the cell where the prince was, James was in the cell next to him. James heard someone being put in the cell next to him, but he didn't know who. The prince didn't leave it at that and constantly shouted:

Gilbert: - 'Let me out of here immediately! You can't keep me locked up here; I'm the prince, son of the king! Do you hear what I'm saying?'- He shouted in despair. James hearing every word what Gilbert shouted. He went to the door and said:

James: - 'My prince! My prince! Can you hear me?' - James asked Gilbert. (James didn't know Gilbert name's yet)

'You are shouting unnecessarily, no one will hear you. They locked us up here and will only come here to give us food, so there's no need to shout so many times.'- He spoke to the prince kindly and calmly.

Gilbert: - 'Who are you? And how did you get here?'- He asked James in surprise.

James: - 'My name is James! I don't know how I got here, I woke up here, and I was probably kidnapped.

Gilbert: - 'How long have you been here?'- He asked back, surprised.

James: - 'I've been here for a day, but it doesn't look like they're going to let us out soon.'

Gilbert: - 'What do you mean by that?'

James: - 'The Evil Witch has a plan for us, that's why she brought us here, otherwise we wouldn't be here.'- He replied calmly.

Gilbert: - 'Do you know the Evil Witch well?' He asked curiously.

James: - 'Unfortunately, I don't know the Evil Witch and I've never seen her in my life.'- He answered after a while.

Gilbert: - 'Then where does this confidence come from; how do you know that we are here for a reason?'- He asked curiously.

James: - 'Why else would she keep us locked up here, we are probably important in her plan.'- He said thoughtfully.

Gilbert: - Probably you're right, but I still don't understand what her purpose is.: - said curiously.

James: - Who are you by the way?

Gilbert: - Oh! My name is Gilbert, nice to meet you.

James: - Nice to meet you too.

James: - 'Gilbert! Do you know the Evil Witch?'- He asked curiously.

Gilbert: - 'I don't know her, but I heard the news that she is capable of a thousand things, I don't understand how I got here, I don't even remember how I got here.': - Gilbert replied.

James: - 'It's typical, of course, that you can't remember, it's all the work of the Evil Witch, a trap.'

Gilbert: - 'But why would she set a trap for us since you don't know her and I don't know her either, it doesn't make sense to me, it doesn't make any sense.' After finishing this sentence, there was a great silence; James wondered what the Evil Witch plan could be by bringing his father here to the cell. James was happy but not at the same time that his father was there in the next cell, he didn't know what to feel, the thoughts in his head were waiting for a thousand answers to see the light of day, but the many questions and thoughts in his head are awaiting the answers for now. Gilbert also thought about everything he had read in that book so far, the many questions in his head didn't let him rest either. They both lay down to sleep to rest as much as they could at that moment. The Witch was very satisfied with the result of her work, now she can relax and plan her revenge as she sees fit. Hanna tried to pull herself together, because if she gave up, there was no point in them reaching this far and so they stayed by each other's side.

Hanna: - 'I'm going out to get some fresh air, I'd like to be by myself for a bit to think, I'll be back soon.'

Evelin, Oliver: - 'Of course, go, we will be just fine!'- They answered at the same time. Hanna went to the side of the stream where James used to go in the morning, she sat down on a big stone sadly and just stared at the trickling stream with tearful eyes, she couldn't really think of what to do and how she could help James. Evelin and Oliver prepared breakfast and waited for Hanna to come back.

Oliver: - 'Listen! What if we could go to the king's place and get a place to stay and plan something together?'

Evelin: - 'That doesn't sound bad! There might be mages there who could help us, let's tell Hanna that too.' They quickly made their way to the stream to tell Hanna about their idea.

His advisor checked in with the king with some pretty bad news.

King: - 'Finally! I thought you would never get here.'- He said excitedly.

Advisor: - 'My lord the king! I have come to you with very bad news, your majesty.'- He bowed properly before the king.

King: - 'What?'- The king was furious. 'What is it that you came with bad news? What does this mean?'

Adviser: - 'With your permission, Your Majesty, I did everything during the evening to help your son in any way I could, but unfortunately I was unsuccessful.'

King: - 'What does this mean? What is it that you did not succeed? Aren't you a mage? A mage always succeeds.'- He replied angrily.

Advisor: - 'With your permission, Your Majesty, I announce that the magic power of all the mages in the area.......' He couldn't finish the sentence because at that moment all the mages in the area appeared in the room and almost at the same time, they started telling the king why they can no longer cast spells because the Evil Witch has deprived them of their spell power.

King: - 'Silence! Silence in the room!' The king shouted very loudly.' Just talk to me one at a time, thanks.'

One of the magicians: - 'Your Highness! I respectfully announce that our magic power is unfortunately unusable. The evil witch took away it from us, and we can't conjure anymore.'- He answered humbly. When the king heard this, he suddenly sat on his throne, his staff fell out of his hand, and he just stared in front of him from the shock that had come over him. The advisor tried to go to the king and a couple of magicians to help the king, but the king gathered strength and pulled himself up from his throne and said:

King: - 'My dear friends! This news is really bad news, but let's not be discouraged, there is a solution for everything, just as we will find something for this too and we will fix it together with common strength, we will not give up, we cannot let the evil witch win. Life is not easy, it is full of surprises, bumpy roads, life puts us to the test, we will need our faith and our strength, we must not lose hope, we will be able to climb out of this crisis together, we will fight to the end, that our families, our children, our brothers and sisters, and neighbours are safe. We have to put an end to this pressure, fear and constant dread, so that we can wake up to a better tomorrow, sleep without fear, be able to walk the streets without anyone disturbing our everyday life.': - He stated firmly. Everyone who was in the room started cheering: -

People: - 'Long live the king! Long live the king! Long live the king!' The mages left the palace late, except for the king's advisor, who stayed by the king's side.

Advisor: - 'Your Majesty! What should we do? I don't know how we can defeat the evil witch, it won't be easy without magical powers, since her power has become as great as ever. I dare to say that we may have made a very bad decision when we separated them....' He wanted to continue but the king interrupted.

King: - 'That's enough!! I don't want to hear another word about this! We will solve this somehow; we will not bury our heads in the sand and watch her win.'- He answered firmly. Yes, but the king really didn't know what was in store for them and his kingdom. The evil witch's vengeance is one which no one has seen or experienced until now, dark times and bitter torments are approaching. Of course, the Evil Witch also heard this, since her ravens are everywhere. The revenge she was preparing for was very sweet to her; her desire to see the king suffer exactly as she had suffered at that time became more and more overwhelming. Evelin and Oliver reached the stream, they found Hanna sitting on the big stone, they went to get her so that they could tell her what the two of them had discussed.

Evelin: - 'Hanna! Oliver had an idea that it would be better for us to go to the king's palace, get accommodation there and help the king with something. He wants his son back and we want James's back, we can find a solution together.'

Oliver: - 'Yes! I think that sounds very good, I'm sure we'll figure something out in the palace together with the king. What do you say?'

Hanna: - 'Okay! So be it, let's go because we're not getting anywhere here anyway.' She answered a little cheered up. Well, they went to the palace to find some solution to this hopeless situation. They arrived at the palace where they were led before king.

King: - 'Welcome! What brought you here?'

Hanna: - 'Your Majesty! We came here to the palace to ask for shelter and to find a solution to this hopeless situation together, with your permission.'- She answered politely.

King: - 'My dears! I will be happy to see you in the palace, my butler will show you to your rooms.'

John goes in search of James.

John finally arrived in the town called Moltius, right in front of the bookstore where James was at the time. He looked around to get a good look at the place and found it quite interesting. The bookseller went out to the front of the shop and greeted him politely, because he knew he was a stranger to the city, but he also knew he was James' father.

118

Mr. Monghur: - 'Welcome to our city, Mr. Alder!'- He welcomed him warmly.

John: 'Oh! Welcome ah...'- He replied as he extended his hand for a handshake.

Mr. Monghur: - 'Oh, sorry! Let me introduce myself, I am Mr. Monghur the bookseller, this shop behind us is mine, I met your son James for the first time in this shop.'

John: 'What did you say? Have you met my son? Tell me, is he okay? Where is he now? Lead me to...'

Mr. Monghur: - 'Mr. Alder!..'

John: - 'Please call John.'

Mr. Monghur: - 'John! Please come to my office and there I will tell you everything, please follow me.': - He invited him to his shop. John was very excited to finally see his son and of course his friends. They arrived and took a seat in Mr. Monghur's office.

Mr. Monghur: - 'Can I offer you tea and biscuits?'

John: - 'Very kind, yes thank you.'

Mr. Monghur: - 'Well, let's start at the beginning, when I first saw James, we met here in the shop upstairs....'

John: - 'Mr. Monghur, if you don't take it as an intrusion, be so kind and get to the point, tell me where James is, please!'

Mr. Monghur: - 'It's ok! Your son is no longer here in our town, he disappeared with his friends, in another world where the evil witch resides, that world is the world of the evil witch, no one has ever been able to get there, and we don't even know how to get there because only those who the evil witch wants to get through can get there. Neither a spell nor a potion will help. This was just one of the bad news, the other bad news is that the evil witch has taken away the magic power of all magicians and sorcerers who

119

are here in this world, they no longer have magic power.': - He finished the sentence sadly.

John: - 'This is terrible news, as I see I came here unnecessarily if I can't even help the children.'- He answered in despair. After the conversation, there was silence in the office, they quietly started drinking their tea and thinking about what they should do.

John: - 'Mr. Monghur! If I saw correctly, this bookstore is quite big, there must be some reading material among all these books that can help us.'

Mr. Monghur: - 'Oh yes, we really have a book that could help, but that book cannot be opened, nobody was ever able to. We believe that only James can open that book, we took him there, but unfortunately, he could not open the book, but we trust that someone will open it one day.'- He answered calmly.

John: - 'Please! Would you show me that book too?'- He asked excitedly.

Mr. Monghur: - 'Of course John! Please come with me.' He also took John to the room where the book was kept locked, opened the door with the rusty key and they entered the room where only the book itself was on a round table. John suddenly took the book in his hand and saw that James had already held the book in his hand, since it had been cleaned of dust. There were beautifully coloured mushrooms on the cover of the book, John knew that this book was a family heirloom, since the small mushrooms are the symbol of his family. He put the book back on the table and grabbed the cover to open it and managed to open it. Mr. Monghur couldn't believe his eyes when he saw this, he immediately went beside John to see what was in the book. But when he got there, he saw nothing but blank pages.

Mr. Monghur: - 'This is strange! I don't understand how this is possible. The pages of the book are empty......'

John: - 'Mr. Monghur! This book is a very old family heirloom, James couldn't open it because the evil witch didn't want him to open it.'

Mr. Monghur: - 'But then I don't understand how it is possible that you opened it yourself!'

John: - 'After all, you said when we met that you can't do magic in this town or anywhere else because the evil witch took away the magic powers. You can open the book because there is no magical power to hold it back. The letters disappeared from it because you can't conjure it up. This is a very old magic book; it contains important spells that can be used to defeat the evil witch. Once, a long time ago, it belonged to my great-great-grandfather, the chief mage of the Alder family. He wrote down every single spell in this book, but especially the ones that could be useful in the future. Since you can't cast spells, we can't read the important spells in it.': - He answered brokenly.

Mr. Monghur: - 'Now that I know the story of the book, there is nothing else we have to do we have to come up with something to stop this process. Let's go up to the second floor and there we might find some book that might help us.'- He replied in despair. They went up to the second floor and started looking for a book that had a dragon on the cover, as it contained important spells.

Mr. Monghur: - 'John! Look for a book with a dragon on the cover, let me know if you find it.' With that, they began to search for the book, since there are no more magical powers they must look around, now he can't locate where the book might be. It took a while for Mr. Mongur to find it, but finally it was in his hand.

Mr. Monghur: - 'John! I found the book!' He said happily. John went to Mr. Monghur and opened the book. As soon as they opened the book, there were only blank pages in this one, just like in the other book.

Mr. Monghur: - 'What did I expect?': - He said angrily. 'This is not going anywhere! I tell you honestly, I don't know what we should do, what we should resort to. This was our last hope, I'm very sorry John.'- He said bitterly.

John: - 'Don't be discouraged Mr. Monghur, we'll figure something out.'- He put his hand on his shoulder to calm him down, not that he was that calm either.

John: - 'Mr. Mongur! Could you show me an accommodation where I can stay, I would really appreciate that.'

Mr. Monghur: - 'Oh! Well of course.' With that, he reached into his pocket and took out the spare key that he then gave him. 'Here's my spare key to my house, I'll take you there.' With that, they walked towards his house. On the way there, John couldn't help but stare, he noticed that the numbers above the doors were marked with colours, and they consisted of two different colours.

John: - 'Mr. Monghur? Two halves of the numbers above the doors are coloured, why?'

Mr. Monghur: - 'Oh! Yes, they represent the family names, it's been like this here since ancient times, it's natural for us, this way we know who belongs to which family.': - He said with a smile. He took John into the house, showed him to his room, where he would sleep, and led him around his house, which may seem interesting, the houses here are not symmetrical from the outside, interestingly protruding parts, ramshackle houses which were not particularly tall, but the situation is different from the inside, they are huge, they are 250 square meters and have 2-3 floors, the layout is also interesting from the inside, the pictures just hang there on the wall, they are not attached with nails, the candles are also standing in the air, everything that can be nailed to the wall is floating in the air. Each room has a separate fireplace and a bathroom, but there is no electric lighting anywhere, only candles and torches are used everywhere. The buildings are made of stone, they are massive and spectacular, and the barriers are also made exclusively of stone and marble. Inside the house, one felt as if one had fallen into a fairy tale. John was delighted by the sight; he couldn't help but marvel at the beautifully crafted railings and walls.

John: - 'Mr. Monghur! I would like to thank you for accepting me into your house and for allowing me to spend my time here until I find the children.'- He said fishily.

Mr. Monghur: - 'Come on, please! The honour is mine. When you are settled in your room, you will find clothes in the closet that you can change into, when you are ready, please come down to dinner in the dining room.'- He said kindly.

John: - 'Thank you!'- He answered respectfully. John went into his room and looked around as soon as he closed the door, the fireplace turned on by itself to warm the room. When John was ready, he went down to the dining room for dinner. Mr. Monghur sat at the table waiting for John to come down. The table was already set, but only for two people. They sat down at the table and began to eat. They ate their food in silence, as both were thinking about what to do, how to stop this whole nightmare.

John: - 'Mr. Monghur? If you don't mind, may I ask where your wife is?'

Mr. Monghur: - 'Ohh! Of course, my dear wife passed away a long time ago, but I don't know exactly when, she was a very good woman, full of serenity and love. An ugly disease took her to our ancestors. That's how it's supposed to be, if we have to go, we'll go where there's peace of mind.'- He answered with a smile.

John: - 'Oh, I'm really sorry sir! I didn't want to upset you.'

Mr. Monghur: - 'Come on, don't bother John, the memory is a phenomenon that no one can take away from us, even if that someone is no longer with us. As long as we live, we can be grateful because we are still here with our fellow humans so that we can help, love and be loved even when it is difficult. Because the love and respect that keeps us alive and the fact that we pay attention to each other can mean a lot when our time comes to leave this world. Our souls will be reconciled, and we will calmly meet our ancestors who will be proud of us just as we are proud of them for what they left behind here.'

John: - 'That's right, Mr. Monghur! This brings out a strange feeling in anyone, it is disturbing and touching that there are such people. You know where I come from, many different types of people live together, good and bad alike, the bad are punished and the good people prevail in life. They will be successful or less successful, it depends on their interest and knowledge. But it is certain that there is no perfect person.'

Mr. Monghur: - 'Hmmm! My dear! The emphasis here is not on whether he is a bad or a good person, because such a person does not really exist. When we are born, we are all the same, only the colour of our skin is different, that's why what you said before develops because the circumstances change it. Not everyone is given what the other has, and it is exactly these which forms good and evil'.

John: - 'Yes! Unfortunately, this is the case! The wicked witch wasn't always wicked either, was she?'

Mr. Monghur: - 'There is no way to know this, it is a question for which we have not found an answer.'- He answered thoughtfully. The reason why nobody knows the answer to this is because at the time when Miriam was separated from her prince, she cast such a spell on everyone that everyone would forget everything about what she really was like, that's why everyone now thinks that she was always evil. Which is true, because when she was born, the raven put tiny grey and black mushrooms in the ears of the previous evil witch to pass on her knowledge, strength, power and all the evil that exists, and that's why she became the Evil

Witch.'

John: '- This story sounds horrifying, how was the previous evil witch capable of this!?

Mr. Monghur: - 'Well, there is a really simple answer to this, she was evil as well. But I can see that you are really tired, I say we rest for tomorrow.'

John: - 'Well with respect, I would like to go back to my room to rest, as I have a long journey ahead of me, good night.': - he said.

Mr. Monghur: - 'Of course! Of course! Just go and relax, I'll be leaving soon as well.'- He said goodbye to John. John went up to his room and got into bed, he got comfortable and fell asleep almost immediately. The next morning came, he went down to the dining room and his breakfast was already laid out for him, but Mr. Monghur was no longer there.

John: - 'Sorry! Could you please tell me where Mr. Monghur is?'- He asked the butler inquisitively.

Butler: - 'Yes, sir! Mr. Monghur already left the house early in the morning; he said that after you have had your breakfast, you should go to the bookstore.'

John: - 'Thank you!': - he said politely. After he finished his breakfast, he also went to the bookstore to meet Mr. Monghur. He began walking towards the bookstore, but he thought to himself that he should look around the area a bit so he could get to know the place better. He wandered back, looked around and admired those interesting buildings, because he couldn't get enough of the sight, he had never seen anything like it before, he made a detour on his way to the bookstore. As he wandered from street to street, he came to the narrow road where only one person can cross to the other side where you can walk normally. He suddenly stopped and looked across the long hallway, as soon as he looked there a strange fog rose up in front of him so that he could no longer see through. He was shocked by the sight and began to feel strange, as if a ghost had passed through him, the cold went through his body, he got goose bumps, he decided to go back to the bookstore. He started walking towards the bookstore, but at the same time he looked at behind him to see if the fog was there? But when he looked at behind him, the fog was gone; in fact, in the distance, he noticed that a certain mass of black clouds was approaching the city. He went into the bookstore where he immediately remembered Mr. Monghur and went to get him.

John: - 'Good morning Mr. Monghur! Sorry for sleeping so late, but really....' He wanted to continue but Mr. Monghur interrupted.

Mr. Monghur: - 'Good morning, John! You have to come here immediately': - He said in despaired. John made his way there and they set off to a secret exit where the other mages were waiting for them. They entered the great hall and closed the door behind them. John didn't dare ask what was going on and followed the events.

Mr. Tregas: - 'Gentlemen! Thank you all for being here, because I have something very important to announce. First, I'd like to introduce you to James' dad, John!' Everyone greeted John.

Mr. Tregas: - 'I would like to continue my speech by saying that everyone must have noticed this morning that a strange mass of black clouds is approaching our city. Since we do not know the reason for what this phenomenon could be, I ask everyone to warn the residents here to be careful. Tell them that everyone should go back to their homes and not come out into the streets until we know more about this phenomenon.'

Mr. Vinthus: - 'After warning the people, we would like everyone to come back here, as we have a lot of work to do.'

Mr. Tegras: - 'Mr. Ambeth! I would like to suggest that after the people have been told and everyone in the bookstore has returned, I should close the door and stay in the store myself in case something happens, so that there is someone who can handle the situation.' Everyone left the room and went out to the people to announce the impending danger. People panicked on some level and started running towards their homes.

Mr. Zathen: - 'Please people! Don't push each other! You have plenty of time to go home! Please! No need to rush!' He shouted to the people. In the middle of the commotion, someone jumped in front of Mr. Zathen and said: -

Civilian: - 'Sir! Sir! Please, I ran all the way from where those black clouds are come from and the darkness covers everything in its wake, please be careful!': - He shouted in despair. Upon hearing this, Mr. Zathen went back to the bookstore and immediately called Mr. Tregas. After the streets were quiet and everyone was safe in their homes, they again walked the streets to check on people's safety. Fortunately, everyone was safe at home, no one was left outside, a cat ran in front of them or a couple of stray dogs or even a mouse or a rat, but everything was fine with that, the birds also hid because birds sense danger and because of that they also went to hide. Each mage went back to the library for further discussion. They were down in the secret room, only Mr. Ambeth stayed up near the door for safety.

Mr. Zathen: 'Dear mages! Out there today, while people were rushing to their homes in a panic, someone rushed to me and warned me that this dark cloud is approaching us and leaving nothing but darkness behind. Since it is known that such a phenomenon is only related to the evil witch, this means that the danger we feared has begun. Unfortunately, James could not stop the evil, or whether it was not possible to stop it for some other reason, we don't know now anyway, the point is that...'

John: - 'What did he mean by that, he couldn't stop the evil witch?'- He whispered in Mr. Monhur's ear.

Mr. Monghur: - 'We helped James on his journey as much as we could, but since he had help there, we didn't worry about him, but something could have intervened, which is why this is happening out there now.'

Mr. Zathen: - (Meanwhile, Mr. Zathen finished his speech) 'Gentlemen? Do they have any questions?'- He asked the mages.

Mr. Onthasy: - 'Since we don't have magical powers anymore, I suggest that we browse the books to see if we can find something there that doesn't require us to use magic. After all, there are options that don't require magic.'- he said imaginatively.

Mr. Monghur: - 'I also agree with this idea. Raise your hand if you agree.'- He said convincingly. Everyone agreed, they went upstairs, and everyone started looking for the kind of books that could be useful in this case. In those regions where the cloud has covered everything, there is complete darkness, and the sun no longer shines. The people were terrified because there was no such thing here in this world, there was always peace, calmness and loving understanding. In one of the small villages where only torches and candles provided light, something strange happened. The man came out of one of the small houses to collect the firewood; he was picking up the pieces when he saw a bunch of dead mice. Suddenly frightened, he threw away the firewood and ran into the house.

Husband: - 'Honey!! Something is wrong out there! I was just gathering the wood for the fire when I found a dozen dead mice.'- He said scared and in despair.

Wife: - 'We should tell the main man of the village! We should warn him!'- She said thoughtlessly. The man looked around first from inside the house and then carefully walked to the front of the house. His son was terrified and sat close to his mother and watched as his father left the house. The Husband hurried to the main man of the village.

Husband: - 'Good evening! Please! I have something to report! I

128

found a dozen dead mice out there while I was collecting firewood, this is not a good sign.'- He said in despair.

Main man: - 'Immediately tell the other people to gather at my place in half an hour:'- He said firmly. With that he left the house and went from house to house to take the message to every man. He didn't have to go that far because the village wasn't big, the total number of people was only 50-60. While knocking on door after door, dead rats were found in more and more places, even dead cats were found, and in one place there were also dead birds. By the time they reached the main man, they saw a lot of dead animals.

Main man: - 'I'm glad you came, please tell me what you saw?'

Man: - 'While we gathered everyone, we saw a lot of dead mice, cats and birds everywhere.'- he said in despair. While they were talking, one of the scribes wrote down each word for documentation.

Main man: - 'I ask the village courier to immediately take this news to the city of Moltius to the great mages.'- He said firmly. The courier left for the city with the news. The people of the village consulted about the phenomenon and there was a magician among them, (every village has a magician) and so the people asked for his opinion. The mage's name is Fimder. The name of the village is Leintes.

Person: - 'Mr. Fimder! What could this all mean? Why are the animals dying?'- He asked in despair.

Mr. Fimder: - 'I don't know why right now, but I'm going home right away and I'm going to look into this phenomenon. If you'll excuse me gentlemen!'- He answered politely. The people consulted for a little while, but not for long, because everyone preferred to go home and wait for the solutions. The next morning came, the courier arrived back at the village and along with Mr. Fimder were making their way to the main man's house.

The people have already gathered in front of his home and waited impatiently for the answer. First, they asked the courier.

Main man: - 'Good morning, everyone! Please tell me what news you brought.'- He said impatiently. The courier took out a scroll and handed it to the main man. The main man opened the scroll and began to read.

Message: - 'Dear fellow citizens! This phenomenon we encounter is the work of the evil witch. The death of animals was brought about by the curse of this dark cloud. For now, we cannot say what it else it brings because magic does not work anywhere in the world. We are trying to find a solution to this phenomenon, we are asking the magicians of every village to find a book that does not contain magic, and we hope to find the solution in these books.' Everyone shouted at the same time to the main man almost at the same time, because of this the mage stood next to the main man.

Mr. Fimder: - 'Dear fellow citizens! There is no reason to panic! We will find a solution for this and everything else, please calm down and return to your homes to your families, only come out of the house if you really have to.': - He said reassuringly. People calmed down as much as they could and went back to their homes. Of course, there was darkness everywhere, regardless, they tried to live a normal life as much as possible. In the town of Moltius, the people reacted with the same attitude as those in the village, even though the black cloud had not fully reached there, they only had a few hours until it will reach there as well. Until then, they tried to divert their attention by getting all the necessary things in their homes. At 14:18 in the afternoon, it covered the entire town of Moltius, everything fell into darkness, only the torches lit the streets and the light of the candles provided lighting inside the houses. Fear slowly took over everywhere, the evil witch felt very good that she could finally rule over everything and everyone. In the prison cells, James and the prince couldn't take it any longer, and so they kept each other's hopes up. The evil witch sent her ravens everywhere so that she could watch how she tormented people. She did not intend such a blow on the people as on the king, she only wants to scare the people, she plays with them like a child with their toy. The mages browsed through almost every book, but finally found the book that did not contain magic. They took it to the great hall and put it on the table so that everyone could see it more easily. This book actually contained descriptions of plants and different stones. Medicines and potions can be made from these precious things, which do not require magic. They had been studying the book for hours, but they couldn't find anything useful in it. They got to page 357 of the book, but the next two pages were missing, and so they were stumped. They started to consult about these two pages and what could be on these pages, almost at the same time they started to say what could have happened with these two pages, where could it have gone? As soon as they had consulted there, John went back to the books and started searching among them as if he knew what he was looking for. During the great search, he constantly thought about what he could do, how this whole thing can be stopped. He was about to reach for the other book when he suddenly remembered something, and he went back to the mages to share his idea with them.

John: - 'Attention! Attention! (Meanwhile, he coughed a lot to draw attention to himself) I have an idea!'- He interrupted loudly. Everyone noticed this and looked at him in silence.

John: - Ahemm, hmm! (He cleared his throat) I'm sorry, but I have an idea, it might be useful.': - He said confidently.

Mr. Tregas: - 'we are listening to John! Out with it!'

John: - Well, I think we should send an animal messenger to deliver letters to James, maybe can still stop the evil witch.'- He explained his idea. All the mages looked at each other and then back at John.

Mr. Onthasy: - 'That doesn't sound bad, Mr. John!'

Mr. Vinthus: 'There is just one catch! How do we exactly execute this? We have no magic! Have you forgotten?'

Mr. Monghur: - 'Yes! Yes! We really don't have magic powers, but we don't really need magic powers to send a letter there.'- He said thoughtfully. 'Let's see, there is a book in which stories about fairies can help us, let's go up and find the book.'- he continued his idea.

Mr. Tregas: - 'Well, that's really a good idea, let's go find that book.'- He said happily. They all went back to the books to look for it, but Mr. Monghur found it right away, since he had read a lot about fairies and knew exactly where that book was.

Mr. Monghur: - 'I found it! I have the book here!'- He said loudly. They all went to him, and they immediately opened the pages of the book and began to search for ways to contact the fairies. They found it right away, Mr. Monghur read aloud: -

"Fairies have such power that no one can take from them or destroy it. In the ancient times, long, long ago, when the fairies were flying happily on the surface of the earth in their own territory, there lived among them a very old fairy who was also the most powerful and the wisest among them. The other fairies respected her greatly for her great knowledge and wisdom. This fairy developed a protective medicine for her fairies so that no one can ever hurt them and destroy their power. This went on for thousands of years until the evil witch (before Miriam) showed. The evil witch attacked the fairies, and they were forced to hide from the world so that the evil witch could not disturb them anymore. The fairies were thus still safe and could continue to develop their powers safer than ever. There is only one way you can contact the fairies; you have to go to the enchanted forest where there is a large tree with many branches. This tree has very many branches, much more than a normal tree. There is a special distinguishing mark on the trunk of the tree: an owl's head can be seen. If the owl's head appears on the trunk of the tree, it means that the tree considers the stranger who strayed there safe. The owl head must be touched as quickly as possible because it is only present for a minute and then disappears."

They read these lines in the book which were really helpful. The mages immediately went back to the great hall to plan the next steps.

Mr. Tregas: - 'Gentlemen! We have to act quickly so that our county and towns are not in more trouble. I am writing a message to James that must be taken to that tree and given to the fairies. It might get shaky, and it won't be easy to get there, but we have to do everything we can to somehow stop the evil witch.' He was about to continue when John interrupted.

John: - 'I'll take that letter! I came here to help my son; I will go to that tree.'- He interrupted firmly. Everyone looked at John, a little silence followed, when they came to their senses, they said this, almost at the same time.

Mages spoke at the same time: - 'It is closed! John can't go there alone! How will he find it, he doesn't know the way there! You will need help! What if you don't get there?'

Mr. Tregas: - 'Silence! Silence!'- He shouted.' Thanks! Well, we need to discuss this calmly, not to guess and judge. I wrote the letter, if John takes the letter, it is only good for us, because he is stronger and younger than us, so we have an advantage. Of course, you won't be going alone, I have a friend who will be happy to help us, who knows the way there and most importantly, you can count on him at any time.': - He told me the plan calmly.

Mr. Onthasy: - 'Well then, I also agree with this, raise your hand if you agree with this decision: - He interrupted. Everyone raised their hands except Mr. Monghur, who refrained because he was afraid that if John was in trouble, there was no point in coming here to help James. Since there was only one absent, everyone agreed with the decision and Mr. Tregas sent a pigeon with the message to his friend to come immediately to the bookstore. They all went up to the entrance to wait for help, until then they prepared everything for John for the trip, with food and good advice. It didn't take long for John to get the help he had been waiting for. They let him in at the door and greeted him with respect.

Mr. Tregas: - 'Good evening my dear friend!'- He welcomed him. Of course, everyone greeted him and introduced themselves to each other.

Mr. Temal: 'Good evening, respect to all.'- He introduced himself politely.

Mr. Tregas: - 'My dear friend! I sent you the message because we have a big request for you! You should accompany John to the enchanted forest to the big tree, you have to take a very important letter to the fairies, if this letter doesn't get there then everything will be lost, we won't have any hope left and then the evil witch will win everything and rule over everyone. What is very important is that you have to get there by midnight, because then the owl's head will appear on the trunk of the tree and remember that it will only be present for a minute, which you have to touch, because after that you will not have any more opportunities to do so.': - He told them the good advice.

Mr. Temal: - 'That's fine, my dear friend, we will take the letter, there will be no problem.'- He said firmly. They said goodbye to each other and set off. They had 5 hours to get to the big tree. They set off through the city on horseback, reached the border of the city and looked back once more, then continued their journey towards the enchanted forest. Once they reached the forest, they stopped for a moment, looked at each other and entered the forest.

John followed Temal because he didn't know where to go, he was paying close attention to everything so that they wouldn't be surprised. Of course, Mr. Temal was also watching everywhere because this forest was enchanted so it wasn't too safe. They went deeper and deeper into the forest, so far everything went smoothly, there were no problems, 2 hours had already passed since they had started, but they only had 3 hours left. They reached a river, where a swinging bridge led them to the other side, and they had to cross to the other side because the big tree is on that side. They tied the horses to the tree and continued their journey on foot. They managed to cross the swinging bridge, so they continued through the forest towards through the tree. They had to go through smaller hills, which slowed down their progress a bit, and the strange noises that sounded around them were quite terrifying. They were heading up a small hill when they reached the top and suddenly something ran away in front of them. They both stopped and looked around at what it could be. They lay on the ground and waited to see if it would emerge again. As they were laying there waiting, that something appeared behind them. They turned around to see what it was. But again, they saw nothing. They were still on the ground, waiting for that thing to appear again. That thing appeared again and abducted Temal with such speed that nothing could be noticed. When John came to his senses, Temal was no longer with him.

John: - 'That's great!'- He said in a low voice. 'Now my journey to the big tree will be interesting, I don't even know where to go next.'- These were his thoughts. 'Well, I have no choice but to listen to my intuition to get there in time.' He stayed on the ground for a while to see if anything was there. But there was nothing there anymore, he stood up cautiously and continued walking, listening to his feelings, he started in one direction, he continued his journey, and he did not give up. He got deeper and deeper into the forest, but the sight there was not encouraging, the forest was quite scary, full of swamps, foggy places, owls hooting, strange animal sounds. But he only had 1 hour to get there, and so he had to hurry up? Something crossed his path again in the knee-high fog, only to notice that something had slipped in front of him. Frightened, he stopped to observe the phenomenon. He looked around but saw nothing. There were strange movements around him, but he couldn't see them because the fog was up to his knees, and he couldn't see through it. He became more and more nervous and slowly fear was eating him up, he didn't know what he should do, because he wasn't aware of what that something could be that was lurking around him. That thing pulled him down to the ground, the mist covered him and disappeared under him. They were face to face, a mongoose looking at John with its yellow eyes.

Mongoose: - 'John! I do not have much time! I have to take you to the big tree, as long as the fog lasts, I can take you for a while, but after that you have to continue your journey alone, it's safe for me anyway, no one can see me here.': - He told him quickly. John's blood froze, a mongoose is talking to him, it was very strange and unusual. Suddenly he didn't know what to say, he thought he was just dreaming, but he realized he wasn't.

Mongoose: - 'Follow me!'- He said firmly. The mongoose started to walk, and John also got up and started following the animal headlong, but he was so surprised that he didn't even look where he was going. All he could think about was how could it be possible for an animal to talk to you, but in the midst of his many thoughts, he also remembered that this is an enchanted forest, everything is possible here, and in fact, in this world, he actually had a lot of strange things that in his world there is no such thing in the world. He reassured himself that it would be better if he got used to it because this would not be the only strange thing he would encounter, since wherever he took that letter, he would encounter fairies. By the way, the mongoose was sent by the fairies on John's path because they knew he was coming, because they see and know everything, just like the witch. His companion was kidnapped by the witch and taken back to the bookstore so that he could not help John. When the magicians saw that Temal had returned to them, they knew that John would not have an easy time out there alone and they also knew that the evil witch had a hand in the matter. Temal begged to be forgiven, but he couldn't do anything, of course the magicians weren't angry with Temal, since it wasn't his fault. The mongoose accompanied John on his way for a long time, but it was not long before they reached the big tree. Before the end of the fog, the mongoose said to John.

Mongoose: - 'John! Just keep going north, don't deviate from your path, if you keep the direction, you will reach the tree.'- He gave him some good advice. With that, the mongoose disappeared before he could thank him for helping him.

John: - 'Thank you for the...' He wanted to continue what he was saying, but the mongoose pulled him down again.

Mongoose: - 'John! Don't talk loudly, the witch is killing everything, just keep going.'- He warned John through telepathy by looking into his eyes so she could give him the important message. Taking his advice, John got up and headed north. He only had 15 minutes left to get to the big tree when John was attacked by an army of black ravens. John tried to defend himself, to chase away the ravens, but there were too many of them, so he fell to the ground and tried to protect himself. In the middle of the big fight, an army of mongooses came and attacked the ravens, the ravens flew away, and John could continue. He could see the big tree and so he walked ten times faster to get there as soon as possible, it was 5 minutes left. He was only 5 steps away from the big tree when a cougar jumped in front of him. John froze because he knew that the cougar was a dangerous animal. They stared at each other as the cougar gritted its teeth and roared. The cougar was getting closer and closer to John; John was looking at how he could defeat the cougar. He saw a pointed piece of wood on the ground that suited the situation. Yes, but that had to be picked up from there, and the cougar is really fast and so he had to come up with something so that from this situation, he can come out the winner. But there was only 1 minute left until the owl's head appeared. They were standing there facing each other when John picked up the piece of wood from the ground with a somersault and with that momentum the cougar jumped and landed directly on John. John was covered by the cougar, he snarled and squealed, but in the end the cougar died, John was successful. The owl's head was still visible on the trunk of the tree, John threw the cougar off him, ran to the tree and finally touched the owl's head at the last moment. When this happened, the trunk of the tree split open, and John went into the tree trunk, which immediately closed behind him. Standing inside the tree, he watched what would happen next. He didn't have to wait long because where he was standing it was like an elevator, it suddenly started going down and took John all the way to the fairy town. When the elevator stopped, the door opened and the fairies were waiting for him, ready to receive John.

Casandra: - 'Welcome John! Come, I will accompany you to my palace. She greeted him kindly.

John: - 'Greetings, dear fairies!' Casandra received John personally because she was very anxious for him to get there safely. The sight that he saw there, John was just amazed and stared in wonder at the little castle that the fairies had built for themselves, it was more beautiful than anything he could ever imagine. They arrived at the palace and sat down at the beautifully laid table.

John: - 'I would like to introduce myself....' Casandra interrupted John.

Casandra: - 'Forgive me for interrupting you, as I know who you are, and so let me introduce myself to you, I'm Casandra, the keeper of the trees, and your name is John, James's father. So, what brings you here?'

John: - 'Nice to meet you, Casandra!' He answered politely. 'I have come to deliver an important letter to you Casandra.' With that, he handed her the letter. Casandra opened and read the letter which read:

Dear Casandra! We are asking for your help in delivering an important message to James that will slow down the activities of the evil witch. Darkness covers everything and the animals also began to die. If this continues, people and children will have nothing to eat. So, we ask that a message be written to James to somehow stop the wicked witch or divert attention from her evil deeds." Thank you for your help, in advance.

Sincerely, Mr. Tregas.

Casandra: - 'Well, there is nothing else left to do, we need to help.'- She stated firmly. 'John! Feel free to eat and drink as much as you like, I'll be back soon and join you, but this is more important than anything else, I have to take care of things now.'- She said to John with respect. John stayed there and saw to the treats, while the fairies watched his every wish if he had one. After a while, Casandra came back smiling as always and joined John. John respectfully stood up from the table while Casandra took her seat.

Cassandra: - 'John! The message that needs to be delivered to James has been taken care of, he will receive it soon and then we just have to wait for what we expect to happen.'

John: - 'Casandra! May I ask if you have met James yet?'

Casandra: 'Yes John! I met James and his friends. When they were here, they were well, we took care of them just like we are taking care of you now, and then we sent them on their way.'

John: 'How many were here?'

Casandra: - 'There were four in total.'

John: - 'Four? Weren't there three here?'

Casandra: - 'No, I'm sure there were four people here, I know their names: - James, Evelin, Oliver, Hanna.'

John: - 'Hanna? Who can that be, I haven't heard of her?'

Casandra: - 'Well, you haven't heard about her because she's not in your world, but in this world. Anyway, Hanna is James' cousin, and James knows that and so they stick together.'

John: - 'I see! Thanks!' With that, they continued their meal.

John: - 'Thank you very much for the dinner and the welcome.'- He thanked her politely.

Casandra: - 'You're welcome! I'm glad I could help, my elves will show you your room, where you'll spend the night tonight, and then tomorrow morning you can head back. Have a safe trip.'- she said farewell to John. With that, the elves accompanied him to his room, where he could relax in peaceful conditions. The next morning, he woke up in a small clearing just like James and the others when they were there. After he woke up, he realized that he wasn't with the fairies, and he started to make his way back. He successfully arrived at the mages in the evening, he entered the bookstore where they were waiting for him.

John: - 'Good evening! Mr. Temal?? How? I saw him disappear!'

Mr. Temal: - 'Good evening! Yes, I disappeared, but the evil witch brought me back here to make things difficult for you. He wanted our mission to fail, but you did it anyway.'

John: - 'Yes! With more or less obstacles, but I did it in the end. I handed over the letter to Casandra and she took care of the rest, the handover was successful.'

Mr. Tregas: - 'This is great, now we just have to wait for the developments. In the meantime, let's all go home to our loved ones and try to rest.'

James buys time

Casandra gave the letter to the underwater fairy Atlindia, who was the guardian of the waters. After receiving the letter, she immediately set out to make sure that the letter reached James. The letter was delivered to James through the channel, by the time James would wake up the letter was in his cell next to him where he was sleeping. When James woke up, he noticed the letter on the floor next to him. He picked up the letter and started turning it to get a good look at what kind of letter it might be and where it came from. There was a seal on it that depicted the fairies, he knew that the letter came from the fairies, and it must be important, he opened it.

Letter: -

Dear James! You have an important mission to complete for the sake of humanity.

We would like to ask you to slow down the witch's activities as much as possible.

Everything was covered in darkness, the animals started to die, we have to stop this.

We are sure that with your sharp mind you will come up with some solution to save us time.

We count on you James!

Kind regards, The Mages

James was shocked after reading the letter, but at the same time he wondered what he could do to the evil witch to buy time. While he was thinking, breakfast was brought to both of them. While eating breakfast, he was thinking about what to do, and he couldn't even finish his breakfast. But lunch was also brought, and nothing useful came to mind. He was constantly walking up and down in his cell when his dinner was also slipped through the door.

Guard: - 'What's up little brother, is the dinner not good enough?! Hahahahaha. Maybe you need help! Or a nice company? Hahaha haha.': - They laughed at him mockingly. James didn't give a damn about them, because they were a bunch of causeless, retarded guards conjured up from enchanted mindless frogs.

The prince heard the guards mocking James and because of this

142

he asked him if everything was alright.

Gilbert: - 'James! Is everything okay over there? Why are the guards mocking you?'

James: 'Everything is fine, Your Majesty. Don't worry about me, I'm just not hungry.'

Gilbert: - 'It's okay! I believe you, then good night, James.' With this, there was silence again in the cells. James couldn't sleep as he thought about how he could distract the evil witch. Morning dawned, and the prince awoke to James shouting at the guards.

James: - 'Guards! Guards! Guards!'- He yelled loudly as he peered through the door.

Gilbert: - 'James? James? What's wrong? What happened? James, answer!'- He shouted to James, but without success because James made such a loud noise that even the dead wake up, he did not hear the prince calling him. The guards made their way to James's cell as well.

Guard: - 'What's going on again!? Are your pants tight? Did you eat too much yesterday? Hahahahaha.'

James: - 'I have to get out of here, it's very important! I have to talk to the witch right away!'- He said to the guard in despair.

Guard: - 'Yes, yes! You want to invite the witch to a date? Do you have too big of a load in your pants, little brother? You'll solve it for yourself here with the walls, or with your cellmate, haha hahaha.'- They laughed out loud. With that, they left the cells there in the middle of a lot of laughter; they didn't even hear James's shout. James fell to the ground hopelessly, sadly, wondering how he was going to help the mages now if they were always such assholes.

Gilbert: - 'James! James! What's wrong? How can I help? If I can, I'll help you, just tell me what's bothering you.'- he said in despair. A little silence followed what the prince asked James, as it took some time for James to collect his thoughts. After preparing for it, he addressed the prince.

James: - 'Your Majesty! Sorry about what just happened, I wasn't prepared to tell you, but I will now. Listen very carefully.... what I am going to say is very important. I received a letter from the mages, it says that I have to get out of here somehow because the evil witch has done such things to the county and to the people out there that I should distract her for a while, it would be very important to get out of here.': - He said. in despair.

Gilbert: - 'Okay! Well, then listen well!'- He said optimistically. He told the plan to James quickly acted.

Gilbert: - 'Help! Help! Help!': - He screamed at the top of his lungs. The guards came down to the cells again.

Guard: - 'What's up again? Are you guys finished with your business, did it hurt too much. Hahahahhahahaha?': - The guard laughed.

Guard: - 'What do you want, Your Majesty??'- He asked mockingly.

Gilbert: - 'Excuse me gentlemen, but I think that my cellmate passed out, something is wrong with him.'- He said in despair.

Guard: - 'Well these guys really did have some heated action in their cells.'

Other guard: 'Yes, well apparently James really exhausted himself.' The guard snorted in laughter.

Gilbert: - 'That's disgusting what you are saying, You should instead open the cell doors.' He snapped at them angrily.

Upon hearing this, the guards rushed to the cell and entered the door. Indeed, they saw James lying motionless on the ground.

Guard: 'Hey, you, there? Get up from there? Heeeeeeey I'm talking to you!'- The guards were calling to James but there was no reaction.

1st Guard: - 'Hey listen! Go up and tell the witch about this, right now!'- He said to his friend.

2nd Guard: - 'Okay! I'm leaving right away; you stay here and watch.'

1st Guard: - 'Okay, will do.'

The guard went to tell the evil witch about what had happened.

2 Guard: - 'Madam! I respectfully report that something happened to James in his cell, he is lying on the ground and not moving.' - He bowed respectfully to her.

The witch was so busy with her evil plan that she didn't even pay attention to the two prisoners.

Evil Witch: - 'What did you say? What happened to James? You absolute brain-dead swine! Where were you that you didn't notice this in time? Did you leave your guard posts again? Inbred mongrels!'- The witch snapped at him angrily. The guard was so scared that he didn't dare speak.

2 Guard: - 'Aaa... No... Yes, ma'am! We went to lunch!'- He said something believable.

Evil Witch: - 'Lunch???!!!! Both of you??? How dare you both leave your guard posts? Stupid bastards!'- She roared at the guard. She started walking out of the room so fast that she pushed aside the guard who proceeded to fall. The guard quickly got up and started to follow the evil witch, as he was afraid of her because he knew that she was so evil and capable of anything. They got down to the cells.

Evil Witch: - 'Open the door immediately!!!': - She ordered the other guard angrily. The guard opened the door, and she entered the cell, of course she found James lying on the floor. She walked to him and checked if he is breathing, checked his pulse, looked at his eyes and gently started slapping him to bring him back to his senses. James began to regain his senses, opened his eyes and sobbed.

James: - 'Where am I? What happened? Is this heaven?' The Evil Witch carefully sat him up and said to him.

Evil Witch: 'Hello, my child! No, this is not heaven, and you are still here in the cell, but now you are better, I think. Tell me dear, what happened?

James: - 'I think it might be that it's too cold here and we don't have enough food, that might be why I passed out.'- He answered nauseously.

Evil Witch: - 'What?'- She snarled at the guards. 'Is this how you pay attention to my prisoners? Stupid fools! This is not what I ordered you fools to do. You will take him up to his room right now immediately, do you understand?!!'- She yelled angrily. 'I'll teach the pair of you how to keep a prisoner later'. The guards immediately took James up to his room, that is, to Evelin's room, which is the only room that the evil witch uses for this purpose, and the guards know this very well. The witch stayed below at the cells, she went to the prince's cell and looked in through the small window, she wanted to see if he was all right. Gilbert sat on the floor and looked up at the small window, because only a tiny bit of light came in from there. In the cell, there was no bed, no table, only a dirty toilet. As she stood there looking at her love, a small spark started to ignite in her heart. The memories just kept spinning right in front of her, how good it was when the two of them were together. But then she closed the window and stormed away. Therefore, in an immediate effect it was ordered to the guards that they bring him a bed and that he receives full care. Of course, the witches' orders were immediately fulfilled. Gilbert was surprised that he received a bed, a blanket, table, candles, and regular food, he did not lack anything in his cell, and the only thing he missed very much was his family. James also got everything he needed in his cell. He looked around the room and what was there matched the description that Evelin had told him. His room was specially designed as a boy's room, but it was just as beautiful as Evelin's at the time. There was also that particular closet, only now it was full of boys' clothes. After he felt better (As he really had fainted, the prince told him what he had to do in order to really faint, only through this way was their plan successful) he went to the closet to open the door and wanted to see what was inside. He immediately remembered what Evelin had told them after the evil witch had let her go. He opened the closet door, and it was full of more and more beautiful clothes. Of course, these clothes were not at all similar to the clothes that people use in his world; their appearance didn't even come close to it. James really liked these kinds of clothes, they were so fitting for a fairy tale, he couldn't help but admire the clothes, and the sight impressed James. He also started to look at the clothes one by one and just admired them; he was about a quarter of the way through them when there was a knock at the door.

James: - 'Go ahead!'- He answered.

Guard: - 'The Witch asks you to change for dinner; we will accompany you down to the great hall.

James: - 'Okay! I'll be ready right away.'- He replied. The guards left the room so James could change. James found a suitable outfit for himself and left the room. James was escorted down to the great hall where the evil witch was waiting for him.

Evil witch: - 'Come, come closer, my dear! Take a seat, please.'- She invited him to the table kindly. This attitude on part of the wicked witch was very unusual for James. James sat down at the table, which was covered to the brim, the table was decorated with more and more delicious foods, their aroma was so tempting that James's stomach rumbled loudly.

Evil witch: - 'I hear you're hungry, my dear, I won't keep you waiting, let's eat, Bon Appetit!'- She said kindly.

They immediately began eating, of course James was very hungry and wanted to eat everything at once, it was quite a funny sight. When they finished dinner, the wicked witch got up from the table and escorted James through to the rest room. They sat down on a bench, which was made of beautifully carved wood and was padded.

Evil witch: - 'Well, my dear, how are you feeling? Are you better yet?'

James: - 'Yes, thank you! I feel much better. The dinner was very tasty, this palace is very beautiful and huge.'

Evil Witch: - 'Oh, thank you so much! But let's not talk about the palace, please tell me what happened down there in the cell?'

James: - 'As I said before, what happened was that very...'

Evil witch: - 'Yes, yes, I heard that once, I know. But please tell me the real reason!'

James: - 'Well okay then! I think that if you have kidnapped us and are holding us here in this palace, where I don't think there is a way out, we can't even get used to it, then why can't we be up here in the palace in a separate room with the prince and maybe we could be of use to you.': - He answered smartly.

The evil witch looked thoughtfully at James deeply looking into his eyes. But she looked at him in vain because nothing was reflected in his eyes, without his magic she couldn't see what was on his mind.

Oliver and Hanna fit in perfectly in the royal palace during this time. Hanna stood outside in the terrace hallway and looked outside, the view was amazing, Oliver was just making his way there and joined Hanna.

Oliver: - 'Hi! What are you thinking?'- He asked.

Hanna: - 'Hi Oliver! I keep thinking about how to stop the evil witch. But I can't think of anything creative.'

Evelin: - 'Hello! I can't sleep! I can see I'm not the only one. What's up? How long do we have to be here? I wonder how James could be. I miss him.'- She said sadly.

Hanna: - Hi Evelin! I can't sleep either, so I come here to think of ways to stop the evil witch, to see if I can come up with something, but unfortunately, I have no idea what to do.'

Oliver: - 'Hi Evelin! I don't know what will happen to us......' He couldn't finish the sentence because suddenly something started to glow in his pocket. All three of them looked there and then Oliver reached into his pocket.

Evelin: - 'I can't believe this! You still have your stone!?'

Hanna: - 'What kind of stone?' Oliver reached into his pocket and took out the stone that shone beautifully.

Oliver: - 'This stone showed us the way to where James disappeared at that time. Maybe even now he can show us the way to where to look for James, because it only lights up when it wants to show something, isn't that right!': - He said with sparkling eyes.

Hanna: - 'Can I ask for the stone?'

Oliver: - 'Well of course!'

He handed the stone to Hanna, and it continued to glow beautifully in her hand. They heard footsteps and quickly started

149

walking towards Hanna's room. They went into the room and put the stone under the blanket because the footsteps were heading towards them. They waited in silence for the footsteps to pass so that they could continue the conversation. When the footsteps were at the room, it suddenly stopped, and they heard a knock at the door. Oliver and Evelin hid under the bed and lay there in silence.

Hanna: - 'Yes, go ahead!'

The door was opened, there was a guard.

Guard: - 'I heard a noise on the hallway; I wanted to know if everything is okay!'- He asked.

Hanna: 'Oh, yes, everything is fine here! Thanks for warning me! Good night!'- She said goodbye to the guard.

Guard: - 'It's okay! Close the door, you can't know what might happen since darkness reigns.'- He warned!

Hanna: - 'I will! I will lock the door and thank you very much for the warning'. With that, the guard left the room and walked away. Hanna closed the door and both Oliver and Evelin came out from under the bed.

Oliver: - 'That was close! There is a little problem! This stone will shine until we get to where it leads us, now what should we do? - He asked in despair.

Hanna: - 'Where is this stone from?'

Oliver: - 'I found it in my large wooden chest when I gathered my things to go in search of James. But it still lit up so beautifully. it led us to the school locker, where James fell in just like us, and then it didn't light up anymore.'

Hanna: 'I understand! Do you know what kind of stone this is?'

Oliver, Evelin: - 'No!'- They both answered at the same time.

Hanna: - 'This stone is an ancient sorcerer's stone, and a long time ago, when the great wise sorcerer cast the important spells on paper, that's when he made a magical stone. The purpose of the stone was to help good wizards in trouble and show them the right way, it only lights up when it finds something useful to help. It means that it has found a useful way that leads us out of the darkness.

Oliver: - 'That's great! But how did the stone get to me?'

Hanna: - 'The stone only chooses a person where it feels safe. The stone chose you, and now it shines only because you are here near it.'

Evelin: - 'Shouldn't we report this to the king? He can still help us in some way! He has mages, maybe they can help!'

Hanna: - 'Evelin! First, we need to know where the stone wants to lead us, if we find out something and the situation gives then we will let the king know.'

Evelin: - 'So far, we would be fine! But how do we get out of the palace with the glowing stone without being noticed? After all, it's always dark and this stone has quite a lot of light.'- She said wisely.

Oliver: - 'I have an idea! Hanna said earlier that the stone only lights up when I'm near it, so this is the solution. I will go ahead, and you will follow me from afar, we just need to discuss the exact plan.'

Evelin: - 'That's not bad! Get to work then!'

Hanna: - 'The plan is as follows!'

"Tomorrow morning, everyone is awake and there is a lot of bustles in the palace, regardless of the constant darkness, the human body still needs rest, doesn't it! So, tomorrow we will have breakfast and if possible, we have to take food without being noticed, because we don't know where the stone will lead us. When we are done, we wrap the stone well in a dark cloth and hide it. Oliver, you go ahead to the cave, we will follow you and we will meet there. The rest will come when we are together."

Oliver: - 'that's fine, but don't forget not to bring the stone down with you when we have breakfast.'- He warned Hanna.

Hanna: 'Don't worry, I won't take it with me. Good night you guys.'

With that, they said goodnight to each other, and everyone went to their own rooms. The next morning, they followed the plan, had breakfast and carefully packed for the trip without anyone seeing them. Oliver set off for the cave much earlier than the others. When the girls were ready, they left the palace without being noticed. Everyone arrived at the cave where the Oliver was waiting for them.

Oliver: - 'Hello! Well, was everything alright?'

Evelin, Hanna: - 'Yes, everything was fine!' They went inside the cave and there Hanna took out the stone, which she handed over to Oliver. The stone lit up beautifully, illuminating the cave, it was a very a beautiful sight.

Hanna: - 'Well, we have nothing else to do but follow the stone and, most importantly, be very alert.' Oliver started walking out of the cave, they started where the stone led them. During their journey, the stone led them to the big tree, but they didn't know why, they just followed the stone. They remembered that there was a reason they went there because the place was familiar.

Oliver: - 'It's like we've been here before, this place is very familiar to me!'

Hanna: - 'Yes, we really have been here, I know where it is leading us!'

Evelin: - 'We really went there, but I couldn't tell you where it's leading us.

Hanna: - 'It's leading us to the big tree where we met the fairies.

Evelin: - 'True! We really met them here! But why did it bring us here?'

Hanna: - 'That will soon become clear!'

When they got to the tree, the stone extinguished its light.

Oliver: - 'I think we have arrived! And now......'

He couldn't finish what he was saying, because the tree immediately split in two and a fairy took them into the tree trunk.

They started down, where the big boss Casandra was waiting for them.

Casandra: - 'Welcome back to us! I hope that my message has reached you and the stone has done its job. I called you here because I have something important to say to you.'- She welcomed them.

'Follow me my dears!' She led them to the great hall where they sat down at the table, ate and then went through to the meeting room, where only Casandra was with them.

Casandra: - 'I know that you don't understand all this, why you are here with me, but I will tell you now.'

James is being held captive by the evil witch, and with this constant darkness that she brought upon us, and as I heard, the animals also began to die is how the evil witch wants to torment the people and teach them a lesson. But something happened that you don't know about yet, James' father came here in this world to save you.

Oliver: - 'Wow! That's cool, this is...' Casandra looked at her with a serious face, and both Hanna and Evelin looked at Oliver

153

sternly, so that he would be quiet. Oliver suddenly cleared his throat and said sorry.

Oliver: - 'Sorry about that!'

Casandra: - 'Okay! Well, James' father sent me a letter written by the mages from the city of Moltius, with the request that the letter should be delivered to James, because it is important to stop the witch's activities, the mages need more time to do something against the evil witch. You three are here because you have to go to city of Moltius and give the stone to the head mage. This is very important to get the stone to where it belongs. You will leave from here tomorrow morning, until then enjoy our hospitality, enjoy yourselves.'- She finished what she had to say.

Hanna: - 'Thank you for this confidential information and of course we will take the stone to Moltius.' With that they left the hall to the fairies and elves. The next morning, they found themselves again in the clearing as before, they got up and set off for the city of Moltius. They arrived at the bookstore in the evening, opened the door and were greeted with great joy.

John: - 'Oh, it's good to see you again, children!'- He welcomed them with great joy. He looked at Hanna and she was so familiar, but he had never seen her before in his life, but still the feeling that came over him was as if they had already met, a real Deja vu feeling, came over him. The Mages led them to their lodgings to rest from their journey. Of course, Oliver handed the stone to the main magician. While the youth rested, the head mage and the others went back to their room and placed the stone in the middle of the large round table. John stayed with the youths at the accommodation and had a catch up. They told John all about their adventure and how sad they were that they couldn't help James. As soon as the magicians placed the stone on the table, the stone glowed like never before. It was important for them to be in the room so that the light of the stone cannot get out of the bookstore, since they are beneath the ground. When the stone shed its light out completely, a writing appeared in the light.

Writing:

"There is only one way to defeat the evil witch!'

'The secret lies within the boy!'

'He carries the key in his heart!"

The mages read this aloud, and when they finished, the writing disappeared. The light of the stone also went out, and so they placed it in a safe place where no one, not even mages, can get to it.

Mr. Tregas: 'Well, gentlemen, here was the key to the secret, we cannot leave it at that, we have to act.'

Mr. Monghur: - 'Yes! We need to do something now. Let's send a letter to the fairies so they can forward it to James. James needs to know this.'

Mr. Onthasy: - 'Sounds good! I will write the letter and send it to the fairies tonight.' They did so, wrote the letter and sent it off with a mongoose.

Evil witch: - 'Bring the prince immediately!'- She stated firmly.

Guard: - 'Yes, my lady!'

Gilbert was taken there to the evil witch.

Evil witch: - 'Well prince! I brought you here because I decided that you would get a room up here in my palace, just like James. If you obey me, you will have a good relationship here with me, if you disobey in anything; you will regret it very much.' And before the prince could thank her, the evil witch waved to the guards, and they took him to his room. When James got up, he found a letter on his pillow, opened it and began to read.

Letter: -

"Dear James! We learned something that could be very important in defeating the evil witch.

We found a letter that said that the secret opens...." He couldn't read it all the way through because there was a knock at the door and he had to answer, so he carefully hid the letter in his bed.

Guard: - 'The witch is calling you to the great hall; you'll get a minute to change. With that, they closed the door behind them. James quickly changed his clothes and left for the great hall along with the guards. He entered the great hall, where the table was beautifully laid, the prince was also at the table, he took a seat and began to scan the at all the food.

Evil witch: - 'Welcome to my palace! Now you're not in your cells, because I decided to give you a chance, and if I ask you to do anything, you have to do it. If you go against anything, there will be consequences. I hope we cleared that up and you took note.' - She smiled to herself. Both obediently agreed to the witch's wish.

Evil Witch: - 'Well! Bon Appetit, feel free and eat.' After finishing breakfast, both of them had to go back to their rooms until further orders. The evil witches heart started to catch fire again, she went upstairs to her own room and started singing, which hadn't happened in a long time. When the guards heard this, they looked at each other and shrugged their shoulders, because they had not heard such a thing in a long time, and it was just unusual for them. Of course, as soon as James got back to his room, the first thing he did was take out the letter from his bed, where he carefully tucked it away.

Letter: -

Dear James! We learned something that could be very important in defeating the evil witch. We found an article in which it was said that the secret lies within you. In order for this to surface, you have to look inside yourself and your deepest feelings and memories have to surface. If you succeed in this, you can defeat the evil witch without causing her any harm."

P.S Don't give up hope and your faith!

After reading the letter, he of course burned it so that no one would find it. He sat down at the window and watched the beautiful landscape in front of him. James tried to decipher what he read in the letter. The prince was just sitting by the window in his room and looking out, thinking what to do, his family must need him, and he missed his family and children very much. In the middle of the evil witch singing, it occurred to her to bring back the prince's memories. She even went down to the magic room to work out the right potion for the prince.

The mages waited helplessly for the time when James would finally defeat the evil witch. But since that takes time, they can't do anything but keep people's spirits up, bring faith, strength and endurance to people's hearts. Hanna and Evelin spent their day together in the bookstore with the magicians and James's father. John tried to get to know Hanna and her family better, which Hanna was happy to tell John. John went about his business with a sigh of relief, knowing where his adopted son was coming from. The evil witch has finished the magic potion that she will give to Gilbert at dinner, and she was very excited about it. After much thought, James still couldn't figure out how to defeat the evil witch, so he left the window and went to the closet to continue looking at the clothes inside. He opened the closet door and began to pull them away one by one. But he was halfway through the clothes when something hit against the window. He suddenly jumped up because he was scared and looked at the window but saw nothing. He stopped looking at the clothes and went to the window to see what it was. He looked out the window and there was a beautiful white dove lying on the windowsill outside. The dove looked into James' eyes as if asking him for help. James opened the window and picked up the pigeon, took it into his room and laid it down on his bed to examine it. The pigeon broke its wing hence why it struck the window. James looked for small tools and a rag to put the wing in a split, and he did it, he carefully put the pigeon's wing in a splint, and he made a place for the pigeon to lie in and he carefully put him inside. When he placed the pigeon in his bed, he looked at James with a grateful look.

James: - 'You will be safe here little pigeon, stay calm and you will recover soon. I will bring you something to eat and drink': - He said kindly to the pigeon. He went back to his closet and continued looking through the clothes. He almost reached the end where that certain secret door was when there was another knock at his door. They were the guards, they called him to the witch. He went down to the great hall where the prince was also waiting. The evil witch led them into the meeting room because she had something important to discuss with them.

Evil witch: - 'I called you here because I have something important to discuss with you. First of all, I'm going to speak with you Prince, I have a certain task for you that you have to carry out immediately. Here's what you have to do, this raven is here, you have to set it off from the window of your room, once you've done that, you have to come back here, we'll wait here until then.

158

Gilbert: - 'That's okay! This will not be a difficult task.'- He said happily. It's just that he didn't know what the consequences would be if he released the raven. So he went upstairs to his room, of course with his guards escorting him, he went to the window, opened it and released the raven. The raven flew away with a loud cawing. The prince happily headed back to the courtroom to tell the evil witch that he had accomplished his task.

Gilbert: - 'I let the raven fly out of the window as you said.'- He said happily.

Wicked Witch: - 'Good! Now sit down because James is next. James! You also have a raven that you need to let out of the window, if you have done that then come back here too.'

James: - 'Okay!'- He answered with pleasure. The evil witch also gave him the raven. James took him up to his room also with a guard escorting him, opened the window and released the raven. The raven flew away with a loud cawing. He also went back to the great hall and sat down again. The wicked witch stood up and walked to the window, looking out and said:

Evil witch: - 'Do you know where those ravens will fly to?'- She asked them. The prince and James looked at each other and simultaneously answered 'No!' 'Well, the raven that the prince released will fly to the king's court to find the king's advisor, after finding him, the raven will kill him.' When the prince heard this, he was immediately shocked and got up from his seat because he wanted to react, but the evil witch immediately motioned him to sit back down. Shock froze on James's face upon hearing this; he couldn't imagine where his raven could have flown after that and who he was going to kill.

Evil witch: - 'Your raven James will fly to the village of Leintes and find the village mage there and kill him.'- To this the evil witch let out a bloodcurdling laugh. In James's mind, ten thousand questions are ringing out in front of him as to how he should react to this. Those certain feelings that arose from anger in James's heart began to surface.

James: - 'So far, it's nice and good, for you of course! But I have a question. Why do these people have to be killed? What harm did they do to you that you have to take their lives?'- He asked calmly. The evil witch looked at James in shock, as she did not expect this reaction from him.

Evil witch: - 'Well! This is a small taste for the king not to mess with me in the future, even if every person on this earth does not bow before me, then I will make sure that this happens.

Prince: - 'It is likely that this was not a smart move on your part, because if you were to announce this all over the country, what your conditions and wishes are, humanity will follow it, don't you think?': - He asked angrily.

Evil witch: - 'Yes! I know that this would be the right way, but if I don't scare them enough, they will ignore my request and then they won't obey.'- She answered calmly.

Gilbert: - 'I will help you write this ad, so that people will understand and take note.'- He said optimistically.

Evil witch: - 'okay then! But the ravens still have to do their mission and then we will send the ad.': - She answered firmly. 'Now, however, I would like to ask you to go back to your rooms until I send for you.'- She said firmly. With that they both went back to their room. The first raven which was on its way to the king's court, arrived and was looking for the advisor. It didn't take long to find him; he was there in the palace at the royal table in the meeting room. The raven flew into the room above the advisors' head, he flew in circles over his head, they tried to shoo him away, but the raven landed on his head and poured into his mouth the liquid that the evil witch had prepared for him. After this was done the raven flew away. They couldn't stop him because the raven was surrounded by a protective shield so that he could carry out what he flew there for. After the raven flew away, they rushed to the advisor to see if everything was okay, but they didn't see anything strange.

One of the advisors: - 'Is everything okay? What did that raven do? We couldn't drive him away; he was surrounded by a protective shield.'- He said in despair.

King: - 'What is the meaning of this? What was that all about? How did a raven get in here?'- He asked suddenly.

Advisor: - 'I don't know! Some kind of liquid...'- He said with a snort, and the life drained out of him. He couldn't finish the sentence because the poison that the raven dropped in his mouth killed him. The advisor is dead. The king fell to his knees and watched the death of his friend, which was very painful for him, since he had known his advisor and mage since he was a child, he did a lot of good for the court and his family, he was almost a second father to the king, because he always looked after him and he was always there when he needed him. For the first time, some of the courtiers saw the king cry. The king fell to his knees sobbing and took his friend's hand, caressed his face and said so.

King: - 'My dear friend! This will not go unpunished, this deed has a penalty, whoever did this will be hanged.'- He stated crying. The king stood up, straightened himself and beckoned to the guards to take the corpse out. The king announced to the people that the person who killed his adviser should be held accountable for his or her actions and that if caught, they would be hanged for it. The councillor's body was also burned on a pyre with dignity, so that his soul could ascend to his ancestors, this was the custom. During this time, the second raven arrived in the village where the other magician was. This magician was also very old, but he put a lot of things on the table, helped and saved many people during his life. They were gathered in the small village as usual to discuss what had happened in the village, of course the magician was also there among them. The raven found him and flew over his head, circled over him, but they couldn't drive this raven away either, he flew on his head and let into his mouth the certain poisoned liquid that the evil witch had prepared. People tried to push him away, but they couldn't get close to him because of the protective shield that surrounded the mage. After the raven finished its mission, it flew on and the magician fell to the ground. The other men who were there rushed to the mage to see if everything was alright, but they saw nothing on him that he had any injuries.

Man: - 'Sir! Sir! Everything all right? What happened? What did that raven do to you?'- He asked in despair.

Mr. Fimber: - 'The raven had some kind of liquid...': - He couldn't finish the sentence because the poison took its affect him very quickly and he died. Everyone stood there in despair and watched this incident and didn't know what to make of this whole thing. The man who knelt down near the mage was very close friends with him, because of this he began to cry, and the others also stood there with sunken eyes and silently watched with their heads bowed and did not understand why it hurt him.

Man 1: - 'Let's take him out and burn him with dignity.'- He said sadly.

Man 2: - 'Come on, people, let's build the pyre.'- He said sadly. All the men got together and started to build the pyre. Yes, but the women also noticed what the men were doing and asked what the pyre was for, who died? The men told them, and then the women began to cry a lot because they loved the mage very much and so they decided to help the men build the pyre. After they respectfully lit the pyre, on top of which the mage was neatly wrapped in a white sheet, they put a tree leaf, a bird's feather and a small piece of paper near his heart, so they paid tribute to the mage. The message that the king announced was the same in their village the next day. The people were shocked that they wanted to know the reason for this and why their mage had to die. This news also reached the mage's of the Moltius city. When they heard this news, they were very surprised and quickly gathered in their secret room to consult.

Mr. Tegras: - 'My dear friends! We've all heard what's going on! Unfortunately, it is not difficult to guess who is behind this. We need to know what is going on here, we need to find out the reason for this.'- He stated firmly. During this time, the evil witch had the prince and the military sign the advertisement and sent it to the king, which was then handed to the king. He unfolded the scroll and began to read the advertisement. While reading, the scroll fell out of his hand, the new adviser picked up the scroll and wanted to give it back to the king, but the king motioned for him to read it. The advisor read it and looked at the king. The king gave the scroll to the herald to read the news to the people. Messanger went out and started reading the advertisement.

Ad: -

"Attention! Attention! Here is my advertisement for you! The deaths of the mages should be a lesson for you.

I want you to submit to me and bow down to me from now on.

If you do this, you will have a good life. If not, you will suffer more.

From now on, everyone, including the king, will be my obedient servants.

If you do anything stupid, I will know and then there will be no mercy.

Have a nice day to you, until my trip!

Evil witch!"

After reading this out loud, people froze. They stood there staring blankly and didn't dare to speak, knowing that if they say something which reaches the ears of the evil witch then it's all over. After a few minutes, everyone gathered their strength and went about their business. There was never so much silence on the streets until now, you could only hear the galloping horses, the dogs' barks, the cats' whining and the people's footsteps echoed throughout the streets, after hearing the news no one dared to speak. The mage watched this misery helplessly and could not do anything about it. The king was so helpless he couldn't do anything to save the kingdom against the evil witch. He also regretted making the decision all those years ago, separating his son from this horrible woman. Everyone felt helpless, lost, lost and unable to find a way out. The mages only believed that James would rise to the next level with that certain courage and strength from which he could save humanity. James was so angry that he wanted to do something that could cause trouble. He was raging in his room, of course, so that the guards don't hear him, because then they will smell bad and nothing good will come of it. The little pigeon watched James, no matter what he did, he didn't take his eyes off him. Of course, James didn't notice this because he was so angry that he couldn't pay attention to the pigeon, of course he gave him food and drink, but that's all. The Evil Witch thoroughly, he always wanted everyone to pay attention to him, and he reached his goal, but there is no end to it any time soon. It was time for dinner in the evil witch's palace, and so she sent her guards to her guests. James was so angry that he didn't bother with the closet anymore, he was walking up and down his room when the guards started knocking on his door.

Guard: - 'Get ready for dinner!!': - They shouted at the door.

James: - 'Right away, I'm coming!'- He replied dejectedly. They went down to the great hall, where the table was beautifully laid with more and more delicious food and sat down at the table to eat. There was a glass in front of everyone, as with every diner, there was nothing strange on the table, at least it seemed. The evil witch placed the potion in the prince's cup to regain his memory. The dinner began, everyone ate in silence, the prince reached for the glass to drink, but then James spoke to him.

James: - 'You're Grace! How was your day?'- He asked cautiously. The prince took the glass from his mouth so that he could speak.

Prince: - 'Oh, thank you for your question! I had a very good day; I was reading a very interesting book that just caught my attention.'- He answered cautiously. James broke the silence! The prince knew that they had to come up with something, so that the evil witch wouldn't notice how angry they were, because then it would be the end of everything.

James: - 'Oh, indeed! What is that book about?'- He continued the conversation. All the while, the prince cannot drink from the glass because James constantly kept asking him something. Of course, the witch noticed it because she was watching when the prince drank from the glass. But the evil witch was out of patience and interrupted.

Evil witch: - 'Come on, my dear! It is not customary to talk at the table until we have finished our food, stop bothering to the prince!'- She said a little nervously.

James: - 'I apologies your grace, it won't happen again!'- He answered politely.

The evil witch sighed and continued her dinner and watched from the corner of her eye as the prince drank the drink. When the prince finally drinks the drink, the witch took a deep breath and ate her remaining food calmly. Everyone finished dinner, and so they got up from the table and went to the rest room to chat. They sat down by the fireplace, where there were snacks and a tea set on the small table. They mingled with each other, but the witch watched the prince in a way that he would not notice it. Not much time passed, and the prince began to feel strange. He sighed, looked dimly, so he said goodbye to everyone and went back to his room. The guards escorted the prince back. The prince went into his room and immediately fell into his bed, he couldn't imagine what could be wrong, since he hadn't drunk enough to be affected by the drink. He fell asleep as soon as he was lying down and couldn't even take off his shoes. James noticed this strange behaviour of the prince, because he doesn't usually behave like this.

James: - 'What could be wrong with the prince? He doesn't usually behave like this!': - He asked in surprise.

Evil witch: - 'Nothing! Maybe he drank more than was necessary and then fall asleep.'- He answered slyly.

James: - 'You're Grace! If you'll excuse me, i will go back to my room because as I am very tired!'- He said politely.

Wicked witch: - 'Of course, my dear! Just go and rest.'- She replied. James also went back to his room and lay down in his bed, scratching the top of his head and thinking about what could happen to Gilbert. The little pigeon got better and better, which James still didn't notice. He undressed and lay down to sleep. While James was sleeping, the pigeon fully recovered, untied its wing and tried them out. Since there was nothing wrong with him, he flew over above James's head, and began to rattle and finally spoke.

White dove: - 'Pay attention to what I'm telling you, I'm only going to tell you once. The strength that is in you needs to be brought to a higher level, open your heart to the world let your true emotions out and then you will see what you are capable of. You don't need magic for this power, because that magic is inside you.' With that, the pigeon flew back into his bed. The next morning, when James woke up, he felt kind of strange.

James: - 'What a strange dream!'- He said out loud. He went over to the pigeon to look at it and saw that it was already completely healed, so he opened the window and let it go. The dream was constantly on his mind, he thought about what kind of power it could have that didn't require magic. Evelin and Hanna where paging through the old magical books hoping to find a solution so that they could help James, but they didn't have much success.

John: - 'Good morning girls! Won't you join us? Come for breakfast, you can enjoy the books later.'- He told them.

Hanna: - 'We're going right away! We'll be there in just a couple of minutes.'- She answered.

Evelin: - 'Is there any news about James?'- She asked worriedly.

Oliver: - 'I'm going because I'm hungry, the girls will join later!'- He said with a smile.

John: - 'still nothing.'- He replied dejectedly. John left with Oliver; the girls stayed there for a short while so that they can sift through more books. Evelin took an old magic book from the shelf called "Unique Spells", a very old book and the pages were also yellow, and the edges of the pages were also incomplete. She flipped through the book, read through everything, and on each page was a drawing next to each description. She turned to a page on which a very strange spell was written, under the spell there was a drawing that depicted a carved cupboard that looked just like the cupboard where she had her room at the evil witch. She started looking at this drawing for a long time because this cupboard was very familiar to her. She just didn't know what the cupboard had to do with the spell. She closed the book and took it with her to the mage, as they went for breakfast.

Hanna: - 'Where are you taking that book? Why didn't you leave it in the library?'- She asked curiously.

Evelin: - 'Nothing special, I just found something in it, it might be important, but let's go to breakfast first.'- She said excitedly. They arrived at the mages, and everyone sat down to breakfast. Everyone was talking to each other at the table, but Evelin kept thinking about this picture she saw in the book, she didn't pay attention to what the adults were talking about. They even tried talking to her, she even nodded her head, but it all landed on deaf ears. One of the magicians, Mr. Zathen, noticed Evelin's strange behaviour, he watched her for a while and saw that the girl, who was thinking about something, wasn't really paying attention to what the adults were telling her, and she wasn't eating her breakfast like she used to. Mr. Zathen sat next to Mr. Vinthus, patted his arm and said:

Mr. Zathen: - 'Vinthus! Just watch Evelin, she's behaving very strangely this morning! I noticed this as soon as she sat down at the table!'- He said warningly. Mr. Vinthus while staying undetected started watching Evelin, and he also noticed that she was really behaving strangely this morning. The two mages looked at each other and were probably thinking about the same thing because they didn't utter a word.

Evelin: - 'Excuse me! But I've finished breakfast, I'm going to leave now!'- She said appropriately. The two mages knew straight away that something was going on in the background as Evelin had never done something like this before.

Mr. Zathen: - 'The girl must be followed!'- He whispered in Vinthus' ear. Mr. Vinthus waved, and the spy mongoose set off on Evelin's path. Evelin went up to the second floor to the library, where she could sit down at the table and read the book. She laid the book out on the table and the way the sunlight shined on the book cast a glow on it. When the mongoose saw this, he immediately ran back to the mage and informed him.

Mr. Vinthus: - 'The girl found a book that contains unique spells: - He whispered into Mr. Zathens ear. Zathen finished breakfast and the others also got up from the table and everyone went about their own business. Mr. Zathen and Mr. Vinthus went up to the second floor together, where Evelin was. During this time, Evelin drew that cupboard on a piece of paper and wrote down the magic spell, closed the book and put it back in her bag. Evelin was just about to leave when the magicians confronted her.

Mr. Zathen: 'Hi Evelin! Can I ask what kind of book you have?' - He asked curiously.

Evelin: - 'Well an old book! I don't think we will get much use out of this book!'- She answered.

Mr. Zathen: - 'Can I, have it? I'd like to see it if you don't mind!' - He said kindly.

Evelin: - 'Oh, of course! The book is here, but I will have to take it back to the library!'- She gave the book to the mage.

Mr. Zathen: 'Thank you, my child! Is there anything interesting in it that you might like share with us?'- He asked curiously.

Evelin: - 'Hmm, I don't think there was anything important in it, it's just an old book.'- She answered a little strangely.

Mr. Zathen: - 'That's okay! I'll give you the book back soon, we'll just have a look.' - He replied kindly.

Evelin: - 'It's fine! See you later'. – With that she left. The two magicians went to the table and put the book on the down so that they could read it. The books cover was simple, it depicted a leaf and a little glass vial. Mr. Zathen opened the book and they started to study it, but since they didn't know what to look for and what Evelin had found, they carefully flipped from page to page, just in case they missed what Evelin found so interesting. During this time, Evelin went downstairs, where she met with Hanna and John.

Oliver: - 'Hanna! What's up with Evelin today, she behaved so strangely at the table!'- She asked worriedly.

Hanna: - 'I don't know! We'll find her and ask her.': -She answered sadly.

Hanna: - 'Where were you? We looked everywhere for you?'- She asked curiously.

Evelin: - 'I was just upstairs! I wrote down something from one of the books. Nothing crazy.'- She answered calmly.

Oliver: - 'Something is wrong! Tell me what's wrong? I've known you for a long time, I know that something is weighing on your soul!'- He asked worriedly.

Evelin: - 'Calm down Oliver! This is not what it seems, shut up!'- She instructed him sternly.

John: - 'Ladies! Oliver! Be careful! Take care of each other, don't hang out on the streets because it's not safe!'- He warned them.

Hanna, Evelin, Oliver: - 'Ok! But we are old enough, we can take care of ourselves.'- They answered once. They looked at each other and started laughing. John also smiled, nodded and said his goodbyes to them. Hanna and Evelin went back together to their rooms.

Hanna, Oliver: - 'What is it? You are hiding something from us, we can sense it! Tell us, what did you find in that book?: - 'They asked curiously at the same time.

Evelin: - 'You won't believe this! I drew a picture from the book and also wrote down the magic spell.'- She said excitedly. She handed the paper to Hanna to look at. Hanna took the paper and began to read it; she read the spell and also saw the drawing of the cupboard. Because Hanna is also a witch, she instantly knew what the magic spell was. She looked at Evelin with a serious face and said:

Hanna: - 'Do you know what you have found?' - She asked

Evelin seriously.

Oliver: - 'Damn! That sounds exciting!'- He interjected excitedly.

Evelin: - 'I don't know exactly what that spell means, but what I noticed there was the cupboard. That's why I drew it from the book to show you first.'- She answered excitedly.

Hanna: - 'Where did you see this cupboard?' - She asked curiously.

Evelin: - 'With the wicked witch in her palace, in the room where she had held me prisoner.'- She said proudly.

Hanna: - 'I can't believe this! Is this cupboard in the evil witch's palace?'- She asked excitedly.

Evelin: - 'Yes! It's there in her palace.'- She said on the proudly.

Hanna: - 'Listen! What's in this cupboard?'

Evelin: - 'When I opened it, it was full of more and more beautiful clothes that I had never seen in my life before. But there was a rickety door at the edge of the cupboard, which unfortunately I didn't have the luck to open.'- She answered.

Hanna: - 'Okay!': - She said thoughtfully.

Evelin: - 'What is it? What's in that cupboard? Do you know?': - She asked curiously.

Hanna: - 'Yes, I know what's in the cupboard.'- She answered calmly.

Evelin: - 'Tell me then, dear, I want to know.'- she begged.

Oliver: - 'Yes! I want to hear it too!'- He wondered.

Hanna: - 'Okay! That cupboard has a door that, if you open it and walk through it, leads you into an old library. In that library, you will find books that can free humanity from the curse and bring back the evil witch in her old form. We can get rid of the evil that dominates her mind. But those books can only be used magically by someone who is a magician or a witch. Because those books are full of magic. They are useless for a normal person. Now, James is also a witch, but he didn't grow up like a witch, he doesn't know how to do the spells, he has to learn them first.

Because even if he gets in there, it is not certain whether those books will be useful for him. We should get into the palace somehow.'- She explained.

Evelin: - 'Then we have nothing else to do, we have to go back to the mages and tell them.'- She answered firmly.

Oliver: - 'Ok, they know for sure what needs to be done!'- He said excitedly.

Hanna: - 'Yes! This is a good idea.'- She replied. James went to the cupboard again to finish looking at what he had started so many times, as if that cupboard had drawn him there. He opened it and began to browse the clothes, when he came to an end and noticed that certain secret door in the closet. He suddenly became curious as to what that door was doing there and he put his hand on the handle to open it, but the door was locked. He thought about how he was going to open the door without the wicked witch noticing. He starts looking for the key in the room, looks everywhere but can't find it anywhere. He didn't find the key because there is no key for the door. The door opens every night exactly at midnight, but James didn't know that, because at that point he is always fast asleep, so there's no way for him to know. He gave up the search and went to the window, sat down on the rather wide ledge and from there he looked outside and looked at the beautiful landscape in which he buried his thoughts. Gilbert's memories of the evil witch came back, he was shaken up by this and it hurt him a lot. After all, he already has a family, and he doesn't know what to do. He knows that the king has tricked him badly, but he can't change the past. The evil witch also knows that Gilbert's powerless for now, but she gives him time, because now what he is going through is rather difficult for him. There Gilbert is sitting in front of the window, and he keeps thinking about how his father tricked him. He was very angry by the mere thought, but at the same time, he was worried because his wife and children, who were waiting for him back at the palace, and were very worried about him. Helpless, he stood in front of the window and looked at the land from which there was no way out, only hope and his faith were left to him. For now, he did not have the mental strength to go down to the great hall in front of the evil witch, because he was not ready for it. However, he doesn't know that he and the evil witch have a child, since he didn't have the opportunity to tell it to the evil one at the time. The evil witch was waiting patiently for the prince to face her. Evelin and Hanna returned to the library to the mages. John greeted them at the door.

John: - 'Hello girls! You came back rather quickly!' - He said surprised.

Hanna: - 'Oh, yes! We have to tell the mages something important, you'd better come there too!'- She said excitedly. The two magicians looked through the book, but did not discover anything interesting in it, because they did not know what Evelin found in that book. John and the girls went up to the second floor where the mages were, everyone reading some kind of book. When the two of them saw that Evelin had come back, they suspected that she was going to tell them something, so they were readily waiting.

Hanna: - 'I would like you to pay us a little attention!'- She stated firmly.

Hanna: - 'Evelin found something very important in an old magic book, in which there is a page about a certain cupboard and a magic spell, if you'll allow me, I will open it on the right page for you.': - She said firmly. The magicians gave Hanna the book that

Hanna then gave to Evelin. Evelin opened the book where the picture of the cupboard with the magic spell was and put it on the table. The mages stood around the book and had a good look at it. They are all muttering something under their breath, but you can't make out what. They looked at Evelin and the mage said:

Mr. Tregas: - 'Evelin! We are very grateful that you brought this book to us and shared this important part of the book with us. Well, this picture that this book depicts is nothing more than the key to the garden of freedom and the freedom garden of humanity. This cupboard has a door, if it opens and you go through it, you have to go through a secret corridor that leads directly to an ancient old library. There is a very important and old book in that library, in that book everything is described in detail, from page to page, how to defeat the evil witch and regain our freedom. Tell me dear, did you see this cupboard somewhere?' - He finished what he was saying.

Evelin: - 'Yes! It is in the evil witch's palace, in that very room where she held me captive.' - Answered.

Mr. Tregas: - 'Hmm, that can only be to our advantage because James is there in the palace. We have nothing else to do; we have to get a message to James.'

Hanna: - 'Yes we can send a message to James, but even if he gets into that library, he won't be able to do anything with the spells, because he doesn't know which one to use, since he hasn't practiced the spells, he has to learn them, this is the big problem.': - She said confidently.

Mr. Tregas: - 'It could be that he doesn't know which one to find, but he was....' He couldn't finish the sentence because Hanna interrupted him.

Hanna: - 'I'm going into the palace!!' - She said suddenly.

Mr. Tregas: - 'That's impossible! You can't just get in there! You are talking nonsense.'- He responded in surprise.

Hanna: - 'We can work out a plan!'- She answered excitedly.

Mr. Tregas: - 'It can't be! You can't get in there; you have to accept that! There is no plan here, if the evil witch realizes then it's the end of everything.'- He finished the sentence firmly.

Evelin: - 'Then all we can do is we send him a message about what's behind the cupboard and maybe he can find some important information.'

Mr. Onthasy: - 'There's just one problem! There is no key to the cupboard, the cupboard door only opens at midnight and only stays open for a hour, then it closes and if James gets stuck on the other side, then the door disappears, you can only see the door from inside the cupboard, but from the other side it disappears and only the wall remains.': - he said.

John: - 'But even if we send him a message, it should tell him that he should know what he's looking for, what kind of book, and maybe you could tell him what he might need.': - He gave a good idea.

Mr. Tregas: - 'This is not such a bad idea! We will do this and then the evil witch will not notice anything about it. Thank you for the good idea, John!'- He thanked him.

John: - 'I'm glad I can help!'- He answered satisfied.

Mr. Tregas: - 'Well, ladies and gentlemen, off to work!'- He gave the order, while smiling. The magicians took a piece of paper and began to write down the message to James with every single important piece of information. After they wrote the letter, they sent it with a mongoose.

The evil witch's heart begins to soften.

'It's time for dinner!' The prince pulled himself together, gathered all his courage, winked and went down to the great hall. The table was crammed with more and more delicious food. When the evil witch saw that the prince was joining them, she was very happy. They all sat down at the table and started eating. Gilbert was still unable to eat so much because his soul was tormented by the many memories that came back to him and knowing that his son James was very distraught by his father's evil deed. He couldn't look the evil witch in the eyes or look James in the eyes at the same time, because he didn't know what he could say to them after all that. The evil witch was patient with him because it was a big shock for him, and it takes time for people to process it. It was very quiet in the room; you could hear a pin drop.

James: - 'I would like to ask a question your grace!'- He broke the silence.

Evil Witch: - 'Well, of course, my dear! Tell me, what would you like?': - She answered kindly.

James: - 'I would like to ask for papers, stationery, and books if possible.' - he asked politely.

Evil Witch: - 'There's no problem, my dear!'- She answered. He nodded in agreement and the guards started to take action. After they finished dinner, all three of them went to the lounge. They sat down by the fireplace and watched the fires' dancing flames. After a while, the evil witch said.

Evil witch: - 'My dears! Since it is already quite late, if you want, you can go back to your rooms, because tomorrow we are leaving the palace, I will take you somewhere.'

James: - 'That's very kind of you! Good night.' - he said goodbye. With that, James left the rest room. But only the prince remained there, but not by accident.

Gilbert: - 'Miriam! (He addressed her by her first name) I'm very sorry for what my father did...' He couldn't finish the sentence because Miriam interrupted him.

Miriam: - 'Tsh, tsh! You don't have to explain! I know it's not your fault, I understand that. The king is responsible for all of this, which he had already paid a portion of its price. He has to suffer what he did to me and you! The king has to learn that not everything can be the way he wants it to be. I know that you have to process a lot because these memories came back suddenly, and you can has as much time as you need and we will come back to this later. Now go and rest yourself, because tomorrow we are going out of the palace.'- She said goodbye to the prince. Gilbert politely said goodbye to the witch and went upstairs to his room. When the prince entered his room, he fell into the bed and just stared at the top of his bed and all his could think about were the memories. The fact that James is also his son made his heart heavier because of this, because none of this is his fault. But the king must somehow find out that his memories came back, that his true love is Miriam. He doesn't know what his next steps should be, since he cannot have two wives. The witch stayed in the lounge and watched the fire in the fireplace and was thinking about her happiest memories. As she was sitting there staring at the fire, she heard some noises and turned around to see who was going there and it was James.

Evil witch: - 'What are you doing here, since it's late?'- She asked in surprise.

James: - 'I couldn't sleep, so I thought I'd come down here to chat!'- He answered.

Evil witch: - 'Well, if you can't sleep, come here and let's chat.'- She invited him there.

James: - 'Your grace! Against my will, I overheard your conversations with the prince, he was your great love, wasn't he?'- He asked tactfully. The evil witch knew that James knew everything because Hanna told her everything and that the witch was James's mother, and the prince was his father.

Miriam: - 'James! I know that you are a smart boy, and I also know that you already know everything about me, since there are no secrets in front me; I think you know that too. Yes, Prince Gilbert is your father, this isn't anything new for you, and neither is the fact that I'm your mother, it can't be easy for you, I know, but fate intervened in my life and so I had to act. I am willing to do anything to have my love by my side again.'- She answered in a slightly sad voice. James began to feel sorry for his mother because she was his mother at the end of the day.

James: - 'Yes, I've known all of these for a while now, but I don't understand one thing, why did you have to subject people to such a fate, why don't you just punish the king who did this to you? Why do people have to suffer because of this?' - He asked.

Miriam: - 'Enough of this now! Go and rest because you will have a long journey tomorrow.' - The Evil witch instructed angrily.

James: - 'I apologize if I hurt you, it wasn't my intention, good night to you.' - He said goodbye politely. With that he went back to his room. When he entered his room, he went to his bed to lie down and found a letter on his bed. He took the letter and started to read it.

Letter: -

'James! Destroy this letter immediately after reading it! There is a cupboard in your room, inside it you will find a door, but there is no key to that door, so don't even look for it, because the door opens by itself once every day at midnight and only stays open for an hour. You should go through that door and look for a book with a heart and a white dove on the cover. When you have found this, you have to look for the page in the book where you see a drawing of a fish and an angel, once you find it, there should also be a spell on that page. If you read this spell out loud, certain memories will immediately come back to you, with which you can defeat the evil witch without having to harm her.'

When he read the letter, he threw it into the fire as he didn't want anyone to find this letter. He looked at the clock, and the time was 23:46, which meant that he only had to wait 14 minutes until the door opened. He decided to wait for the right time and walk through the door. He laid down on the bed to wait for the door to open. The time soon came because in the meantime, he was constantly thinking about everything; there was not even a minute's rest. It was twelve o'clock and he could hear the click of the cupboard. James immediately went there and opened the door. He went to the other side, where he found himself in a narrow corridor, to which there was only one path. This corridor was winding, and 50 steps long to get at the library. When he got there, he went into the kitchen, which was filled with a lot of old books. There were so many books in the library it was like looking for a needle in a haystack. He had no choice but to start from the beginning, and he nicely kept moving forwards. Yes, but he only had one hour to find that particular book, because of this he constantly had to keep an eye out for time so that he doesn't get stuck there, because then he would get caught. He only had 9 minutes before the door closed, and he marked the book where he could continue his search tomorrow. He made his way back to the door and went back to his room. As soon as he stepped through the door, the door closed shut behind him. He went to bed to sleep because the next day the witch wanted to take him somewhere. When he got up the next morning, James couldn't believe his eyes, he hurried to the window and his heart was filled with happiness, it was bright outside again.

James's thought: - 'Apparently, that evening chat worked and there is still hope, the witch's heart has softened. This is only a good thing and so he will continue to play his cards as he sees fit. he went down to the great hall to have breakfast. Everyone was there and were waiting for James.

James: - ''Good morning, everyone!'- He greeted everyone happily.

Gilbert: 'Good morning to you too James! You're in a good mood this morning!': - He answered with a little surprise and relief.

Miriam: - 'Good morning, everyone! Let's eat as we have a long day ahead of us.' - She answered with a smile.

When Hanna opened her eyes, she screamed so much that Evelin immediately leapt out of her bed.

Evelin: - 'What is it? What happened?' - She woke up suddenly. 'Wow!!! I do not believe it! James did it! He made it! Yupeeee! Yupeee!' - They hugged each other and started jumping around the room in joy. Oliver also woke up to the loud screeching and when he saw that it was now light outside, he was very happy.

Oliver: - 'Hello girls! He did it! He actually made it! I can't believe it!' - He was overjoyed.

Hanna: - 'He really did! This is incredible!' They thought that James had finally defeated the evil witch, that's why they were so happy. They quickly tried to get to the mages so that they can all celebrate the success. When they went out to the Street, everyone was very happy, people chatted and shouted in the streets. When they got there, they went to the mages in the bookstore, and everyone was smiling.

Mages, John: 'Good morning girls! Oliver! Today we dawned a new day! Let's go to breakfast.' - John finished his sentence.

Hanna, Evelin, Oliver: 'Good morning, everyone!'

Hanna: - 'I can't believe that James did it! Unbelievable!' - She said happily.

Evelin: - 'I'm so proud of James!'- She said happily.

Oliver: - 'Well yes! He's my best friend!' - He pulled himself out proudly.

John: - 'Let's have breakfast!' - He invited them to the table. They sat down at the table for breakfast, happily eating, but Oliver was watching the mages, who were by no means so happy. Oliver noticed this immediately. He bumped Hanna, who was sitting next to him at the table.

Oliver: - 'Listen Hanna! Something is wrong here! Look at the expressions on the faces of the mages; they are not as happy as we are! We need to know the reason for this.' - He warned Hanna. Hanna also started watching them, and indeed Oliver was right. They finished breakfast and everyone went to the secret room. They closed the door behind themselves and Mr. Tregas said:

Mr. Tregas: - 'Everyone listen! As we can see there is no more darkness outside, this is a good thing, but not as good as it seems.' Suddenly Hanna and Evelin and Oliver started whispering to each other.

Mr. Tregas: - 'It may be that there is no more darkness, but the problem is still not solved. This means that James has failed to defeat the evil witch. I know this for sure because we still don't have magic. James managed to convince the evil witch of something, that she finally returned the light to the people, but not our magic. I urge everyone to be patient because it is more than likely that James will not give up on saving us. It's just a matter of time and then everything will be back to normal.'- He said confidently.

Oliver: - 'Maybe we screamed before, but it's still not over!' - He said a little disappointed.

Mr. Monghur: - 'be patient, my child! Trust your friend, this is not such a simple task that he can solve in a day. When the time comes, he will succeed.' - He answered reassuringly.

Mr. Zathen: - 'There you go kids! Time solves everything; we just have to be patient! We did everything we could; the rest is up to James. Until then, we will wait with patience; we will continue our daily work, which we have been doing until now, because the constant darkness is over. Let's enjoy the fact that we got back the light, which is important to everyone.' - He said wisely. Everyone talked about it among themselves and then everyone went about their business. The king by this point has realized that the three good friends are no longer in the palace, but he did not attach great importance to this because he thought that they left because it was important, and they did not dare to tell him, he thought that if they ever needed to return, he would be happy to see them. The king and the people of the royal court were very happy when they saw the light, and they threw a big party. Gilbert's wife and two children were not so happy, since the father of the children and the love of the princess were not there. But they were very happy at the fact that its was now light again. Princess Anna and her children sat next to the king. The names of the children were: the boy's name: - Arastis, the girl's name: - Annabell.

Annabell: - 'Mom, when will dad come home? I miss him a lot!'-

She asked sadly.

Arastis: - 'Yes, mother! When will dad come home?'- He asked sadly.

Anna: - 'Children! I miss your dad too, but he had to go on an important mission, and then he will come home soon, you will see.' - She said reassuringly. While she knew that it was not certain that they would see Gilbert in the future, but she did not give up hope. The king overheard this conversation and intervened.

King's name: - Devilus.

Devilus: - 'Children! Be patient my dears! Your father will be home soon, you will see! Until then, let's celebrate.'- He said with a smile. The evil witch, the prince and James got ready for the journey; the guards opened the gate and lowered the bridge. They drank out of the gate and walked all the way across the bridge, when they got to the end of the bridge, the witch laid three dragon eggs on the ground, she waved at them and huge dragons flew out of the eggs, they were beautiful and powerful. The dragons began to flap their enormous wings, and then lowered their huge wings so they could climb on its back. The prince looked at the witch and the witch warned him to calmly climb up to its back. Both James and Gilbert climbed up on the back of the dragon, and the witch as well, once they were all on the dragons back, they immediately flew up into the air. The prince and James were very excited because the view from the top was breathtaking, they could see the whole landscape and the prince could see his castle from where he was, he also saw that there was partying almost everywhere, this made him a little sad because he thought that everyone had forgotten him, and that his family are no longer waiting for him to come home, but it wasn't the way he thought. James also noticed that people are very happy because there is light everywhere again, and James was very grateful for this. The dragons took them to places they had never been before. They flew to a lot of huge mountains where snow covered everything, it was a beautiful view from above, James noticed smoke in the distance and so he pointed the dragon towards it, he wanted to know why there was smoke there. The Evil witch instantly noticed that James deviated from the target and that he changed directions because of the smoke, and so they all followed James. A small village located at the foot of the mountain was where the smoke was coming from. When the people realized that the dragons were getting closer, they panicked, and everyone ran into their homes. The three dragons landed near the village and the witch also went to the village. People did not dare to leave their homelands because they were afraid of the evil witch.

James: 'Why did the people hide? What are they afraid of? Is it the dragons?'

Evil Witch: - 'No, my child! They are afraid if me! Let's find the head of the village.'

They found the person they were looking for, as he was waiting for them at the door.

Head man: - 'Welcome! What are you doing here with us? We weren't expecting guests.' - He asked in dismay.

Prince: - 'Good morning! We're just passing through, we saw the smoke and wanted to make sure everything was okay.'- He answered kindly.

Head man: - 'Well, now you can see that everything is in order, you don't have to worry, we only use the fire for the pot and to warm up. But if you've come this far, I'd like to invite you to a warm tea, if you don't mind.' - He invited them in respectfully.

Evil Witch: - 'Don't worry about us, because we're leaving, we won't disturb you in your daily tasks, good day' The Evil Witch interjected. With that, they went back to the dragons and flew on.

They were heading further and further east, where everything was covered in snow, and in the distance, they saw a huge castle, the kingdom of the northern king was the Erminus kingdom. King Erminus had a daughter and a son. His daughter was called Karnita and his son Zulante. Karnita was already married, Zulante was not yet married because he was still making the king wait, but he had a good reason for it. The witch knew the reason why she brought everyone here, she had a very good reason for it. The prince did not react in any way to this empire, rather he was indifferent. The prince's kingdom was located in the southern region, his wife is from the western kingdom, his father's name is Nyaritius and his sister's name is: - Nivita, who is not yet married. There is the eastern king whose name is: - Koldvir, and he also has two sons who are called: - Robnis and Valtinus. They were fraternal twins, which means that one looked like his mother and the other looked like his father. The witch hid such a secret that if she tells the prince, it can lead to a huge scandal, or it could turn out okay. They arrived at the royal court where they were greeted. The dragons flew away while they were there visiting.

Gilbert: - 'Why did we come here?' - He asked curiously.

Evil witch: - 'You will know everything in time.'- She answered with a smile. After that, James didn't even ask why they came here. The king greeted them.

Erminus: - 'Welcome to my palace! What brings you here?' - He asked curiously.

Evil Witch: - 'King Erminus! I thought that I would bring the prince here so that he could get to know the northern kingdom a little and we also brought a traveller with us, whose name I would like to introduce to you, his name is James Alder.

Erminus: - 'Greetings to you all! The guards will show you where you will be staying, stay as long as you wish: - The king said politely. With this, the guards escorted them to their rooms where they can rest for the remainder of the night or as long as they like. They all got a beautiful room, James was very satisfied, and he likes this kind of adventure. Gilbert still did not understand why they had to come here, he kept thinking what was the point of all this, he would rather be at home with his family.

Gilbert: - 'I don't understand why we are here? My children must be worried, Anna, I miss you so much!'- He said these things while standing next to the window. He was standing in front of the window when someone started knocking on his door.

Gilbert: - 'Yes! Here, it's open.' - He shouted. The door opened and James came in to see the prince.

Gilbert: - 'Come inside James!' - He invited James inside. 'Tell me, do you understand why we came here?' - He asked a little angrily.

James: - 'No I don't get it! But there must have been a good reason that she brought us here, I think.' - He answered calmly.

Gilbert: - 'So far it's fine that she brought us here for a good reason, but what could be the reason for that...' They just knocked on the door again.

Gilbert: - 'Yes! Come in, it's open.' The door opened and it was one of the maids.

Maid: - 'Excuse me, the king called you to the meeting room.' She passed on the message, then bowed before them and went out.

Gilbert: - 'Well, then we have to go, let's not make them wait.'- He said a little nervously. They started walking towards the meeting room and on their way there almost everyone secretly looked at them, of course they noticed this but did not pay attention to it. Some of the ladies of the court were whispering when they passed by them, but they went on to the discussion room. They went in, and the king, his son, and the evil witch were waiting for them there, and they sat down at the table.

Erminus: - 'Welcome, my dear guests! I'm so honoured to finally get to know you Gilbert. I've heard a lot about you, of course people only say good things about you, and you don't have to worry': - The king smiled. While you are here, I'll be happy to show you my kingdom after you've rested, in the meantime, enjoy my hospitality, you can look at every part of the palace, the maids will escort you everywhere if needed, or if you don't want a maid, yes, you can explore this great palace for yourself. Dinner will be at 8 o'clock sharp, be there.'- The king finished his speech.

James: - 'Thanks for the warm welcome; I will be there at dinner your grace!'- He bowed and left.

Gilbert: - 'Thank you your majesty for your kind hospitality, of course I'll be there at the dinner your grace!'- He also bowed before the king and left the hall. The witch stayed there to talk with the king. James waited for the prince at the door.

Gilbert: - 'let's get something to eat and then we will leave the palace until dinner.'- He said angrily.

James: - 'Okay! I don't mind let's go.'- He answered with a little surprise. They got something to eat and went out in the palace garden. The garden space was very nice, it's true that everything was covered by snow, but the garden was beautiful. There were places in the garden where different types of garden pagodas were built, it was stunning. Both James and the prince loved the look of the garden and although for a little while, but they forgot that they can't be with their loved ones. Zulante started behaving rather strangely after seeing the prince in the palace. He was constantly walking back and forth like the flying Dutchman, he didn't even know what he was doing, one of his concubines saw this.

Zulante's concubine is called Zahen.

Zahen: - 'Darling! Something is wrong. I can see you're worried about something! Maybe I can help you?'- She asked worriedly.

Zulante: - 'No, no! I'm fine, I'm just too tired, I didn't get much sleep, nothing serious.'- He answered a little confused. ''Go now, if I need you, I'll call you, my dear! I would like to relax a little.' With that, he stormed away. Zulante stormed away so quickly that Zahen couldn't even get another word out. The prince and James enjoyed their visit to the garden, they even had a snowball fight and also built a snowman. The children who saw them immediately joined them and helped with the snowman. The King opened the window and laughed at what he saw, his heart filled with joy after seeing this. Zulante was just about to lie down on his bed when someone knocked on the door.

Zulante: - 'I told you not to disturb me!'- He shouted angrily. But the door opened, and the Evil witch entered his room. When Zulante saw her, he looked at her forebodingly.

Evil Witch: - 'Hello Zulante! How are you getting on? I hope you understand why I came here and brought the prince with me?'- She asked with a sarcastic laugh.

Zulante: - 'Yes, I know! But why now? What did you have to bring him here in the first place?'

Evil Witch: - 'Come on, come on! The situation has changed a little, my dear, a lot of things have happened which is the reason why I'm here. I think you know what you have to do, or if you don't do it, I will help you to do your duty.'- She answered sarcastically.

Zulante: - 'But then it will be a big scandal, my father will disown me.'

Evil Witch: - 'He won't disown you from the family if there is an agreement, and then everyone will benefit, including us.'- She answered convincingly.

Zulante: - 'Gibert will not agree, and neither will his father, he will shine a negative light on our kingdoms.': - He answered nervously.

Evil witch: - 'Let this be your concern! But time is running out! With that, the evil witch left the room. Zulante jumped up from the bed and walked up and down the room, there was not even a minute's rest. He went to the window and saw that Gibert was making snowmen with the children, he was very angry and had no idea how he was going to solve this. When dinner time came, everyone took their seats at the table, Zulante and Gilbert sat opposite each other. Zulante tried to avoid Gibert's gaze, he didn't dare to look her in his eyes, but of course he couldn't do that for long.

Gilbert: - 'Tell me Zulante, why are you avoiding eye contact? Is there something wrong?'- He asked curiously.

Zulante: - 'Oh! There's nothing wrong! And I wasn't avoiding eye contact, but the guests were needing my attention, I can't ignore them.'- He replied with a nervous chuckle.

Gilbert: - 'I would like to speak with you after dinner.'- He said with a smirk. Zulante could only muster a small smile and nodded. Zulante was so angry that he lost his appetite. Dinner was over and everyone left the table. When the evil witch stood up from the table, she looked at Zulante as a reminder about his duty. Zulante nodded and looked at Gilbert. Gilbert immediately looked at Zulante as everyone left the room.

Gilbert: - 'Well! I feel that you are not telling me something because you have been behaving strangely all day, I would like to know the reason!'

Zulante: - 'It's okay! Anyway, I wanted to talk to you, but, if possible, let's not talk here, let's go out in the garden, there's no one there and I can tell you more easily.'

Gilbert: - 'Okay then, then let's go.' With that, they got up from the table and started walking to the garden. The evil witch watched them from a distance. They went outside in the garden to one of the pagodas and sat down there to talk about the problems.

Gilbert: - 'Well, I'm curious about the explanation!': - He said with interest.

Zulante: - 'Well okay then! Then I will tell you what has been weighing on my heart for years, it won't be easy to say, but I will do everything I can to somehow release this burden. I don't really know how to start, it won't be easy for any of us, nor for the kingdoms.' Gilbert began to worry a little.

Zulante: - 'The truth is that... me and Anna your wife, so the two of us..., well we've been together for a long time......and soo....' When Gibert heard this, he stroked his hair backwards nervously and started looking everywhere because he already knew what he wanted to say.

Gilbert: - 'Continue!' - He told him angrily.

Zulante: - 'Listen! I'm very sorry that you have to learn this like this and here, but you should know that this happened before you got married. We loved each other back then, only because of our fathers we couldn't be together because they thought it was better if she gets married to you and not to me. I don't know why, because they didn't say, they just said that it should be like this, and that the country would be stronger this way. But unfortunately, there is no end to this because there is something else that you need to know, and I will tell you this because I consider it my duty that you also know this and that you will do whatever you want with me and rightfully so. The children are also mine....' With that, Gilbert punched him twice because he couldn't hold himself any longer, and one more punch as a bonus which he deserved because of the secrecy and the fact that they both took him for a fool. Gilbert became very angry, he punched the pagoda one more time, Zulante got up, picked himself up from the floor and stood in front of Gilbert.

Zulante: - 'Please forgive us for all these years of secrecy, I'm very sorry, from now on it's up to you how to proceed.': - He said sadly and with that he started back to the palace. Of course, the evil witch saw everything and smiled at the fact that she finally got back the love that she had lost all those years ago. Gilbert stayed outside because he had to collect his thoughts, all the moments that he had spent with Anna all these years were being replayed in front of him, he tried to understand all of this, but he had to formulate his memories so that he could make sense of it. While Gilbert was out there, Zulante went back to the palace and of course the evil witch was waiting for him.

Zulante: - 'Are you happy now?': - He asked nervously. And with that he continued walking.

Evil Witch: - 'Hahaha! Oh, of course I'm happy, but you don't look like it, hahahah.'- She laughed. Zulante was very angry; he immediately went to his room and was walking up and down his room. He didn't know what he should do, if the Kings find this out then surely, he will be cast out from the kingdoms. James saw Zulante go to his room angrily, from which he knew that something had happened, and he went to find Gilbert to find out the reason. Gilbert was still out in the garden walking back and forth, visiting every nook and cranny to pick up his memories and put the missing pieces together. After an hour, he managed to put together the missing pieces and was angry with himself that he did not notice these signs that were right in front of his nose. Well, those children loved Zulante very much, only Gilbert didn't know why, but now he knows the reason, he knows everything about it, but there is a big problem, what will the kings do about it. It was a huge burden on his shoulders, but as a prince he will solve this too. James did not find Gilbert anywhere in the palace, he asked one of the servants if he had seen him somewhere, and he told James that he was out in the garden. James went out into the garden where he found Gilbert.

James: - 'Good evening my prince! What are you doing out here in the cold? Is something wrong? You seem very angry! I saw Zulante angrily running into his room, did you guys argue?' - He asked curiously.

Gilbert: - 'I would rather not talk about this now James! You'll find out in due time, but thanks for worrying about me, go and rest, we'll get back to it tomorrow.' He patted him on the shoulder and started walking back in the palace. James doesn't like that he saw Gilbert sad, he didn't leave at that, so he went back to the palace and was headed straight towards Zulante's room. Gilbert also met the evil witch who was waiting for his arrival. The Evil Witch walked towards him, she grabbed his face and looked deep into his eyes.

Evil Witch: - 'My dear! What you just found out is all your father's doing, he's taking revenge on us because he doesn't want to accept me, but don't worry, everything will be fine, I promise.'

Gilbert: - 'How could anything possibly be fine!? This whole lie which lasted for years, how can I look my father in the eyes while Anna and the children are there, how can I tell them what I know!: - 'He said in distress.' With that, he went on to rest in his room if he could even rest at this point. Miriam watched him leave and she let him go, as it was a huge shock for him that he had to deal with, he needed time to process it all. Miriam also went to rest in her room and thought about what to do next. James reached Zulante's room and knocked.

Zulante: - 'Don't disturb me!'- He shouted angrily. But he kept knocking.

Zulante: - 'I told you not to disturb me now! Get out of here!'- He yelled back angrily. But the door opened, and James entered.

James: - 'Excuse me your grace, but this urgent, it won't wait until tomorrow. – he said calmly.

Zulante looked over and saw that it was James.

Zulante: - 'Come in James! I thought someone else was knocking.'

Zulante: - 'Tell me, what are you doing here so late, why aren't you in your room?'- He asked curiously.

James: - 'Well first of all because I saw you running angrily to your room and after that I talked to Gilbert, I thought I'd ask you what the hell is going on between you two?': - He asked curiously.

Zulante: - 'Oh come on kid, this doesn't concern you, this is for adults, it's nothing, just a little misunderstanding, that's all. Go to bed and don't worry, we'll take care of it. Good night.'- With this he said goodbye to James. Yes, but Zulante does not know that James is Gilberts' son, because how could he know. James said goodbye respectfully and left Zulante's room. But he didn't let it rest, and so he made his way towards the Evil Witches room. When he got there, he could hear her voice coming from the room and he stood in front of the door to listen.

Miriam: - 'My plan was completely successful, I can sleep peacefully now, now nobody can stance between us, I won once and for all, hahahah.' – her voice echoed out of the room. James began to think about what the evil witch was trying to say, so he thought it would be better if he went back to his room.

Evelin and Oliver were very worried about James, what would happen to him when they would see their friend. They also went to bed because they were tired. Evelin fell asleep quickly because she was very tired. As soon as she fell asleep, she had a very strange dream, it was as if it was real. She dreamed that James came back to get her and the three of them were together again and she finally met her father after all this time, everyone was very happy. She also dreamed that they succeeded in defeating the evil witch; suddenly a huge, big light came out of nowhere and so she woke up. She sat up in her bed and looked at the clock, the time was 03:47, she was really sweaty and so she lay back down so that he could sleep some more because it was way too early to wake up yet. But the dream was constantly on her mind and so she was rolling around restlessly until she fell asleep. The next morning, when they got up, Evelin quickly dressed and left the room to tell Oliver about her dream. They met together in the corridor.

Evelin: -'Good morning, Oliver! Listen, I had a very strange dream last night, I dreamt that James came back to us and that he also defeated the evil witch, but then something else happened, but I don't remember what it was.': - She said happily.

Oliver: 'Good morning to you too, Evelin! Well, this must have been a very interesting dream, although if only it were true, then everything would be solved and we wouldn't have to be here anymore, but we could finally go home.': - He answered a little brokenly. After all, he missed his loved ones very much.

Evelin: - 'Believe me, I wish the same, you are not the only one who misses their loved ones, I miss them too, but don't forget that we chose this, James didn't ask us to come here, we came after him on our own. That's why we have to stand by him until the end, as a true friend stands up for another.': - She answered Oliver reassuringly.

Oliver: - 'You are absolutely right! And yes, we will stand by him until the end and thank you for being here with me, I don't know what I would be here without you.': - He said to Evelin calmly and they hugged each other.

Evelin: - 'Well! Come, let's go to breakfast and tell the others what I dreamed okay?!': - She said cheerfully.

Oliver: - 'Okay! That's a good idea, let's go.' They went to breakfast with the others, and Evelin was looking forward to telling them about her dream. After they finished breakfast, everyone went over to the library to talk and read.

Evelin: - 'Now that everyone is here, I would like to tell you what I dreamed last night, it is important to me because it was so realistic that I almost thought it was true. The main thing is that I dreamed that James came home and that he defeated the evil witch. But after all this, something strange happened that I can't explain, a huge light came out of nowhere and then I woke up. I don't really understand what that could mean, but this dream was good.':- She finished the sentence happily. The magicians listened to Evelin the whole time and looked at each other. John was also apparently cheered up a little by this dream because he smiled.

Mr. Vinthus: - 'Evelin! Come here for a bit, please!'

Evelin: - 'Of course! Yes! What do you want to say Mr. Vinthus!'

Mr. Vinthus: - 'Evelin! I want to talk to you about your dream. When you said there was a big light in your dream and you didn't know what it meant, how big was that light? Think about this carefully because what you say may be important.': - He asked knowingly.

Evelin: - 'It's fine! The light I saw was blinding, so much so that I woke up immediately after it, and everything was wet, I could hardly go back to sleep after that.': - She answered in surprise. He didn't think this dream would be so important.

Mr. Vinthus: - 'Thank you Evelin! You can go now, if there are any developments, we will let you know.': - He said thank you.

Evelin: - 'It's fine! See you later then.' As Oliver waited for Evelin, he couldn't imagine what they could have been talking about, so he quickly asked Evelin a thousand questions.

Oliver: - 'Evelin! What is he talking about.....': - He couldn't finish the sentence because Evelin interrupted.

Evelin: - 'About what else, my dream! They believe that what I dreamed can only be important, isn't that cool? Then they'll tell us its meaning later, we can go hang out somewhere until then, what do you say?': - She asked happily and jumping.

Oliver: - 'Okay , we can go, I say yes to a new adventure, why not.': - He laughed.

John: 'Just say Mr. Vinthus, does that dream have any meaning?': - He asked curiously.

Mr. Vinthus: - 'Oh yes it does! We are already looking into what exactly it means.': - He answered excitedly. 'Come, let's go to the row where there are books about dreams and find out their meaning.': - He continued what he was saying.

John: - 'That sounds good! Then get to work.' Everyone started browsing the books to decipher Evelin's dream.

James couldn't wait to talk to Gilbert, he was very curious about what happened yesterday and what the evil witch might have been referring to.

James: - 'Gilbert! Are you going to tell me what happened yesterday?': - He asked curiously.

Gilbert: - 'Listen James! I want to tell you, but I don't know how you will react, so I ask you not to ask me to tell you again, when the time is right, I will tell you. Now I don't feel like that time is here, you have to be a little more patient, okay!': - He said somewhat calmly.

James: - 'It's okay! I understand, no problem and thank you.': - He answered clearly. James went out of the palace to walk and get some fresh air. Miriam heard every word of their conversation, so she went out into the garden after James. Gilbert went to the library to find something to read, but Zulante was there too.

Gilbert: - 'Good morning!': - He greeted him dejectedly.

Zulante: - 'Good morning, to you too.': - He replied sadly.

Zulante and Gilbert wanted to talk to each other at the same time, then they smiled to themselves.

Gilbert: - 'You start, I cut you off.'

Zulante: - 'Alright! Listen Gilbert! I'm really sorry about yesterday, honestly! It's not easy for you to process these things and it's not easy for me to see you suffer like this either, because it wasn't a nice thing from us, I agree, and also that we made you a fool for so long. But I promise that I will accept the consequences of this, I will stand in front of my father today and let him know all this, and then what happens….. well will happen'.: - He finished what he had to say dejectedly.

Gilbert: - 'Yes, I think that it will be the best for everyone! I gathered my thoughts about this yesterday and all the pieces fell into place, I was the blind mouse who didn't notice the signs that were right in front of my nose, I didn't pay too much attention to the external signs that were given, but it happened and this you can't undo anymore. There is only one solution left, the king must be told.': - He answered in agreement. They shook hands and left the library. Zulante sent word to the king to receive him because he had something important to discuss. The king accepted his son of course.

Erminus: - 'Well , my son, what was so important that I had to leave the important things to discuss there?' The door closed behind Zulante and he was left alone with his father, who told him the whole story from beginning to end. Meanwhile, Gilbert went out into the garden to clear his mind, to forget all this for a minute if possible. He noticed James int he garden and that he

197

was also walking outside and went over to him.

Gilbert: - 'Hi James! I was hoping to find you here, as I have something to talk to you about.': - He said firmly. With that, he told James the whole story and that Zulante was telling the king at the moment as well.

James: - 'I'm glad you finally told me, now I understand why you both were angry, but hopefully everything will be alright.': - He answered with a smile. 'There's just one problem! Miriam!'

Gilbert: 'Why? What about her?': - He asked curiously.

James: - 'I visited Zulante that evening to ask him what happened after you didn't tell me anything. But I didn't have much luck because Zulante didn't say anything either, so I tried to go back to my room when I heard voices from one of the rooms, it was Miriam's room. I stopped and began to listen, and she said something like "Finally my plan succeeded, I can sleep peacefully now no one can come between us, I won once and for all". I don't know what that might mean to her, but she had a good laugh at the end. Well, that's what worries me the most and the fact that she's still evil and I'm here to defeat her, I have to stop her evil because it's a matter of moments and she can fall back into the situation where she can't control herself and then all hell will break loose again.'

Gilbert: - 'You are absolutely right about that! I 'll look into it, don't worry about it, okay?': - He asked seriously. James nodded, Gilbert patted his shoulder and headed back to the palace. As soon as he arrived at the palace, he met Miriam, who was very happy.

Gilbert: 'I need to talk to you right now! Come, let's go to the library.': - He invited her to talk hurriedly.

Gilbert: - 'Miriam! I want you to be honest with me! Tell me, are you the cause of this whole story? Did you bring us here to make all this happen? Why did you wait so long?': - He asked desperately.

Miriam: 'I've been waiting for these questions, my dear! As i can see, you are ready to accept your fate. After all, your destiny is for the two of us to be together! The first unfulfilled love brought a curse on everyone and everything. Your father is the cause of everything, he was so blinded by his royal duty that he didn't pay any attention to the prediction that if he separates us, then nobody will be happy until we two belong to each other forever. After all, we met each other by chance and fell in love like that, didn't we? This was because fate is inevitable and what should have happened did not happen, especially since I was still pregnant with your child. Why am I so mean? It just comes from me! The revenge I cooked up against your father took years, it didn't come about in a day. And I had to give our common child to a certain Alder family to be raised because I couldn't look at him without you by my side. I chose the Alder family carefully; their descendants were wizards just like me. James can also do magic, because he was born with it. But I took away everyone's magic power so that no one can cross me, that's why now everyone obeys me and does what I say, so that the balance is restored as it should be. I hope I expressed myself clearly.'

Gilbert: - 'Yes! Totally understandable! I just don't agree, if my father was responsible for what he did to us, then why did you punish everyone, why didn't you just punish my father?': - He asked inquisitively.

Evil witch: - 'It wasn't just your father who had to be taught a lesson here, but everyone who helped him. The wizards and mages all helped your father to remove me.': - She replied patiently.

Gilbert: - 'Um, I see! Now that you've revealed this secret to me, you can let James go, right?': - He asked curiously.

Evil witch: - 'I might as well do that, yes! After all, it can't hurt me anyway, I'll think about it.': - She answered. 'But now we have to worry about what decision the kings will make, then we will see what will be the fate of James.': - She continued the sentence.

Gilbert: - 'Okay! Then we'll wait until then.': - He said with satisfaction.

In the meantime, the magicians looked through the books about dreams and found the solution in one of them.

Mr. Ambeth: - 'I found the solution to Evelin's dream! It's written here, I'll read it. Dream decipherer, the light!: - ' The huge blinding lights meaning is a deep underwater crystal which is so powerful that if it falls into the wrong hands, it creates the endless reign of evil. If, on the other hand, if it falls into good hands, it can lead to the prosperity of the world and a new age, happiness will return to its place."

Mr. Ambeth :- 'I have already heard about this crystal, it lies at the bottom of the great Ocean Gilebart, in a very well-guarded area, it is almost impossible to get there, even magic does not help to get that crystal, because its magic power is even greater. Yes!!!! The crystal has magic power that even the evil witch can't destroy! But if it falls into his hands, then it's all over.':- He said a little cautiously.

Mr. Tregas :- 'Now that we know what this dream means, there is a reason why Evelin dreamt this, a sign of how to put an end to all this. Now let's look for the book in which he writes more about the crystal, to see if we can find some solution on how to get that crystal. It's almost time for lunch, so

King Erminus called Gilbert and Zulante before him.

Erminus: -'It's good that both of you are here! We have an important conversation together! Well, I was sorry to hear that my son is in big trouble, he destroyed everything that we had built up together with King Devilus , because please, he fell in love with Princess Anna, and what's more, he even fathered children, this should be reported to Devilus immediately so that we can have a discussion about this whole incident. As for you, my son, I have not yet made a decision about your fate, we will discuss this with Devilus first and then make a decision. My son Gilbert, you are rightfully angry with my son, I completely understand if you want to make the judgment, but as I said before, we will discuss this together with your father, and you can leave until then.': - The king finished what he had to say. Zulante left the room, but Gilbert remained there because he wanted to speak with the king.

Erminus: - 'Yes, my son! Do you want to say something?': - The king asked.

Gilbert: 'Yes, my king! All I want to say is that after the conversation we will go to my father to clarify this and bring the meeting together for further discussion.': - He finished his sentence.

Erminus: - 'Don't worry about it, my child! Your father will be here in three days, as Zulante told me what happened, I immediately sent for your father. Stay calm until your father gets here.': - He finished the sentence with a smile.

Gilbert: 'Yes, Your Majesty!' Gilbert also left the room and went to the library to find something to read for himself until dinner. When he got there, he met Miriam.

Miriam: 'I heard that you were with the king! And that your father is coming here, it will be good fun! Hahahah.': - She laughed proudly.

Gilbert: - 'Yes, that's right! But how do you know all this?': - He asked curiously.

Miriam: 'Come on my dear! I know everything, there are no secrets in front of me!': - She answered proudly.

Gilbert: 'Well, that's true! I already forgot how far your magic power extends .': - He replied mockingly.

Miriam: - 'Take it easy, my dear! I believe you are angry, but this needs to be resolved once and for all! Or do you see it differently?'

Gilbert: 'No, no! Of course, I want this to be resolved too, I'm just so confused that I can't think straight. I still have to process all this information, I hope you understand.': - He finished his sentence depressingly.

Miriam: 'Well, of course I understand, there's nothing wrong, I'm sorry my dear, you're absolutely right, I didn't take into account the fact that in such a short time you got too much information that it's not easy to process it. I promise I won't make fun of you again, okay?' With that, they hugged each other for a long time, and as soon as they touched each other it brought up the old memory in Gilbert when they were still together and loved each other, it filled him with a very good feeling.

Gilbert: - 'Thank you for understanding, and I really need more time, especially since my father is also coming here, I'm even more tense than I should be, I'm sorry my dear, but now I'm going outside to get some air.': - He answered a little confused. With that he left the library and went out into the garden. Word had reached James that King Devilus would be visiting soon to discuss Zulante's fate, so he set out to find Gilbert. He didn't have to look for long, he found him in the garden where he used to go since they were staying here. That place was kind to him for some reason.

James: 'Hi Gilbert! I heard King Devilus is coming! I guess you are upset. I'd be the same if I were you. I'm sorry for snapping at you like that, I think I'd rather leave now, I don't want to bother you.': - He said understandingly. With that he turned to leave, but Gilbert addressed him.

Gilbert: 'No, you're not bothering me! Please stay here with me, as you are my son, how could you bother me. It is good that you are here with me and that I got to know you. It's true that it's a bit strange, but the point is that you're here. He hugged him by the shoulders and they both stood there scanning the beautiful snow-covered landscape.

During this time, the magicians found the book about the crystal, which they immediately opened. In the book it was said that 'The crystal is located at the deepest point of the ocean and is guarded by creatures that are impossible to defeat, even magic power does not help. But everything has a weak point, so do the creatures, one that could be used to defeat them. If you can successfully get close to them, you have to hit their heart, yes, but it's not that easy to hit their heart, as they are protected by several layers of armour, you have to use a special sword to break through the armour. Well, it's not so easy to handle a sword underwater, that's why you'll need that particular special sword. The sword can be found in the stomach of a volcano, it is made of an alloy that does not melt or break. That sword has enormous power, and getting to it will not be an easy task either, since the volcano lies in the belly and is surrounded by hot lava." Reading these lines, the magicians thought that it would not be as simple as they had imagined.

Mr. Tregas: - 'Well people, you heard what the book says! I think it won't be easy to get that crystal, but we'll figure something out together.': - He said a little broken. Evelin and Oliver walked around the neighbourhood to distract themselves from all the troubles. They were in a nice clearing where there was a small playground. They were swinging, laughing and even sliding.

There was no one there except them because people were afraid to leave the house, they only went out for the necessary things, but they spent the rest of the day at home, there were not many people out on the streets. Evelin and Oliver went back to the magicians because it was lunch time. After they had lunch, Evelin immediately asked him about the meaning of her dream.

Evelin: - 'Did you manage to decipher my dream, Mr. Tregas?': - She asked curiously.

Mr Tregas: - 'Yes, we managed to decipher your dream, the big light you saw was a crystal lying at the bottom of the ocean...' He told her what they found out.

Evelin: - 'Wow, this will not be an easy task! But you should also figure out how to solve this, right?': - He asked inquisitively.

Mr. Tregas : - 'We will do everything to find a solution, my child .': - He answered with a smile. King Devilus arrived in the northern kingdom where he was warmly received. Gilbert was very upset because he didn't know how to look in his father's eyes after this. He gathered strength and stood in front of her.

Gilbert: - 'Welcome, father! I'm glad you got here safely, and I would like to talk to you later.': - He greeted his father.

Devilus: - 'Welcome my son! Of course, we will definitely talk later.': - The king replied calmly. After they greeted each other, the king settled in his suite, rested and later joined the lunch. The two kings sat next to each other at the table and clearly butted heads quite a few times during lunch. After the lunch was over, everyone left the room. The two kings discussed the process to get revenge for Zulante's actions. Of course, Anna didn't go with the king because the king wouldn't let her. Late in the afternoon, the two kings summoned the two princes to a meeting.

Devilus: - 'Well, come and take your seats, I think we have come to an agreement regarding your case, and we hope that our decision will be satisfactory to everyone. Well, here is our decision, my king!': - With that he gave the floor to King Erminus.

Erminus: - 'Zulante! You can't undo what you did, it's a fact and true, what's done can't be undone. The country will be shocked by the news, but they will get used to it like anything else. In any case, I intended you for Princess Nivita, because she is a kind, correct and good-looking woman. As we can see, this is unfortunately no longer possible. Of course, Anna found out about everything and apparently took it well, as she was happy with the news, "I'm sorry Gilbert" Anna would like to marry you Zulante, since you even have the children, right? We can somehow sweep this under the carpet, but the biggest stumbling block is Gilbert. After all, it is well known that the one Gilbert loves is the evil witch. Well, we know what the evil witch has done to this world so far, and we don't take kindly to that. There could be consequences for Gilbert and the evil witch to become one. This marriage does not comply with the regulations, although a prince must marry only one princess, which means that Gilbert cannot marry the evil witch only Nivita.': - With that he ended his speech. There was great shock in the room and deathly silence. But the great silence was soon broken by Gilbert. None of the kings, however, know that Gilbert has a son from the evil witch.

Gilbert: - 'Well, I have a couple of things to add to that too!': - He broke the silence.

Gilbert: - 'There is something that some of you here do not know! The evil witch did what she did because of my father.': - He continued the sentence. When King Devilus heard this, his mouth fell open in surprise, as he did not expect this.

Gilbert: - 'King Devilus, my father, was kind enough to sabotage my connection with Miriam, that's the evil witch's name if you didn't know by now. We both really loved each other and we still love each other. After Miriam gave me back my memories , everything became clear to me and what method my father used to take it away from me. Yes! Here, not only Zulante did something that shouldn't have been done, but also me, but I only got this memory back from Miriam two weeks ago. I found out what Zulante did a few days ago. My father used magic to erase from my memory the fact that I was ever in love with Miriam, he made me forget every single moment that was related to Miriam, so that we could not accidentally become one with my love. But like everything else, this one also saw the light of day! I was angry with Zulante because it took me a long time to find out, but after I found out what really happened, I felt that I was free again and I have Zulante to thank for that. Miriam and I have a son together , who is here with us in the palace. His name is James Alder ." Everyone in the room was shocked at this, King Devilus paled at what was said, so much so that he almost passed out in his chair. King Erminus also found what was said interesting, so he knew that something very interesting would come out of it. Zulante , on the other hand, breathed a sigh of relief that he will not get exiled yet, he was filled with happiness.'So since we have a child together with Miriam, in the name of our law, i must marry her, this is the regulation. And you cant deny that Father. 'The many bad things that have happened so far are all thanks to you, my dear father.':- With that he finished what he was saying and proudly pulled himself out, satisfied that he could finally reveal these things to his father. King Devilus was so shocked that he was suddenly speechless.

Erminus: - 'This story has taken quite an interesting turn, in this case I invite your son and Miriam as well .': - He interrupted. King Erminus invited James and Miriam there. They both entered the room and took their seats. King Devilus looked at Miriam with bloodshot eyes when she sat down at the table, but he couldn't do anything, he had to accept what happened.

Erminus: - 'Take your seats! We discussed a couple of certain things, but another thing was brought up that we only just found out about. Miriam, I think you know what it's about. James, I'm glad I know who your mom and dad are now. We have to get to a certain agreement to hear this story, so let's not delay any longer and cut to the middle of it. My king, I give you the floor.': - With that, he gave the floor to king Devilus because he has to make a decision in this. King Devilus couldn't speak for a while because he was in shock after hearing the news, so he collected all his thoughts and finally started his speech.

Devilus: - 'Hmmm (he sharpened his voice)! In this case , what we learned here today affected us quite deeply and surprised us, of course. I don't really know how to react to this yet, but I'll try to do my best to come to an agreement. First of all, I would like to welcome you, James, although we have already met, and as for Miriam, I don't even know what to say. We didn't do much good, it's true, but what I did then, I wouldn't do it differently now. But this situation is different now because we have a situation in front of us that cannot be ignored and it is none other than James. Since James is their common child, my son and Miriam, unfortunately, the law really requires that they must marry, and I can't do anything about it either. In the near future, hopefully, everything will turn out differently and everything will turn out well , but for this to happen, Miriam must die.

Hearing this, everyone was shocked and looked at King Devilus . Miriam became so angry that black clouds gathered over her head.

Gilbert: - 'Everyone calm down! This conversation is going nowhere if we can't come to an agreement. The fact that King Devilus wants to get rid of Miriam at all costs will not help anyone in this case. Yes! Miriam causes many headaches for people , but I ask, why did she do what she did? I'm asking you most of all, father? Why did you cross us at the time, wouldn't it have been easier to sit down with us then and talk like we do now?

Maybe then all these things won't happen, right? The other day, Miriam told me something that you, my dear father, did not take into account at the time, you knew very well the risk involved in ending this relationship. You also knew that a curse would fall on everyone if you ended our love, yet you took the risk by putting human lives at risk just so that you could fulfil what you set out to do. Well, this irresponsible decision had consequences. The time has already come to put an end to this and fix what my father messed up at that time. If you agree with me, raise your hand, thank you .': - With that, he sat down . Of course, no one raised their hands.

Devilus: - 'That was a very powerful speech, my son! We really didn't sit down to discuss this at the time because I didn't see the point in you marrying a poor witch. But the fact that everyone will be cursed is pure fiction. Only Miriam thinks this way to punish me. The law stipulates that you must Marry if you have a child together, because that child is more important than anything else. So the curse you talked about, my son, is Miriam's invention. She cursed everyone in order to bring everyone under her control, which of course she succeeded. What I said before, that Miriam must die, I still stand by that, because a witch with such evil must be put to an end once and for all. Miriam jumped up from the table in a terrible rage and lashed out at the king.

Miriam: - 'Well , my dear king, if you want to get rid of me so badly, I will stand before you! But I will see how you want to execute me, because there is nothing that can defeat me. With that, she lifted the king from his chair and he disappeared with one movement. Everyone watched the event in shock and no one dared to speak.

Miriam: - 'Well! Now the king won't cross anyone again, I guarantee it, he's in a place where he belongs. If there is anyone else who might have objections, say so now, or stay silent forever.': - She finished the sentence angrily.

Erminus: - 'I think I have closed the meeting, there is nothing more to discuss, I feel that what happened here today was a testimony for everyone. In the future, we will also discuss with Anna how this should be announced, and we will arrange everything so that it is good for everyone, thank you, they can go.': - He finished his speech with a trembling voice. Everyone left the room. James was shocked at what Miriam was capable of, he never thought she had that much power. In another room, Gilbert and Miriam were engaged in conversation.

Gilbert: - 'What you did in the room was amazing! But let me ask you where you put my father?': - He asked curiously.

Miriam: - 'Don't worry about that, my dear! He's in a place where he belongs. He is not hurt, that I can promise'.

James goes back to his friends.

Everyone returned to their own palaces, King Erminus had arranged everything about Anna and Zulante, announced the news to the people, and of course the people were no longer surprised at anything. They also accepted this just like everything else that has happened around them. Miriam was of course very happy with Gilbert; they could be together again like before. Gilbert moved into Miriam's palace so they could finally be

209

together. James, they let him go back to his friends, because he wanted to go back to them at all costs. This was all fine and good until now, but there was always evil in Miriam that had to be driven out of her. For now, because of her happiness, she was not so dangerous because the beloved triumphs over everything. The evil little mushrooms, on the other hand, fought against goodness, because they had a goal and they will achieve it at all costs, it's only a matter of time before they surface again. The Mages and witches got their magic back, thanks to Miriam's happiness, but let's not forget that she can take it back from them at a moment's notice, if they try anything, she immediately takes back their magic. They were preparing for the big wedding in the northern kingdom. It was a lengthy procedure, they didn't create the wedding in one day, knowing that it would be a wedding of true love. Anna's children were a bit hurt by the news because they loved Gilbert and they still had to get used to the new situation. Anna was completely happy by Zulante's side, she can finally be with her great love. Zulante finally surrendered to the complete happiness that he can freely enjoy without any remorse, everyone was doing well, only King Devilus suffered the whole thing. King Devilus was locked by Miriam in one of the highest towers of her palace, where he lacked nothing. Guards guarded his door and if he needed anything, he got it. King Devilus was very angry that he was separated from his family and most of all his kingdom, he thought about how he could get out of there. The tower was very high, and it was impossible to escape from there, only a miracle could help him escape from there. Sadness and anger boiled in the king to such a level that he could not even sleep at night. Of course, he didn't know that everyone got their strength back because no one reported any events to him, this was his punishment for putting his son's happiness in the crosshairs. The mages and witches could enjoy their power again, but unfortunately they could not use it against the evil witch, so they had to resort to other methods. The weeks passed and the time of

210

the big wedding came. The palace was teeming with guests from the rich to the poor, as everyone could go to the big celebration. Anna and Zulante were very anxious to make sure everything went well. Everything was ready for the wedding to begin, the church was full of people, there were even many people standing on the street. The bride also walked to the church and was escorted to the groom. Everyone looked at Anna in amazement, she was such a beautiful bride. The ceremony lasted for an hour, after they said their vows and they were already declared married, everyone cheered and cheered the newly married couple. They went back to the palace and the big wedding started, where everyone had a lot of fun. Of course, King Devilus was left out of this wedding, as Miriam did not allow him to attend. The fun lasted until breakfast the next day, where everyone had a great time. When James got back to his friends, of course his dad was waiting there too. They didn't attend the wedding because they didn't think it was important. They were very happy for each other; they were happy that they could finally be together and that he could see his friends again. James: - 'Dad? How did you get here? I'm glad you're here with us, but how did you get here? Is everyone okay at home? Mom must be worried about me.': - He asked a lot of questions.

John: - 'Hello son. I'm also happy to finally see you and see that everything is fine with you, which I'm very happy about. How I got here is a bit of a long story, but I'll keep it as short as possible. Of course, we parents were worried about you, since you disappeared, so we set out to search for you together with the parents of Evelin and Oliver. After that, we had an adventurous trip to get here, we even made it all the way to Mexico so that I could come here to you. There, an old witch helped me get here into this world because an adult cannot get here. The fact that Evelin and Oliver are here with you is possible because they have not reached adulthood. Everyone is worried about you, but hopefully you have calmed down a little knowing that I am here with you. I will help you in any way I can. I've heard that you know about everything, I hope this news doesn't hurt you because your mother and I haven't been able to tell you the truth, we've prepared to tell you many times, but we didn't know how it would affect you. I want you to know that we did everything we could to raise you well, we were also aware that the day would come when we are where we are right now, but we did not expect that it would come so quickly.': - He hugged James.

James: -'I know, dad, you don't have to worry about me, I understood everything here thanks to Hanna. Of course, I'm not judging you because you didn't tell me the truth, but it would have been better if I knew all about it. The only thing that matters now is that I have to defeat the evil witch, as just because she's calmed down a little doesn't mean she's changed. It all quietened down for a while.': - He answered seriously.

The mages didn't stay idle, they worked on a new method so that the evil witch wouldn't know they were all working, they spent almost most of the day in the secret room.

Evelin: - 'James! I can't believe you're here with us again! But I don't understand how the evil witch let you go, since she knew very well why you went there, and still she let you go?': - She asked curiously.

James: 'Yes! She really let me go, because now she is very happy and the happiness that dominates her, you wouldn't be able to tell that she was once evil. It was strange to see her like this. But we must not forget that the evil is still in her, for now we are safe as long as she is happy, but if something happens, it will be over.': - He answered.

Oliver: - 'Dude, it's good to see you here again, this place was empty without you, hihihi.': - He patted his shoulder and laughed.

James: - 'Oh man! It's great! It's great to be with you again. But where is Hanna? I haven't seen her yet?': - He asked curiously.

Evelin: - 'Aah! Hanna is in the process of reading the books at the accommodation to see how she can help defeat the evil witch.': - She replied happily.

James: - 'So what are we doing? Let's go to and greet her.': - He answered excitedly. They went to the accommodation where Hanna was up to her neck in books. When they saw each other, they fell for each other with great joy and hugged each other for a long time, then sat down to talk.

Hanna: - 'James! You are finally here with us again! But the evil witch ???': - She asked in despair.

Evelin: - 'Calm down Hanna! Everyone is working on it, researching how to defeat evil.'

Oliver: - 'Well! I just feel that we are moving backwards in this matter!': - He said jokingly.

James: - 'Believe me, Hanna, that it is not as simple as we imagined! I was there with her for a very long time, and it just wasn't feasible. The fact that I trusted her was only a good point, but the situations themselves did not turn out the way I imagined. But I think what I have achieved so far is a start!': - He answered.

Hanna: - 'Of course! Of course! You've done this really well so far, I'll give you that, but tell me that from your point of view, how can this be done, because it's well known that it wasn't easy to get there and when we finally succeeded, we fell into a trap.'

Oliver: - 'There is a solution for everything! There are things that can be solved or that are right there in front of our noses, but we don't notice them.': - He interrupted.

James: - 'Well! This is so true! There really is a solution for everything, and we will find it together.'; - He answered.

While they were talking, the mages didn't have a moment's rest since they got their powers back. The young people knocked on their door while they were talking. It was James' father, he came to tell them about dinner, since they were talking so much that they missed lunch. Days passed, but nothing clever was planned. Christmas was slowly approaching, for which there was a lot of preparation. The streets were beautifully decorated, the houses inside and out, it was a fascinating sight, something like this the good friends had not seen in England, since it is a completely different world, with different customs than here where they are staying. The outside of the houses was decorated with the colour of every family that matched their family name. The stars and snowflake decorations were stunning, and most importantly, everything was covered in real snow because it snowed almost every day. The children really enjoyed the Christmas period, the atmosphere and the sight made people extremely happy, it made them forget the evil witch's deeds and wickedness. The good friends have been there for so long that it was already discussed among the adults that when school starts, they too will have to go to school, otherwise they will miss out on a lot of things. Christmas Eve has arrived, this is the most important part for families, when they sit down at the table and have dinner and talk together. But what was also interesting in this world was the Christmas custom. This means that on December 24, after everyone had dinner, they talked until midnight, told each other all kinds of stories, sang Christmas songs together, and opened the presents together before midnight. After opening the presents, the family members went to the relatives and friends and sang Christmas songs in front of their door, after the resident welcomed them with love, they offered the visitors cakes and sang Christmas songs together. This went on until morning, everyone had a good time, they celebrated Christmas. When 5 o'clock in the morning came, everyone returned home and went to bed. They put the wicked witch case aside for the Christmas season because they didn't want to deal with it during the holidays. The days passed and they slowly welcomed the new year. A lot of fun and a good atmosphere made them forget the bad things, but last but not least, someone had to remind them that the work must continue, because the evil can return at any time. The new year began, and people went back to their old ways, adults went to work and children to school. Well, the good friends also started school, because if they're already stuck here, they might as well go to school too. The children there helped them find their class, which seemed quite a maze at the beginning until they got used to it. They quickly fit in because almost everyone knew them, and they were famous for their actions. They also helped them in their lessons, since they were quite behind. But they caught up pretty quickly as they had help. Oliver didn't really like the fact that he had to go to school again, since he wasn't really a fan of it, but he was comforted by the fact that in this kind of school there was a class where magic was also taught. After all, sorcery was natural here, there are many sorcerers in this world. Miriam and Gilbert were overjoyed. Gilbert couldn't stop thinking about his father, because he was alone in the tower, and no one cared about him. No matter what his father did then. One day he went up the tower to visit him. The guards let him in because they were instructed that Gilbert could go to his father at any time to talk.

Gilbert: 'Good morning, father! How are you doing here in the tower?': - He asked breathlessly.

Devilus: - 'Good morning my son! Well, how would it go? I've been here alone for a while now, I already know that it's all my fault, I'll give you two that, but I can't take back what I did or what I said. On the other hand, I would appreciate it if you would talk to Miriam about me, that I have changed my mind and that I won't stand in the way anymore, I give you my blessing, just let me go home.': - He begged.

Gilbert: - 'My father is fine! I'll talk to her and see how she decides about you. But I'm glad that you think so because our love is getting stronger and no one can break it, not even you.': - He answered with joy. With that he left the tower and went back to Miriam.

Gilbert: - 'Honey! I just came back from my father's, I talked to him again and he has changed since he was there alone for so long. He had time to think it over and changed his mind. He said that he regretted everything he had done and said that you should let him go home to his loved ones.': - He told Miriam.

Miriam: - 'It's fine! But before that, I will also go up to him and talk to him.': - She said firmly.

Gilbert: - 'Of course! Just go and talk to him.': - He answered with a smile. Miriam went up to the tower to speak with the king.

Miriam: - 'Welcome Devilus! I hear that you have reconsidered your actions and that you want to go home. Well, I want to hear what you came up with?': - She asked the king.

Devilus: - 'I apologize for every rude act and speech I have made against you. I had time to think and consider these things, I decided to give you my blessing, be happy, I will not stand in your way, I give you, my word. I would like to ask you to let me go so that I can go back to my palace where I am needed and to my loved ones.': - He confessed honestly.

Miriam: - 'Okay! I'll let you back but only on one condition, if i found out that you're up to something, I'll find out sooner than you think, and then I won't be so kind to you anymore, I hope you've understood that.': - He stated firmly.

Devilus: - 'Of course, I understand! I promise I won't try anything, just let me go back to my loved ones.': - He replied in despair.

Miriam: - 'Well okay! What you said was quite persuasive, so I will arrange for you to go back to your palace.' Miriam went back to Gilbert, informed him of the incident and arranged for the king to leave the tower and return to his loved ones. The king was very happy that he no longer had to languish in the tower and could finally go back to his home. When the king returned to his palace, he was welcomed with great joy and a small feast was held to celebrate this. The king decided to give up on his organized plan regarding Miriam, and he didn't even want to talk about it anymore. Thus, he could continue to rule peacefully without any problems because he kept his word. The mages called a meeting in the secret room where only mages could participate.

Mr. Tregas: - 'Gentlemen! I have called this important meeting because we must do something about the evil witch before it is too late. You must have remembered the crystal and its power, whose existence we know thanks to Evelin's dream not so long ago. Married! We have to get that crystal somehow. If we get it, we can defeat the evil witch once and for all. Since everyone got their magic back, it won't be that hard to get the sword we need. In order to get to the belly of the volcano, we will need to use a simple protective shield. But for this deed that we will carry out, it must remain invisible the whole time, so that the evil witch does not notice anything, because if she notices what we are preparing, then everything is over. We need to find a volunteer for this task and then we can start the adventure. Does anyone have an idea who that particular volunteer could be?': - He announced the plan.

Mr. Monghur: - 'That sounds like a very good plan and feasible! We have to choose someone who is worthy of this task and will certainly not fail. I would have a suggestion for this task, I think it should be Oliver.'

Mr. Onthasy: - 'Yes! I also agree with that.'

Mr. Zathen: - 'I also agree.'

Mr. Vinthus: - 'I agree.'

Mr Ambeth: - 'I think it's a bad idea to choose Oliver. He is a bit hesitant and scattered, I don't see how he will accomplish this task, I think it should be James. He has already reached the evil witch and changed a lot of things, and he even has magical powers that can help him.

Mr. Tregas: - 'Yes! But it must also be taken into account that if our chosen one goes on this task, he cannot cast a spell there, because if he does, the evil witch will notice him immediately and then it's all over. Then we can never get the crystal.'

Mr. Ambeth: - 'And what if the evil witch already knows about this crystal? No one has ever thought of that, have they?'

Mr. Tregas: - 'That was a smart question, Mr. Ambeth! This really hasn't occurred to us yet, what if the evil witch really knows about the crystal? This important question must be investigated somehow first, and then we will be able to decide more easily.'

Mr. Monghur: - 'I also agree with this, let's find out first because even people's lives may depend on it. The mages got into an important conversation about what Mr. Ambeth said, he asked an important question that they hadn't even thought about, the only problem was how to find out so that the evil witch wouldn't be suspicious, because she would immediately know that something was brewing against her again. In the midst of much discussion, Mr. Monghur remained silent for a while, so much so that he could no longer hear what they were talking about. He came up with a good idea on how to find out, it's a bit risky but worth a try.'

Mr Monghur: - 'I have an idea!': - He suddenly interrupted the magicians' conversation. The magicians suddenly became silent and all of them fixed their eyes on Monghur .

Mr. Monghur: - 'I had the idea to fly a pigeon to the evil witch's palace and take a small piece of shiny crystal in the pigeon's mouth and leave it in the evil witch's room, in a clearly visible place, so that she can find it. After finding the crystal, the pigeon waits for its reaction and also waits for what the crystal will say afterwards, and then we will find out from the pigeon whether it knows about the existence of the crystal or not.'

Mr. Tregas: - 'Hmmm! This seems like a good plan, not that dangerous, and we can cast an inaudibility spell on the pigeon, so she doesn't even notice it's there. This can be done; I don't see us failing in this. That was a good idea Mr. Monghur ! Congratulations!' The other mages also liked the idea, and they already saw the implementation of the plan. The next morning, after breakfast, the magicians arranged part of their plan, told the pigeon the invisibility spell and put the small piece of crystal in its mouth and then let it go. They were very anxious to see their plan succeed because it was very important to everyone. Of course, they didn't tell anyone about their plan until they were sure of the outcome. The pigeon flew to the evil witch's palace and placed the small crystal on her table. Then the pigeon flew to the windowsill and waited there. Miriam did not suspect anything of the whole thing, since no one noticed the invisible pigeon. When evening came, Miriam and Gilbert went up to the room to go to bed. When they reached the door of the room, Miriam turned back in the library to bring up a book for them to read a little before falling asleep.

Miriam: - 'Oh dear, I'm going back to the library, I'll get a book for each of us to read before going to bed, I'm not going to join you.

Gilbert: 'It's fine my dear! I will wait for you in the room. Miriam went back into the library and Gilbert went into the room. When Gilbert entered the room, he immediately noticed the small crystal piece. He took it in his hand and began to look at it, he rolled it around and took a good look at it. He thought about how this small piece of crystal got on the table, the window was ajar, but he didn't really pay attention to it, because it was always ajar.

He sat down on the bed and stared at the small crystal piece. Then he thought about it and put it away to make some kind of surprise for his beloved. Meanwhile, Miriam arrived back in the room with the books.

Gilbert: - 'Hello my dear! I thought you'd never come back, come lie down with me.

Miriam: -'I'm coming, dear!' With that, they cuddled up in bed and started reading together, talking, frolicking, laughing and finally went to sleep. Gilbert didn't say a word about the little piece of crystal. It's past midnight and the pigeon is nowhere to be found. The magicians began to worry that something must have happened, that's why the pigeon didn't come back.

Mr. Ambeth: - 'Gentlemen! No need to worry! We have to be patient, maybe the evil witch didn't find the crystal piece, that's why the pigeon isn't here. I think it will be better if we also rest and tomorrow we will be able to think better with new strength and freshness.'

Mr. Tregas: -'Mr. Ambeth may be right! I agree, let's go home and see you here again tomorrow, good night gentlemen.' With that, they said goodbye to each other, and everyone went home to rest. The pigeon continued to wait there, as it cannot return without news. The next morning came, and everyone went to breakfast. After breakfast, Gilbert took the small piece of crystal to the goldsmith to make a beautiful ring for his love. The ring will be ready in the afternoon when Gilbert can go get it. The magicians were already very nervous about where the pigeon was for so long. But they reassured themselves that the evil witch still hadn't gotten it, and that's why the pigeon hadn't come back yet. Which, of course, was the case, since Miriam still hasn't received the crystal. The evening came again, and Gilbert couldn't wait to ask for Miriam's hand in marriage, although seeing the little crystal he immediately thought that now was the time and that this was a good opportunity to do so. They entered the room again and Miriam was about to go to bed when Gilbert stood in front of her.

Gilbert: - 'My dear! (He took Miriam's hand and knelt before her.) Here and now, I want to ask you to be my wife!'

Miriam: - (With a numb face and surprised, she was suddenly overcome with such happiness that her heart was pounding in her throat.) 'Oh, my dear! Of course, I'll marry you!': - She replied happily. With that, Gilbert put the ring on her finger, which was beautiful, the small crystal shone beautifully on her finger. Miriam cried tears of joy when she saw that beautiful ring. She sat down on the bed and began to look at the ring on her finger.

Gilbert: - 'Do you like it my dear?': - He asked excitedly.

Miriam: - 'Of course I like it, dear! This ring is very beautiful. Where is this beautiful ring from?': - She asked curiously.

Gilbert: 'I made it for you today my dear! It's time to get married and finally be each other's forever.': - He answered proudly.

Miriam: - 'Oh yes! This is really a very good feeling that we can finally be together, my dream about you will come true, after the wedding, no one will separate us anymore, I love you my dear Gilbert!': - She said happily.

Gilbert: 'I love you too my dear! Now come and lie here next to me, my dear.' With that, they cuddled up in bed and talked for a long time about the wedding, which will be announced soon. It was already very late; Gilbert was sleeping soundly. Miriam couldn't sleep, she was looking at her ring. She got up and left the room. She went down to the great hall and sat down by the fireplace and stared at her ring, speaking in a low voice.

Miriam: - 'I wonder where you got this little crystal from? This crystal reminds me of something. With that she got up from her chair and went to the kitchen, took a very old book and opened it.

The book was about that certain crystal that is hidden in the depths of the ocean.

Miriam: - 'Ah! I knew that the crystal was familiar to me, this crystal will be mine one day and no one can take it away from me.': - She said out loud and giggled. When the little pigeon got this information, it immediately flew back to the magicians. The magicians were looking forward to the arrival of the pigeon and welcomed him happily. After learning what the evil witch said, they immediately had to rethink their every move.

Mr. Tregas: - 'This is not good news! The evil witch knows about the crystal, and as we've heard, she's going to get it. We have to think carefully about what we do because our lives depend on it.': - He said in despair.

Mr. Onthasy: - 'We will do everything to prevent the evil witch from getting the crystal.': - He said encouragingly.

Days and weeks passed, but no results were achieved. In the meantime, James and his friends heard the news of what the magicians were planning.

James: - 'Listen! Today I listened in on the magician's conversation and they were talking about some kind of crystal! They said that it won't be easy to get them to beat the.... and I didn't hear the rest because someone came just then, and I left.

Evelin: -'Oh yes! The crystal! We really haven't even told you the story about what I dreamed about; this will be good! I dreamed that you came back to us, which did happen, but there was also an interesting chapter that ended with a very blinding light. But since this was very interesting dream, I thought I would tell the mages who also found it very interesting. They deciphered it and they mentioned a certain crystal after it and that you can defeat the evil witch with it.': - She told the story.

Hanna: - 'Yes! I've already heard about that crystal, but it won't be easy to get it.'

James: - 'What makes that crystal so special? How do you defeat the evil witch with it? After all, we are here for a reason, as I have to defeat the evil witch, and everyone knows that!': - He suddenly asked a few questions.

Hanna: - 'That's right James! Only you and no one else can defeat the evil witch! But the way I see it, the mages don't pay attention to this, hence why they can't come up with a solution. It could also be that the power of the crystal could easily defeat the evil witch without harming her, but for some reason the mages are confused. I 'll find out what the reason for this is, see you, see you later.': - She said goodbye to them.

Oliver: - 'Can I go with you too? I would like to help! I won't be into he's way, I promise!': - He asked with big innocent cat eyes.

Hanna: 'I don't even know! Not sure if .... She couldn't finish the sentence.

Oliver: - 'Please! Let me help! Please!': - He folded his hands and begged her.

Hanna: -'You can come on one condition!'

Oliver: - 'Yes, I will do whatever you say!': - He promised.

Hanna: 'Come on you idiot! You will only speak if I ask....' Meanwhile, they have already left.

Evelin: - 'I have a better idea! Let's go to the school library and look through the books, see if we find something clever, we'll help with something.'

James: - 'Okay! We can go to the library, but if we can't find anything smart, we'll turn to plan B!'

Evelin: - 'Okay! Well, that's that.': - She smiled. (Meanwhile, she looked at James, and suddenly she realised that James said that they will turn to plan B.)

Evelin: - 'You listen! What is Plan B? Would you initiate me too?': - She asked curiously.

James: -'Yes, of course! Sorry! Plan B is that if we don't find anything clever, we go to the teacher who teaches magic, you know Mr. Oxternt, he can help us.'

Evelin: - 'It's not a bad idea! Let's try because we still have a lot to do.' They arrived at the school library and saw him browsing the books. Hanna and Oliver also went back to the magicians in the bookstore. There were only two mages in the shop because the others were browsing the books to no avail. Hanna and Oliver went up to the second floor to pretend they were also looking for a book, while they could observe the mages. The magicians were so engrossed in browsing the books that they didn't even notice that Hanna and Oliver were there. The wicked witch was in a very good mood after Gilbert asked for her hand in marriage, the wedding day slowly came, so she turned all her attention to the preparations.

Miriam: - 'Darling! I'm so excited about the wedding! Only a few days separate us from being each other's forever! Isn't it wonderful?': - She giggled happily.

Gilbert: - 'Of course it is! Very wonderful, my dear!': - He picked up Miriam and they spun around a few times with happiness. Hanna knew that now would be the big opportunity to act, even though the evil witch was all about the wedding. If they don't act in these next few days, then it will be too late. She didn't have to wait long to notice that the magicians were talking gibberish to each other as if they were bewitched. This usually happens when someone casts a spell on them so that they don't understand each other. But the big question was, who did this to the mages? Since they were pressed for time, it was easier if she solved this little problem herself. That's why she used a spell to untie the confused mages so that they could go about their work more easily. The magicians were a little confused and did not know what had happened to them, as if they had lost a whole lifetime worth of time, but since they saw that Hanna was there, they already knew that she had helped them.

Mr. Tregas: - 'Thank you, Hanna, for lifting this superstitious curse on us, we are grateful for it.': - He thanked her with a sigh.

Hanna: - 'It's only natural! I'm glad I could help': - She answered with a smile.

Mr. Tregas: - 'Well, ladies and gentlemen, we have an important task! We have to try until the evil witch has her eyes on us. Even though it happened that she bewitched us so that we couldn't cooperate in this matter, even though she wants to get the crystal, we only have a few days left people!': - He said excitedly. Everyone started browsing in harmony to finally find the solution to get the crystal. Oliver and Hanna looked for a description of the crystal in books, but they didn't get very far either. Well, there is a reason for this, that no one finds anything because Miriam has hidden all the books related to the crystal in her secret library, so that nothing about it will be found. Everyone has already given up the search and gone home, the school has already closed, and the magicians have also closed the shop. The next morning, when they were all having breakfast together, Hanna brought up this topic at the table.

Hanna: -'Well people! I feel that now is the time for this, because we are very pressed for time. We didn't find anything in the books, at least we didn't find any books about crystals! How successful were you?': - She asked James and Evelin.

James, Evelin: - 'No results!': - They answered at the same time.

Mr. Zathen: - 'Well, there can only be one reason for this! The wicked witch has overtaken us. Even if you remember, it wasn't that long ago when we flipped through the book about the crystal, now it's gone too. Isn't that a bit strange?': - He said questioningly.

John: 'Hmm! But yes! Indeed, it is! And we only noticed this now !?': - He said in amazement.

Mr. Tregas: - 'Yes! Unfortunately, that's true! She found out from somewhere what we wanted to accomplish here, that's why she got ahead of us, and that's why she confused us with the confusion spell so that we couldn't work together. But I don't understand something? If she found out about this, then how-how did she not take back our magic power?': - He asked curiously.

Oliver: -'Phh! What a question that was! Because she is head over heels in love!': - He replied clearly smiling. Suddenly everyone was looking at him. Oliver stuffed his head because he was hungry, he couldn't imagine how they could talk so much when they could eat instead. When he noticed that everyone was looking at him, the toast fell out of his hand.

Oliver: - 'Now what! Maybe I said something wrong?': - He asked with his mouth full. Everyone at the table started laughing, but because of what Oliver said, the magicians are considering it.

James: 'Come on mate! We have to go to school!': - With that he patted his back and smiled. Everyone went about their business. There was a girl at school who liked Oliver, that girl was called Jessy, Oliver also liked this girl, but he didn't dare approach her, even though this girl was very beautiful and also smart. Jessy had two girlfriends with whom they hung out all the time. No matter how many times they passed Oliver, she always smiled at him, which embarrassed Oliver. What Jessy liked about him was that he was a funny and a laid-back guy. When they reached the school, Oliver immediately spotted Jessy. But he hadn't told his friends about this girl yet, because he didn't dare tell them that he liked her. In February, a carnival ball was held at the school, and the ads were posted on the bulletin board. Raffle tickets could be purchased in the principal's office. Of course, everyone had to dress up in some kind of masked outfit. The three good friends were just reading the ad about the carnival ball when Jessy also stood there with her friends. The girls started giggling standing behind Oliver. Both Oliver and his friends turned back to see who was giggling. Of course, Oliver was embarrassed again and walked away from his friends and the students standing there. James immediately noticed Oliver's reaction and went after him.

James: -'Oliver! Don't you want to say something? You don't usually behave like this!': - He asked curiously.

Oliver: - 'James! Please! There's nothing wrong with me, it's just that there were suddenly too many people there and I rather stood aside, that's all.': - He answered shyly.

James: - 'Okay mate! If you say so!': - He smiled in disbelief.

Oliver: - 'Let 's go to class before we're late because of this stupid ad!': - He said a little nervously.

James: -'Come on guys, let's go, and then we'll look at the ad later!': - He said to the others. Everyone went to their classes; Jessy took one more look at Oliver and smiled at him. Of course, Oliver noticed and wanted to smile, but James dragged him to class so they wouldn't be late. They sat down for magic, everyone took their seats and there was still an empty place where you could sit, Jessy came into the class and took the empty place. When Oliver noticed it, he was embarrassed again. James hasn't noticed any of it yet. The teacher entered the class, and the lesson began. Oliver sat in the penultimate bench in the middle row, Jessy sat in the first row in the third bench. Oliver was constantly watching when Jessy didn't notice. During this time, the teacher continued giving her lecture James was sitting on the last bench in the row where Jessy was. At a certain moment, he noticed that Oliver was constantly staring at Jessy. He was very curious about this, because he knew that Oliver was hiding something from him, so he didn't say a word. Jessy looked back at Oliver and said something to him that of course Oliver did not understand. Jessy wrote something for him on a piece of paper and passed it on to Oliver. The teacher turned back and told the students not to talk. The piece of paper finally reached Oliver and was about to unfold it when the teacher stood next to him.

Mr Oxtern: - 'Do you have an important message for me, Oliver?': - The teacher asked him.

Oliver: - 'Oh, no, teacher, it's just a small piece of paper of no importance.': - He answered suddenly. The whole class started laughing.

Mr Oxtern: - 'If it is not of any importance, then give me that piece of paper and you will get it back at the end of the class, I would be happy if you would pay attention in the meantime because this topic will be on the exam next week.': - With that he confiscated his little piece of paper. The Oliver looked at the Jessy, smiled and shrugged his shoulders that he didn't manage to look at the message. James looked at Oliver and gestured to him what was all this. Oliver told him that he would tell him. The lesson continued, but Oliver couldn't pay attention, the message kept going through his mind, wondering what Jessy could have written in it. Finally, the class ended, and the teacher called Oliver over, waited until everyone left the class and then spoke to him.

Mr. Oxtern: - 'Oliver! I'll give you back your paper slip, but you won't get it back next time. You have to pay attention in lessons, we don't send love messages to each other, you can sort that out in your free time, I hope I was clear!': - He warned sternly.

Oliver: - 'I completely understand, sir! It won't happen anymore, I promise.': - He replied politely. As soon as he got the little piece of paper back, he left the classroom where James was waiting for Oliver.

James: - 'Dude! What are you hiding from me? You and Jessy? Since when are you two together': - He asked suddenly.

Oliver: - 'Dude! It's not what it seems! Jessy and I are not together, but the truth is that I like her, and she likes me. But I don't know what to do, I'm really bad at this.': - He answered a little confused.

James: 'Hey man! You? You don't know what you have to do? You're taking the piss right! It's obvious that you have to do, go to the girl and ask her out on a date.': - He answered firmly.

Oliver: - 'Yes, that would be so obvious bro! And when schools done, I'll ask her on a date.': - He answered excitedly.

lesson was over and, as Oliver said, he went to Jessy's to ask her out on a date.

Oliver: -'Hey Jessy! Would you come here for a minute?': - He called her to him.

Jessy: - Okay then girls, I'll see you later, bye!': - She said goodbye to her friends and went to Oliver.

Jessy: - 'Hi Oliver! What do you want to say?': - She asked awkwardly.

Oliver: - 'Would you come on a date with me?': - He asked briefly and firmly.

Jessy: - 'I thought you would never ask! Tonight at 19:00 come pick me up and we'll go to Brontus, okay?'

Oliver: - 'Okay! I'll be there!': - He answered happily. Brontus is a restaurant with separate billiard rooms. In this place, they made the most delicious cheeseburger in the whole city, and you could even have fun at the same time. What you should know about this place is that the restaurant itself looked very cozy from the outside. When you enter the restaurant, the place where you will sit changes into whatever mood you're in right now. It is full of magic, which is why it is so interesting and, moreover, they cooked delicious food.

James: - 'Did you talk to Jessy?':- He asked accidentally in front of everyone.

Oliver: - 'thanks man! Now everyone ....'. He didn't finish the sentence because everyone there were curiously questioning him.

Hanna: - 'Are you not going on a date?': - She asked with a smile.

Evelin: - 'Oliver! This really excites me!': - Jumps into his neck.

Evelin: - 'Who is the lucky girl?': - She asked back suddenly.

Oliver: - 'fine, fine! Well! Her name is Jessy, and I asked her out on a date today.': - He answered with a half-smile.

Hanna: -'Well, Oliver! You didn't waste your time! How long has this been going on between you two?

Evelin: - 'Yes! Where are you going tonight?': - He asked curiously.

Oliver: - 'We are going to the Brontus.': - He answered.

Hanna: - 'Wow, that's a very good place, man! When you go in there, its writhing with magic. It was a good choice, Oliver.': - She said excitedly.

Oliver: -'I didn't choose it, Jessy did. But what makes just a restaurant with billiard rooms so magical, right?': - He asked in surprise.

Hanna: - 'You'll see when you go in, it'll be great.': - She answered with a smile.

Oliver: - 'And what should I take now, this is the question?'

Evelin, Hanna: - 'I will help!': - They answered at the same time.

Oliver: 'Okay girls! Then choose something and I'll put it on, but don't make it too conspicuous, just put on simple clothes.': - He told them a little nervously.

James: - 'Calm down mate! It's just a date, there's no need to be nervous.': - He reassured Oliver.

Oliver: -'I know! Just a date!': - He answered even more nervously. Finally, they managed to choose the right outfit and it was time to go to Jessy. He said goodbye to his friends and left for the date. He arrived at Jess's house, whose family colours were yellow and light green. He knocked on the door and waited for it to be opened. Someone came to the door and opened it. A large man opened the door, Jessy 's father Mr. Zathen Derras.

Mr. Derras: - 'Good evening, young man! Come in!': - He invited him into the house.

Mr. Derras: - 'My daughter will soon be ready. Let me introduce myself! I'm Mr. Derras, welcome!': - He introduced himself.

Oliver: -'Good evening, sir! Nice to meet you! I'm Oliver!': - He introduced himself respectfully. After they introduced themselves, Jessy came down the stairs, and she was so beautiful. Oliver's breath stopped when he saw Jessy.

Jessy: - 'Hi dad! We'll be back soon, kisses!': - She said goodbye to his father.

Oliver: - 'It was nice meeting you sire, goodbye!': - Thank you.

Mr. Derras: - 'Be home by ten at the latest!': - He said after them.

Jessy: - 'okay then, bye dad!': - She shouted after him. With that they went to Brontus. When they reached the door of the restaurant, Oliver politely opened the door for Jessy. Jessy entered, followed by Oliver, the door closed behind them, and they walked up to the reception desk where they were directed to their table. They were greeted at the welcome desk by a lady with a beautiful white owl on her shoulder. The owl directed each guest to their own table by hooting in the lady's ear and with that the lady knew which table they should be sent to. Oliver and Jessy received a table with a lily of the valley finish. Each table was separate and had a different look. A beautiful table setting was waiting for them on the table, decorated with candles and lilies of the valley. The look of the table itself was dazzling. There were menus on the table that you could choose from. They did not have to hold the menu with their hands, because as soon as they sat down at the table, the menus rose into the air and opened in front of them, dazzling the guests with loud speech and three-dimensional images. Oliver was impressed, he suddenly couldn't find words, he liked this place so much.

Menu: - 'Oliver: - I wish you a good evening, sir! Welcome to Brontus! Today we are treating our guests to something special! Appetizer, stuffed meatballs, casino eggs and ham and olive snacks. Our main menu is sour cream chicken with steamed vegetables and dumplings. And the unmissable cheeseburger with fries sprinkled with cheese. Drink selection: - Love syrup, beautiful waterfall, rainbow cloud, crystal string of pearls. If you have decided about what you would like, just tap me and you can order.': - It listed the selections for Oliver. Of course, Jessy's menu also listed the same items.

Oliver: -'I can't believe this! This is a very nice restaurant Jessy! It was a very good choice. Did you manage to choose?: - He asked excitedly.

Jessy: - 'I love this place; it always disconnects me from the reality outside. I already know what to order because I've been here a couple of times, if you want, I can help you order too.': - She answered with a smile.

Oliver: - 'It's fine, then I'll leave it to you!': - He answered curiously. Jessy tapped on the menu and began placing orders.

Jessy: - 'We would like to have two servings of cheeseburgers with fries sprinkled with cheese and two rows of crystal pearls, thank you.'

Menu: - 'We have placed your order in the pick-up line, the waiting time is ten minutes. Thank you for your order, in the future if you want to order something else, please indicate with the usual tap, Bon Appetite.': - The menu replied.

Oliver: - 'Jessy! I am very glad that we came to this restaurant, it is very well thought out, cozy and you don't have to wait long for the food.': - He said calmly.

Jessy: - 'I'm glad you like it! But the evening is just beginning, the best is yet to come.': - She answered with a smile. The server was nothing more than a tray flying by itself, bringing the drinks they ordered to the table. The drinks flew off the tray straight in front of them. Oliver was also surprised by this and by the way their drink looked.

Oliver: - 'Jessy! This is very serious service! And this drink! It looks amazing. As if it were full of crystals.': - He said in surprise.

Jessy: - 'Don't worry, it's just an appearance! Everything here is full of magic, that's why this place is good.': - She reassured him.

Jessy: - 'Listen Oliver! Tell me something about yourself! I want to know how you got here to us?': - She asked curiously.

Oliver: - 'Ohh! Yes, it's a long story!': - He answered with a smile.

Jessy: - 'We have time till 10! Tell me the bottom line, I want to know more about you. Where were you born? Which city did you come from?': - She asked.

Oliver: - Okay then! We've got time after all, don't we?': - He answered with a smile. Oliver began to tell Jessy how they got involved here and what they came to this world for. In the middle of the big story, they also brought out their food and ate it slowly, and it didn't seem like they wanted to go play billiards or snooker, they felt completely comfortable at their table. Their table, which was decorated with lilies of the valley, slowly began to open and released a very delicious fragrance. This scent almost embraced them and drove them to each other. When they were already sitting next to each other, Oliver hugged Jessy and continued his story. Jessy seemed to be having a great time with Oliver. But time ran out quickly, so they had to prepare to leave. They paid for their order and were ready to leave. When they got up from the table, a hanger appeared at their table with their coats. Oliver was completely impressed by the restaurant, he felt so good that he grabbed Jessy and kissed her on the lips. Jessy didn't even have to excuse herself; she returned the kiss to Oliver. When this kiss clicked, the place where they were sitting turned into a rainbow waterfall, but of course nothing was wet because it was all magic. The marigolds opened completely and hovered above them, circling the loving spa. Both of them left very happy, laughing and walking out the door with a tight hug.

Jessy: - 'It was a very good evening, Oliver! Thanks! Could we do this more if you're in it?: - She asked with a smile.

Oliver: - 'I had a good time with you too, Jessy! And we can repeat this evening at any time.': - He answered happily. He accompanied Jessy home, they said goodbye and Oliver started walking home, but he was so happy that he didn't even know how he got home. At home, everyone was waiting for Oliver to arrive because they were curious.

Oliver: - 'Hello, guys!': - he greeted everyone with a smile. 'It was a really great evening!!! Sweet, sweet sauce!! Who would have thought ......?': - He started humming and threw himself on the bed.

Evelin: -'Well, well! Tell me how it was?': - He asked curiously.

Hanna: -'Well, I think it's clear that the date went well! He's seemingly happy.': - She said with a laugh.

Oliver: - 'It was the most beautiful evening of my life! That should be enough for you, share it until the near future ...': - He said with a sigh.

James: - 'It's okay guys, let your date rest, and we'll get back to it tomorrow!': - He said laughing. With that, everyone went to their room laughing. Miriam was only one day away from the wedding. That's why she sprung into action and set out to get the crystal without Gilbert even knowing about it. The mages weren't idle either, but they also figured out how to get the crystal. When everything was prepared, they sent the firebirds on their way to get the sword. Yes, but the evil witch preceded them, and the sword was no longer there when the firebirds arrived on the scene. So, they flew back to the mages and told them that there was no point in going after the crystal.

Mr. Tregas: - 'This is incredible!! I can't believe the wicked witch has beat us again. It's all over now, we have to tell the children the bad news immediately.': - He gave the instruction to the other mages. Mr. Monghur immediately rushed to the accommodation to tell them the bad news.

Mr. Monghur: - 'Children wake up immediately!! I have very bad news!': - He woke them up.

James: - 'What's wrong Mr. Monghur? What's so urgent that it can't wait until morning?': - He asked sleepily.

Mr. Monghur: - Everyone get up immediately! Right now!': - He shouted in despair. When everyone woke up and went downstairs in the hall, they waited curiously to hear what Mr. Monghur wanted to say.

Mr. Monghur: - 'Good to have you all here! I came to you tonight with some very bad news. The evil witch got the sword, it was already too late when the firebirds got there, we think she got the crystal since then.....' As soon as he said this, a huge light covered the whole part of the earth, the crystal was so bright, just like in Evelin's dream.

Evelin: - 'Damn!!! It's just as bright as in my dream!': - She said with her mouth open.

Everyone just marvelled at the sight, but the light went out after a minute.

Mr. Monghur: - 'Well, we missed this completely, now we can only hope that the evil witch will have mercy on us and not spill our lives, because this crystal has such a great power that if it falls into the wrong hands, it's all over.'

James: - 'Maybe it's not all over yet!! There is another solution that might come in handy.': - He spoke wisely.

Oliver: - 'God damn, that was really cool!! This is crystal is awesome! It has a little light, that's for sure.': - He interrupted in amazement. Evelin nudged Oliver not to say so much nonsense. Oliver looked at Evelin and shrugged his shoulders, wondering what he had said wrong again.

Hanna: -'I don't think all is lost! James is right! It is known that the wicked witch is very much in love now and her wedding is tomorrow, so we have an ace of trumps'. James can go back to the palace whenever he wants, can't he? After all, his mum and even his father are there, so James is the only one who can prevent this from harming anyone. James! Tomorrow is the big wedding, which you are also official, you have to go there anyway. Well, the plan is as follows': - When you arrive at the wedding, you will observe Miriam's every step and movement. He can only keep the crystal in the palace, as this is her realm. You show up at the church for her to see you, when the ceremony starts you turn around and sneak out of the church. When you came out of the church, you go into the palace and start looking for the crystal. If you find the crystal, try to get back to us immediately, okay?!!: - She told her idea.

James: - 'That idea sounds good! But do you think that the crystal is not guarded by its guards? Surely, she won't let anyone get to it!': - He answered thoughtfully.

Mr. Monghur: - 'That's right! The crystal is sure to be guarded, she won't leave it in plain sight!! That's why you have to be very careful and don't forget that you have now magic power, use it if you need to!': - He gave him good advice.

Oliver: -'I'll go with you too, buddy! I won't leave you alone in this adventure!': - He interrupted with immediate effect.

James: - 'It's nice of you, Oliver! But you can't come here with me, I have to go through this alone! Sorry mate.': - He answered confidently.

Oliver: -'You know better! I will be happy to help if needed!': - He answered bravely.

Mr. Monghur: - 'Well my son, get ready because you have to get there on time! Don't forget that if something goes wrong, use your magic power!': - He provided good advice.

James: - 'It will be fine! I will do my best.': - He replied confidently. Evelin walked over to James and hugged him. James returned the hug and whispered this in his ear.

James: - 'It will be fine! I promise to bring the crystal.'

Evelin: - 'So be it! Be very careful! I don't want to lose you again.': - She whispered in his ear.

Oliver: - 'Okay now! Enough of that! He's not going to a funeral or something!': - He interrupted sarcastically. They said their goodbyes and James set off to get the crystal. The next morning came when James arrived at the palace. He was allowed into the palace as he was one of the most important guests. Everyone welcomed James.

Gilbert: -'Good morning, James! So, this is where you ended up? I thought you weren't coming! Go up to your room and change because we have to go to the church soon.': - He greeted him happily.

James: -'Good morning, Gilbert! Alright, I'm going to change! See you soon!': - He answered back. On the way, half of his room met Miriam.

Miriam: -'Good morning, James! It's good to see you here again! Hurry because the ceremony will start soon, don't be late!!': - She greeted him happily.

James: -'Good morning to you too, Miriam! I'm on my way there, see you soon!': - He answered back. Everyone in the palace was buzzing for the big ceremony, the servants were in shock. The time had come to set off in the church, the riders lined up and waited for the guests to board. Gilbert was the first to be taken to the church, followed by the other guests, although the bride was the last in line. When everyone was there in the church and settled down, after a little while the bride arrived. The wedding music played in the church when the doors opened and Miriam the bride entered. Everyone's breath was taken away, she looked so beautiful in her wedding dress. Gilbert was also breathless when he saw his bride. Miriam walked over to the altar and faced Gilbert. The Priest began the ceremony. The wedding ceremony lasted an hour and a half, during which time James had plenty of time to do his important mission. But there was a small hitch, he had to sit in the first row because he was the son of Miriam and Gilbert, so unfortunately, he couldn't leave the church, he had to resort to another method. While the ceremony lasts, there is plenty of time to figure out how to find the crystal. Finally, the ceremony was over, the bride and groom were the first to leave the church, followed by the guests. Everyone got into the horse-drawn carriage and headed back to the palace to celebrate the newly-weds. Now was the big chance for James to finally find out the whereabouts of the crystal. There was a lot of activity in the palace because today was very important. James had an idea about where to look for that crystal. He also went down into the basement, which was a pure labyrinth, there were lots of small rooms down there and it would take a while to find the crystal, if it was in the palace at all. Since there were guards standing in front of the door leading to the basement, as in front of all other doors, it was necessary to figure out why he wanted to go down there.

Guard 1: - 'Where, where young man?': - He asked curiously.

James: - 'Oh! Nothing special, my mother asked me to bring them a glass of special wine!': - He answered suddenly.

Guard 1: - 'Okay! But don't stay too long': - He warned.

James: - 'I won't!': - He answered relieved.

With that, the guards lowered James into the basement. Long rows of stairs led down to the basement, from which more than half of them had an exit, and the rows of stairs continued down, a real labyrinth. At the first exit, he couldn't decide which way to go, because there were so many paths leading in all directions. He sat down on the steps and pondered which direction to go, because he couldn't waste much time down here as then it would be conspicuous for the guards. He had a good idea, so he went back to the door where the guards were standing and cast a forgetting spell on them.

James: -

MIASERIUM ALIENTUM!

FORGANUM SECTUM!

IMALLIUM PERISENDRUM!

He read these lines on them and now he can safely search down there because the guards won't know he's down there. So, he started, one at a time, but he also paid attention to Miriam's intuition, since he wouldn't have had enough time to check the entire basement, because then Miriam would have noticed it. He went into quite a few rooms and found nothing, so he tried to use his magic again because he would never find that crystal without it. When he was about to start the spell, he suddenly stopped because he remembered that if he starts using his spell now, the crystal will most likely light up and he will immediately be caught. So, he had to find another solution, so he sat down on the floor and closed his eyes. He started concentrating on the crystal to find it, but unfortunately, he didn't see anything, the crystal was simply not in the line of shapes. He got up from the ground and started walking back, but when he got to the door where the guards were, he had to say a spell again to restore the guards' memories.

James: -

BACKFINDEM REVIRENTUM!

REMINTEM WHAHTUS!

SWEPIREM FOUNDATION!

When he recited the spell to restore their memory, he came out of the door with a bottle of wine in his hand and started towards the ballroom. When James was out of the guard's sight, James made a quick turn and carried the wine up to his room and sat down on the floor, wondering where the crystal could be. Well, the crystal was in a place where no one would find it, even though Miriam had cast a hiding spell on it precisely so that no one would find it, and if someone did find it, she would know about it immediately, because then the crystal would emit a huge light, so it won't be easy to get to him. Miriam took care of everything so that no one would accidentally steal it from her. James was sitting on the floor in his room and was thinking about where the crystal could be, meanwhile he took the bottle of wine in his hand and started to turn it around, looking at the bottle. A white dove knocked at her window with a message. He opened the window and took the message.

Message: -

'Dear James!

Don't even try to look for the crystal any further, because if you do find it, you'll be in big trouble!

The evil witch made sure that the crystal did not fall into the hands of others.

Come back to the bookstore as soon as you can and we'll discuss the rest.

Destroy this message!

James immediately knew where the crystal was hidden after reading the message. But since it was dangerous for him to go there, he preferred to go down to the guests, so that Miriam's didn't notice his absence.

Miriam: -'Well James! Where have you been dear, I missed you from the fun! Come and dance with me!': - She asked happily.

James: - 'I was just walking in the garden!'

They went to dance in the middle of the hall, everyone stood around them and clapped, laughed and had a good time. When they finished the dance, James thanked her politely and then he walked over where everyone else was standing. Gilbert walked over to James and said:

Gilbert: - 'James, are you all, right? I can see that something is pressuring your heart!': - He asked seriously.

James: - 'Aah! There is nothing wrong! But I've never danced in front of so many people, especially not in the middle of the crowd, and I'm quite embarrassed!': - He pulled himself out of the truth.

Gilbert: -'Aha! I get it now! Come enjoy the party too, you don't have to be shy!': - He said with a smile.

James: - 'Yes, of course! I'll come in a bit; I'll just have to work up some courage!': - He answered with a little smile. Gilbert caught his bride, and they danced in the middle of the crowd, everyone applauded them and cheered. James went back to his room and lay down on his bed looking at the pictures on the wall which surrounded him, but he couldn't fall asleep. It must have been around midnight when James was still not asleep, simply no dream came to his eyes. He heard a small click on the west side of his room, he sat up and began to listen. He didn't have to wait long because there was another click in the wall. James went over to see what the clicking was. He took the candle with him so he could better see what the clicking was. He looks at the wall where the clicking came from, but he doesn't see anything. When he turned around, a goblin named Bonty was standing behind him. When James saw him, he was very scared because he didn't expect to meet a goblin, and almost dropped the candle from his hand.

Bonty: - 'Don't be afraid, master! I will not hurt you! I am a goblin, and I was sent by the great boss of the goblins to serve you and help you when you are in trouble. Not many people can say that they have a goblin, only those people who have earned it. Master, i am at your disposal, whatever you ask of me, I will do it for you as long as I live.': - He said with a smile.

James: - 'Ah! Yes, I see! But I still don't understand! Why do I need a goblin? What did I do to deserve a goblin?': - He asked in concern.

Bonty: - 'Well, master, I am at your disposal, I will fulfil anything you ask!': - He said with a smile.

James sat down on the ground and just stared at the goblin, suddenly not knowing what to do with him.

James: - 'Okay! Can you take me back to the bookstore?': - He asked him curiously. The goblin took him back to the bookstore with one movement. James just stared in astonishment out of his head, unable to believe that such a thing even existed.

James: -'Well God damn! Well, that was very fast, I'll give you that! I didn't think you could get me here so fast! I appreciate that!': - He said with a smile.

James: - 'And what else can you do?': - He asked the goblin curiously.

Bonty: -'Oh! My master, anything you ask me!': - He answered, bowing his head respectfully.

James: - 'But are you going to tell me what I did to get you assigned to me?': - He asked curiously.

Bonty: - 'Master! You saved our world from evil, and as I said, goblins are not assigned to everyone, only those who deserve it, my master!': - He answered humbly.

James: 'Ah, I see! But this world is still under a curse, I haven't saved it completely yet, the best is yet to come!': - He said inquisitively.

Bonty: - 'Yes, master! Even the boss goblin knows this! Everyone knows this! But I was sent to help you and protect you from the trouble that lies ahead, my master!': - He answered politely.

The Dark Power of the Crystal!

The next morning everyone wakes up from their deep sleep! Nature was covered in ice by the cold, cruel snow. The carnival ball at the school came slowly, there were only two days left until the big ball started. Everyone prepared for this special day, because here in this world, every ceremony is very important, passing on and maintaining the local culture means a lot to every resident. At this time in February, it is very cold, and winter is in full swing, which means that snowfall is inherent. Children who are only in kindergarten or even younger play outside together and sled and make ice slides with their feet, the longer the merrier. The local large park serves well for this purpose. Parents are not afraid to let their children out in the big park because there are many of them together and there has never been an instance of the children having any trouble other than falling down while sliding. Those who sled play on steeper hilly places, everyone has their own place to play, even skaters. Together as one big family! James and his friends had already gone to breakfast in the library because they had to go to school.

John: -'Good morning, guys! Only two days until the carnival ball starts!': - He said happily.

Hanna: 'Yes! You can be sure that it will be very beautiful!': - She said proudly.

Evelin: - 'I'm looking forward to it too! I've never been to a carnival ball before!': - She said excitedly.

Oliver: - 'It's sure to be fun! I'm looking forward to it'!: - He said laughing.

Mr. Tregas: - 'James! Please call me after school, I want to have a word with you!': - He said firmly.

James: - 'Yes sir!': - He answered seriously.

Of course, no one knew about James' goblin because no one was supposed to know that there was a goblin with him. James respected the goblin's request, not wanting to get him into trouble. After they had breakfast, they went to school. There was a rush to the school, everyone was very excited about the carnival ball, even the teachers. All the students went to their classes, there was silence on the streets, only the voices of the teachers could be heard from the classrooms. James and his friends were in magic class, the teacher was teaching them the concealment charm. In another class, they practised magic. Everyone was engrossed in great learning. And Hanna and John worked on the last prom dresses at home to make them in time. At school, the first lesson ended, the bell rang, and the students poured out of the classrooms. There was a rumour going around the hallways that something very dark and evil was coming. James and his friends were talking in a huddle when four students walked past them and were talking about just that. Oliver heard what they were saying and noticed it immediately.

Oliver: -'James, did you hear that? Did you hear what these guys said?': - He asked very upset.

James, Evelin: - 'No?!': - They answered at the same time.

James: - 'What did they say? I wasn't paying attention!': - He asked excitedly.

Oliver: - 'Come with me!': - He grabbed James's arm and pulled him after the guys.

Oliver: - 'Listen here guys! Did I hear correctly what you said earlier? Darkness is approaching and something...': - He didn't finish what he had to say because one of the guys had already spoken.

Guy 1: - 'Oh about that! Yes, of course, haven't you heard what will happen soon?': - He asked seriously.

Guy 1: - 'Well, the evil casts darkness on us again, but everyone already knows that.': - He told them clearly.

James: - 'What? What evil? What kind of darkness were you talking about?': - He asked in surprise.

Guy 1: - 'Come on James! Don't say that you don't know .....' He wanted to continue the sentence, but the bell rang, and they had to go to class, so he didn't have chance to say the full answer. James went to class with the others confused and kept thinking about what the others were talking about and where this news was coming from, what they were basing it all on. The potion lesson began, the students took their places at the table where everyone had to be in pairs. Of course, James was paired with Evelin and Oliver was paired with Jessy. James could not pay attention to what the teacher was explaining to them, so Evelin worked hard for him.

Evelin: - 'James! Maybe it's all just a bad joke, don't worry, we'll find out everything from the mages!': - She whispered in is ear.

James: - 'And what if it's not a bad joke?': - He answered in despair. The teacher immediately noticed that Evelin and James were whispering, so he told them.

Mrs. Embrine: - 'James, Evelin! All right with the magic potion? I see I'm whispering a lot about something; may I know what it is? If something is important, share it with us!': - He interjected inquisitively. Evelin wanted to speak, but James grabbed her arm so she wouldn't say anything, and he wanted to speak about her.

James: - 'Teacher, please, I want to ask something very important!': - James spoke up.

Mrs. Embrine: - 'Yes James, go ahead!': - She said firmly.

James: - 'Something really worries me about what I heard on the hallways today!': - He continued what he was saying.

Mrs. Embrine: - 'What kind of talk was on the hallway?': - She asked curiously.

James: - 'It is being spread that the darkness is striking again and something very evil is coming….: - He gave the information to the teacher.

Mrs. Embrine: -'Come on James! You don't have to believe everything you hear on the hallways!': - She cleared her voice and lowered her head.

Mrs. Embrine: - 'Children! You don't have to believe everything you hear in the hallways, there are malicious rumours, but you don't have to be afraid of anything, I don't know of anything bad that is coming. Everyone should return to the given task because we still have a lot of work to do.': - At the end of her sentence she took a deep breath and lowered her head again and turned her back to the class.

Evelin: - 'Well, I told you it was just a bad joke!': - She said with a smile.

James: - 'Well , bad joke!':- He answered with satisfaction. James knew that the teacher wasn't telling the truth, he saw it in her behaviour, but he didn't say anything about it to Evelin, because he first wanted to make sure it was true, which he has no doubts about, since he was almost sure based on the teacher's behaviour, that something is in the works. The class was over, everyone left their class, and the students went out to the hallways.

Evelin: - 'James, don't worry, I think it's just bad news!': - He tried to calm her down.

James: - 'I'll be right back, see you in the next class!': - With that he disappeared on the hallways. James went to see Mrs. Embrine, the teacher, as he didn't let what he heard rest.

James: -'Mrs. Embrine, please! Do you have a few minutes? I would like to talk to you, please!': - He addressed the teacher.

Mrs. Embrine: -'Of course James! Tell me, don't you want to ask me about what you asked me in class, right?': - She asked stressed. She took him by the arm and brought him to a safe room where no one was there, and no one could hear them.

Mrs. Embrine: - 'Listen carefully James! What I'm about to tell you, you can't tell anyone here at school, okay!'

James: - 'Okay, I won't tell anyone, I promise!': - He answered in despair.

Mrs. Embrine: - 'Well then, listen carefully! Unfortunately, the news you heard in the hallways is all true! I can't imagine how this information was leaked, but I also think that someone leaked this directly to cause panic in the school. Unfortunately, since then, I think this news has spread throughout the school, since then everyone knows about it and it is impossible to stop it. I, on the other hand, ask you to make the students believe as much as possible that this is just a bad joke and that all of this is not true, because if panic breaks out, then there will be no carnival ball.': - She asked in despair.

James: - 'It's okay, I'll do everything to make them forget this! But if this is true, where does this information come from?': - He asked curiously. In the meantime, one of the students noticed that James and the teacher had entered the room, so he crept in front of the door and began to listen, listening to every single word of the conversation.

Mrs. Embrine: - 'This information came to us from a very reliable source, but there is someone among us who leaked it and more...' The student who was listening at the door dropped a book from his hand and of course got scared, so he picked up the book from the ground and immediately ran away. By the time the teacher got to the door to see who it was, no one was there.

Mrs. Embrine: - 'Well, we're in big trouble! I'm sorry James! I don't know who eavesdropped on our conversation, but if this continues to spread, it's all over!': - She said desperately.

James: - 'I have an idea of what we can do about it! Let's use the forgetting spell against the one who was here and then the problem is solved!': - He replied proudly.

Mrs. Embrine: - 'Yes, this is also a solution, and it's not even a bad idea.'

MIASERUM ALIENTUM!

FORGANUM SECTUM!

IMALLIUM PERISENDRUM!

With this, he recited the forgotten spell, hoping that it was successful and that the news he heard here would not spread further.

Mrs. Embrine: - 'I hope that this will be useful, and that the news will not spread any further.': -She answered a little relieved.

James: - 'Well, the magic spell has been said, I don't see why it shouldn't stop .... if only ...!

Mrs. Embrine: - If only what???: - She asked immediately. 'Oh no...' Continued the teacher in despair.

James: - 'Let's hope that no one used the protective shield magic on the students!': - He said dejectedly.

Mrs. Embrine: - 'Yes! Let's go to class because we're late, we'll find out later anyway!': - She said dejectedly. James went back to class and the teacher went to her class. Evelin was already very worried about James and so was Oliver.

Evelin: - 'Where were you? We were already very worried about you!': - She asked desperately.

Oliver: - 'Oh man! Where have you been for so long? You were absorbed like swill in the pig!': - He asked nervously.

James: -'Calm down guys! I'm here aren't I! It's okay for you to worry, but don't worry unnecessarily, okay!': - He answered with a half-smile. Evelin did not let all this rest; she knew that something was wrong. School was over and the students were getting ready to go home. Almost everyone on the hallways was talking about that certain bad thing and the coming of darkness, so what they feared with the teacher came true, that the forgetting magic didn't work, someone deliberately wants to make everyone aware of this, its confirmed. They arrived at the bookstore where the mages were already waiting for them.

Mr. Tregas: - 'Finally, that you are here! I have something very important to announce to you!': - He received them impatiently.

James: - 'Yes, we know!! Everyone is already talking about this at school!': - He answered suddenly.

Mr. Tregas: - 'What do they talk about at school, my son??': - He asked surprisingly.

Oliver: - 'About the coming of something dark and that the evil ...'

Mr. Tregas: - 'So the news has already arrived! This is spreading faster than I thought!': - He took hold of his beard thoughtfully.

Evelin: - 'What do you mean that it spreads faster than you thought? Is it true then? I thought it was just a bad joke!': - She asked dejectedly.

Mr. Tregas: - 'Unfortunately, it's not a bad joke! It's all true what you heard at school today! The big question here is why all this is happening, why we are back where we were a few months ago! The difference is that we have magical powers, but how long will it be like this is the big question!': - He said desperately, stroking his beard.

Hanna: - 'I think she just wants to scare us so that we know where our place is!': - He said in between.

James: - 'I agree with that too!': - He replied.

Mr. Monghur: - 'I hope you are right!': - He interrupted.

John: - 'I don't think there's anything bad to fear, come and see the costumes to see how they turned out.': - He diverted their attention for a while.

Mr Tregas: - 'Yes, yes, look at the costumes!':- He said thoughtfully and headed upstairs.

Oliver: - 'I don't know why you're there like that, it's just a rumour, doesn't mean it's true, you've believed everything you hear, that's it!': - He interrupted, shaking his head.

Evelin: - 'James! Tell me what you talked about at school with Mrs. Embrin?': - She asked curiously.

James: -'How do you know I talked to her? Oh yes, I think from where, someone could have listened to us, I think he spread what he heard at school based on what he heard.'

Evelin: -'Yes James! But I don't understand why you are hiding this from me! Maybe you don't trust me? The three of us came here together, remember? We've already been through a lot together, I feel that you could only honour me with your trust.': - She said sadly and wanted to leave with that, but James caught up with her.

James: - 'Evelin wait! It's not that I don't trust you, on the contrary, I do ... it's that if I tell you anything, I'm afraid that the evil witch will get into your thoughts and then find out everything from you, unfortunately even if it's a protective shield I would also cast a spell on you, it's not sure that it would protect you completely, since you are not wizards, you cannot hold the power of the spell like me, I'm very sorry Evelin, I would have liked to tell you, but I couldn't.':- He replied dejectedly.

James: - 'But what Mr. Tregas said is all true, the darkness will come again, is better if you only know this much, please trust me.': - He said sincerely and hugged her.

Evelin: -' It's fine James, I believe you and I trust you; I think you know what you're doing.': - She hugged him back reassuringly. The mages and wizards still showed no signs that their powers were gone, they were still able to cast spells, which was reassuring to them on some level. The good friends tried on their costumes, and everyone liked them very much and were completely satisfied. So, the Carnival ball arrived, everyone was very excited about it, because the locals here really liked this kind of celebration, the streets and houses were decorated in honour of the celebration. The young people were getting ready in the big ballroom that was held in the castle town. At the carnival ball, all participants can nominate someone who will be the king and queen of the carnival, in addition to the raffles, there will be smaller prizes. The costumes were related to the carnival, according to local custom, people dressed up as kings and queens, princes, princesses, clowns, cooks, vegetables, fruits, or wizards. Most of the decorations were vegetables, fruits, crowns, and jewels decorated the houses and the town hall ... Everyone had already arrived for the evening entertainment, the road leading towards to the town hall was a beautiful sight and the town hall itself was also very beautiful.

Evelin wore a princess dress and looked beautiful in it. James wore a royal outfit, Hanna wore a queen outfit, Oliver wore a military outfit with a dragon shield and Jessy dressed as a mage, everyone looked very good in their outfits. The leader of the ball was, of course, the president of the town hall, whose name was Mr. Vinthus Almer.

Mr. Almer: -'I wish everyone a good evening! I would also like to welcome our new residents, as this is their first carnival ball here. During the evening, in accordance with local customs, there will be a raffle, in which we will give these gifts to each winner. (He pointed to a table full to the brim) After that, there will be games that can be played to win prizes, but last but not least, there will be the election of the king and queen. The lucky winner of this title will receive a free evening at Brontus!' Everyone starts cheering after hearing this, because it is one of the best restaurants in town.

Mr. Almer: 'Attention! Attention! The evening's king and queen election will take place at midnight! In the meantime, I wish everyone who comes here a pleasant evening and have fun!': - He announced the important events of the evening. James went to the bathroom, when he entered the door, the little goblin appeared.

Bonty: - 'James! You need to get out of here immediately! The evil darkness has arrived! Get out of here immediately!': - He warned in despair.

James: -'What are you talking about? When does darkness come? And what will happen to the others?': - He asked surprised.

Bonty: - 'You must leave here immediately! Go to the library to the secret place, you will be safe there!': - He warned again. With that, the goblin disappeared. James suddenly didn't even know what to do, because the party was in full swing out there, it must have been around ten o'clock, the party started at nine in the evening. he finished his business in the washroom and went outside to speak to Mr Tregas about it. He tried to push himself through the dancing crowd and suddenly someone pulled him back, that someone was Evelin.

Evelin: - 'James! Where have you all been looking for you? Dance with Me! The atmosphere is very good, I feel great! Come on!': - She called excitedly.

James: -'Evelin! I'll come right back and dance with you all night but first I have to talk to Mr. Tregas!': - He answered with a smile.

Evelin: - 'Okay! I will wait for you here! Don't be late!': - She replied smiling and gave him a kiss on the lips. James also returned the kiss, grabbed her by the waist and hugged her tightly and kissed her. James looked deeply into Evelin's eyes and smiled to himself then he went to speak to Mr. Tregas. Evelin got so excited that she raised both her hands in joy and started spinning around, laughing and dancing.

James: -'Mr. Tregas! We need to talk right away!': - He spoke seriously.

Mr. Tregas: - 'The time has finally come! Come, let's go to a quieter place!': - He said seriously. They went upstairs to an office where they were sure that no one would disturb them. When they left the room, James' father noticed that they were leaving the room, so he secretly followed them to see where they were going. They entered the office, closed the door and sat down to discuss important matters. In the meantime, James' father also came to the office and started listening.

Mr. Tregas: - 'James my child! Pay close attention to what I'm going to tell you. The evil darkness is coming here tonight, I don't know what it will bring with it, but I'm sure it won't be good either. We have to plan how to save these people and where they will be safe. Yesterday in the library I read a book about what this crystal can do if it falls into evil hands, and what I learned about it was creepy. If we don't do something about it right now, everything and everyone here will disappear from the face of the earth.': - He said nervously.

James: - 'Yes, I know about it! We must warn everyone about this, and the carnival ball must be cancelled immediately, because human lives are at stake here. However, I would like to know where the crystal comes from.': - He was interested.

Mr. Tregas: - 'The crystal was forged by our ancestors in the depths of a cave very far away from here. Back then, that cave was full of all kinds of crystals. But there was a special crystal that was dug up from the depths of the earth, even when it was dug up it had such a huge light that it blinded everyone, they quickly threw something at it so that they could see. The mages and witches of that time began to study this crystal in a strictly secret place and, of course, with protective glasses. But before they could see it for his study, they put on their protective glasses and were able to see the crystal itself, what it really looked like. Then and now, the scribe was always there and wrote down everything about what happened and drew it so that the next generation would know about it. So, when they put on the goggles, they only noticed that it wasn't just any crystal, they didn't even have to study it, because they immediately knew that it could be dangerous and could even be used for good. This crystal was hidden deep underground by the goblins so that no one would find it. Back then, goblins and mages and witches worked together. The goblins had that particular crystal, they didn't talk about it because they were aware of the crystal's power and didn't want it to fall into the wrong hands, they rather hid it well, but apparently not well enough. The people who found it were curious about what kind of crystal it was that glowed so beautifully, so they didn't leave it at that and constantly harassed the magicians and witches about it to get an answer and of course they demanded back what they found. At that time, they brought together a big meeting with mages, witches and goblins to figure out what to do and tell people not to give the crystal to them. Then the goblins said that they would now take it to a place where no one would be able to get to it again, so they took her to the depths of the ocean and the goblins developed a protective shield that even mages and witches couldn't break through with their magic, since that was the goal. But then, when all this happened, people had to invent something and even show them, of course, so that they would believe it and not deal with the crystal anymore, so they invented a lie, showed them a special crystal that was completely different from the original, and luckily for them, they believed and accepted it. Therefore, it was quickly forgotten, so the crystal lay peacefully at the bottom of the ocean until now. However, the evil witch managed to get it somehow, because as we have seen, her power is unsurpassed. Well James we have to go back and stop the ball immediately and send everyone to a safe place if we want to save them.': - He finished what he was saying.

James: -'Mr. Tregas! This was a very interesting story, I completely agree that the ball should be stopped immediately, let's go right now.': - He answered excitedly. When he opened the door, he caught his father because he couldn't leave in time.

James: - 'Dad! Were you listening?': - He asked in surprise.

John: -'I'm sorry, son, but I followed you, and while I'm...'

Mr. Tregas: - 'There is nothing wrong! Come on, we need to act immediately, you can help if you already know everything.': - He hurried them.

John: - 'All right! I'll help in anything I can! Come on!' They ran down the stairs, of course Mr. Tregas couldn't keep up with them because he was already old, so he used his magic and overtook them.

Mr. Tregas went on stage and took the microphone, but in the meantime James and John told the people in line to leave the room and go to safety.

Mr. Tregas: -'Attention! Attention! I would like to ask those gathered here to leave the town hall immediately. I'm closing the ball with immediate effect here and now it's over. I ask everyone to go home and put yourselves in a safe place. Unfortunately, the evil darkness will arrive here soon and then it will be too late to do anything. Thank you for your attention, now home immediately.': - He warned the people. The people were outraged by what was said, but everyone started to put on their coats and were ready to go home. Yes, but there were a few who didn't agree with that, they didn't even want to go home, they wanted to stay there to continue partying and enjoying the carnival ball. Mr. Tregas couldn't talk them out of it, so they stayed there at their own risk, twenty people stayed at the ball, they didn't want to go home, and they weren't even willing to. This all happened at 10:48. By the time the large hall was empty, it was 11:37 minutes, people did not go out faster because they had to stand in line for coats, so it all took time. Of course, the twenty people who refused to go home continued to have fun. People went home and hid in their safe place, as every house had a safe place, if something bad was coming, they should have a place of refuge. But in this great effort and haste, James forgot to mention to Mr. Tregas whether everyone should go to the secret room in the library, of course the mages and James and his friends all went there, but the townspeople hid in their own houses. The people who stayed there, who continued to have fun at the ball, didn't even care about the impending danger, at least for them what Mr. Tregas said was unbelievable. The time showed 11:59.

Teenager 1: - 'Attention! Attention! It won't be long before the election of the king and queen! There is only one minute left!': - He announced on stage with great joy. The others cheered and clapped.

Teenager 2: - 'Yes! Yes! Let's draw a winner!': - He shouted. As soon as he said this, the evil darkness arrived and everything was covered by endless darkness, and at that moment those who remained there suddenly all disappeared. The people, who were hiding in their houses, terrified and full of fear, waiting for the long-awaited darkness to pass, unfortunately everyone was taken away and not a single soul was left there. Everyone disappeared from the face of the earth. Not only people but also animals. Nobody in Devilus' kingdom was hurt. The explanation for this is that his vow and promise to Miriam protected the kingdom and it is also due to the fact that Gilbert was Miriam's husband. Gilbert knew nothing of it all, as Miriam had told him nothing of it. What's more, what's most interesting is that he didn't know how to find out, since he lived there with Miriam, they didn't go out of the palace right, so Miriam did whatever she wanted. King Devilus didn't notice any of it either, since they were completely covered by darkness. The goblin appeared to James again and called him aside where no one could see them.

Bonty: - 'James! I'm very sorry for what happened! But I'm glad that you're safe.': - He said happily.

James: -'I don't understand this now! What are you sorry for? After all, we told everyone and everyone went home to their safe place, only a few stayed in the town hall because they were not willing to go home.': - He answered confused.

Bonty: - 'James! Everyone wouldn't have fit in here anyway, you know that, in order to save everyone they should have been brought here instead of hiding in their own houses, no one is safe there.': - He replied sadly.

James: - 'Are you saying that the people who stayed outside or hid have all disappeared?': - He asked indignantly.

Bonty: - 'Tsh! Tsh! Quietly, they might still hear us, and then we will be caught. Yes James! Unfortunately, everyone has disappeared and only the evil witch knows where she has put them.': - He replied sadly.

James: - 'That was enough!': - He spoke loudly. Everyone turned their attention to James.

John: - 'Son! Is everything okay?': - He asked in despair.

James: - 'Oh, yes! Of course, everything is fine, I was just thinking out loud!': - He answered suddenly.

James: - 'Bonty! Bonty! Please come forward, let's talk about this calmly!': - He asked. But the goblin didn't show up because it wasn't safe since quite a few people turned their attention to James.

Evelin: - 'James! Are you okay? I'm afraid! What should we do now? Is everything okay with everyone else out there? Why doesn't anyone say anything?': - She asked in despair.

James: - 'Everything is fine, I hope!': - He replied depressingly and hugged Evelin, pulled her to him and they sat down on the floor close to each other.

Oliver: -'someone say something! What the hell is going on here?

When can we finally go out? How long do we have to stay here?':
- He asked nervously.

Mr. Tregas: - 'Pay close attention to what I am going to say now!
What just happened out there is very sad, those who were out
there unfortunately all disappeared from the face of the earth, not
only the people but also the animals.'

Oliver: -'Not everyone! Those people who hid in their own
homes are still there!': - He interrupted.

Mr. Tregas: - 'Oliver!...... Those people who hid in their own
houses, unfortunately they also disappeared.': - He answered
sadly.

Oliver: - 'What!!! How?? What is he talking about? They couldn't
have just disappeared if they were safe? Isn't it true?': - He asked
indignantly. James noticed something that Mr. Tregas said that
for a moment he was suspicious of all this.

Mr. Tregas: - 'I'm very sorry, people, but this is the only place
where we can be safe, no one is safe anywhere else on earth.':-
He answered breathlessly.

Oliver: -'You tricked everyone at the ball, didn't you? How can
you be so heartless! Why didn't you do something about it to stop
it, then Jessy disappeared along with everyone else!!!': - He
yelled nervously.

Mr. Tregas: - 'I'm sorry! I'm really sorry!': - He answered with
his head down.

Oliver: - 'Well, you can be sorry all you want! A heartless old
man!': - He shouted angrily.

John: - 'Calm down, Oliver! There must be some solution to this,
isn't there?': - He reassured him.

Oliver: -'What would be the solution to this? They are not doing
anything about it, don't you see!!!': - He shouted angrily.

James: -'Oliver! Come here with us for a while!!': - He took his arm and tried to calm him down.

Oliver: -'I'm not going anywhere!! Let me out of here immediately, I don't want to stay here for a minute longer.': - He yelled angrily.

Mr. Zathen: - 'Unfortunately, we can't open the door yet, only in the morning, until then we have to spend the night here.': - He replied calmly.

Oliver: - 'And I won't stay here with you for even a minute longer!!!': - He howled angrily and tried to open the door without much success of course. He collapsed on the ground and started sobbing from the sadness and pain he felt in his heart. He was very angry with everyone, he blamed everyone for what happened, he didn't want to talk to anyone, he went aside alone and lay down on the ground and sobbed. Unfortunately, they couldn't open the door for him, because then they too would suffer the same fate as the others, having to wait for the morning. Everyone tried to rest as much as possible because everyone was scared and angry about what happened. James and Evelin slept next to each other, at least James tried but no dream came to his eyes. He kept thinking about what Mr. Tregas said and thought about it until he solved the mystery. The next morning when everyone woke up Mr. Vinthus opened the door, at this sound the Oliver immediately woke up and jumped up and was already outside the door with that movement. He ran out of the building straight to Jessy 's house and immediately knocked on their door. He waited for a while and then knocked again and only knocked. In despair, he sat down on the stairs and started to cry, as he was sitting on the steps and crying, behind him, he noticed a door opening, he immediately turned back, and Jessy and her family stood at the door. Oliver jumped up from the ground and jumped on Jessy's with one movement. They were very happy for each other, hugged each other for a long time and then invited Oliver into the house.

Oliver:- 'I don't understand this!! How, how!! My God, I can't believe it! I must be dreaming!': - He said hesitantly.

Mr. Derras: - 'Oliver! You're not dreaming, it's real! We are here, we didn't disappear!' And five more families came to the room because they also escaped to Mr. Derras' safe bunker.

Mr. Derras: - 'You know, Oliver, I built a safe bunker under our house for cases like this, I read a lot about our ancestors and their culture and their deeds, so I like to keep my family safe. That's why I was able to save these people, but unfortunately not anymore because the bunker can only accommodate two families.

Oliver: - 'Well, there are more than two families here!!': - He said surprisingly.

Mr. Derras: - 'Yes! There are really more of us, we pulled together a bit and now we are here.': - He answered with a smile. Oliver was both happy and at the same time very angry because why didn't the magicians do what Jessy's parents did for others.

Jessy: - 'Oliver! Come on, let's go and look for more survivors, to see if there are others who survived this!': - She asked kindly.

Oliver: - 'Of course I'm going! We can go!': - He answered proudly and calmly.

Mr. Derras: - 'Take care of each other!': - He spoke after them.

Oliver: - 'We will Mr. Derras! See you later!: - He said Goodbye. So, they set off and knocked from house to house to see who had survived this disaster. In the evening, they returned to Jessy 's house and sat down to dinner.

Mr. Derras: - 'How many survived?'

Oliver: - 'Well, we managed to count 400, but unfortunately the others did not survive.': - He answered breathlessly.

Jessy: - 'Listen Oliver! I think something is wrong here, because I was thinking that if the others are not here, where are they anyway? They didn't just vanish off the face of the earth. I think the wicked witch hid them somewhere! It's only me who thinks this way, of course, what do you think?': - She asked.

Oliver: - 'I don't know what to say, but I think that there is certainly something wrong here! I have to go back to the others now, but we'll meet and talk tomorrow, okay!': - He said goodbye. During this time, the others also searched the population to find out how many survived this disaster and they also counted 400 people. Everyone was in despair as to what this was about, and everyone wanted answers to what happened. People lived in fear, they didn't dare to go out into the street, the city and the surrounding towns and villages seemed to have died out, but the people who survived were afraid to go out of their homes, which was completely understandable. James was constantly wondering why Miriam did this when she already got everything she wanted, what was the point of all this, what did she want to prove? These thoughts tormented him and did not let him rest, he kept walking up and down in the library without even a minute's rest. As he was walking, in the midst of great thinking, he found himself where he first arrived here in this world. He was standing at the door where there was that certain big book in the room that he couldn't open, he suddenly stopped and started to think, he tried to open the handle but of course the door was locked. James had an idea, so he went to Mr. Monghur to ask for the key to the door.

James: -'Mr. Monghur! Ahem, ahem ... (he sharpened his voice), I would like to ask for the key to the door where that big book is in that big room, you know what I couldn't open!?!': - He asked.

Mr. Monghur: - 'Oh yes! Of course, I know, yes, but why would you go in there, there's nothing there except the book.': - He answered surprisingly.

James: - 'Yes, yes! But I still want to go in to look at that book if it's not a problem?!':- He asked.

Mr. Monghur: - 'Alright then! I'll give you the key, but when you're done, I'd like it back right away, okay?!': - He answered with a little attention.

James: - 'All right Mr. Monghur! I'll bring the key back afterwards!': - He said with joy. With that he took the key and started walking towards the door, but someone followed James, so he is not alone. When he got to the door, he inserted the key and turned the lock and the door opened, he entered the room and the book was there on the table, closed. He stepped closer to the book and felt a great urge to open that book. He put his hand on the book and stroked it all over, and the mushrooms that decorated the cover of the book started talking about James. The person who followed him hid in a shadowy corner so that James couldn't see him, and of course he didn't even hear that he was there. While caressing the cover of the book, James finally took hold of the cover and opened the book, but as he opened the book he closed his eyes, the book opened and James opened his eyes, he slowly began to look down at the book, only he could heard the humming of the little mushrooms no one else, of course, they didn't stop what they were saying, they just kept humming and humming, when he finally looked down at the book, the letters were there, all the ones he hadn't seen before. James watched with wide eyes and couldn't believe what he was seeing, at first, he rubbed his eyes, thinking that his eyes were just dazzled, but the letters were really there. That someone hiding in the dark was none other than Mr. Monghur, when he saw this, he immediately came out of hiding.

Mr. Monghur: - 'Well, this is incredible!! James how is it possible that you can see the letters in it?': - He asked suddenly. James was a little scared because he didn't expect anyone, he thought he would be there alone.

James: -'Oh my god, Mr. Monghur!! You scared the crap out of me! I don't know how the letters appeared in it, but here they are clear as day.': - He answered proudly. Mr. Monghur walked over to James, and he took a closer look at the book so he could finally see what was inside. But when he looked at it, he didn't see anything in it, the pages were empty just like before. He frowned and didn't understand why the pages were blank, since James said the letters were there clear as day.

Mr. Monghur: - 'James! Are you looking at the letters now?': - He asked curiously.

James: -'Yes, of course I can see the letters! Why don't you see them yourself?': - He asked back with a smile.

Mr. Monghur: - 'No, I don't see them! There are only blank pages in front of me, nothing more.': - He answered breathlessly.

James: - 'That's weird! How can you not see the letters since they are here.':- He said in surprise.

Mr. Monghur: - 'Um, um!! That could mean something! Listen, my son, if you see the letters in the book, then tell me what is written on this page?': - He asked curiously.

James: - 'Here, for example, on this page (page 12) there is a drawing that depicts an underground cave, and next to the picture it says, "The only treasure that can keep good and bad in balance".: - He answered.

Mr. Monghur: - 'What exactly can be seen in that picture?': - He asked.

James: - 'There are rocky walls everywhere, the earth is dark brown and grey, but where this treasure is, there is dark green and dark purple and very dark blue earth.': - He answered.

Mr. Monghur: - 'I understand! That's just interesting!': - He muttered.

James: - 'Why, what does this mean?': - He asked curiously.

Mr. Monghur: - 'Well, in this place they found, a long time ago, the certain crystal that the goblins hid at the bottom of the ocean and the evil witch stole, which caused all this.': - He answered thoughtfully. Meanwhile, the mushrooms kept whispering to James, making him turn the pages of the book, and he began to turn the pages. When he got to page 24, he noticed something very interesting that made him smile. Mr. Monghur noticed James' smile immediately.

Mr. Monghur: - 'James! What did you find? Why are you smiling?': - He asked curiously. James looked at Mr. Monghur and began to dance in joy. Mr. Monghur didn't understand what was wrong with James all of a sudden, why he was dancing with joy.

Mr. Monghur: - 'James! What did you see on that page?': - He asked smiling.

James: -'Mr. Monghur! You won't believe what's on this page!!' Here is another drawing of a certain island with houses and people. Here in the writing, it says that the people whom the crystal dematerialized don't die but are teleported there, far from their home in a completely magic free zone.': - He answered happily.

Mr. Monghur: - 'Well, this is really interesting! And of course, good news indeed! But where is this island? Because I don't know of any island here in this world!': - He said in surprise. James's smile froze on his face and as he watched Mr. Monghur, he could not answer.

Mr. Monghur: - 'Okay then! We need to find out where this island is! And then we will find the people who disappeared as well.': - He said firmly.

James: - 'Yes, that's a good idea! But where can we find this island if there are no islands here in this world?': - He asked curiously.

Hanna: - 'This is not an island!! But a sphere.... these people are locked in a sphere from which there is no way out, only if Miriam lets them out of there and that seems impossible in this case!': - She interrupted.

Mr. Monghur: - 'How do you know all this?': - He asked curiously.

Hanna: - 'I followed you here and eavesdropped on your conversation, as soon as I came to the conclusion that while you were searching here, I used my magic power and it showed me this sphere where people are locked, it is in a well-guarded place in Miriam's room, where to enter is impossible.': - She answered firmly.

James: - 'And what if I could still get to in, after all, I'm her son, right?': - He asked.

Hanna: - 'You may be her son, but it is not yet certain that you will be able to get to this sphere, as I said before, it is in a very well-guarded place in her room.': - She answered.

Mr. Monghur: - 'Hmm! What James said is not such a bad idea! Even if you can't access the sphere, you can look around the room and find out how carefully it is guarded, and with this we can come up with some solution on how to get them out of there.': - He replied.

Hanna: - 'This could also be a solution to find out how securely she guards this sphere!': - She said thoughtfully.

James: -'Well, then we'll tell the others and I'll get ready right away so I can go there as soon as possible.': - He answered excitedly.

Mr. Monghur: - 'No! You leave now, Hanna and I will go back

and tell the others.'

James: - 'Okay then! Then I'm not even here anymore!': - He said goodbye to them.

James went back to his room to prepare his things for the trip, Hanna and Mr. Monghur went back to the others and told them what they found out and that James was preparing for the evil witch. James is putting the last of his things in his bag when the goblin appears.

Bonty: - 'James! I know that you are going to see your mother right now and why. Please pay close attention to what I am about to tell you. When you get to the palace and enter the gate, you will of course be greeted as always, but don't stop, just go straight to your room, no matter who stops you as soon as you cross the palace gate, don't stop until your room, even if your own mother is stopping you.': - He warned him seriously and disappeared before James could ask anything. He stood there dumbfounded, wondering why the goblin could have said that to him. James left the bookstore and was on his way to towards his mother's palace.

Oliver: - 'I don't understand this now! How is it possible to enclose people in such a sphere? Why would someone do that?': - He asked confused.

Mr. Vinthus: - 'This is all the work of the crystals power and this is just the beginning, a small taste of what this crystal is capable of, if we don't get it back and put it back in its place, a disaster will break out here and then we won't be able to talk together here anymore because then there will be nowhere to run away and hide because what we just experienced was just a small taste of it, I hope everyone understood this.':- He interrupted a little angrily.

Mr. Ambeth: - 'Okay! Everyone should calm down and let's calmly think about all this, what and how we will solve this together!': - He calmly interrupted.

Evelin: -'Mr. Ambeth is right! We need to calm down in order to find a solution together, don't we!': - She said in a slightly trembling voice.

Oliver: - 'And yet, how do you want to fix this, if this crystal has so much power and is also in the possession of the evil witch, ha, ha!!! How are you going to get it back, James just walks over there and just takes it and brings it to us? Well, it's not that simple! I hope you see this as well where ...'

Hanna: - 'Oliver!! You are a genius! While you were arguing about how to get the crystal back, I flipped through a few books and what did I find??? So!'

Oliver: - 'So what did you find, a lottery jackpot? Phh, phh!': - He said puffing.

Hanna: - 'Yes, Oliver! Believe it or not , it's a jackpot. Look at what it says in this book.': - She continued what she was saying. Hanna showed everyone what was written about the crystal in that book.

Oliver: - 'Now, not to make a fuss, but wasn't it the case that all the books about the crystal disappeared? Then how is it here?': - He asked surprisingly.

Hanna: - 'Oliver, this book is mine and it was here at the bottom of my bag, I was looking for something in it and I found it, so I quickly looked for the important thing to know, for which you should be grateful now.': - She answered.

Mr. Tregas: - 'So here we have to focus on the fact that what he writes here can only be good for us, but unfortunately we can't tell this to James because he's already making his way to the palace, that's why I'm writing a ....' And he didn't finish the sentence because he remembered that he couldn't send a message to James, since all the animals on earth were inside the sphere.

Oliver: - 'Yes, Mr. Tregas! What did you want to write?': - He asked curiously.

Mr. Tregas: - 'Nothing! I don't want to write anything anymore! We can't message James even with the fairies, because if they come to the surface from there, they immediately disappear in the sphere and they know this very well, that's why we have no chance to message James in any way.': - He said in despair.

Bonty: - 'But yes there is!!!': - He interrupted.

Suddenly, everyone looked at the goblin and watched him with their mouths agape in deep silence, how did he get there and how does he know about everything.

Bonty: - 'I would like to introduce myself first, my name is Bonty, and I am here because I got permission from my boss to help people once again, because as we can see here, you need help. I have already spoken to James and told him what he needs to know, so I ask you not to worry about him.

Mr. Tregas: - 'It is an honour to see you here! I would like to thank you for alerting James to everything for which we are very grateful and thank you. What can we do to help?': - He asked with a smile.

Bonty: - 'A very kind gesture from you, Mr. Tregas, but I have to go back, I still have a lot to do.': - He answered and then disappeared.

Oliver: - 'That's a joke!! I could imagine such a goblin as my helper!': - He said with a smile.

Evelin: - 'Oliver! Please, won't you be a little quiet, please!': - She asked a little nervously.

John: - 'Good! Then if James knows what to do, it's a bit reassuring, isn't it?': - He said nervously.

Mr. Zathen: - 'I think we wait for the end and then we get to be angry afterwards if something doesn't work out as we hoped. I think everyone is occupying themselves with something until James returns.': - He said soothingly. Everyone accepted Mr. Zathen's advice and they went to find something to do. Evelin and Hanna went home, and Oliver went to Jessy's.

Evelin: - 'Hanna! Do you think James will succeed in getting the ....' Hanna suddenly covered Evelin's mouth so she wouldn't say anything. Evelin suddenly didn't understand why she kept her mouth shut, but she didn't say a word after that. Hanna wrote on a piece of paper telling Evelin not to say a word out loud about anything they talked about in the secret place, because words are not safe out here and whatever they say, the witch is sure to find out. Evelin nodded and corrected herself.

Evelin: - 'So do you think James will succeed in getting his mother's love? I mean, does she love James enough, after not seeing him for so many years and because she didn't raise him, I don't think it's going to happen overnight to win back someone's love.': - She asked breathlessly...

Hanna: - 'I think time will solve everything for us, because the bond between a mother and her child is stronger than anything in the world, it can overcome anything.': - She answered with a smile.

These words that were spoken between Evelin and Hanna naturally reached Miriam as well and hearing these words something great happened in Miriam that had never happened before, she even sat down on the chair because they were very heartfelt words, as she sat there on the chair something changed in her a for a minute. But the evil mushrooms that lived in her did not let the good feelings get the better of her. That's why the good feelings didn't affect her for long, she got up from her chair and went on with her head held high and did what she was doing at the moment, boiling evil. The evil mushrooms slowly ate up Miriam's mind, she was already treating the one she loved very much, Gilbert, badly. Gilbert was a little scared to see this, but he accepted that he was just tired and had a lot to do, so he let her do what she saw fit. James was already close to the palace, he was very anxious not to do something wrong, so he thought everything through and made good progress towards his goal. Finally, he reached the palace and just as Bonty told him, everyone greeted him kindly and tried to talk to him and ask him questions, but James tried to go on and not pay attention to what was asked of him. Gilbert also went over to him and greeted James and even hugged him.

Gilbert: - 'James! It's good that you're again! We can finally have a good chat and we can go fishing if you want! At least we have something to occupy ourselves with! We do whatever you want!': - He said very happily. James could not resist this and looked into Gibert's eyes and stopped. He put down his bag and returned the hug and said with a happy smile.

James: -'Welcome Gilbert! It's good to be here again and to see you! Yes, we can go fishing right away if you want?': - He replied very happily. Gilbert waved and the servants immediately took his luggage to his room. Gilbert hugged him and they already went fishing to the river. This was the biggest mistake that James made by talking to Gilbert, although he shouldn't have talked to anyone or Gilbert, but because he did it now James also fell into the trap of one of the special powers of the crystal, as once someone steps through the door of Miriam's palace and mingles with whoever they talk to, they are instantly enchanted and there is no way back from that, only Miriam can help with this. Of course, Miriam watched all of this as James walked into the trap, and she was filled with joy because her mind was so overwhelmed by the magic mushroom that she didn't have much control of her goodness left. Bonty watched all of this, of course, invisibly, and suddenly became very sad that the plan had not been carried out, so he went back to the Head of the goblins.

Bonty: - 'Menthis! I regret to share the bad news that our plan has failed.': - He said kneeling down, and head down.

Menthis: -'All is not lost yet! This can still be fixed!': - He stood up from his chair and said firmly.

Menthis: - 'Get up immediately and go back to the palace and make him go back to his room, go!': - He said in a raised voice, firmly.

Bonty: - 'Yes, will do sire!': - He answered with his head still down. Bonty stood up and immediately went back to James, invisible of course. James was busy with his fishing rod to rig it up ready for fishing. Gilbert was also busy fitting the fishing rod and humming as he was happy to have James with him. Bonty took advantage of the moment that Gilbert wasn't paying attention and was humming, so he quickly whispered an important message in James's ear, invisibly of course. James looked up to see who was talking to him, but of course he didn't see anyone. Because he was enchanted, he also forgot that he has a goblin named Bonty who is trying to help him. Bonty was aware of this, so he whispered in his ear once again, but this time much more decisively and convincingly than before, he knew that it had to succeed, because if it didn't, then it was all over. James noticed again who was whispering in his ear, but he didn't see anyone. Gilbert happened to glance at James and saw that he was looking around as if he was looking for someone.

Gilbert: - 'James! Everything all right? Are you looking for someone or something?': - He asked with a smile.

James: -'No, no! It's just that the place is very beautiful, and I was just looking at why we haven't come out here to fish before.': - He answered smartly. All this fishing was just an illusion, even though there were no fish in the river, they disappeared from the surface of the earth like all animals, but because of the spell they still saw the fish like all other animals. The fact that James did not tell the truth to Gilbert is because Bonty's words were only effective for James.

James: - 'Gilbert! If you'll excuse me for a little while, I forgot to take something out of my bag that I intended for this occasion, I'll go get it and I'll be back in no time, okay?': - He said smiling.

Gilbert: -'Alright then! But hurry if you don't want me to catch all the fish!': - He said laughing.

James: - 'Okay then! I'll Hurry back and leave some fish for me too.': - He said back laughing. He was about to leave when Miriam appeared.

Miriam: -'Oh, you're here! I've been looking all over for you! Hello dear James! It's good to see you here again!': - She greeted him with a smile, and she hugged him. This was the biggest mistake that could happen by hugging James, the only consequence was that James was under a spell again, but this time not just any spell, even the goblin can't get him out of it.

James: -'Oh Miriam! It's good to see you again! We're just hanging out with Gilbert, but I don't even know why I got up from here anymore... it's not that important anymore, let's continue where we left off Gilbert!': - He answered with a smile. With that, he sat back where he had been and completely forgot why he got up from there and where he should've gone back to. Bonty became very angry and unfortunately had to go back to report on what happened.

Bonty: -'Menthis! I'm very sorry, but the evil witch must have sensed something, because when she was about to go back to her room, suddenly she appeared out of nowhere and so the plan had failed.': - He said, bowing his head sadly.

Menthis: - 'Hmm! Hmm! Let me think! Summon Gorth here immediately!': - He issued an immediate order. What you need to know about this Gorth is that he is one of the oldest goblins and one of the wisest, he has special magic powers so he can help with this problem.

Gorth: -'Menthis! You called me!!'

Menthis: - 'Yes! I called you here because you need to fix an important matter. Unfortunately, James has been captured by the power of the crystal, so I need you to help him carry out his task.': - He issued an order.

Gorth: - 'I understand! Hmm, let me think about that for a minute! Aaaah! I know what to do! The plan is as follows.......' James and Gilbert had a lot of fun, and the time passed so much with the fishing that it was dinner time, so they went back to the palace. Everyone was already sitting at the table, so they were the last two. When everyone had dinner, they left the room.

Gilbert: -'Well today was a very good day, James! We could repeat this tomorrow!': - He said very happily.

James: -'I agree with that too! Tomorrow we can go fishing again, but now let's go somewhere else, let's not go back to that lake again.': - He replied happily.

Gilbert: - 'It's fine! We go where you want! Get some rest for tomorrow!': - He shouted after him with a smile.

James: - 'Will do!!': - He shouted back.

James was walking towards his room to go to bed, he opened the door and went in, he closed the door and hummed happily and started to change. The invisible goblin was already waiting for him in the room. As soon as James sat on the bed, the goblin began to recite a special spell on him to lift the enchantment. The goblin was successful, so James suddenly looked at the stone and did not know how he got there, because it was already dark outside and when he arrived it was still broad daylight.

James: -'How did I get here so late? What happened to the rest of the day? I don't understand this?': - He asked himself, shocked.

Gorth: -'Hi James! I'm here by your side, don't be scared, you can't see me because it's dangerous. I was sent to help you! Now pay close attention to what I say, your mission failed at first, it's dark because you were under the power of the charm, but don't worry because it's not too late to fix this. The plan will be as follows, I will read you a spell that can help you get the crystal and then you will have nothing else to do but take it home.': - He whispered in his ear.

James: - 'It's okay! I'm ready.': - He answered quietly. The goblin read the special spell on him and with that he disappeared. Miriam and Gilbert were still walking outside in their huge garden, talking. During this time, James sneaked into Miriam's room to get the crystal, but the crystal was so protected that it wasn't that easy to get. As soon as he went near the crystal, it cast such a strong spell on James that the special spell was immediately released and James was again under the enchantment to such an extent that this time the little mushrooms left James' ears, and they left the palace and made their way to the goblins for help. James went back to his room because he wondered what he was doing in Miriam's room, so he went back to his own to finally go to bed and rest. The next morning, Evelin, Hanna and Oliver went to have breakfast in the bookstore, they hoped that James would be there too.

Mr. Tregas: -'Good morning children! Come for breakfast, it's already laid, come inside.': - He invited them in a little sadly. The good friends already knew that James was not there yet, so Evelin started to worry.

Evelin: - 'Hanna, I have a very bad feeling, I don't think James is here yet, maybe he didn't succeed in completing his mission.'

Hanna: -'Don't worry! Maybe he will join us a bit later. But I have an idea to find out if everything is okay with James, come with me.': - He answered excitedly.

Evelin: - 'Okay! Let's go!': - She answered excitedly.

They went upstairs where they could safely cast spells. They sat in a room and Hanna began to work her magic.

Spell to find a person: -

SEMERITUM SHOWHUM!

PERSONTUM ACTIVE!

IMEDIUM PLACEITUM!

When she finished the spell, nothing happened because it had no effect.

Hanna: -'I don't understand this! This should work but nothing happened! Something is wrong.': - She said worriedly.

Evelin: - 'Try again, maybe it will work this time!': - She said encouragingly.

Hanna: - 'I won't lose anything by saying it again, right?': - She asked a little nervously.

Spell: -

SEMERITUM SHOWHUM!

PERSONTIUM ACTIVE!

IMEDIUM PLACEITUM!

She said it once more, but much more passionately than before, but it had no effect either. At that point, the two girls started to worry a lot.

Hanna: - 'This is very strange!': - She said in deep thought.

Evelin: - 'Is there something wrong?': - She asked in despair.

Hanna: -'Yes, we have a big problem!': - She answered nervously and with that momentum she pulled open the door and started running downstairs to the others. Of course, Evelin ran after her, terrified.

Evelin: -' Hanna! Wait! Where are you running to? What's wrong?': - She asked breathlessly.

Hanna: - 'You'll find out soon!': - She answered panting. They entered the room where everyone was waiting for them at the table. When they entered the room, everyone fixed their sad eyes on them and as they were sitting in silence, they didn't say a word, waiting for them to finally sit down at the table. They took a seat and Evelin already knew from the sad looks that there was big trouble here.

Mr. Tregas: -'Well, now that everyone is here, before we start having breakfast, I would like to announce to you that James failed, our plan did not work. He is stuck there in the palace, He's under a very strong enchantment, just like everyone else who stays inside the palace gates. But there is something else that is a very sad case, which is that we no longer have magic power, so James has no way out. The evil witch set this trap, as she already knew about everything and was prepared for our action. One of the oldest goblins was here with me and he let me know what happened to James, so we really have to stick together and work together. The Head of the goblins sent me a message that he will house the people who are left for this critical situation in the hidden world of the goblins until we find a solution. The remaining people already know about it, so we all have to be at the main square at 11:00 today to make this possible. The rest will be worked out together with the goblins. But now let's have breakfast.': - He announced the important things to know. Evelin and Hanna looked at each other and could not say a word because they were both in doubt that the evil witch had so much control over their world. King Devilus was very happy in his kingdom, because they were not harmed there, but the charm spread there too because he was not left out of it either. The mushrooms who escaped from James' ear climbed into the ear of the head goblin and asked him for help, that's why he made the decision to house the people who remained in the world of the goblins so that they wouldn't get hurt. The time had come for people to move down in the world of goblins, everyone was already there in the main square, they were just waiting for the right time.

Oliver: - 'What is happening here is not good! I hope that they will find some kind of solution to this and that this will all stop.' So, the time came, when the clock struck 11, everyone who was there in the main square disappeared at the same time, there was no one left. People were already there in the goblin world. Everyone already had their own little place where they will live for this temporary period. The cottages that were there consisted of three rooms, a living room, a kitchen, a toilet and a bathroom. The largest building was given to the mages together with the young people, which means that it had three floors and twenty rooms. This was the place where they gathered to discuss what to do next against the evil witch. There were a lot of goblins living there, at least two thousand of them, if not more. Each goblin had his own task, who did what, and they did their daily work very diligently. The chief of the goblins was in the main palace, who was just like a king. Even that day, the mages went to the head of the goblins to discuss what to do next.

Menthis: - 'Come inside!': - He invited them in kindly. Take a seat and we can even start the discussion.': - He invited them to the table. So, they sat down at the table and began the discussion.

Evelin and the others set out to discover the world of the goblins, which seemed quite interesting to them, since it was not a place like their world, everything here was different, the land, houses, trees, animals, water, everything had an interesting appearance. Miriam was so happy that she had finally put all of humanity under her feet that it was impossible to express it in words, of course Gilbert knew nothing of this and neither did James. Miriam went up to her room and took the crystal in her hand, placed it near the window and said:

Miriam: -'My crystal! I want complete darkness to reign on this earth, the Devilus kingdom to remain as it has been, everything else to perish!': - And she laughed very loudly, but so loudly that even King Devilus heard it. As soon as she said these words, the crystal immediately began to work and covered the earth in complete darkness, destroying all living things, nothing was left alive on the earth, only the bare earth, it even destroyed the houses. The two palaces were completely barren, of which the people living in the palace did not notice anything. From the barren, harsh darkness, the witch summoned monsters to keep order in case someone somehow strayed there. The sounds of the monsters were terrifying, but for whoever wandered in would surely not survive the blow caused by the monsters. She put the crystal back in its place, smiled and walked out of her room completely happy and joined her love and son as if nothing had happened. The sight of the Earth was frightening, that there was no life on it, only monsters roamed this god forsaken land, the sight was saddening. Miriam was under the control of evil to such an extent that it was quite difficult to get out of it.

Menthis: - 'So, I want to start this whole conversation by saying that you have to come up with a very good strategy......'

He couldn't finish what he was saying because one of the goblins who was his advisor whispered something in his ear. Until then, the others sitting at the table looked at each other and waited to see how this would end.

Menthis: - 'I'm sorry, but I received some very terrifying news! My counsellor just told me that the world above is completely destroyed, there is nothing above but darkness and the monsters that rule the darkness. This is very bad news, which we unfortunately expected, which is why it's good that we evacuated everyone here. The other bad news is that anyone who strays into the world above will surely die. Therefore, we have to come up with a very smart plan so that no one gets hurt.': - He spoke to those sitting at the table.

Mr. Tregas: - 'Well, this is very sad news, it must be said! But there's still something here that might help. Your goblin are lucky enough to have a special ability. Which means you can turn invisible, that means you can even go up there without anyone noticing you. Now, in my opinion, we should assemble an army and sneak into the witch's palace so that we can finally steal that crystal.': - He came up with a very clever idea.

Menthis: - 'Hmm! It's not such a bad idea as you say here! I'm already announcing their task to my goblins.': - He said with a smile. 'I will close the meeting, everyone can leave!': - He finished his speech. The head of the goblins called the councillor there and issued an order to call all the goblins together with immediate effect. The goblin councillor immediately took action on this matter. After an hour, the head of the goblins stood on the terrace and spoke to his goblins.

Menthis:- 'My dear goblins! I called you all here today because I have something important to say to you! The big situation is that everything in the world above has already been taken over by darkness, there is nothing up there but pure wasteland and the monsters of darkness, which have enormous power. Since we goblins cannot leave it like this, it is now our task to fix it and restore order to its original state. In the world above, the darkness is now ruled by the monsters of darkness, two kingdoms are left above under light. Well, since you know that we goblins can help with this, I ask everyone to prepare for war, because we are going to fight. But before we go into battle, the goblin delegates will go to the other clans and call for help from everywhere, because we will need all the help.': - He finished his speech.

Clans unites!

Envoys of the underground goblins went to ask for help, as the goblins formed four kinds of clans. The first kind were famous for their magical power, the second kind mastered the power of fire, the third kind mastered the power of water, and the fourth kind of goblin were famous for their fighting style. The four goblin clans didn't keep close relations with each other as their state of peace never required any of the clans to contact each other. The fairies haven't really had a rest since darkness descended on the land. They had a lot to do because of this, they worked day and night to prepare for the long-awaited battle. King Devilus calmly lived his everyday life, unaware of what was happening around him. In the two kingdoms, animals were given so that they would not lack anything, and Miriam made sure that it was so. The people locked in the small sphere were aware of what was happening with them, but they were safe, with the difference that they were worried about their companions who could not be there with them. Gilbert was very happy because the charm was already in full force and so that Miriam could work on her evil in peace. Miriam has created something so evil that it will be very difficult for anyone to defeat it. The evil mushrooms that were parasitizing in Miriam's ears gave her the evil magic power to continue what she started. James' little mushrooms were still in the ear of Menthis and they were working to make everything go their way. James also felt good in Miriam's palace, he had something to do every day. The day when the goblins set out to unite the clans and to also go looking for other help. James and Gilbert came up with a fun game, so Gilbert called the people in the palace together and announced the game.

Gilbert: - 'My dear friends! Today is a special day! My son and I would like to announce a game for you! Starting today, we will play this game once a week. This game will have to be played in a labyrinth, there will be three different types of balls that we will hide in the labyrinth. Of course, there will be traps and you will have to get through places that will not be easy. One ball will consist of glitter, the second ball will consist of flowers, and the third ball will consist of water. The maze will be full of surprises and illusions. There will be four teams that will be selected for this game, only those who are suitable for this game can start this game. The team as a whole will consist of 5 members, and the most important thing is that they have to pass the test first. The most important rule is that one team cannot help the other team under any circumstances, but if they do, they are eliminated. I hope that everyone understood the rules and essence of the game. So let the selection begin!': - He stated cheerfully. People liked the game, so many signed up for it. The selection process took a while, as the right people had to be sent to the game. The goblin's envoy arrived at the clan with the power of fire. The head of the fire goblins was a female called Fyrra.

Envoy goblin: - 'I welcome you Fyrra! I was sent to you by head Menthis for help, the time has come to unite against evil and reclaim the world above!': - He said, kneeling and bowing his head.

Fyrra: - 'I welcome you, messenger! Yes, I know why you came here, we already heard what happened up there, and my advisor and I already had a meeting before your arrival here. Go tell Menthis that we will join in the fight! Go now, take the news!': - She said firmly. The goblin envoy naturally bowed and left and tried to continue to the next clan. King Devilus arranged a great celebration in the palace. The king was so happy that he celebrated his birthday like never before. Everyone in the palace had to make sure everything was perfect. The king wanted to send a pigeon to his son to invite them to the celebration, but of course the king was not aware that if the pigeon flew out of the palace, it would not get far, as the monsters would immediately devour it. Of course, Miriam also sees what King Devilus is up to, so she told Gilbert.

Miriam: - 'Gilbert dear! Your father sent a pigeon in the palace with a message that we are invited for his birthday!': - She said with a smile.

Gilbert: -'Oh! That's great dear! Then let's get ready for the big celebration! I'm going to tell James about the good news, dear!': - He replied happily and kissed Miriam.

Miriam: - 'All right, dear! Tell James, I'll take care of the rest in the meantime.': - She said firmly. Gilbert slapped Miriam's bottom and left smiling. Miriam immediately set about the preparations for the trip, so that their journey would seem so that they would not notice anything from what the real world looks like now.

Gilbert knocked on the door of James's room and waited for

James to answer, but no one answered. Since he wasn't in his room, he looked for him in the palace, he could only be at the selection for the games. Well, he didn't have to search a lot because he was where he thought he was going to be at the game selection.

Gilbert: - 'James! It's good that you're here, I have something to say to you! A white dove just arrived with a message from my father that we are celebrating his birthday, I would like you to come with us.': - He made the message known.

James: - 'Ohh! I think that's good news! But if it's okay, I'd rather stay here and supervise the selection so that we can be ready on time! You just have a good time with Miriam, have a little fun because I think it suits you, I'll have fun here, and give my best wishes to the king.': - He answered excitedly.

Gilbert: - 'As you wish! But if you change your mind, come and tell me, okay?': - He asked with a smile.

James: - 'will do! I will definitely tell you!': - He answered with a smile. Gilbert went back to his room and told Miriam about James' decision.

Gilbert: - 'Honey! James decided not to go with us, he said he wanted to supervise the selection because he wanted to know everything was in order. He's a really resilient kid, you have to give it to him, he knows what he wants, I like that, he is determined, confident, smart.': - He said with a smile.

Miriam: -'Oh yes, of course! Our son is just like that, he has someone who he inherits from, isn't that right! It's okay if he doesn't come with us, he's doing well to occupy himself with something, if he likes to do that then we'll let him get on with it.': - She answered with a smile.

Gilbert: -'Yes dear! Come here to me, let me love you a bit.': - He called her to him and hugged her tightly and they kissed each other. The next day they set off for the ceremony in the palace. The way to the palace was as if nothing had happened to the outside world, Miriam made sure it was like that until they got there and, on the way, back, of course. Gilbert enjoyed the journey to the palace, just admiring everything and liking the sight. The journey to the palace takes them one day. During this time, the Goblin arrived at the second goblin clan for those with waterpower.

Envoy goblin: -'Greetings to you, Watim! I was sent to you by Chief Menthis for help, the time has come to unite against evil and reclaim the upper world!': - He said, kneeling down and bowing his head.

Watim: -'I welcome you, messenger! Yes, I know about this, I learned about the world above before you came here. But my decision is that we will not go to war for the world above, it does not affect us in any way, so take the news to the Menthis that we will not join.': - He said firmly. The messenger goblin bowed and made his way to the next clan. Gilbert and Miriam successfully arrived at the palace of King Devilus, where they were warmly welcomed. The king personally went out to meet them, he was so happy about their arrival.

Devilus: - 'Welcome my dear children! Come inside and enjoy yourself during your time here. Let me ask, where did you leave James?': - He asked curiously.

Miriam: - 'He had something very important to do, but don't worry, he sends his greetings to you and even sent you a gift!': - She answered with a smile.

Gilbert: -'Welcome, father! Well, this day has come again, your birthday! I see that you are very happy, which makes me happy too. Tell me, how are your days here? Aren't you lonely? Do you have duties that you attend to?': - He asked with a smile.

Devilus: -'Oh my dear son! You don't have to worry about me,

I'm here in my little corner and of course I'm busy, I'm not bored. Is everything okay with you? I am very happy, and you've made me very happy by coming all the way here to me.': - He hugged Gilbert and Miriam. They entered the palace and took their seats in the great hall, then talked to each other.

Devilus: - 'Just tell me, any news from over there? Tell me something new!': - He asked them excitedly.

Gilbert: - 'Actually, there is something new that I would like to tell you! James and I came up with a new game that we announced in the palace not so long ago.' He told his father about the game, which the king seemed to like very much.

Devilus: - 'This is a very interesting game! After my birthday is over, I'd like to watch this new game when it's available!':- He replied excitedly.

Gilbert: 'Well, of course you can watch it! We are very happy to see you in our palace! When your birthday is over and we're getting ready to go home, you'll come with us, how does that sound?': - He asked excitedly.

Devilus: - 'Absolutely perfect! What do you say, Miriam?': - He asked excitedly. But Miriam was not in the room, as she had left the room in the meantime so that they could talk freely. Miriam went and made arrangements about everything to make everything appear normal and make everything perfect. It was time for dinner, everyone was already sitting at the table except Miriam. Gilbert went to find her to invite her to dinner. He found her in the garden, sitting on a bench in the pagoda.

Gilbert: - 'Well, you're here, my dear! I've been looking for you everywhere! Come, let's go to dinner my dear.': - He invited her in the palace.

Miriam: -'I'll go right away dear! Just give me a minute and I'll join you, okay? I would like to be here alone for a while!': - She answered with a smile.

Gilbert: - 'As you wish my dear! We'll wait with the dinner for you!': - He replied happily.

Miriam: -'Oh, that's very nice of you! But for once, don't wait for dinner, I've already eaten it in the kitchen, I'm not hungry, start without me.': - She answered with a smile.

Gilbert: - 'Okay then, as you wish, my dear! But if you change your mind, come and join us!': - He said with a smile.

Miriam: - 'Will do my dear! Now go and enjoy your father's company, there are still many things to discuss!': - She answered with a smile.

Gilbert: -'Oh yes! Before I forget, my father and I just talked about the fact that when his birthday is over and we would go back, he would like to see the new game that we will launch soon.': - He said excitedly.

Miriam: -'It's fine, my dear! Then he will come back with us too!': - She answered with a smile. Gilbert kissed Miriam and went back to the palace to have dinner. He came back into the room and sat down at the table.

Devilus: - 'Well, my son! Where is Miriam?': - He asked curiously.

Gilbert: - She will join a little later! She said to start without her!': - He answered with a smile.

Devilus: - 'It's okay! Bon appetite to everyone then, let's eat.': - He started the dinner. With that, they started to eat, the musicians played soft music for those who were there. The table was full of all kinds of delicacies. Miriam was still out in the garden at the particular pagoda where she had dined with Gilbert at the time. She sat there and the memories kept coming back about how good her life was back then. But the evil mushrooms injected so much evil into her that this memory was also slowly killed. That's why she stood up and looked up at the sky, but she couldn't see the stars because the evil cloud of darkness completely covered the sky and everything else that was on earth. In Miriam, there was a pinprick of goodness left in her, only the rest was consumed by evil. She went back to her room and took out the evil sphere and started stroking it, she wanted to see how it looked and also whether the monsters of darkness were doing their job properly. In the other sphere, where the remaining part of humanity was locked, they were not hurt, of course, each of them was aware that the place they were in was only magic and not their real home. The goblin emissary arrived at the last of the goblin clans, who were famous for their fighting prowess.

Stranger Goblin: - 'Greetings Bathes! The head Menthis sent me to you for help, the time has come to unite against evil and reclaim the upper world!': - He said, kneeling down and bowing his head.

Bathes: -'I welcome you! I was already informed of your arrival, and we were waiting for you! I heard what happened and we stand by you, and when the time is right just let me know and we will join in the fight, because this cannot go on like this. Take the message to Menthis. You can leave!': - He said firmly. The messenger goblin respectfully left with his head bowed. Worried John simply couldn't find his place because of the war, his mind was constantly on James, what kind of turn he might have with the evil witch. Hanna noticed something that she shared with one of the mages.

Hanna: -'Mr. Zathen please! If you have a minute, I'd like to say something!': - She addressed him inquisitively.

Mr. Zathen: -'Hi Hanna! What worries you so much?': - He asked reassuringly.

Hanna: -'Mr. Zathen! I thought so much about this whole thing, in the world above, and now here we are, worried about the people who disappeared! So many things are swirling inside me, the point is that we don't have any more magic power, but what about the goblins? They have magic down here, but what if they go up? Do they have magic up there?': - She asked curiously.

Mr. Zathen: - 'Hmm! This is a very good question! I will find this out, no matter what it takes because if they don't have magic up there, then everything is lost.': - He answered thoughtfully.

Mr. Zathen: - 'Now go and somehow keep the spirit in the others because they are quite restless lately.': - He added.

Hanna: - 'Of course, sir!': - She answered.

Mr. Zathen thought about his business and met Menthis on the way.

Mr. Zathen: -' Oh, but it's good that we ran into each other! I have a very delicate question for you.': - He addressed him.

Menthis: - 'Greetings to you Zathen! What would be your question?': - He asked with a smile.

Mr Zathen: - 'The truth is that what I am about to ask actually did not occur to me but to Hanna.': - He said.

Menthis: - 'Go ahead, feel free to ask!': - He answered.

Mr. Zathen: - 'So, since the war is approaching now, it means that you have to go up to the world above to fight, but the big question is, do you have magic powers up there?': - He asked worriedly.

Menthis: - 'Hahaha! This was an interesting question, of course I didn't expect this, but the answer to your question is that we do have magic up there. Why did Hanna think we didn't have magic up there? But I appreciate your concern, I reassure you that you have nothing to worry about, everything will be fine.': - He answered with a laugh.

Mr. Zathen: -'Well, that was a really reassuring answer! I wish you a nice day, if there is any news, let us know.': - He asked with a smile.

Menthis: - 'It will be my friend, and don't worry....': - He replied as he was leaving. Mr. Zathen was not let down by this question and tried to go to the arch mage to tell him. Menthis thought about what Mr. Zathen told him, and for the sake of safety, he sent one of his goblins to the surface to test his magic. On the way to his accommodation Mr Zathen met Mr Tregas.

Mr. Zathen: -'Oh, it's good that we ran into each other! I would like to have a word with you, Mr. Tregas!': - He addressed him breathlessly.

Mr. Tregas: -'Come on, what's the hurry! Take a deep breath and then tell me what's so urgent.': - He reassured him.

Mr. Zathen: - 'Sir! I think this is very important, let's go to our accommodation immediately! I'll tell you on the way.': - He answered calmly.

Mr. Tregas: - 'alright, let's go!': - He answered.

Mr Zathen: - 'Listen carefully! I spoke with Hanna today; she made an observation that I think cannot be ignored. It's certain that there won't be a war here, but what if the goblins don't even have magic up there? What if the evil witch thought of everything and then it's all over.': - he said in despair. When Mr. Tregas heard this, he immediately stopped and looked at Mr. Zathen.

Mr Tregas: - 'I didn't even think of that! If the evil witch really thought about this, then there is a big problem here. But we have to figure something out if this is true, because we have to defeat evil in all forms, at any cost if necessary. Let's go back to Menthis, I need to talk to him right away.': - He answered excitedly.

Mr. Zathen: - 'Wait! I already talked to him!': - He grabbed his arm and stopped him.

Mr. Tregas: - 'Really? And what did he say anyway?': - He asked curiously.

Mr. Zathen: - 'He told me not to worry because they have magic up there and to go home calmly because they have everything under control. I wanted to talk to you about this because I think the evil witch is capable of anything and somehow, we need to know this before it's too late.': - He answered reassuringly.

Mr. Tregas: - 'Yes, yes! Indeed, you may be right, that's why we have to go back to Menthis and talk to him, that's for sure!': - He answered.

Mr. Zathen: - 'Alright then, let's go back and talk to him .': - He said excitedly.

 In Miriam's palace, everything was ready for the game to be announced by James and Gilbert, they just had to wait until Gilbert returned home and then the big game could begin. In the palace where Miriam was staying with Gilbert, the big birthday party started the next day. Both the palace and the ballroom were beautifully decorated. The musicians played music for those present, and everyone seemed to have a good time. The big party was in full swing, and the music was so loud that it could be heard very far away. The monsters outside didn't appreciate this properly, so they made terrible noises. But it was in vain because those who were in the palace did not hear anything because Miriam took care of this as well as everything else. The birthday party went perfectly normally without any problems.

Miriam: - 'Darling! I would like us to go back tomorrow because I have a lot to do in the palace.': - She said charmingly.

Gilbert: -'Okay, my dear! We'll go back tomorrow if you want, I'll go and talk to my father! I love you dear'! - He answered happily.

Miriam: - 'I'm waiting for you here, hurry back my love!': - She said with a smile. Gilbert went to his father and talked to him, his father was obviously very happy to hear the news and so he waved to Miriam smiling, and Miriam waved back with a smile. Miriam motioned for Gilbert to go back to her. Gilbert saw Miriam's warning and immediately went back to her.

Gilbert: - 'Honey, it's very kind of you to allow my father to come with us tomorrow, but at the same time, I'm very excited about the trip tomorrow, because when we get home, we'll be able to start the game we've been preparing so much for, not to mention our son James.

Miriam: - 'Yes dear, I know that the game is important to you, and I absolutely agree with you, it should be left as a good pastime and also exciting. It was a good decision my dear! Well, we're going home tomorrow, that's for sure, the birthday party was a great success, everything was perfect, wasn't it?': - She answered with a little smile.

Gilbert: -'Oh, yes dear! Come with me to our room and I'll cheer you up a bit.': - He replied with a chuckle and picked up the Miriam.

The envoy goblin came back to the goblin palace with the news, but the boss goblin wasn't there because he had something important to attend to. The guards told the messenger that he will be back soon, and he could wait for Menthis in the forecourt. The messenger goblin did so, sat down on a chair and waited for Menthis there. Menthis was having a meeting with one of his confidential goblins.

Menthis: - 'Listen carefully, my friend! I know that what I'm about to say will sound a little strange to you, but you have to do what I'm asking you to do. This news comes from a very interesting source, that if we go to the surface, we no longer have

293

magical powers! Well, I want to get to the bottom of this because if this is true, then we are done for. I hope I was clear!': - He stated firmly.

Confidential goblin: - 'Yes, I understand, boss! I will act immediately and inform you of the developments as soon as I come back!': - He answered firmly.

Menthis: - 'All right, go now, hurry!!': - With that he said goodbye to his confidential goblin. Menthis tried to return to his palace, as he still had a lot to do.

Menthis: - 'Oh, you're back, that's great, come on in and tell me about the developments.': - He greeted with a smile.

Guest: -'Greetings! The news is as follows!': - He began his speech by taking out a shiny diamond pen about a 5 centimetre long and playing the response of the heads of the clans to Menthis with a click of the button.

Menthis: - 'Hmm! I understand! So, Watim doesn't want to join the fight, too bad!! He would have been very important in the fight, and even he would have an interest in it, since the evil witch harmed him as well as everyone here, somehow, I don't understand why he backed down, there must be a reason!': - He muttered loudly.' It's okay, messenger, you can go now, thank you for your help.': - He finished what he had to say. The envoy left the palace. Menthis walked up and down the room listening to the humming of the little mushrooms. As he was walking down the hall of the palace, a white owl flew in through his window with an important letter in his mouth, carried it directly in the hands of Menthis and with that flew out of the window. Menthis was surprised to see the letter and started to turn it over, to take a good look at who the letter came from, but the letter only said "Important!" Open it right now!" Menthis opened the letter and started reading.

Letter: -

'We heard about the coming war! We would like you to know that we would also like to join you, we will do everything we can and everyone who lives and moves will participate in the fight at any cost. I believe that if we come together, we can defeat the evil witch once and for all. We have also notified each of our clans to join in the big fight and they are all in, so you can definitely count on us!

Kind regards, Fairies!

Menthis read this, he immediately sat down on the ground where he was, because he was so surprised by this letter that he could not believe what he read. But after that, he gained even more courage and self confidence in the fact that together they will definitely defeat the evil witch. After a couple of hours, Menthis's confidant goblin returned.

Confidential goblin: - 'My friend Menthis! I'm back with some bad news! I was up there, and that world has completely changed, it's not the same as it was before. Night monsters lurk everywhere, there are so many of them that we will need a lot of fighting power for this fight. But most importantly, I tried my magic on one of the night monsters and unfortunately it didn't work, sir! I'm very sorry, but what Hanna said is unfortunately true, the evil witch is prepared for anything.': - He wanted to continue what he was saying, but Menthis interrupted.

Menthis: - 'This is really very unfortunate news, my friend! But I don't think all is lost, I did receive a letter from the fairies, and they also stand by us at any cost in the big fight, which means we have a better chance.': - He answered a little depressed.

Confidential goblin: - 'My dear friend, that's not all! We do know that Miriam's palace is intact and healthy, just like the other palace where Gilbert's father rules.'

Menthis: - 'Yes, I know! But what do you mean by that?'

Confidential Goblin: - 'My friend, the only thing is that whoever enters that palace will surely be enchanted and their personality will be completely transformed, they will no longer be themselves, because the magic that surrounds the palace is secured at the whim of the evil witch. All magical powers cease, and you are no longer master of anything, we must not break through the gates of the palace.': - He replied brokenly.

Menthis: - 'Don't worry my friend, we will figure something out together! In a week, the fairies and the members of our clans will arrive here, until then we will work out something to make the war go well': - He answered reassuringly.

Confidential goblin: - 'So be it my friend! I support you in everything!': - He finished what he had to say and left. Menthis was constantly thinking about how to carry out the great war, so he didn't hesitate and visited the high-ranking Mr. Tregas.

Oliver: - 'Listen Jessy! It could be that we are down here now, I think it's really cool, much better than up there! What do you think?': - He asked excitedly.

Jessy: - 'Oliver! I don't know what to say, it's not that bad to be here, but I miss my home, my friends from school, even the teachers, I don't think it's right, but we have to accept the current situation, trusting that we'll survive this somehow!': - She answered sadly.

Oliver: - 'Yes, I know it's not the same! I still like this place; I think it's very adventurous to be here! I could explore this place; everything here is so magical! If it's any comfort to you, I miss my parents too, I haven't seen them in a long time. To be honest, I don't know if I will see them again at all.': - He answered a little sadly.

Jessy: - 'You're right! You know what? Come, let's go and take a walk where we haven't been before, but just the two of us, no one else can know that we are going out! Are you in?': - She asked excitedly.

Oliver: - 'Oh, of course I'm in!! Let's go!': - He answered excitedly and happily. With that, they sneaked out of the house without anyone noticing and set off on a journey of discovery. Evelin and Hanna were together in the living room and talking.

Evelin: - 'What do you think will be the end of this?': - She asked in despair.

Hanna: - 'Listen! I can't answer that for you, because the truth is that I don't know, but I hope that there will be a good ending, as the evil witch can't win in any way. We can see what she has already done to our world above, she has destroyed everything, and she will not rest until she destroys everything in her path.': - She answered a little sadly.

Evelin: - 'But I am very worried about James! He's stuck up there with the Wicked Witch and we have no idea what happened to him, maybe he's not even ali...... And she began to cry bitterly because she loved James very much and was very worried about him. Hanna hugged Evelin and tried to calm her down.

Hanna: -'Listen Evelin! I believe that we are where we are for a reason! The goblins will do anything to defeat the evil witch, I'm sure of it. I don't think you should....' She couldn't finish her sentence because there was a knock on the door. John went to the door and opened it. Standing in front of the door was Menthis.

John: -'Greetings! Come on in.': - He kindly invited him in.

Menthis: -'Greetings to you to! Have you seen Mr...' Meanwhile, Mr. Tregas just came down the stairs.

297

Menthis: - Oh, I'm looking for you, my friend! We have to talk!: - He said excitedly.

Mr. Tregas: -'Greetings! Come inside please! Can I offer you refreshments and cookies?': - He asked politely.

Menthis: - 'Oh, very nice, but no, thank you. If you'll allow me, I'll get to the point.'

Mr. Tregas: -'Of course my friend, what is so urgent?'

Menthis: - 'Is everyone here? Because everyone needs to hear this.'

Mr. Tregas looked around the living room and everyone was there except Oliver and Jessy.

Mr. Tregas: - 'Everyone is here except Oliver and Jessy! Did anyone see them?'

John: - 'They were just here, but I'll go and find them, it only takes a minute, I'll be right back.' He went to look for them but couldn't find them anywhere, so he went back to the living room.

John: - 'I can't find them anywhere, maybe they went out for a walk, and we'll tell them when they come back.

Menthis: - 'It's okay, then I'll start! When we met with my friend Mr. Tregas, and he drew my attention to something, what if we go up to the surface to fight and we don't have magic power, and I told him not to worry because we also have magic power on the surface, so… I take it back now. Of course, after our conversation, I sent one of my confidential goblins to make sure of this, and unfortunately, he returned with bad news. We don't have any magic up there and the worst thing is that we can't go beyond the palace gates because the entire palace area is enchanted. Whoever puts his foot there completely forgets who they are, they transform into a person who is no longer himself. However, today I received a letter from the fairies in which it was said that they

298

support us in the fight and will do whatever it takes to defeat the evil witch together!': -He finished what he had to say. Everyone started grumbling to each other after hearing this news.

Mr. Tregas: - 'My friend Menthis! This is just sad news! But I'm sure that we have something together...' Evelin couldn't bear to listen to this anymore, so she ran out of the living room and ran up the stairs straight to her room.

Hanna: - 'I apologize!!': - She interrupted. She went after Evelin in her room.

Hanna: - 'Evelin!! Please! Don't give up hope!': - She reassured.

Evelin: - 'What hope, Hanna! There's no hope left; can't you see? The evil witch has won, there is nothing left to do against her. I still have to get home somehow; my parents must be worried to death about me! There's no way out of this, we're going to die too, and I couldn't even say goodbye to my parents!!': - She cried in despair. Hanna, she didn't say anything, she let her cry on her shoulder, because whatever you say at this time is useless, she let her cry but didn't move away from her.

Menthis: -'I'm glad we discussed this! Then see you tomorrow at my palace. Have a nice day.': - He said Goodbye politely.

Mr. Tregas: - 'See you again tomorrow my friend': - he said goodbye politely.

John: - 'Wait, where did Oliver and Jessy go?'

Mr. Derras: - 'They will be back soon! They're just taking a walk because they're bored here, passing the time somehow!': - He calmed them down.

John: - 'Okay! I 'm going to see how Evelin is!': - He finished what he had to say. Oliver and Jessy arrived at a lookout point. The sight itself was amazing from such a height, I'm sure you can only see something like this in a fairy tale.

Jessy: -'Oh my God, Oliver! I'm so glad we finally got out of the house and went exploring. This sight is simply indescribable, it's a shame that the others can't see it.': - She sighed with happiness.

Oliver: - 'I'm glad that you decided this way, my dear! This sight is really wonderful, and we can be a part of it.': - He finished his sentence and hugged Jessy, and they enjoyed the amazingly beautiful landscape.

John knocked on Evelin's door.

Evelin: - 'Yes, come in!': - She replied with a sniff.

John: -'Hello! How are you, Evelin? All is well. Can I help you with something?': - He asked politely.

Evelin: -'Hi John! Feel free to come in! You can't help me with that, it's very kind of you to ask! But the fact that we are stuck here, so to speak, I don't see a way out of this, or even how I will ever get home to my parents! Unfortunately, you can't help with these, but thank you for your concern!': - She answered sniffling, with teary eyes.

John: - 'Evelin! I know you are in doubt, everyone here is in doubt, it's just that we react differently, but that does not mean that there is no way out of this. There is a way out of everything, everyone has a weakness, even the evil witch. Therefore, don't give up hope and believe that we will win, and not the evil witch, and then we will figure something out together, okay!!': - He reassured her kindly.

Evelin: - 'Okay! But now I would like you guys to leave me be, I want to be alone.': - She answered sadly but she was no longer crying.

John, Hanna: - 'Good night' They went out of her room and let her calm down a bit and get some rest. As soon as they left the room, Evelin kept thinking about what John had told her, about everyone having a weak point, even the wicked witch. This sentence played in her mind at least twenty times, she sat there on the bed and this sentence just rang in her head back and forth several times in a row. She fell into bed and fell asleep in these thoughts. A dream came over her again, she dreamed that James was there in the palace, and he was feeling very well, absolutely happy and cheerful as if nothing had happened. He is preparing for a big game with Gilbert, for which they have prepared so much. The next scene in her dream was the crystal falling to the ground and breaking into small pieces and the light completely disappearing. But Evelin woke up from her sleep from the loud crashing of the crystal, it was already morning anyway. She sat up in her bed and remembered her dream and realized that it would again be a message just like her previous dream, so she tried to change her clothes and hurried to the others to tell him about her dream. As soon as she opened the door to her room, she ran into Hanna and Oliver and Jessy.

Evelin: - 'You won't believe what I dreamed again!! Everyone needs to be told this immediately, come quickly.': - She said excitedly. They started running down the stairs so hard that the whole house was shaking. But everyone was already in the living room, they were just waiting for them.

Evelin: - 'I had a dream again, just like last time, only that it was a completely different kind of dream. Excuse me, good morning, everyone!': - She said very excitedly.

Mr. Tregas: - 'No problem my child! Calm down and tell us what you have dreamt of!': - He reassured the panting Evelin.

Evelin: - 'I dreamed that James was very comfortable in the palace and that he was very happy, they were preparing for some kind of game with Gilbert and the next phase was that the crystal would fall to the ground in some way, I don't know how, but it breaks into small pieces and its light goes out.': - She told them excitedly. Everyone in the room looked at each other and started

301

whispering in unison.

Mr. Tregas: - 'Hmm! This is a really interesting dream; I'll give you that! We have to go to Menthis for a meeting today anyway, so I'm going to tell him this story, it will probably be very important later on. Thank you, Evelin, you had a vision again just like last time. Now let 's have breakfast.': - He answered thoughtfully.

Hanna: -'Evelin! This dream has a very important meaning, that's for sure! The fact that the crystal breaks into small pieces is a message, we just have to decipher its meaning.'

Oliver: - 'I think if it's true, that the crystal breaks, it means that we will defeat the witch, right?': - He asked with a chuckle. Jessy nudged him to stop him from giggling at that. Oliver immediately put on a serious face.

Oliver: -'I didn't mean it that way! I meant that it must have some good meaning if it breaks, because then it no longer has the strength, right?': - He asked with forced seriousness. Hanna also thought about this, because there was some truth in what Oliver said. After all, if the crystal breaks, it loses its power and then everything returns to its original state as it was before. Everyone took their seats at the table and started breakfast, but everyone ate their breakfast in silence and thought about what Evelin had told them. But the thought of the crystal did not let Hanna rest. Everyone was obviously thinking about this whole thing. Finally, Hanna broke the silence.

Hanna: - 'What Evelin said today about her dream and what Oliver said afterwards, does not let me rest, I have to say something now. Quoting Oliver, she said that if the crystal really breaks, it loses its power, and this is indeed the case. If the crystal breaks, it loses its power, that's for sure, the big question here is how and when the crystal breaks? After all, Evelin dreamed that the crystal would break, didn't she? Her last dream also came true,

I think it's a sign and not a dream. Something will happen soon with that crystal; you just have to wait for the right time.': - She interrupted wisely.

Mr. Tregas: - 'That's true Hanna! If the crystal breaks, it really loses its power, only a simple crystal remains and the evil witch can no longer destroy the world, but we forgot something very important. The crystal only gave the evil witch extra power, so she still has a lot of magic power, and we can't really do anything against that, the one who will be able to stop the evil witch, it's none other than James. Today we have been invited to the goblins for lunch and there will be an important meeting afterwards, I would like you all to be there because this meeting is important for everyone. Let's finish breakfast now and then we'll meet in the palace of the goblins.': - He spoke to everyone. Menthis was out in the forest with his advisors, and they discussed that what awaits them up there will not really be a walk in the park, they will need all the helping hands. In the middle of the big conversation, they were already in the middle of the forest when they came to a place where big hill blocked their way. The vegetation was sparse, and the trees were close together, hardly any light came through because of the foliage of the trees. They stopped to look around when suddenly the ground beneath them began to shake. They held each other and watched what was going to happen. Countless, even more beautiful mushrooms came out from under the ground. When the area was already covered, the shaking stopped and finally a much bigger mushroom came out from under the ground, it was the head mushroom. The head mushroom climbed onto a larger piece of rock and stopped there. All the other mushrooms did not move, waiting for the command of the head mushroom. The head mushroom turned to Menthis and spoke.

Head of Mushrooms: - 'Menthis, listen carefully to what I say!

The little mushrooms in your ears relayed every bit of information to me. Those little mushrooms belong to James Alder who help him when he is in trouble. Unfortunately, they crawled out of his ears because the evil witch enchanted him with the magic spell, because of this the mushrooms could no longer stay in his ear. I decided that they should crawl into your ear and listen to you and lead you on the right path and make the right decisions, which they did. You will need a lot of help for the above battle you are preparing for. Knowing that if you go up to fight, you'll have no magic power because the evil witch took care of that, but she didn't expect that I could provide the mushrooms with magic power that even the witch couldn't face. Therefore, what I'm going to do now is that all the goblins who go up to fight will get the right mushrooms in their ears and I'll give them the right magic so they can fight. Those little mushrooms in your ear Menthis will go back to James because he will need their help. If you have any questions, you can ask them now.': - He spoke impressively.

Menthis: 'Greetings, Head mushroom! I didn't even know you existed until now! I didn't even know that there were mushrooms in my ears (He put his finger in his ear) but now everything is clear to me why I behaved like that, and I am grateful for every good thing, but most of all I want to thank you for your help. My question is, if we go up to fight, how will the spell above be able to resist your magic?': - He asked curiously.

Main mushroom: - 'That's a very good question! My magic is different from anyone else's, we have been helping people for centuries, but one day when I was preparing an important magic potion, something fell to the ground with such force that it created a huge earthquake, more of the potion was added than needed, that's why those mushrooms they became evil and I couldn't turn them back because they ran away immediately. Those evil mushrooms crawled into the ears of the then reigning evil witch and her power grew to such a level that she kept humanity in complete terror. But one day, that wicked witch died due to a botched potion. The mushrooms immediately crawled out of her ear and into the ear of the corresponding witch who is currently terrorizing the world. That's why we have magical power up there while no one else has it. I hope my answer was satisfactory.': - He answered smartly.

Menthis: - 'I have one more question, if that will be, okay?': - He asked again.

Head of Mushrooms: - 'Go ahead!': - He answered calmly.

Menthis: - 'How is it possible that those little mushrooms that were in James' ears could not protect James, since they had magical powers or not?': - He asked smartly.

Head of Mushrooms: - 'Those little mushrooms didn't have that much power when they crawled into James's ear, since it happened in James's world, and then they only had as much magic power as was appropriate for the given situation, that's why they had to be rescued from there. but now they will have the magic power they need to win this battle. There will probably be those who fall, as you also have to take into account that the witch's strength has greatly increased due to the crystal, but you can defeat her regardless. I hope my answers were satisfactory. Now go back to the palace and prepare for battle.': - He said goodbye to them.

Menthis: -'Yes, the answers were satisfactory, goodbye! Thanks for your help!': - He said goodbye to the head of mushrooms. Menthis and his councillors went back to their palace to prepare for lunch and the big meeting. They arrived back at the palace, and everything was ready for lunch, and even the guests had already arrived.

Oliver: - 'Hanna, where is the big boss, I don't see him anywhere?': - He asked curiously.

Hanna: - 'He's here somewhere, he's probably getting ready for lunch, we'll find out! Why do you ask?': - She was interested.

Oliver: -'I don't even know! I have such a strange feeling, don't you? It's as if everything is so different here, not like when we first came here!': - He noted.

Hanna: -'Come on Oliver! You are just imagining things, what would make everything different? Everything is still the same you idiot.': - She replied laughing.

Oliver: -'Well, if you say so, then you're probably right!': - He answered with a smile.

Jessy: - 'Oliver! What did you mean that something has changed here, I don't see anything strange either, I think it's the same as when we came here!': - She interrupted the conversation.

Oliver: - 'Hmm, I don't know, it's not the same as when we came here, as if something has changed, but I can't say what it is, I just have a premonition, that's all.': - He answered with a smile. Meanwhile, they arrived in the great hall, where the important goblins were already sitting at the table. Everyone took their seats, and the lunch was served, and everyone had a look at the magnificent lunch. When they finished lunch, everyone went through to the meeting room to start the important negotiation. Everyone took their seats, and the trial could begin.

Menthis: -'Greetings to you all! I called you here today because this negotiation will be the last. Today I went for a walk in the woods with my advisors to freshen up a bit. But something very interesting happened, which makes today's hearing interesting and, above all, important. I'm guessing some of you here have heard of magic mushrooms? If yes, raise your hands.': - He asked seriously. Almost all of those present raised their hands, except for Jessy and her family members, because they had not heard about it yet.

Menthis: -'Well, for those who may not have heard of magic mushrooms, now is the time to learn more about them. Today in the forest, millions of small magic mushrooms came out from underground and at the very end a bigger mushroom came out from under the ground, it was the head magic mushroom that controls the other little mushrooms. Today I learned something from the main mushroom that was reassuring for me and for the other goblins who will go up to fight. After all, the main mushroom can also give us back our magical power up there if the little mushrooms climb into our ears. Which you can't really feel that they are there, only that they constantly radiate the power. I didn't even know I had magic mushrooms in my ears until the main mushroom told me. Well, these magic mushrooms will help us defeat the evil witch, which in itself is very good news. We will start the War a week from today, until then we will try to gather some clans to help us. If anything, new happens in the coming days, I will of course notify you immediately. Thank you for staying with me, you can go now.': - He finished what he had to say.

Mr. Tregas: - 'Menthis, I have a question!'

Menthis: -'Of course! Go ahead, feel free to ask.': - He answered with a smile.

Mr. Tregas: - 'How will we know if these little mushrooms will definitely have magical powers up there?': - He asked curiously.

Menthis: -' Well, that's easy! The main mushroom said that his spells had no correlation with the evil witch. His spells are completely different from humans, so it is absolutely certain that they will help us up there.': - He answered with a smile.

Mr. Tregas: - 'Alright then! Then I wish you good luck for the big battle and that you succeed in defeating the evil witch. But there is something important here, I almost forgot, today Evelin had a vision again. She saw that the crystal would break into small pieces and lose its power.': - He finished what he had to say.

Menthis: - 'Hmm! This is extremely interesting! To what extent can these visions be trusted?': - He asked curiously.

Mr. Tregas: - 'She already had a vision that came true, I think we can believe in this too.': - He answered calmly.

Menthis: - 'Okay then! It was very important that you said this because it is definitely a sign that we don't yet know what it means. But when the time comes, we will find out, as this cannot be found out that way.': - He finished what he had to say.

Mr. Tregas: 'Well, we really won't know until the time comes. Thank you for today, we wish you a nice day.': - He said Goodbye. Everyone went back to their little corner and thought about what Menthis told them today.

~The Labyrinth games! ~

So, the long-awaited day that James and Gilbert announced not so long ago has arrived. Everyone in the palace is already prepared for the big game day. People were excited about what this game would be like. Everyone gathered in front of the palace. The balcony door opened, and Gilbert and James stepped out onto the terrace, the people started cheering and cheering for their king. Gilbert raised his hands and motioned for silence. People were silent and listened to his announcement.

Gilbert: -'I wish everyone a nice day! We have gathered here today because it is well known that I am opening the labyrinth game today. (People started cheering again) This game was carefully crafted and designed with James and of course a few other dedicated designers. The essence of the game is that there will be three different types of balls hidden in the maze, which you have to find, but the balls will be well hidden to make the game more difficult. This means that there will be traps, illusions, monsters and magic that will make things difficult for the contestants. What is also very important is that the teams cannot help each other, because if they do, they are out of the game, each team is responsible for their own. We will give the winning team a chest of gold and a gold cup. Well, I hope everyone understood that! Let the game begin!!!': - He shouted.

People cheered and were excited about the game, so everyone went to the designated place where they could sit and watch the game unfold. The players were already very excited about the game, everyone wanted to win, of course. The players had a separate building in which there were four separate rooms, in those rooms they could prepare and put on their appropriate clothes, even though each team had a different colour of clothing and had a symbol on it. Team One was dressed in red and blue, Team Two in Black and Orange, Team Three in Green and Yellow, and Team Four in Indigo and Pink. The emblem of the first team was the chameleon, the emblem of the second team was the dragon, the emblem of the third team was the lion, and the emblem of the fourth team was the butterfly.

Names of red-blue players:

Beneth

Carl

Eric

Mitch

Zoe

Names of black and orange players:

Norbert

Patrick

Mark

Adam

Doris

Names of players in green and yellow:

Jason

Kurtis

Alice

Emy

Liam

Names of indigo-pink players:

Mason

Carter

Betty

Kyle

Grace

The teams were all ready and waiting for the signal to come out of the house. It didn't take long because the signal was given by King Gilbert, and the troops came out one by one in the forecourt, which was full of people. When the people saw them, they immediately burst into cheers and applause. Gilbert and James stood on the podium where they welcomed the players. Each team stood in a neat order in front of the podium and waited for further instructions.

James: - 'Welcome to the maze game. As you can see, the players are all ready for me to start the game, that's why I shall not stop them, let them go and start the game. We wish all players' good luck.': - He exclaimed happily. People applauded, rejoiced, cheered and shouted: - 'GO! GO!' This made the players even more excited and eager to start playing.

Gilbert: - 'Even before the players enter the labyrinth, I want to give them a self-defence weapon, which is nothing but a sword. This sword will be put to good use against the monsters in there. Good luck to you!': - He concluded his speech. The guards opened the gate leading to the labyrinth and the players started entering the labyrinth.

Red and blue player.

Beneth: - 'Listen now! What awaits us in there? I'm very curious, aren't you?': - He asked excitedly.

Mitch: -'Oh i am! But it will become clear when we are inside, relax!': - He answered with a smile.

Black and orange player.

Patrick: - 'Damn it's so exciting! I can't wait to start this game, are you excited too?': - He asked impatiently.

Norbert: -'Of course I'm excited for it! But you know what, I'm telling you now that we'll win the game for sure.': - He replied confidently.

Green and Yellow's player.

Jason: - 'This shows that it will be a very good game! But we have to be sure not to help the other teams.': - He said excitedly.

Liam: -'That's right! We won't even help anyone, let's play!': - He encouraged the others.

His indigo and pink player.

Carter: - 'Watch what you're doing because it's going to be full of traps!': - He warned them.

Grace: - 'Calm down! We just do what we have to, and it won't be a problem.': - She encouraged them. When the players were all inside the starting line of the maze, the door closed behind them. The initial starting point was divided into four possible paths, the players could decide which path to choose. Each starting path had traps, illusions, monsters, and magic built into the maze to make things difficult for the players. The teams were ready to start and had to wait for the signal given by Gilbert and James. Gilbert and James started counting down from ten and the people who supported the teams counted along with them.

Gilbert and James: - 'Ten, nine, eight, seven, six, five, four, three, two, one!!!!' With that, the horn was blown, and the game could begin. The players went into the labyrinth. The red-blue team chose course two, the black-orange team chose course four, the green-yellow team chose course one and finally the indigo-blue-pink team chose course three. The players carefully entered the labyrinth because they knew it would be full of surprises. The three balls were hidden separately on each field, the point is that the team that finds the balls first will win. The teams can also meet each other, since the paths were not closed because that would have made their job easier, but they had to follow a certain line to find the balls, of course no one knows the line, since they had to figure it out and decipher the path. The green and yellow players who were on each field moved forward quite slowly, they were quite careful because they wanted to do well. The hedges were at least twelve meters high on both sides, and they had no chance to see through to the other side or even to climb it and find the right direction.

Carl: - 'Guys listen! What if we somehow try to climb the hedge wall and spy the way?': - He asked curiously.

Erik: - 'I think this is a good idea, let's try it.': - He answered excitedly.

Zoe: - 'You can't climb this hedge wall, you morons! What will you hold on to, the leaves? That was a good joke!': - She said laughing. As soon as she had said this, unnoticed by them, an upwards leading tendril appeared.

Zoe: - 'Look at this hedge, what would you hold on to if not one...?': - And she pointed to the hedge wall.

Mitch: - 'Well, we're going to hold on to this! Look at this, there is a tendril along the hedge wall! This is something!': - He warned them.

Carl: - 'Right! Well, we will hold on to this!'

Beneth: - 'Hey, this tendril, wasn't here before, was it? Or is my memory failing me?': - He asked in surprise.

Erik: - 'Really! It really wasn't here before!': - He answered in surprise.

Zoe: -'It could be a trap! I think we should move along.': - She answered in surprise.

Carl: - 'Come on! Don't be such coward, I'll climb on it.': - He expressed bravely.

Beneth: - 'okay then! We will be here, not going anywhere.': - He said encouragingly.

Zoe: - 'I think we are wasting our time, let's move on.': - She told them firmly. With that Carl grabbed the tendril so he could climb it. As soon as he started up the tendril, the tendril transformed into a giant snake, which Carl did not immediately notice. He realized that it was a snake when it started to move and became slimy and slippery. The others from below, when they noticed that it was a huge snake, immediately started screaming and encouraged Carl to let go and jump down. But the snake began to wrap itself around Carl, from which it was quite difficult to escape. The others took out their swords and attacked the snake to free their companion. After a little struggle, they finally managed to free Carl, who fell to the ground and coughed suffocatingly because of the snake's grip. The snake immediately disappeared from there, but the others ran away because they were terrified.

Zoe: - 'Well, I told you to move along!!! These are all traps here, have you already forgotten?': - She said breathlessly. Carl didn't say anything because he was still under shock. They continued into the labyrinth. The black and orange team also moved forward cautiously, noticing strange sounds as they got deeper into the labyrinth.

Adam: -'What are these sounds? Do you hear it too?': - He asked very startled.

Mark: -'Of course we hear it! Keep quiet, just in case they disappear from here.': - He said softly.

Doris: - 'I think we should all stay close to each other, if something happens then we can protect ourselves.': - She answered in terror.

Norbert: - 'Just keep quiet, don't say a word!': - He spoke to them quietly.

Patrick: - 'Look up guys!': - He warned them in fright. They all looked up and a huge spider was standing on top of the hedges, its fangs snapping at them. When they saw this, they stood closely with their backs to each other and cautiously took out their swords to protect themselves. The sticky saliva dripped out of the spider's mouth right at them, and then the spider attacked to devour them. They all attacked the spider with their swords, slashing as hard as they could. The spider was not so easy to hit because it jumped all of the place. But with joint strength and solidarity, Patrick and Norbert finally wounded the spider so that it finally fell to the ground and Doris, Mark and Adam continued to mow it down with their swords until it crumbled to dust.

Mark: -'Guys! This was a very hard fight, and we are only at the beginning, what will happen next?': - He wiped the sweat from his forehead.

Adam: - 'That was really shocking! I thought he was going to eat us!': - He answered tiredly.

Doris: -'Well, boys, it was a very serious fight! We have to prepare for everything because this track is still very long, it shows what awaits us! - He said breathlessly.

Norbert: - My god guys, does anybody have any toilet paper…. We did it well though, it wasn't easy, but we did it! Let's stay close to each other so we can prepare for further surprises. Oh, and one more thing! I think it will be best if we only speak quietly to each other from now on.': - He said panting.

Doris, Patrick, Mark, Adam: - 'I agree!......oh…. I agree': - they all whispered at the same time. With that, they set off in nice silence, and for now they were just pointing at each other, because they were moving forward with preparation and strategy. The green and yellow players perceived the field in front of them in a slightly rattle-brained way. They laughed a lot and fooled each other; they even scared each other. They were having a lot of fun, it must be said, and because of their loud laughter, they didn't hear what was waiting for them. They kept laughing when Kurtis slipped and fell on a dark green sticky slime.

Kurtis: - 'What the hell is this green stuff?': - He asked with disgust. The others started laughing at him. Kurtis struggled to his feet from the ground and was covered in pure green sticky slime. The others couldn't avoid the green sticky slime either, because it was all there. They walked with disgust, but they were no longer laughing.

Emy: -'What the hell is this green shit? How did it get here?': - She asked, looking down in disgust.

Alice: - 'It's disgusting, and it's also sticky.': - She said with disgust.

Liam: - 'There seems to be something in this slime, just look!': - He warned them.

Jason: -'yeah something is in it alright! Your fat head is in it. But what else would be in it, pieces of earth and leaves, your brainless idiot.': - He said mockingly.

Liam: - 'This is no joke! There really is something to it! Look.': - He said firmly. Jason leaned closer to look and Liam slapped the green sticky slime in his face with that movement. Everyone started laughing so hard that they couldn't stop, of course Jason didn't find it funny at all. So, he wiped it off his face and started fighting with Liam to teach him a lesson. The others were laughing so hard they couldn't intervene to separate them, but in the end, they were separated.

Emy: - 'What's with you guys? That was a good joke! Jason, anyway, you started it all, you made fun of Liam, you can only blame yourself.': - She said laughing.

Jason: - 'This dude is a bastard; I have no idea why he's on this team! How did it even get in here? He can't even lift his big ass, he can't even run, he's just holding us back.': - He said aggressively. Liam didn't like this very much; he was saddened by it.

Alice: - 'Listen! Those who are in this game are here for a reason, right? Everyone had to pass the test and Liam got in, so there is a reason why he is here with us. Now it would be good if you stop this childish argument and find out what.......' She couldn't finish the sentence because the certain monster from which the green sticky slime comes from attacked them. It happened to be a giant soft bodies insect that had a million teeth and eight eyes, green slime flowing out of its mouth in streams, snapping its teeth and coming at them so fast that they couldn't even draw their swords. Everyone got scared and slipped on the slime, fell into a neat line and tried to crawl away. Liam managed to get to the side of the hedge, clinging to it, managed to stand up and took out his sword. The monster snapped its teeth back and forth at its companions to devour them. When Liam was on solid ground, he swung his sword at it to injure the monster. The monster made a terrible sound from its mouth and the monster turned its head towards Jason and was about to bite the head with its mouth wide open, but then Liam cut off the monster's head with one big movement which then fell right on top of Jason. The monster lay sprawled on the ground and after a moment turned to dust and disappeared. Liam sat down on the ground and just looked straight in front of him, wondering how he had the courage to do this for his companion who actually made fun of him.

Jason: - 'Liam! I want to apologize to you! I was a jerk to you, don't be angry! Thank you for what you did for me, it was really a very brave thing to do, I promise you that I won't tease you again. Are we friends?': - He apologized to him and held out his hand.

Liam: - 'It was nothing after all! I think you would have done it for me too, wouldn't you?': - He held out his hand and finally they shook hands and became good friends from then on.

Alice: - 'These guys!': - She shook her head.

Kurtis: - 'Listen! I think it's time to take this game seriously! Who knows what else awaits us, it will be better if we are on the lookout from now on and don't put the swords away, but rather hold them in our hands!': - He said confidently.

Emy: -'I agree with him. No more laughing, listen! Seriously, otherwise we won't win.': - She replied seriously.

Jason: -'Come on fatty, let's go! Just kidding! But I can call you fatty, right?': - He poked his shoulder with a smile.

Liam: - 'Okay! You can call me fatty, I'm fat after all! I won't get offended.': - He answered with a smile. With that, they continued on the path, but now they didn't laugh out loud, they just talked in a normal voice. The indigo blue-pink team were more serious and shyer than the others. Carter went in front and the others followed, Kayl was at the back, thinking. Kayl was looking around when he noticed something shiny in the hedge. He started walking towards it to see what it was, as he got closer to it, it glowed brighter and brighter. The Betty constantly looks back to see if Kayl is okay. But she noticed that Kayl was heading to the wall of the hedge because he noticed something.

Betty: -'Stop! Kayl noticed something on the hedge wall.': - She warned the others. The others stopped immediately and watched Kayl. Kayl didn't tell the others because he was enchanted by magic. His companions moved closer and closer to Kayl to see what he had noticed. When they got close enough to Kayl, the magic took a hold of them too, except for Carter because he got away from it and therefore couldn't get as close as the others. The others who were already under the spell turned to Carter and grabbed his hands and dragged him towards the shiny object. But Carter had his eyes closed so he couldn't see what was really there. Hearing so much that a very strange voice spoke.

Strange voice: - 'Carter! Open your eyes and I will hand you of one of the winning balls! I'm holding it here! You only need ask, but for that you have to open your eyes!': - He seduced him. But Carter knew that it was just a trap and that if he opened his eyes, they would definitely be out of the game, so he fought his way out of the others' hands and ran far away. But the others ran after him. He took out a handkerchief from his pocket and put it over his eyes and thus somewhat protected himself from the temptation. He could see dimly through the handkerchief, and he saw that the strange voice was a monster with a ten-legged female body, which the others of course did not see because they were under the power of magic. The monster was closing in on Carter. He carefully took out his sword and was ready to fight. His job was difficult because not only the monster attacked Carter but also his companions, so he had to act smartly. After a quick thought, he took out two more handkerchiefs from his pocket and managed to put one over Mason's eyes and the other over Grace's eyes, so now there were three of them together, which meant that they had a better chance of defeating the monster. They fought the monster and their other two companions because they had to, they punched and shoved until Mason managed to hit the monster in the heart, who collapsed to the ground and turned into dust. The spell ended and the others regained consciousness.

Betty: - 'What happened? I don't remember anything!': - She asked scared.

Kayl: - 'Really, something happened, didn't it?': - He asked surprised.

Carter: -'Oh yeah! It was all nothing actually! He had you under the power of magic. But we're over it, that's all that matters, let's continue our journey and be alert.': - He sighed tiredly. They continued on the path, going much more carefully than before. The spectators enjoyed the game very much, cheered the players on, waved flags and shouted encouragingly, as the spectators could see the entire labyrinth. During this time, Miriam could calmly deal with her evil plans. She went into her room and took out her crystal ball in which most of humanity was locked, placed it on the table and began to look at it. The people there lived their everyday lives without any worries, since they were not hurt there. Zulante and Anna have been extremely happy ever since they got together, even the children were happy because Zulante played with them a lot. King Erminus lived his days with complete peace of mind, seeing that his children were safe and very happy together, he enjoyed the company of his grandchildren, as he loved them very much. King Nyaritis received notice from the courier.

Notice: -

Dear King Nyiaritis!

I am writing this letter to you because my son Robnis wants to marry your daughter Nivita!

I would like to invite you and your wife and of course your daughter Nivita to lunch, so that we can talk about the youths' futures.

I believe this offer will benefit both kingdoms for the future.

In two weeks, we will warmly welcome you and your family to my palace.

Kind regards

King Koldvir.

After reading the letter, King Nyaritis immediately wrote back to King Koldvin and sent the reply letter with his courier, in which he accepted the invitation.

King Nyaritis called his daughter Nivita to him.

Nivita: - 'Yes, father! Why did you call me?': - She asked curiously.

Nyaritis: -'Yes, my daughter! I called you because we want to discuss something important with you. Not so long ago I received a notification from the courier that we are official in the kingdom of Koldvir: - The purpose of our visit will be to marry you to Robnis. King Koldvir has made an understudy, so we will take advantage of the opportunity. The meeting will be in two weeks at King Koldvin's palace.': - He explained what he had to say.

Nivita: - 'Thank you, father! Then I'll prepare for the meeting, which I'm really looking forward to!': - She bowed in front of her father and left. Nivita left the room and immediately a smile appeared on her face, because she was in love with Robnis, but her father didn't know that. This news made her very happy, so she quickly went to his mother to tell her the great news.

Nivita: - 'Mother! Mother! listen, I just talked to my father, and he said that in two weeks we will visit Robnis, he will ask for my hand in marriage! Isn't it wonderful? I can't wait to go there.': - She announced happily.

Martha: - 'Oh, my daughter! This is very good news! I am very happy about this, that you will marry the person whom you also love very much. Well, then we have to prepare for the trip, we can't forget anything at home. I entrust this task to you, but if you still need my help, just let me know.': - She answered with a smile. Miriam watched all this, how happy the people were and what event they were preparing for, so she planned something very evil to make things difficult for them. The road to King Koldvir's palace was filled with obstacles that no one knew existed. After all, Miriam had fun with this, for her it was like a game to cause pain to others. King Koldvir also wrote another letter to King Erminus, in which he asked the hand of the daughter of Carnita to the son of Valtinus. King Erminus accepted the invitation; therefore King Koldvir brought the two under the same hat, on the same day. King Koldvir made alliances with both the King of the West and the King of the North. King Koldvir not only invited the kings to a traditional dinner, but also organized a huge ball in honour of the proposal. The two kings carefully prepared for this important event, as the future of their children was important to each king. After carefully planning everything, Miriam put the sphere back in its place and left her room laughing. Gilbert and James really enjoyed the game, wondering which team would win the competition. The red and blue team moved forward cautiously as much as possible, but even though they were on the lookout, there were things hidden that you couldn't really prepare for, that was the exciting part. Carl and Beneth walked side by side in front, Erik, Mitch and Zoe followed behind them. They reached a junction where they met the green-yellow team. The road became such that they could only go on together from there. They all looked at each other and kept going because they didn't really have any other choice. This challenge was one of the most difficult parts of the game, because here if any of them help the other team, elimination is certain. They were somewhat relieved because they saw the junction in front of them, which meant that their paths would diverge there. This was what they saw, but in reality, the road in front of them did not split, it was just an illusion to test them. As they moved forward, a large sea of water separated them from the illusive junction. They all stopped to decide what to do next.

Jason: - 'Well, we have no other choice, we have to go to the other side on those sunken ships that are next to each other, like a crossing! Otherwise, we won't get any further.': - He said firmly.

Liam: - 'But I can't swim! And this already seems quite deep.': - He said with dread.

Zoe: - 'Lame!': - She spoke softly.

Kurtis: - 'Calm down, I'll help you!': - He encouraged.

Jason: - 'And I'll help you too, don't be afraid!': - He encouraged with a smile.

Erik: - 'The thing is, I can't swim either!': - He interrupted sadly.

Mitch: - 'I can't swim either!': - He interrupted in despair.

Zoe: - 'This lame company! How did you get into this game anyway? It's all bullshit.': - She snapped at them angrily.

Emy: - 'I can't swim either!': - She said shyly. Well, the two teams stood separately and held a meeting in a pile on how to help those who can't swim. But they didn't count on whether there might be any surprises in the water.

Red-blue team.

Carl: - 'The plan is as follows! Erik will start first, followed by Mitch, then Zoe, followed by Beneth and I will be the last in line, so that if something bad happens, we can help those who can't swim.': - He said firmly.

Zoe: - 'Why do you have to go in that order, there is a passage anyway, what can happen to us?': - She said sullenly.

Carl: - 'We have to go in this order because it is safe and if something happens, there will be someone to help!': - He said sternly.

Zoe: -'Well! What would happen anyway? There is nothing in the water, only water!': - She answered with a laugh.

Carl: - 'Okay! Pay attention! We are together to solve this task, we just have to win together, if we don't do it this way then it was a shame to start this competition. If you are not a team player, we can even go back, and we will be the first to be eliminated. Decide what you want.': - He replied angrily.

Zoe: - 'Alright then! Let's do it then!': - She answered somewhat grumpily.

Green-yellow team.

Jason: - 'I think the primary thing we should pay attention to is that there are no surprises in the water. When we make sure that everything is in order, Kurtis will be the first to go, followed by Emy, then Alice, then Liam and finally I will close the line.': - He said confidently.

Kurtis: - 'That sounds really good, there is no shortage of surprises again.': - He agreed.

Alice: - 'I'm a very good swimmer and underwater too, so I think if you think about it, I'll go ahead and scout the terrain.': - She said bravely.

Jason: 'That's a good idea! Then I think we should ready up and get started': - He answered excitedly. The red and blue team were already standing at the passage where the ships joined, so they will be the first to leave.

Carl: - 'Well then, as we discussed!': - He started walking ahead. As he said this, they already set off one by one across the ships, which of course sank down as soon as they stepped on them, so that it would not be possible to cross to the other side. They were halfway there when something grabbed Zoe's leg and pulled her under the water. The others from the green-yellow team didn't see anything because the illusion didn't make this possible, they only saw that they were moving nicely and calmly to the other side. When Beneth saw that Zoe had disappeared, they immediately started shouting and stopped to look for Zoe. They started looking around, down and in the water, but they didn't see anything.

Carl: -'Zoe! Zoe! What happened to her, where could she have gone?': - He looked for her in despair. Beneth panicked and started shaking.

Erik: - 'Beneth! Don't panic, we're here, don't worry!': - He shouted nervously. But Beneth was so frightened that he could not control himself. Zoe finally climbed up the ships and tiredly tried to warn them.

Carl: -'Where did you go Zoe! I looked everywhere but I just didn't see you anywhere!': - He asked scared.

Zoe: - 'Something pulled me down, but I couldn't see what it was! There's something in the water guys, we have to be careful.' Beneth could hardly control himself because he panicked, this made things difficult for all of them. Mitch also panicked because he couldn't swim either. The others who were waiting for their turn on the other side didn't notice anything, they just saw that everything was fine, and they were moving smoothly to the other side. In the meantime, Beneth was also pulled into the depths by the same thing that pulled Zoe down. Beneth's eyes were open, and he saw the thing that pulled him down into the depths, an evil Siren with sharp teeth and large claws was about to devour Beneth. Zoe immediately noticed that Beneth was dragged under the water by the monster.

Zoe: - 'Guys Beneth is gone!!': - She shouted and with that movement she already jumped into the water. The others then also jumped in the water to free their companion Beneth. Mitch stood there on the ship and sat down with trembling knees because he could no longer stand on his feet. There was a huge fight under the water, it was not easy to fight the siren because they had to swim to the surface for air. Beneth passed out under the water, so he began to sink to the bottom, which made their situation even more difficult. Erik came to the surface and after taking a big breath of air swam back under the water, swimming straight for Beneth to catch him in time. After a big fight, Zoe and Carl managed to defeat the siren and rescue their companion from the water. As soon as they defeated the siren, the water and the siren disappeared, and they lay there exhausted on the ground with the first water ball next to them. They looked at each other laughing happily and got up from the ground panting and shouted with joy that they had the first ball.

Zoe: -'Mitch! Is everything alright? We left you here, but I think you were better of up here!': - She said panting.

Mitch: - 'I was really afraid that you wouldn't come back from there.':- He answered in horror.

Beneth: - 'Guys, you saved my life, for which I am very grateful, thank you!': - He thanked them trembling.

Carl: - 'It was nothing!!': - He answered panting.

Erik: - 'You owe us one!': - He said with a smile.

Zoe: - 'Let's go boys, we have the first ball, there are only two more to go, this is a good game!': - She said excitedly.

The green and yellow team only saw that they got through to the other side.

Jason: - 'Then we're next! Are you ready?': - He asked.

Alice: - 'Then I'll jump in the water and look around, wait here until then.': - She said seriously. With that she jumped into the water and began to swim down to make sure everything was okay. But as as she didn't see anything out of the ordinary, she swam back to the surface.

Alice: - 'I didn't see anything out of the ordinary, I think you can proceed calmly.': - She said encouragingly. They started to the other side one after the other, so that they could keep an eye out if something happened. Alice made sure that everything was in order, but even though she was so careful, the unexpected happened. A giant octopus with huge teeth and sticky tentacles emerged from the water. Everyone was in awe when they saw the big monster. They were so scared by the octopus suddenly rising out of nowhere that Emy fell onto the ship and did not dare to get up from it. When Liam saw this, he farted in fear, but almost five in a row.

Liam: -'Oh my God, what will happen to us now? This monster is going to eat us! Let's turn back!!': - He shouted in despair.

Emy: -'Help! It's eating us! Now what are we going to do?': - She shouted in horror.

Jason, Kurtis and Alice fought the octopus, the fight was huge.

Jason: - 'Kurtis, let's aim for the heart!!': - He yelled tiredly.

Kurtis: 'I'll try! Distract it somehow!': - He shouted back.

Alice: - 'Be careful! He will catch Emy! Be careful!!': - She shouted warningly. With that, the octopus grabbed Emy and pulled her under the water with one of its tentacles, and with the other tentacle, it grabbed Liam and pulled him under the water as well. Of course, the others didn't leave it at that, they immediately swam after them to free them. Alice distracted the octopus, until Jason injured the tentacle in which Emy was held, thus freeing her from its grip. He brought her to the surface and put her onto the ship. Mitch started stabbing the octopus in the eye with his sword, so the octopus released its other tentacle, and Liam was also freed. Alice brought him to the surface and helped him onto the ship, then went back to fight. The octopus caught Alice, but her hand was free, so she stopped its tentacles with her sword.

Alice:- 'Attack now!! Try and get to its heart!!': - She shouted in the middle of a fight.

After a long fight, they defeated the octopus together, so both the water and the octopus disappeared, they fell to the ground. After they were over the big fight, they looked at each other and continued to lie on the ground smiling with a big sigh.

Liam: - 'Guys, you saved us from that big, huge monster, thanks! It was an illusion course! Look, the water ball is over there, we got the first ball!!': - He said with a smile.

Alice: - 'Well, it was, and served with a huge octopus as an extra side dish.': - She replied laughing.

Kurtis: - 'Finally, we have the first ball!': - He answered with a smile.

Alice: - 'Hey! Emy are you okay? Did you get hurt?': - She asked caringly.

Emy: -'Thank you, I'm fine! But I don't want to see water anymore, that's for sure. Thank you for saving me, I'm grateful for it': - She answered in horror.

Jason: - 'We suffered for it, but finally we did it, here is our first ball guys, yuppie!! I think it's ok now, let's go on, we did this too!': - He said with a smile.

Kurtis: - 'It was a bit of a struggle, but it was worth it! Let's go on!!': - He said with a smile.

They got up from the ground and started slowly.

The black-orange team reached a junction where they also met the indigo-blue-pink team. Since they didn't have any other choice, they also had to continue together to the next junction, the teams looked at each other but didn't deal with each other much, so everyone stayed with their own teammates. The end of the road ahead of them could be seen, which was a relief for everyone. Yes, but they also had an illusion course waiting for them, just like their peers, only that it was a different kind of wet task, not like the previous one. On two sides, the hedges turned into water. Suddenly everyone stopped and looked to both sides because the water was rising on our side. The two groups gathered separately to discuss this phenomenon.

Black and orange team.

Norbert: - 'What we see here is nothing but a trap, we have to be very careful! Who can swim?': - He asked.

Patrick, Doris: - 'I can swim!': - They said at the same time. Both, Mark and Adam remained silent meaning they could not swim.

Patrick: - 'I can swim very well underwater.': - He said enthusiastically.

Doris: - 'Fortunately, I also swim well under water.': - She interrupted excitedly.

Norbert: - 'Okay! I don't know what will happen but be very careful and stay very close to each other, and Mark and Adam, hold on to us because if something goes wrong, we can catch you and don't let us go.': - He told the possible plan.

Mark: - 'And what if we drown?': - He asked scared.

Adam: -'If I suddenly go under water, I panic!'

Norbert: - 'We'll solve it somehow! Try not to panic because then it will be easier for us too.' That was easy to say, but even harder to do. The indigo blue-pink team stood in front of the black-orange team, and they also held a meeting.

Indigo Blue-Pink Team.

Mason: -'Listen up, skunks! I don't know what will happen, but now tell me who can't swim?': - He asked seriously.

Betty: - 'I can't swim and I'm very afraid if the water is too deep!': - She said in horror.

Kayl: - 'Unfortunately, I can't swim either, I'm terrified of water!': - He said nervously.

Mason: - 'It's okay! Then it's good if only you two can't swim, because then the three of us can help you more easily. The point is that you two stay close to us so we can catch you.'

Betty: - 'But what if we drown, because you won't be able to help?': - She asked in despair.

Kayl: - 'Yes, what will happen then?': - He asked him scared.

Mason: - 'Calm down, we'll solve it like we did before.': - He answered reassuringly. After the teams discussed the strategy, they stood close to each other and watched closely what was going to happen. Beautiful fish swam into the Water Wall, they even saw a turtle, but nothing else strange. The indigo-blue-pink team slowly moved forward and looked around. The black and orange team waited a little longer because they didn't want to follow them closely. When the indigo-blue-pink team was halfway to the middle, they heard a big tremor, but this tremor was also heard by the black-orange team. Suddenly, the indigo-blue-pink team stopped to observe what the tremor was. The black and orange team didn't even move. The shaking got stronger and stronger, and finally the walls of water on the sides merged and took everyone who was standing there with it. The players of the indigo-blue-pink team did not have time to react to the event, so they all were thrown in every direction. The players of the black and orange team held on to each other and held each other tightly. Partick broke away from them because the water pressure hit him directly, but since he could swim well under water, his quick thinking helped him, and he swam to its companions.

Betty didn't even open her eyes under the water because she was so terrified of the water. She startgrabbed;hing to escape and grabbed someone or something, but she didn't know who or what she grabbed, all she knew was that she wasn't going to let go. Kayl was also under the water with his eyes closed and thrashed to hold on to something, but he did not succeed. Betty latched onto a two-headed, six-legged water snake. Her companions saw this and immediately tried to help her. Kayl was finally caught by Carter and brought to the surface, but he couldn't leave him there alone because then he sank back under the water, so he had to stay with him on the surface, there were only two people who could help Betty. Norbert saw what kind of monster they were dealing with and brought those who couldn't swim to the surface, but quickly took advantage of the fact that one of the players from the other team was caught by the monster, so they quickly started swimming to the other side. But they swam in vain because another monster was waiting for them as well. This monster was none other than Cathulu, it looked very terrifying, it was extremely huge.

Patrick: - 'Oh my god, this is just a joke, right??': - He asked, horrified.

Norbert: - 'No, this is not a joke!! Let's catch the monster.': - He said bravely.

Mark, Adam: - 'And what will happen to us??': - They asked at the same time.

Doris: - 'Don't worry, we are here to protect you!!': - He said to them smiling. Meanwhile, Norbert constantly poked and prodded his sword to see how it should fall to his hand, so that he would have a good grip. As he was spinning his sword, he accidentally pressed something on it and it transformed into a three-bladed sword.

Norbert: -'Holy shit guys! Look what happened to my sword! I don't know what I did, but it turned out like this!': - He said excitedly.

Patrick: - 'I also found the opening point, mine also changed, very cool!!': - He answered with great joy.

Doris: - 'I have mine too, let's hit him, let's destroy the monster!': - She said belligerently.

Patrick: - 'Let's give it to him!!': - He said in agreement.

Norbert: - 'Let's cut it into small pieces!!': - He said, ready to go. Mark and the Adam were clinging closely to each other in a protruding tendril and watching their companions as they fought, but they were terribly afraid. The Monster caught Patrick with one of its tentacles and pulled him away from the others, but luckily his sword didn't fall out of his hand, so he was able to injure the monster's tentacle. Norbert cut off one of the monster's hands. In the midst of the great fight, a large pirate ship suddenly appeared. They watched in awe and wondered how it got here. Of course, the monster still wanted to catch them, but the pirate ship got in the way.

Doris: -'Holy shit! How did it get here??': - She asked in surprise.

Adam: - 'Good God, even this is here, we will never get out of this!': - He said terrified.

Mark: - 'Now what on earth are we going to do, we need to find something too!': - He said trembling.

Adam: - 'The problem is that we can't swim, so we can't really do anything.': - He answered in despair.

Mark: - 'But if we climb on the ship, we can deal with the

pirates!!': - He said imaginatively. Meanwhile, Norbert, Patrick and Doris were already on board the ship.

Norbert: -'Well, guys, it's going to be a good party!! Listen, there are five of them, just like us, I think they will also take part in killing the monster': - He said enthusiastically.

Patrick: -'I agree with you Norbert! I think we can easily handle the monster together! Don't be sorry, let's give it to him.': - He answered enthusiastically. In the meantime, Adam and Mark also arrived on board.

Mark, Adam: - 'We are here too guys! We won't miss this party!!': - They said at the same time, ready for battle.

Pirate 1: - 'Guys! Ready for battle!!!': - He shouted. With that, the pirates ran at the monster and the fight began. Everyone started sword fighting to defeat the monster.

Norbert: - 'That's all you've got, come if you dare!': - He shouted at the monster.

Cthulu: - 'You are funny my friend! This was just a warm-up for me, I will only really fight now!': - He replied laughing.

Norbert: - 'We'll see who laughs at the end!': - He answered with a smile.

Patrick: - 'That's for you, you goofy-eyed freak!': - He shouted excitedly.

Doris: - 'What's up, little one, come if you dare!': - She annoyed the monster.

Mark: - 'Well, I like this when we don't have to suffer under the water, these pirates were sent here at the right time!: - He said aloud.

Adam: - 'Of course, I also like this better than suffering in the water, I agree with you Mark, let's give it to them!': - He said with a smile, and they fought hard.

Norbert fought very well with the pirates and his companions in unison, it was not as easy as Norbert had imagined, but they did not give up. The monster knocked the sword out of Norbert's hand three times, and of course it wasn't easy to get it back because he was waving his tentacles everywhere. Norbert bent down to pick up his sword and when he was about to take it, the monster knocked him into the water with one of his tentacles.

Pirate: - 'Now what? You don't have a sword mate?': - He asked in surprise. But Norbert swam under water over to another ship to retrieve his sword which was stuck in a broken mast, the others who saw it happening were careful that the monster would've notice, because then it would catch Norbert.

Then Norbert climbed up to the other ship and got to his sword, he pulled it out and ran back and jumped on board the other ship to fight on. Patrick somehow climbed up the back of the monster and started attacking from there, which was a good idea. Two other pirates also followed Patrick's example and climbed the monster's back with great difficulty.

Adam: - 'Guys, try to tire him somehow!!': - He shouted.

Pirate 1: - 'That won't be an easy task, this beast is huge!': - He shouted back. The monster has already broken the ship to such an extent that it begins to sink.

Chief Pirate: - 'watch out!! The ship is sinking!!' Meanwhile, Patrick and the other two pirates who were on the monster's back managed to gouge out its eyes, which meant that they had a better chance of winning. After his eyes were gouged out, the monster started to stumble because he couldn't see anything, so he tripped. Taking advantage of this, Doris, Mark and Adam quickly reached its heart to kill it, but the monster was using its spikes to protect itself, which is why it was not easy to kill it even though its eyes were pierced.

Mark: - 'Doris!! Doris!! Adam!! Come here!! I'm here! Help!!': - He got up in despair. The monster surrounded Mark with one of its tentacles so much that he could not move.

Doris: - 'I'm coming, hold on!!': - She shouted.

Adam: -'I'm coming mate!! I'm here!!': - He ran over to help. Doris and the Adam simultaneously cut off the monster's tentacles, which surrounded Mark, and finally they managed to free him.

Mark: - 'Thanks guys, I could barely breathe!!': - He said gasping for air.

Norbert: -'I'm here Patrick!! Come here!': - He called him there.

Patrick: - 'I'm right behind you!!'

Pirates: -'We are here too!'

Patrick: - 'Hold on to his tentacles and climb up!!': - He said hurriedly.

Norbert: - 'I'm on it!!': - He answered tiredly.

Patrick: - 'Come on, I'll pull you up!!': - He held out his hand. Both of them held on to each other and swung towards the monster's heart with a great momentum and plunged their swords into the monster's heart at the same time. The monster didn't die immediately as it was huge, after the stabbing it started to stagger back to such an extent that it sent Doris and Mark into the water, but both of them fainted due to the blow, which can be quite dangerous. One of the pirates immediately noticed and jumped after them to help them.

Adam: -'Norbert, Patrick!!! Quickly, come here, Doris and Mark fell into the water, the monster hit them with its tentacles, so that they flew into the water, I think they fainted!!': - He warned them in despair.

Patrick: - 'Come on, Norbert, let's jump after them!!: - He called for help.

Norbert: - 'I'm coming!!': - He answered enthusiastically.

Pirate: - 'I'm going too, wait!': - He shouted. All three jumped into the water to save Doris and Mark. The Mighty Monster destroyed everything in its path even though it was dying. It even dragged one of the pirates under the water. They pulled Doris and Mark out of the water just when they noticed this, Patrick and Norbert immediately swam back under the water to pull the pirate out of the grip of the tentacles. They couldn't pull him out because his tentacles stuck to the pirate, so they cut it off and freed him. Everyone was there and no one was missing.

Chief pirate: - 'Good job son!! You fought well, with great difficulty, but we defeated the beast Ahoy!!!': - he said goodbye to the team.

The team: - 'Ahoy captain!!!': - They said goodbye to them. 'Thanks for the help.' With that, the water and everything else disappeared from the scene and they sat on the ground again.

Adam: - 'That was tough, guys!': - He said breathlessly. They all looked at each other and then at Adam and started laughing, they didn't have energy for anything else.

Doris: -'I can't believe this, guys We did this course too! Thank you for saving me from the water and not leaving me there!!': - She said gratefully.

Mark: - 'Thank you guys for not letting me down!! Watch this! Here is the water ball, our first ball, we got it, woohoo!!!': - He shouted happily.

Adam: -'That's right! We did it guys, we have our first ball, great!!': - He said with a loud smile.

Norbert: - 'We finally have the first ball; we only have to get two more and the game is over.': - He said tiredly but smiling.

Patrick: - 'The good thing is that we have the first ball, I don't think there is much left, let's go on, let's play this game': - He said firmly but still smiling.

Mason and Grace went back underwater to help Betty who was being held captive by the monster and was about to be devoured. Grace grabbed Betty's arm and started to pull her out of the monster's claws until Mason started poking the monster's eyes with his sword, as soon as he stabbed one eye, it immediately released Betty so that Grace could bring her to the surface. Mason continued to fight the monster, but he couldn't last long under the water, so he had to swim up for air. Grace got Betty to safety while Carter looked after them both. Grace immediately swam back under the water to continue fighting the monster. Grace also managed to injure the monster, but she also had to swim to the surface for air, so Mason continued the fight. At the cost of a great struggle, they defeated the monster and then the water disappeared, the monster turned to dust, and they found themselves on the ground. They were very exhausted, they just lay there on the floor and looked out of their heads.

Carter: -'That, guys! This was a very tough fight! But we did it, you two were very good, I congratulate you.': - He said panting.

Mason: - 'Well! We did it! But you weren't bad either, keeping two people in such a way that they were panicked, and you were under the water almost the whole time to save them, that's awesome.': - He answered panting. Betty and Kayl could barely speak, still in shock.

Carter: - 'I think we should get up and go on, let's not waste time, we will catch our breath on the move.': - He said tiredly.

Betty: - 'Look what I found, here is the water ball, we got the first ball, guys!!': - She shouted with great joy.

Carter: - 'The ball is really here! This is really cool guys! We finally have the first ball! Congratulations to everyone!!': - He said happily.

Kayl: - 'Great! You were great, that's for sure! Congratulations to you!': - He said breathlessly.

Grace: 'We were really good! The point is that we have the first ball, and nobody got hurt.': - He said with a smile.

Mason: - 'I agree, guys, we were good, we were able to work together, which matters a lot in this game, we have the first ball, there are only two left, let's keep going!': - He encouraged them. The teams progressed nicely on the field. The audience had a lot of fun, they liked the game, the atmosphere was great, there was silence in the audience only when they were in the middle of such important events, but when they solved the task, they cheered the players ecstatically. Among the spectators, it was clear which team they were rooting for, so the atmosphere was frenetic.

~

Elisa: - 'Robnis my son! You're going to meet your future bride soon, I'm sure you're excited, aren't you?'

Robnis: -'Yes, mother, I'm looking forward to it! The only thing is that we are condemned here, this is not very reassuring. I have a very bad feeling about this marriage proposal, there is too much silence, everything is so perfect, I don't like it.': - He answered thoughtfully.

Elisa: -'Come on, you're seeing horrors, son! Nothing has happened so far, why would it now? We are safe here; we don't have to worry about anything.': - She answered reassuringly.

Robnis: -'I hope you're right, mother! But I will still prepare for

338

this, I will post guards in the towers for the day when the guests arrive here.': - He said thoughtfully.

Elisa: - 'okay my son, as you see fit.': - She answered understandingly.

Nivita: - 'Father! It's good that you're here, I want to talk to you!': - He said excitedly.

Nyaritis: - 'Tell me, daughter, what are you so excited about?': - He asked with a smile.

Nivita: - 'Father, I can't wait to see Robnis, I'm so excited that I don't have any more patience. Why do we have to wait two weeks, why can't the big event be tomorrow?': - She asked excitedly.

Nyaritis: -'Oh daughter! It's not as easy as you imagine, you have to plan it carefully so that everything is perfect and that takes time, you know that!': - He answered with a smile.

Nivita: - 'Yes, yes, I know, but even then, those two weeks are so long, that time will never come.': - She said with a withered smile.

Nyaritis: - 'Come on, Nivita, you're an adult, you're no longer a child, you just have to endure this little time, after that, when you get married, you'll have a whole life ahead of you to be with your love, right?': - He asked with a smile.

Nivita: - 'You are right my father, somehow I will survive and thank you for taking the time for me!': - She said with a smile.

Nyaritis: - 'It's just natural my daughter and perseverance to you!': - He shouted after her laughing.

Karnita: -'Mother! What do you think Valtinus will be like? I mean is he good looking? Because I haven't been lucky enough to see him, only when we were kids and that was a long time ago.': - She wondered.

Julia: - 'My daughter! I can assure you that Valtinus is a very handsome young man, you will like him very much, I guarantee that. In the meantime, we have to prepare well for the trip, because time passes quickly, you don't even notice it, and we have to go.': - She reassured her with a smile.

Karnita: -'I believe you, mother! But I'm very curious about how he looks like.': - She replied dreamily.

Julia: - Haha! My dear child, when the time comes, you will see! Now you better get ready, so you don't forget something at home.: - He said with a laugh.

Karnita: - It's fine, mother! But I'm still very excited about the meeting.: - He answered thoughtfully.

Julia: - 'Don't forget to come down for lunch!': - She said with a smile.

Karnita: - 'Of course, mother!!!': - She answered while looking out the window. The mother left the room and went to the king.

Erminus: -'Oh, it's good that we ran into each other, dear! I want to discuss something important with you. Come let's go to our room to talk face to face.': - He said smiling.

Julia: - 'Is there something wrong?': - She asked curiously.

Erminus: - 'No dear, there's nothing wrong!': - He answered with a smile. They reached their room and closed the door on themselves.

Julia: - 'My dear, you scare me! What's happening? There's something wrong, right?': - She asked the questions.

Erminus: - 'Dear, take a seat, please! I invited you to our room because I want to ask you to do something that you have to agree to! Now that our daughter is also getting married, it will be just the two of us here in this big palace. What would you do if we had a child? We are still young, and it would be nice if we had a

340

little lurker at the house.': - He asked with a smile.

Julia: -'Oh my dear Erminus!! But since we already have grandchildren, we are no longer too young to have a child! Soon we will have grandchildren again and we will be able to play with them as much as we want. I'm already too old for that!': - She answered with relief and surprise.

Erminus: - 'Come on, dear, we're not old, we could easily fit another child into our lives.': - He said with a smile.

Julia: - 'Darling! I appreciate your desire for children, but if we go to King Nyaritis, we will meet our grandchildren there and then you can be with them as much as you want. But from my part, this i no longer want any, I'm sorry, but I don't want anymore children.': - She answered with a smile.

Erminus: - 'Okay then, my dear! If you don't want more, I respect your decision. But we're going to have a little fun tonight, right??': - He caught her hand and hugged her, smiling.

Julia: - 'Well, I'll think about it, you little heartthrob!!': - She giggled and collapsed in his arms. The players continued on the field in silence, everyone was watching so they wouldn't be surprised again. But the labyrinth was full of surprises, so you can't really prepare for it. The red-blue team reached a junction in the road and had to decide which path to take. They left path comes to a dead end, but the other path continues on.

Beneth: - 'Guys, now we have to decide which way to go! Which do you think is the right way?': - He asked thoughtfully.

Zoe: - 'I think we should go to the right, so far we have always gone to the right.': - She replied confidently.

Carl: - 'Zoe is right, let's go to the right.': - He answered in agreement.

Erik: - 'I don't even know what will happen if we fall into some kind of trap again.': - He answered nervously.

Zoe: -'Erik! Are you serious? You can't be that big of pussy, you signed up for this game, didn't you?' No one forced you to apply, then be a man and not a bunny.': - She answered while rolling her eyes.

Mitch: - 'I also agree with Zoe, I also think we should go to the right.': - He agreed.

Beneth: - 'Well, the majority decided, so we go to the right.': - He closed the topic. So, they started to the right as they wanted. Zoe went ahead because she wasn't afraid of anything, she actually enjoyed it all, finally something exciting is happening in her life. As they went further inside, suddenly everything around them started to get so dark that they couldn't see anything but heard sounds and the rustling of leaves.

Erik: - 'Guys!! Guys? Are you still here? Someone say something?': - He asked, terrified.

Beneth: -' Im here Erik! Can you hear me?': - He asked.

Erik: - 'Yes, I hear you, where are you?': - He asked back. Meanwhile, he was feeling around because he couldn't see anything. They were waving their arms around in case they walked into someone or something, until they finally found each other and held each other's hands tightly.

Mitch: -'What could this be again? I can't see anything God dammit.': - He said nervously.

Zoe: - 'Oh and i wonder what it could be? A little darkness, what else. You aren't afraid of the dark, are you? Fate has brought me together with God damn weak ass men!!': - She muttered aloud.

Beneth: - 'I think we should find something with which we can make a fire, so that we can see something!: - he said thoughtfully.

Zoe: - 'look for something!! Are you serious? It's very dark, if

you hadn't noticed yet you little genius, we won't find anything!':
- She replied angrily. As soon as she said this, a sudden light flew
past them and disappeared.

Erik: -'Did you see this? As if a light had flown past us!': - He
said scared.

Zoe: - 'Oh, a light that flies! How could we have missed it, your
head suddenly lit up from all the fear.': - She scoffed.

Erik: - 'Make fun of me, I still saw it!': - He defended himself.
With that, it flew past them again, but now there was more of
them which all of them witnessed.

Erik: - 'I told you, didn't I!': - He answered proudly.

Mitch: - 'What kind of phenomena are these?': - He asked in
surprise.

Beneth: - 'That's just interesting! Let's stay close to each other
and take out your swords.': - He said prepared.

Zoe: - 'I don't think our sword will be useful against them, it
seemed to me as if they were ghosts, the sword wouldn't work on
them.': - She interrupted wisely.

Erik: - 'Then, how do we defeat them?': - He asked terrified, he
was very afraid of ghosts.

Beneth: - 'I'm sure there will be a solution for this.': - He
answered reassuringly.

Zoe: - 'Look, here they come!!!': - He warned them. The ghosts
attacked again, but now there were more of them than before,
they were attacked from several sides. Suddenly they all fell to
the ground and looked at how many there were. There were quite
a few, but there was one that was different from the rest. This
spirit was red and blue just like the colours of their team, but this
spirit flew high enough that it was impossible to even catch it. In
the meantime, the other teams also arrived on the course of

darkness just like the red and blue team.

Black and orange team: -

Norbert: - 'Stay on the ground, don't get up yet, we have to watch how high the orange ghost flies.': - He said warningly.

Green-yellow team.

Jason: - 'Let's stay close to each other, but, if possible, sit on the ground. We need to spot that green-yellow ghost, how low it flies, and then we can catch it.': - He warned them.

Indigo Blue-Pink Team: -

Mason: - 'Listen, if the indigo blue and pink ghost comes out again, be on the lookout, because we have to catch that ghost. Well, each team captain warned his teammates that they had to catch the right spirit, everyone was aware of this now, but that spirit was not so easy to catch because it flew very high. But if those ghosts are caught, they get the second ball, which means that there is only one ball left to win.

Norbert: -'I have an idea guy! I think that spirit should be lured down somehow in order to be able to catch it, otherwise it will not come down because the other spirits are protecting it so that it can fly higher.': - He spoke wisely.

Doris: - 'This is correct so far, but still, how are we going to lure it down?': - She asked thoughtfully.

Patrick: 'Is this serious! Are we going to luring ghosts? Fuck me, I can't believe we have to do this. Let's hope it works, because for now it seems that the other spirits are quite protective of that one.': - He said with a laugh.

Mark: - 'This will be a good party! I'm so into this whole ghost luring malarkey, let's kill us some ghosts.': - He interrupted.

Adam: - 'Okay then! Time for some ghosts! We'll capture the

beast. Well then, how do we get started, guys?': - He said bravely.

Norbert: - 'For now, let's keep an eye on them to see where they're moving and then I'll get up to see their reaction, and then we'll decide, you just watch, okay.': - He said quietly.

Patrick: - 'Norbert, we won't budge, just do it!': - He answered softly.

Mark: - 'I'm ready!!': - He interrupted.

Adam: - 'Yeah, yeah, I'm ready too, let's push him!!': - He said softly. Norbert began to stand up very carefully so that he could see the reaction of the spirits, as soon as he stood up the spirits almost completely surrounded Norbert so that he could not get close to the main spirit, so Norbert lay back on the ground.

Adam: -'Well, guys, it won't be easy, that's for sure!': - He interrupted.

Doris: - 'Listen! What if we disperse and Norbert stays here near the main spirit. We then stand up and attract the attention of the other spirits and then Norbert could attack the main spirit, since he is the tallest among us.': - She said her idea.

Mark: - 'This seems like a good idea; it won't take long to try it!': - He replied with a smile.

Norbert: - 'After all, we can try it out, if it doesn't work out, we'll come up with something else!': - He answered. With that, everyone spread out and slowly started to stand up to distract the spirits. This worked well so far because the spirits surrounded them and protected the main spirit. As it seemed, Norbert got a free pass to hunt. Finally, Norbert slowly stood up and with the sword in his hand began to climb the hedge wall, since the protective spirits were not near the main spirit, it went lower and lower and thus Norbert could easily catch it.

Adam: - 'I'm here ghosts, come here!': - He shouted loudly.

Mark: - 'Come and get me if you can!': - He shouted loudly.

Doris: - 'Here, here, little ones, come, my dears, this is what I'm here for!': - She shouted loudly. Thus, the spirits did not hear Norbert climbing up the hedge wall. Finally, Norbert easily caught the main spirit and swung it in two with his sword, as soon as this was done, all the other spirits disappeared and out of the main spirit a beautiful ball of glitter fell to the ground. They were the first team to get the second ball. But as this happened, the main spirit poured out sparkling fireworks, which was a breathtakingly beautiful sight. The others cheered with joy that they managed to get the second ball.

Doris: - 'Yehhhh!!! That's it, we have the second ball, we did it boys!': - She cheered in joy.

Adam: -'That's it, the ball is there!!! We are good, I'll give us that.': - He said happily.

Mark: - 'This is how it should be done!! We showed those spirits that we are the best!': - He shouted with a smile.

Patrick: - 'That's good!! Teamwork guys! Just keep going and we'll have the last ball!': - He said smiling, they shook hands.

Norbert: - 'This team effort was great, it was a good job guys, Doris, I congratulate you on your idea, it finally came together in the end!': - He said happily.

Doris: -'I'm glad it worked out! Well, there's only one ball left, and we'll have that as well, I'm sure of it. I don't know what awaits us yet, but if we work together, then anything is possible. Let's go on!': - She said happily. They all said, 'let's go on an adventure, guys, let's keep going, nothing can stop us !!' With that, they continued.

Red-blue team.

Carl: - 'There are a lot of these ghosts! How are we going to catch that master ghost?': - He asked in surprise.

Beneth: - 'I think we should stay here on ground for a while, and we can observe how many spirits surround the main spirit.': - He answered.

Erik: - 'After all, it's not a bad idea, then we'll figure something out!': - He interrupted.

Zoe: - 'Let's not waste time, let's come up with something quickly!': - She interrupted. They lay there on the ground and watched the movements of the spirits.

Mitch: - 'Listen now, see how calm the ghosts are? Because we are not near the main spirit, but as soon as we stand up, they attack to protect the main spirit.': - He said imaginatively.

Beneth: - 'That's right! But the question here is, how can we distract the spirits?': - He asked.

Erik: - 'Well, if it's not a problem, then I can try, if it doesn't work, we'll come up with a plan!': - He interrupted.

Carl: - 'And what do you want to do anyway?': - He asked curiously.

I'll get up slowly while you stay here, we'll see how the spirits react!': - He answered seriously.

Zoe: - 'That sounds good! Let's do it and see what comes out of it!': - She interrupted excitedly. Erik then slowly stood up and tried to catch the main spirit with his sword, but at that moment all the spirits surrounded him and did not allow the main spirit to come near him. Erik fell back to the ground with that momentum.

Erik: - 'Well, it didn't work, guys, but we already know that only I was attacked by the ghosts.': - He said bravely.

Beneth: - 'Well! This is a good sign, but if we divert their attention, we could catch the main ghost!': - He spoke wisely.

Carl: -'I have an idea! Mitch is the tallest among us, he could catch the main spirit more easily, the only question is how?': - He spoke imaginatively.

Zoe: 'I also have an idea, boys! I say that Mitch should stay here near the main spirit, the four of us should be a little further away from Mitch to distract the spirits and then Mitch can catch the main spirit!': - She interrupted.

Beneth: - 'Hmm! We can try this too, Zoe that actually sounds pretty good! Well then, let's move away from Mitch and when I give the signal, we will all stand up and loudly drive them towards us!': - He said the plan. They did so, creeping aside away from Mitch so that he could catch the main spirit, when they were a good distance away, they all stood up and started shouting loudly.

Carl: - 'Come here ghosts, I'm here!!': - He shouted loudly.

Zoe: - 'I'm here, catch me if you can!!': - She shouted loudly. Of course, the spirits all gathered around them to protect the main spirit. Until then, Mitch calmly and of course quietly started to climb the hedge wall.

Beneth: - 'Come on, my little ones, I'm here, catch me!': - while waving his sword he shouted loudly.

Erik: -'Here, here my dears! Come on, daddy's here!' He also wielded his sword and shouted as loud as he could. Mitch managed to get to a height where he easily reached the main spirit and swung his sword and split it in two, at that moment the spirits disappeared and the glitter fireworks sprung out from the main ghost, from which a ball of glitter fell to the ground. The Others started cheering and jumping for joy.

Zoe: - 'We did it guys!! We did it!! Yupeee, yupeeee!!!': - She jumped in joy.

Beneth: - 'That's it, we did it!': - He shouted.

348

Carl: -'We have the ball guys! We got the second ball!!': - He shouted happily.

Erik: - 'We got the ball!! Awesome!!': - He shouted happily.

Mitch: - 'It's finally here!! We killed them together guys, it was good teamwork!': - He said happily.

Beneth: - 'We exterminated the beasts! The point is that we have the ball, we can continue the game, there is only one ball left.': - He said happily.

Mitch: -'That's right! Let's go on, let's get the last ball!': - He said excitedly.

Zoe: - 'Let's go boys, we'll win this game for sure!': - He said confidently. With that, they moved on.

The green and yellow team sat on the ground and discussed.

Jason: - 'There are quite a lot of these spirits and the main spirit flies very high, I don't know how we will catch it?': - He asked thoughtfully. Alice lay down on the floor while the others were still sitting. Kurtis noticed that where Alice was lying, the ghosts did not go at all, but where they were sitting, they hovered quite low, almost above their heads.

Kurtis: - 'Listen guys! I think we should lie down on the ground because then the ghosts won't come near us, look at Alice, the ghosts won't go there because she's lying on the ground.': - He said imaginatively. The others then lay down on the ground and began to watch the spirits. Kurtis was really right in this, because at that point the spirits started to fly higher. Liam didn't tell anyone, but he was very afraid of ghosts, he was already completely sweaty, and his heart was pounding in his throat. For some reason Emy looked at Liam and saw his scared face. He crawled next to Liam and said softly.

Emy: - 'Liam! Are you afraid of ghosts?': - She asked softly.

Liam: - 'Can you tell? I can't even look at them.': - He answered in horror.

Emy: - 'Yes, everyone can tell! But don't worry, we're here and we'll figure it out somehow.' Yes, it's just that Liam was the tallest in their team, but they don't know yet that Liam has to solve this task.

Jason: - 'Well guys, it's a good sign that the ghosts won't attack us like this, now we have to figure out how to surround the main ghost!': - He said seriously.

Kurtis: - 'Listen, I'll stand up alone, so we can see what the ghosts will do then, and then we'll plan something!': - He said firmly.

Alice: - 'Okay! Then we'll watch, let's do it!': - She answered excitedly. But Liam didn't dare to open his eyes to observe what was really happening. Kurtis slowly stood up, and then the spirits completely seized him and did not allow him to do anything, so he fell back to the ground.

Jason: -'Well, that was interesting, the ghosts only attacked Kurtis and left us alone, which means that if we are standing, the others will protect the main ghost at all costs. Well, does anyone have an idea of what to do?': - He asked thoughtfully. As they lay there on the ground, they kept thinking about how to distract the other spirits from the main spirit.

Emy: - 'I had an idea about how to divert the spirits from the main ghost!': - She said.

Kurtis: - 'How?': - He asked back.

Emy: - 'I think it could be that one of us stays here near the main spirit while the others divert the spirits much further away and then that person can take down the main spirit.': - She answered smartly.

Jason: - 'That sounds good! But who will that someone be?': - He asked curiously.

Kurtis: - 'I think we would only have a chance if the tallest among us carried out this task.'

Alice: -'That's sounds like a plan, guys! But who is the tallest?': - She asked curiously. At this, the others immediately looked at Liam. And Liam was lying on the ground with his eyes closed.

Jason: - 'Liam! What's up mate? Didn't you hear what we talked about here? You are the tallest among us, you have to carry out this task!': - He said warningly.

Liam: -'I'm sorry, guys, but I can't do it! I'm very scared of ghosts, I can't even look at them, can't you hear the scary sounds they make? I'm sorry, but I won't be able to do this, you have to appoint someone else for this task.': - He replied trembling.

Jason: -'Come on dude! You don't have to be afraid; we are here with you, we will distract the other ghosts while you only have to fight one ghost. Listen, let's do a test and then you'll see that the spirits won't hurt us, they'll just scare us to keep us away from the main spirit, we're here by your side, okay. And only you have to deal with the main ghost, until then we 'll take care of the other ghosts, you have to trust us, you know it's a team effort. Let's start by opening your eyes, okay?': - He said encouragingly.

Liam: - 'Okay! I can try!': - He said in a trembling voice. He slowly opened his eyes and when he saw how many ghosts are around them, he farted in fear and immediately closed his eyes again.

Liam: - 'I can't do this, I'm sorry, if I get scared, I always have to fart and then how would you distract the other ghosts?': - He asked in despair.

Emy: -'Listen Liam! What we're going to do is that we're going to crawl much further away from you, and then when we're far

351

enough away from you, we're going to stand up and shout at the top of our lungs at the same time to drive all the other spirits towards us, until then you only have to focus on one spirit, which I don't think is a bad idea. You will only be able to deal with that one, so what do you say?': - She asked reassuringly.

Liam: - 'Yes, and what if I fart again, the other spirits will attack me!': - He said desperately.

Emy: - 'Calm down, Liam! Plug your ears with something and then you won't hear these sounds, maybe then it will be easier for you!': - He answered smartly.

Kurtis: - 'Well, that sounds good!': - He interrupted.

Alice: - 'Here is this rag, plug your ears with it, it will really help, try it first!': - She interrupted. Liam tried the rag and put it in his ear and barely heard anything, he liked it, he calmed down to some extent.

Alice: - 'How is it? Do you hear something?': - He asked.

Liam: - 'It was much better this way, I can't hear them as much, in fact I can barely hear anything, I think this will be good! It's fine, I'll do it, just give me a signal when I should go and then I'll attack!': - He finally gave in.

Jason: - 'That's what I'm talking about man! Let's do it together, don't be scared!!!': - He encouraged him. The others carefully crept away from Liam, and Liam plugged his ears and watched for the signal. When the others were at a certain distance, they stood up and started shouting loudly, then all the ghosts flew around them and then Jason gave the signal to Liam to go. Liam got up from the ground and started to climb the hedge wall, which was a little difficult for him because he was very afraid of ghosts. Once he even fell off from the wall, so he had to climb up again to get closer to the main spirit.

Liam: -'Damn, I'm not going to make it! I'm really afraid of these ghosts, my goodness, I'll try somehow, I don't want to let the others down, I have to do it! Courage Liam! You can do it, you can do it!': - He encouraged himself while his eyes were closed. He opened his eyes and saw the ghosts, so he let out another huge fart from fear. He looked at the others and saw how much they were fighting against the ghosts, so he leaned against the hedge wall once more. Unfortunately, he fell off the wall again, but this time he didn't leave it at that.

Liam: -'I can't believe this! They won't be able to hold the ghosts for much longer, I have to do it, I have no other choice, Liam, close your eyes and concentrate!': - He encouraged himself enthusiastically and with that he began to climb the wall again.

But in the end, on the third attempt, he managed to reach the main spirit and then he sliced it in two, from which glitter fireworks erupted and the glitter ball fell out, then at that moment all the other spirits disappeared and of course the darkness along with it. Everyone was very happy that they finally managed to do this task and got the second ball.

Jason: - 'Liam! You finally did it! You know that you are a king, don't you !!!': - He shouted happily.

Alice: - 'Liam, you were great mate, congratulations!': - She said smiling while patting him on the shoulder.

Kurtis: - 'I knew you'd do it, I'm proud of you mate!': - He said smiling while shaking his hand.

Emy: - 'Liam! You did very well! You are a real team player, congratulations!': - She said with a smile.

Jason: - 'We only have one ball left, we'll get it just like we got this one, with teamwork, let's go, let's go, we're awesome!': - He shouted happily.

The audience enjoyed the game with huge cheers, the atmosphere was frenetic.

Gilbert: - 'James! This game turned out better than I imagined! The audience likes it and I enjoy it too, I think it wasn't a bad idea, right?': - He asked with a smile.

James: - 'It's been really good so far! In fact, I think this game is very good and we will launch this game next year at the same time and on this day! What do you think about it?': - He asked excitedly.

Gilbert: - 'But didn't we say that we would play this game every week?': - He asked, surprised.

James: -'Yes, I know we talked about this, but what if we announced this as a national game, because the audience really likes it, it went better than we expected, I think if we play this once a year, it's more than enough, because the players are also exhausted they are under quite a lot of pressure, I say that it will be enough to play this once a year.': - He replied thoughtfully.

Gilbert: 'You're right after all! It could also be the national game, okay then, I will announce the details about this game at the end of this game.': - He answered in agreement.

James: - 'Listen, where is Miriam? She was here not long ago, where did she go? Maybe she doesn't like this game?': - He asked surprised.

Gilbert: - 'She must have had something to do, because you know what she's like! I think she'll be back soon!': - He answered with a smile. Meanwhile, Miriam was still in the palace preparing her traps for the people living in the sphere and after that she checked her crystal to make sure everything was in order, and no one could accidentally access it. The people who lived in the sphere had no idea what Miriam was doing because they felt too comfortable there, they could finally live peacefully without being threatened by anyone. Miriam was looking at the crystal, admiring it, because the light of the crystal was very beautiful. She was thinking of what evil to do as she stared at the crystal.

The evil mushrooms poured out their evil in Miriam's ears.

The evil mushrooms whispered: -

The world must be destroyed!

All must perish!

Darkness will be reborn!

The evil mushrooms kept whispering this in Miriam's ears as the evil spell engulfed her mind. The love she felt for Gilbert was still there, which even the evil mushrooms couldn't erase. But the most important thing is that she has done most of the evil, as the mushrooms make sure that evil is carried out. After admiring the crystal, Miriam put it back in its place and joined her love, Gilbert.

Gilbert: - 'My love, where have you been? I missed you! James was worried about you too! Is everything okay?': - He asked with a smile.

Miriam: 'Oh, of course dear, everything is fine! You don't have to worry about me, I can take care of myself! How is the game? Has everything gone smoothly so far?': - She asked firmly.

Gilbert: -'Oh, of course! But there is one more team left who haven't got the ball yet, I think you should watch this too! The other teams solved the task very cleverly.': - He answered excitedly.

Miriam: - 'I'll be here with you now, I'm not planning anything, so I'll be watching the game all the way through.': - She answered with a half-smile.

James: - 'That's great!! Then let's sit back and let's enjoy the game.': - He said happily.

Indigo Blue-Pink Team:

Mason: -'Guys, there are more and more of these ghosts! The main ghost is flying very high, I have no idea how we will catch it!': - He said thoughtfully.

Betty: - 'Let's sit on the ground until we can think of something against them!': - She said.

Carter: - 'I agree, as long as we're standing here, they won't leave us alone and we can't even think.': - He answered nervously while waving his arms trying to get rid of the ghosts.

Grace: - 'That was a good speech, Carter!': - She interrupted and sat down on the ground.

Kayl: - 'So what should we do now?': - He asked curiously while lying on his back on the ground. The others followed his example and lay down on the ground. While they were staring at the ghosts, they noticed that they were no longer approaching them.

Grace: - 'Do you also see that the spirits no longer come so close to us now that we lied down on the ground?': - She asked, surprised.

Betty: - 'Really! You're right Grace! Maybe that means something, doesn't it?': - He asked curiously.

Grace: - 'It is certain that the spirits are protecting the main spirit so that we cannot catch it! The big question here is how do we go about capturing the main spirit?': - She asked thoughtfully.

Carter: - 'This is really interesting guys! I think we should come up with something quickly, because our time is running out.': - He interrupted.

Mason: - 'We need something very powerful to capture that ghost, but how?': - He asked thoughtfully.

Carter: - 'What if we divert them, would the main ghost follow them?': - He asked wisely.

Betty: - 'Carter, how do you get these ideas? That's it! Let's distract them from the main spirit and then we can capture it!': - She interrupted excitedly.

Carter: -'Well then, let's try it first to see if it works! Are you guys in?': - He asked excitedly.

Mason: -'Of course we're in! Let's distract them, I'll give it a go!': - He answered excitedly.

Carter: -'Okay! But until then, let the others stay lying on the ground and see what will happen!': - He interrupted.

Betty: - 'Okay then! We'll stay here, don't worry!': - She answered with a smile. Mason slowly stood up and held out his sword, at that moment all the ghosts rushed around Mason to protect the main ghost, but the spirits left the others alone. Mason quickly lay back on the ground.

Kayl: - 'Well, that's something! Only Mason was attacked by the ghosts, which is a good sign.': - He said excitedly.

Grace: - 'It was really interesting that only Mason was attacked, and we were left alone.': - She interrupted in amazement.

Carter: - 'Well then guys, here's the plan! In order to distract the ghosts from the main ghost, someone has to stay here near the main ghost and the others have to distract the other ghosts somewhere further away.': - He spoke with a good plan.

Mason: - 'This is a great plan but does the person who will take down the main ghost have to be the tallest, because he has to climb the hedge wall in order to reach the main ghost.': - He interjected smartly. At this statement, everyone looked at Betty, as she was the tallest of them all.

Betty: - 'It's fine, I'll do it, you can depend on me!': - She answered enthusiastically.

Mason: - 'Alright then! Then the plan is as follows! Betty will stay here until we are far enough away where Betty can easily capture the main ghost. Until then, we all stand up and make as much noise as humanly possible, so that the ghosts don't notice Betty and then I think she can capture the main ghost.': - He told them the plan.

Betty: - 'I think this plan is perfect, and I 'll keep an eye out on you guys for when it's time to go and then I'll pounce on it!': - She answered enthusiastically.

Kayl: - 'Well then, let's do it!': - He said excitedly. Everyone crawled far away from Betty and when they were far enough away, they stood up at the same time and started yelling loudly with their swords so that Betty could catch the main ghost. Betty immediately got up from the ground and started climbing the hedge wall.

Betty: - 'god damn! This stupid hedge wall is not that easy to climb!': - She scolded the wall. But she didn't give up, and when she reached the top, she split the main ghost in two, and glitter fireworks came out of it and the glitter ball fell out of it as well. All the ghosts then disappeared along with the darkness. Everyone was very happy that they finally got the second ball, so their team could continue.

Grace: - 'Oh Betty! You're one hell of a girl, you did it, you're great! Congratulations!': - She jumped on her neck, rejoicing.

Kayl: - 'You were great Betty! Congratulations girl!': - He patted her shoulder.

Mason: - 'You did well, girl! Congratulations!': - He grabbed her shoulder.

Carter: - 'You cut the beast in half really well, congratulations girl!': - He grabbed her shoulder.

Betty: - 'Thanks guys, but I couldn't have done this without you, so congratulations to you as well.': - He answered with a smile.

Mason: - 'Thanks Betty! Well, that's how a real team works, but now let's move on because there's still one ball left that we have to get.': - He answered with a smile. The team members all said at the same time while facing each other: -

'Get on the ball! Let's get it! We will win the game! Go! Go! Come on!': - They then jumped up and clapped their hands together. All competitors have already won their second ball, now it just depends on who will win the last ball. The players continued on the field, where everyone now gets a break to refresh themselves. Food and refreshments were placed in the way of the competitors so that they could blow off steam a little.

Red-blue team.

Beneth: - 'Just look! Do you see what I see! A table with delicious food and soft drinks awaits us! Well, this comes in handy now because I'm starving!!': - He said with a sigh.

Erik: - 'Food! Food! I'm hungry!!!!': - He yelled and started running.

Carl: - 'Finally some rest, I needed it!!': - He said calmly.

Zoe: - 'To the trough!! come on guys, time to stuff food into face holes!! We can recharge with a little extra power!! I'm already hungry, let's eat, hmm, it looks delicious!!': - She said with satisfaction.

Mitch: - 'God damn, it looks so damn good!! I have already devoured it all with my eyes!!': - He said starvingly.

Zoe: - 'Let's eat!!': - She said hungrily.

Beneth: - 'This place is very beautiful! Cozy!': - He said.

Mitch: - 'Ahem!! That...! - Meanwhile, he stuffed his face.

Carl: - 'This is delicious!! My goodness, I don't even know when was the last time I ate something so delicious!!': - He said with his mouth full.

Erik: - 'Ahem!! Very delicious!!': - He said with a full mouth.

Zoe: - 'Not even while you're eating can you guys just shut up??': - She glared at them.

Beneth: - 'Alright! Don't tire yourself up, eat and don't pay attention to us!!': - He said with a smile. Zoe just shook her head that they were going to be irreparable like this.

Black and orange team.

Norbert: - 'Look over there!! There is a table spread, with food and soft drinks until you drop!! Let's eat quickly!!': - He said loudly to his companions.

Patrick: - 'Good!! Finally, we can eat something!! This is my place!!': - He said hungrily.

Doris: - 'hey hey hey not so fast gentlemen!! Ladies have priority!!': - She said laughing.

Mark: - 'Wow!! The directors really showed themselves today!! Hmm, what a delicious aroma!!: - He sniffed the air.

Adam: - 'That one will be mine!! Pass that bowl of thighs here, please, thanks! I'd like the soft drink too, thank you!!': - He asked for the food and the soft drink.

Doris: - 'Hmm, it's very tasty you hear!! Please put the bowl of potato salad here, thank you!!': - She said with a smile.

Norbert: - 'We deserve this!! Listen, pass the bacon wrapped chicken here! Thanks, buddy.': - He asked for one of the food bowls.

Green-yellow team.

Jason: - 'Come on, quick!! Look, there is a big table full of delicacies!!': - He addressed his companions.

Alice: - 'Yes, I can see it too!! yooo, look how many delicacies are here!! Well then, let's eat the delicious food!!: - She said hungrily.

Kurtis: - 'You're right!! So many good-looking foods!! Why was this put here?? Isn't this a trap??': - He asked in surprise.

Emy: - 'Come on!! Trap?? I think it's time for lunch, since we haven't eaten anything since morning!! I think we should enjoy all these delicacies while we can!!': - She replied, rubbing her palms together.

Liam: - 'I agree with you Emy! We can eat in peace, now it's time to rest.'

Kurtis: - 'Well, if you say so, then it must be true!! Let's eat!! Bonn appetite everyone!!': - He replied hungrily. Spectators could also go to lunch and enjoy refreshments while the players were having lunch.

Indigo Blue-Pink Team:

Betty: - 'Guys!! There is a big table full of food!! Come quickly!!': - She called the others.

Mason: - 'There really is a big table full of food!! That's awesome!! I'm as hungry as a wolf!!': - He said enthusiastically.

Kayl: - 'Let's go eat quickly!! I'm hungry, I'm thirsty, aaaaaaa!!!!!': - He yelled as he ran to the table.

Carter: - 'I'm sitting here!! I will be closer to delicious meats!! Pass that chicken here, please!!': - He asked with wide eyes.

Grace: - 'Betty I'm sitting next to you!! Us girls stick together!! Oh, my goodness, there's so much goodness in here!! I don't even know which one to take first!!': - She said in amazement.

Mason: - 'Bonn appetite everyone!!': - He said with a smile. The teams all calmly ate the many delicacies from the table, when everyone had eaten their fill, they got up from the table, stretched out and talked to each other, when the last player also got up from the table, then the tables disappeared, and the game could continue. The audience was already in their seats to continue monitoring the progress of the game. The players started on the path in front of them, everything was full of flowers, they saw more and more beautiful things along the way. There were arch gates that they had to pass through, and they were full of even more beautiful flowers. The teams really liked this sight, but they didn't know what to expect. The black and orange team arrived at a large clearing that was full of beautiful flowers and the large clearing was surrounded by huge trees. The next path continued in the eastern half of the clearing, as soon as they saw this they started towards the path. Yes, but as soon as they reached the middle of the clearing, the wolves came out of the trees. One of the wolves was white and they had to kill it.

Adam: - 'Watch out, wolves! Bring out your sword's guys!!': - He warned his companions.

Mark: - 'My sword is already in my hand!! Let's give it to them, don't pity them!!': - He shouted belligerently.

Patrick: - 'Fight, guys!! Let's kill them!!': - He shouted excitedly.

Doris: - 'Let's stay close!! It's easier to take them down that way!!': - She shouted excitedly.

Norbert: - 'Press the switch on your swords!! Then it will be easier to defeat them!!': - He yelled at them in warning.

Patrick: - 'Attack!!!!': - He called out. After this, they all started running against the wolves, of course the wolves also ran against them. There was a total of 5 wolves, of which 1 of them was white, each wolf chose a suitable opponent and attacked in this way. The White Wolf chose Doris. A big battle started between them, and they have already wounded some of the wolves, but they were still attacking.

Norbert: - 'Partick, be careful!!': - He warned.

Patrick: - 'Thanks mate!!': - In the meantime, Patrick killed his wolf.

Mark: - 'Come on!! I'm here!!': - He addressed it so that they were facing each other. The wolf jumped at Mark and then Mark jumped in a such a way which that he split the wolf in two.

Mark: - 'I killed this one!! Game over for this one!!': - He said tiredly.

Adam: 'What will happen!! Come if you dare!! He said with his knees bent and the sword in his hand, they were looking at each other with focused eyes. The wolf ran at Adam growling and gnashing his teeth, they jumped on each other and fell to the ground, they turned and fought when the sword fell from Adam's hand. Adam didn't hesitate either, he quickly rolled after it and picked up his sword again and with a sudden movement split the wolf in two. With that he fell back to the ground panting and smiling. All that was left was Doris to defeat her wolf.

They were just eyeing each other, circling each other so that she could catch it in a good position. The wolf didn't wait any longer and jumped at Doris. Doris was about to attack when she tripped and fell, but as she fell, she turned backwards so that the wolf wouldn't catch her. But her sword fell out of her hand, and she could not reach it, she had to go and gte it. The Wolf jumped over Doris and stopped right above her head. Doris slowly stood up and slowly walked towards her sword without taking her eyes off the wolf. The others watched in silence to see what the outcome of this would be. They knew that they would not be able to help in this, since everyone had to kill their own wolf. The other teams were already fighting with their wolves.

Doris: - 'Just one more step and I have my sword!': - She thought to herself. As soon as she reached her sword, she carefully crouched down for it and raised it slowly, but as soon as she raised her sword, the wolf immediately attacked and smashed Doris to the ground with such force that the others thought that the wolf had killed Doris because the wolf towered over her. They then rushed to Doris to see what happened, then a sea of butterflies flew out of the white wolf, and they landed wherever they could. The wolves disappeared and the black and orange team became the winner, they got the last ball.

Norbert: - 'Oh my goodness Doris!! We thought the wolf had killed you, you really scared us!! I'm glad you're not hurt!': - He held out his hand to help her up.

Norbert: - 'Doris!! Look!! The last ball is right next to you!!': - He told her surprised.

Doris: -'That's right!! The last ball is here!! Yupeeee! Yupieee!': - She shouted with great joy.

Adam: - 'We have the last ball!! We did it guys!!': - He shouted in joy.

Mark: - 'We did it!! We finished the game; I can't believe it!': - He shouted with a big smile.

Patrick: - 'King!! We did it!! It's game over for us! This is it guys!' They stood in a circle and threw the ball up into the air and laughed with joy. Since they had already found the last ball and won the game, the road in front of them changed completely, the exit gate stood in front of them, which they went through cheerfully and rejoicing. They were already waiting outside for them with huge applause and cheers.

Red-blue team.

Beneth: - 'Be careful!! The wolves are coming closer, be ready!': - He warned them.

Zoe: - 'We are all alert! Let's wait until they come closer, then prepare your swords.': - She replied quietly.

Erik: - 'They can come all they want!! I'm waiting with open arms!!': - He answered excitedly. The wolves had already chosen their opponent and were already attacking. In all the other teams, the wolves had already chosen their opponents and each team needed a white wolf to fight for the last ball.

Carl: - 'Come on!! Aaaaaaa!! Damn it!!': - He yelled. The white wolf of the red-blue team chose Carl. Zoe: - 'I'm going to catch you now, come closer!!': - She lured it towards her, while focusing on it. The wolf jumped at her and laid her on the ground, tried to bite her, only for Zoe to turn away from her. The Wolf constantly tried to scratch her and succeeding as the sword fell out of her hand, so she rolled forwards and picked up her sword again. The wolf immediately attacked her, but Zoe held her sword in front of her and stabbed it in the heart.

Zoe: - 'Well, that's enough!! I'm sorry, little one, but I had to do this!!': - She told the wolf.

Beneth: - 'Oh my goodness!! This bastard hurt me!! Aaah, that hurts!!': - He got to his feet.

Erik: - 'You are very beautiful, little one!! Can't we discuss this in private?? You know, just you and me! And the..... He couldn't finish what he wanted to say, the wolf already attacked him. He caught Erik, and the fight went on, teeth snarling, but he lost his sword in the middle of it all. He got down on one knee and looked to see where his sword had gone, but he couldn't see it anywhere. He was completely in despair, he didn't even know how he was going to defeat the wolf, so he began to think about what he could do to defeat it. Not far from him, there was a small piece of iron in the grass, it looked like a good weapon, but he had to take it. He tried to slowly there, while staying close to the ground, but in the process, he looked the wolf in the eye. When he got to a point where he could safely pick up the piece of iron, he picked it up slowly and carefully, and when he had the piece of iron in his hand, the wolf immediately jumped at Erik. Erik was so in control of himself that he managed to stab the wolf with it. The wolf fell on Erik in a way that he could not move, he managed to push the wolf off him, and he could finally breath. Only Carl was left, the others were watching to see how the fight would end. The White Wolf didn't really let him think, he kept attacking him, so he had to be very alert. When the wolf jumped up to attack him, Carl jumped and cut him in half through its stomach. As soon as this happened, all the wolves disappeared, and butterflies flew everywhere. Carl was lying on his back on the ground and laughing with joy, he spread his hands and grabbed the ball, he looked at what he caught and when he saw it, he immediately jumped up from the ground.

Carl: - 'We have the last ball!!! We did it guys!! That's it!!': - He yelled as loudly as he could. The others also ran to Carl and hugged him with joy and shouted.

'We are awesome!! We are damn awesome!! We won! We won!!' In their great joy, they didn't even notice that the road in front of them turned into a big gate, which was the final part of the track.

Zoe: - 'Guys, look!! There's the gate, we've reached the finish line, let's go out!! Game over!!': - She said to them.

Beneth: - 'Come on guys, let's go out!! The game is over for us here!': - He said with a big smile.

Erik: - 'I wonder who was the first??': - He asked curiously.

Carl: - 'We'll find out soon!': - He answered with a smile. Finally, they went out the gate and everyone greeted them with applause and cheers. As soon as they stepped out of the gate, it immediately closed behind them.

Erik: - 'Yes, I can see now who was the first!!': - He said with a smile.

Beneth: - 'Come, let's go to them, let's congratulate them.': - He said to the others. The red and blue team went to congratulate the winning team.

Beneth: - 'Congratulations!!': - He held out his hand to Norbert. Of course, they all shook hands.

Norbert: - 'Congratulations to you guys as well!! You guys came second and there is a prize for placing second, and its one hell of a prize!!': - He answered with a smile.

Zoe: - 'Is this serious? Doesn't only the winning team get a prize?': - She asked in surprise.

Patrick: - 'Well no!! Everyone gets a prize only according to how they finished.'

Zoe: - 'That's good to know!! But how do you know this?': - She asked surprisingly.

Mark: - 'From what the directors said! They said that because the course was quite difficult and everyone fought very hard, therefore everyone will receive a prize based on what position they finished, I think this is very correct, because the course was really hard.': - He answered with a smile.

Carl: - 'But according to this, they also changed the prize for the first arrivals? Or only on the others?': - He asked.

Adam: - 'We don't know exactly, but I think they had to change it because then it would be fair.': - He answered with a smile. One of the directors overheard their conversation and approached them.

Director: - 'Hello! I would like to congratulate you, you fought very well, I appreciate everyone! I happened to hear what you were talking about, and I would like to answer your questions, yes everyone will receive a prize and yes, we have changed the prize for the first arrivals as well. This is because the course turned out to be more difficult than what we had planned, you had to fight a lot and you guys had very serious struggles, but with King Gilbert we decided that everyone gets a prize because they deserve it.

Zoe: - 'That's great, really! And I also agree, because it was really hard to do, but we did it, we are finally here!! There are only two teams left and then they can relax as well.': - She replied happily.

Director: - 'Go there in the gathering tent, you can rest there, there are refreshments and snacks for you, please wait for the others there, okay?': - He directed them.

Green-yellow team: -

Alice: - 'Oh my god, I lost my sword!! Damn it, what now?' The white wolf of the Green-yellow team chose Emy.

Liam: - 'I'm afraid of this wolf, it growls at me and gnashes its teeth! Help?': - He despaired, in the process he farted again. The wolf sneezed upon hearing this and continued to grind his teeth and then began to attack. Liam fell backwards but held the sword in front of him. When he hit the ground, the wolf jumped right into the sword and died as a result. Liam was very lucky, he didn't have to fight much, but the wolf fell right on him, so he had to take it off of himself somehow.

Liam: - 'Damn it!! This beast just fell on me! Great, now it won't be easy to get it off, but I'll try! I killed the beast without a fight, now that's something!': - He told himself.

Jason: - 'Where's my sword? Aaah, there you go!! Come here you little bastard!!': - He muttered to himself.

Kurtis: - 'Aaaah!!! You're done!!': - He thrust his sword into the wolf.

Alice: - 'Come here, just a little more, great!! Now!!!': - She shouted. The wolf immediately ran at her and caught Alice, yanking the sword out of her hand and throwing it aside, Alice rolled under it and then further away from it. But she couldn't find her sword, so she had to resort to another method. Since the wolf didn't notice where she was rolling, which came in handy for her because she went right behind the wolf, jumped on its back, put her arms around its neck and squeezed tightly until she finally strangled it.

Alice: - 'Phew!! That was close!! My goodness, I can't believe I killed a wolf with my bare hands!': - She told herself. Liam lay there on the ground panting and smiling. Only Emy was left, everyone was watching her to see how she would defeat the white wolf. There was a big fight there as well, they were both in an offensive stance.

Emy: - 'I hope that I will be able to defeat you! - She said in a low voice. The wolf attacked her and both of them fell to the ground. The others silently watched what was going to happen and who was going to get up from there and finally, Emy got up from the ground, but in that moment hundreds of butterflies took off high up and covered the clearing. Emy found the ball on the ground and picked it up from there.

Emy: - 'We have the last ball!!!': - She shouted in joy. The others shouted in joy at the same time.: -

'Amazing!! We did it, we have the last ball!!': - They shouted. At that moment, the big gate appeared in front of them, through which they finally went out. They were already waiting for them outside, and they were welcomed with loud cheers, and applause.

Kurtis: - 'I can't believe we did it guys! We finished the track!!': - He shouted with joy.

Jason: - 'We did it mate!! Finally, we're out!': - He grabbed Kurtis by the neck.

Director: - 'Hello guys! First of all, I would like to congratulate you, you played very well. I ask you to join the others in that tent, because you have to wait for the last team.'

Emy: - 'Thank you very much!': - She answered breathlessly.

Liam: - 'Come on guys.': - He addressed the others as well.

Director: -'Oh, and there's refreshments in the tent, snacks as well, hurry!!': - He said after them.

Alice: - 'Now that's exactly what we need!!': - She interrupted.

Indigo Blue-Pink Team.

Betty: - 'Damn it! It bit me, ssssss, it's hurts! - He grabbed her arm. Mason was chosen by the white wolf in the indigo blue-pink team. Only Betty and Mason are left here, the others have already defeated their wolf. One problem was that Betty couldn't fight with one hand, because the wolf bit her so badly, in order for her wolf to disappear, Mason has to defeat his wolf first.

Carter: - 'Mason!! You have to defeat your wolf first, Betty can't fight anymore, man!!': - He yelled at him. This round will be interesting, that's for sure, because Betty's wolf will not stand there and wait until it defeats the other wolf, so Mason had to be very cunning. Before Betty's wolf attacked, Mason's wolf attacked Mason by provoking him and Carter sneaked up to Mason's side to help him. The wolves attacked them, Carter and Mason waited for the wolves in the attacking position, when the wolves wanted to jump for them, they both pulled to the side and split the wolves in half at the same time.

Carter: - 'We have finally killed the wolves with our combines power, it was a good strategy, I'll give you that.': - He said panting.

Mason: - 'We are unbeatable with teamwork.': - He answered panting.

Betty: - 'I'm really grateful to you guys, I couldn't have done this

370

on my own, thank you!

Carter-Mason: - 'You're welcome!'

Mason: - 'We are a team, so we help each other.': - He said with a smile.

Carter: - 'Betty, it's only natural that we help, we just couldn't let you fight wounded!'

Betty: - 'Thanks again guys.': - She said in gratitude.

Here too, the area was flooded with butterflies, it was a very beautiful sight.

Mason: - 'We have the ball guys!!': - He shouted with joy. Betty fainted from the pain and fell to the ground. The others noticed this and immediately ran to her. The gate was already wide open in front of them, and the doctors rushed in to treat Betty's arm.

Carter: - 'Help her, she's hurt!': - He said desperately.

Doctor: - 'Stand aside! Leave the space around her free!': - He instructed the others.

Director: - 'Congratulations to you! You played very well, now go into that tent and meet the others, there are refreshments and food. Relax, the award ceremony will take place in an hour.'

Grace: - 'Thank you very much!': - She thanked him.

Kayl: - 'Come on guys, let's go!': - He addressed them. Meanwhile, Betty regained consciousness and the doctors attended to her wound. The game is over, all the players have arrived, and the award ceremony, which the players have been waiting for, will be held soon.

Gilbert: - 'Dear audience! Dear players! I would like to congratulate you, you all played very well! During the game, we decided with James and the game organizers that everyone will receive a prize based on the position of your arrival. We decided this way because the course through which you have played turned out to be a little more difficult than planned! As we can see, unfortunately, we also have wounded people, but that's one of the outcomes of this game!! The wounded have been treated and are doing well. So! The first finishers are the Black-Orange team! (The audience cheered and applauded) Our second finisher team is the Red-Blue team! (The audience cheered and applauded) Our third finisher team is none other than the Green-Yellow team!(The audience cheered and applauded) Our last finishing team is none other than the Indigo Blue-Pink team!(Audience cheered and applauded) Well, the prize for the first team is none other than a gold cup and a whole year of free dinners at Brontus!(Everyone cheered) And the prize for the second team is a silver cup and half a year of free dinners at Brontus! (Everyone cheered) And the prize for the third team is a bronze cup and a quarter of a year of free dinners at Brontus! (Everyone cheered) Well, the prize for the final team, is none other than a crystal cup and a month of free dinners at Brontus!' (Everyone cheered): - He announced their prizes. Gilbert waited until everyone was bursting with joy. All the players were completely satisfied with their winnings and were very happy, so they were jumping for joy.

Gilbert: - 'Dear audience and players, since the game is over, I ask everyone to go home and we will repeat this game next year at the same time, because we want this game to remain as a tradition. in this city. Thank you to everyone who came and supported our players, we wish everyone a nice rest of the day!!': - he said goodbye to the people. Everyone went home, the players were very excited about their prizes, as they can have a free dinner in one of the most famous restaurants. Well, yes, but the restaurant is no longer anywhere because Miriam made sure that it no longer exists, but unfortunately, they don't know that.

~   Parents are trying to connect with their children!   ~

Kev: - 'Good morning, dear!': - He said hello to his wife.

Jenifer: - 'Good morning, dear! But still not that good! I miss Oliver very much! When will we see my son again, I can't wait any longer! Let's finally do something, this can't go on like this!'

Kev: - 'It's okay! I agree with you, this cannot go on like this! I'm going over to the Timbers right now and talking to him! Hi, see you later!': - He said goodbye.

Jenifer: - 'See ya dear! Tell me what you have arranged! - She shouted after him.

Kev: - 'Okay, I'm on it! Hi, I love you!': - Finally he said goodbye. Kev went over to his friend's house to talk to him about the kids. The phone rang in Kev's apartment.

Jenifer: - 'Hello, this is Jenifer speaking, to whom am I speaking? - She said into the phone.

Mrs. Hildred: - 'Good morning, its Mrs. Hildred, I am calling to ask if there is any news about Oliver?': - She was interested.

Jenifer: - 'Good morning, Mrs. Hildred! Unfortunately, there is still no news about him! But my husband just went over to the Timbers to discuss what should happen next, because this cannot go on, that they have disappeared for so long and we don't know anything about them!': - She answered desperately.

Mrs. Hildred: - 'I'm glad that your husband is not leaving it be, but I'm not happy that there's no news from them yet. I apologize for the inconvenience and have a nice day!': - She said farewell.

Jenifer: - 'Thank you too, goodbye!'

Timber: - 'Hi Kev! Well, you? Isn't it too early?? What's wrong?': - He asked.

Kev: - 'Hi Timber! Listen, we can't take this anymore, man! I don't know how you feel about it, but I say we should somehow get in contact with the kids and find out if everything is okay with them!': - he said in despair.

Timber: - 'Come in, we'll talk here!': - He invited him into the house.

Timber: - 'Take a seat! Would you like a tea or a coffee?': - He asked reassuringly.

Kev: - 'No thanks, I'm fine!!': - He answered breathlessly.

Timber: - 'Is there something wrong? You look so broken!': - He asked seriously.

Kev: - 'Listen, buddy! My wife and I are already very worried about Oliver, they disappeared a long time ago and even John along with them. There is still no sign from them and John hasn't sent any sign back telling us we don't have to worry, so my wife and I talked about how it would be good to get in touch with them in some way. Don't you have any idea how to get in touch with them?': - He asked worriedly.

Timber: - 'Hmm! Yes, this worries us too, I won't deny it! It's fine! Listen, let's go to dinner tonight and discuss this with our wives. What do you think?': - He asked with a smile.

Kev: - 'Sounds good, I will go and tell my wife! Thanks Tim!': - They shook hands.

Timber: - 'No problem! Then we'll have dinner at the usual place in the evening!': - he said goodbye.

Kev: - 'Evening it is then!': - He raised his hand as a goodbye gesture. Kev went home to his wife and told her what he and Timber had talked about.

Jenifer: - 'Hello, my love! So, what did you come up with?': - She asked curiously.

Kev: - 'Hi, honey! Tonight, we will go to dinner together at our usual place and we will discuss together what to do.': - He answered with a smile.

Jenifer: - 'Alright then! I'm off to work, see you later!': - She said goodbye to Kev.

Kev: - 'Bye, honey, I'm coming right this second, I'll just look for my tie. I love you!': - He said out loud.

Jennifer: - 'I love you! I'm off!': - She finally said goodbye. After Kev left, Timber looked up Abby's phone number and called her.

Abby: - 'Agent Abby, what can I help you with?': - She asked.

Timber: - 'Hi Abby, I'm Timber! How are you? Is everything okay over there?': - He asked.

Abby: - 'Oh, hello Tim! What's up with you? Was the last time you were here with me successful?': - She asked with a smile.

Timber: - 'Oh, that! Of course, it did, everything went well! Well to be honest, nothing is really okay, Listen, there's a problem....': - He complained.

Abby: - 'Come on Tim! I don't know you as someone who is in trouble! Tell me, what can I help you with?': - He asked with a smile.

Tim: - 'No, no! That part was successful, everything is fine, the only thing is that John has not returned since then and has not given us any sign of life. The truth is, it would be nice to know if everything is okay with them. You were the first person that came to my mind!': - He said seriously.

Abby: - 'I see! Listen, I can't help much in this matter, but the person you've met in Mexico could help you again, you just have to contact her. I could help you to the extent that I would contact her for you and call you once its sorted!': - She said.

Tim: - 'Thank you Abby, then call me and thank you again!': - He was grateful.

Abby: - 'I'm happy to help. I'll call you in a bit!': - She hung up the phone. Tim finally went to work.

During this time, Abby called the witch Naiara to tell her what problem Tim was having.

Abby: - 'Hello! Greetings Naiara! I'm Abby, we've met before! One of my good friends needs help......' After the conversation Abby called Tim.

Tim: - 'Yes! What did you come up with?': - He asked curiously.

Abby: - 'In two days, you will meet Naiara in London at the Sky Garden Cafe at exactly 12:00, if possible, don't be late because she won't wait for you for a minute.': - She said firmly.

Tim: - 'Abby, I don't know how to thank you again for what you do for us, it's amazing! Thanks Abby! We'll talk later!': - Thank you.

Abby: - 'Come on Tim! It's an honour to help you. We'll talk later, I have to go now. Be careful!': - She said goodbye.

Tim: - 'Will do, and thanks again.': - He switched off the phone. The evening arrived where they finally met in the restaurant. Everyone had already taken their place at the table and started drinking.

Jenifer: - 'How are you guys these days?': - She asked while clearing her throat.

Tim: - 'Listen, we all know why we're here tonight! Well, the situation is as follows! Kev, today after you left, I didn't hesitate either, but I called Abby and asked her about this, whether she could help. Since she helped me last time, I thought I'd try again. She said that in two days we have to go down to London and that we will meet Naiara in a cafe at exactly 12:00. If we are not there on time, she will not wait for us even for a minute.': - He finished what he had to say.

Amanda: - 'To London??': - She asked surprisingly.

Tim: - 'It's closer than Mexico!!': - He answered with a smile.

Jenifer: - 'That just sounds better!! Okay, as soon as you find out something, call me right away, okay?': - He said excitedly.

Kev: - 'It's only natural dear! I'll call you right away, you can be sure of that.': - He answered while holding her hand.

Tim: - 'That's right!! We will call you right away to see what we were able to arrange!! Of course!!': - He said smiling.

Amanda: - 'Jennifer!! We could even go to London as well, right?': - She asked with a smile.

Jenifer: - 'Yes, yes!! We really could go too! While you have a meeting with the old crone, let's look around the Buckingham Palace.': - She said with a big smile while clapping his hands together.

Amanda: - 'And we'll walk in the park, feed the squirrels, hmm, that'll be perfect. What do you say, dear?': - She asked firmly.

Tim: - 'That's a great idea!! After all, why not. We will book a hotel room for two nights and combine the pleasant with the useful.': - He answered with a smile.

Kev: - 'Well then, it's decided!! Off to London!!': - He said with a smile. Amanda and Jenifer were very happy that they could go with their husbands, so when they went home, they immediately booked the accommodation and packed for the trip.

Martha: - 'Nivita, do you have a minute dear?': - She asked.

Nivita: - 'Of course, mother!': - She answered.

Martha: - 'Come, my daughter, I want to show you something!': - She invited her into her room.

Nivita: - 'Mother, what is it!': - She wondered.

Martha: - 'You'll know right away, patience!': - She answered with a smile. Martha walked over to her closet and opened the door, took out a large box from the bottom and opened it. There were a lot of things in the box, but what Martha took out was a beautiful dress.

Martha: - 'Here, my daughter, here is this wonderful dress that I've been saving for you for years, now it's time to give it to you. Here, now it's yours!': - She handed it over with a smile.

Nivita: - 'Mother! I don't even know what to say! This is a beautiful dress! Are you sure this can be mine? Why am I getting this beautiful dress?': - She asked happily.

Martha: - 'You know, my daughter, this dress is not just any dress, if you wear it on the night of your engagement, it will shine in a colour that no human eye has ever seen. At the time when I wore this dress, I remember everyone talking about this dress for years, it radiated such beautiful colours. This dress reflects what you are currently feeling and will shed its colour based on your feelings.': - She told her with a smile.

Nivita: - 'But this is wonderful! Why didn't you tell me about this dress until now? Oh mother, I can't wait to go there and put on my beautiful dress.': - She said happily. Robnis and Valtius sparred with each other just for fun, as they were bored and thought they would pass the time a little.

Robnis: - 'Be careful bro, you're going to walk into the pillar, hahah...': - He was laughing.

Valtius: - 'Are you sure about that?? You can't even catch me, I'm too fast! What are you going to do now!!! Hahah!!': - He laughed.

Robnis: - 'Listen now! I don't really like this great silence!!': - He said doubtfully.

Valtius: - 'What are you thinking??': - He asked in surprise.

Robnis: - 'I don't like this! Everything is so nice and good, but what if it doesn't last long either?': - He asked.

Valtius: - 'Come on! You see horrors, you need someone who really captures your attention, so you don't think about stupid things anymore. But don't worry, you don't have to wait much longer!!! Hahaha!!': - He laughed.

Robnis: - 'Haha, you're funny!': - He answered with a smile.

Valtius: - 'Come on, let's refresh ourselves with some delicious wine!!': - He laughed.

Robnis: - 'Little brother!! You know what's good!': - He asked laughing.

Karnita: - 'Estel?? Would you please help me?': - She asked hurriedly.

Estel (maid): - 'Yes miss!': - She answered humbly.

Karnita: - 'Please do my hair, I'm going to dinner soon and my hair isn't in such a good state, thank you!': - She said kindly with a curtsey.

Estel: - 'Of course miss, I'll do it right now!': - She bowed courteously.

The phone rang at Amanda's house.

Amanda: - 'Hello! This is Amanda, who am I talking to?': - She spoke into the phone.

Jenifer: - 'Hi Amanda, it's Jenifer. I only called you because I can't decide whether you think I should take a hair dryer there or is there one in the hotel?': - She asked as it was very important for her.

Amanda: - Jenifer!! The answer to this is simple, go to their website and see if they have a hair dryer in the room and if not, take one with you!': - She answered patiently.

Jenifer: - 'Why didn't i think of that! Thanks Amanda, you are a genius!!': - She thanked her.

Amanda: - 'Come on, that's what friends are for, right??': - She asked with a smile.

Jenifer: - 'Oh, of course, dear! Alright then see you tomorrow!!': - She said goodbye.

Amanda: - 'Hello tomorrow, if you have any questions about anything else, feel free to call me, ok?': - She said seriously.

Jenifer: - 'Okay, bye!!': - She said goodbye and hung up.

Tim: - 'Who was that darling?': - He asked curiously.

Amanda: - 'Ah, just Jenifer!!': - She answered.

Tim: - 'Okay!! Come to bed my dear, I'm waiting for you here in the pre heated bed!!': - He shouted with a smile.

Amanda: - 'I'm coming, dear!': - And with that momentum she jumped into the bed next to Tim. They laughed, frolicked, tickled and hugged each other. They lay close to each other and stared at the ceiling.

Tim: - 'How strange that Evelin is not here! I still can't get used to it and I don't intend to. The house is so empty without her, it's not good, I miss her a lot and worry about her. Who knows what's up with her? Especially since John didn't show any sign of life either, this is what worries me the most! I hope that Naiara can help us, I would like to receive at least some sign of life from them!': - She said worriedly.

Amanda: - 'Don't even start, I haven't been able to sleep properly for months! When I do, then I'm just having nightmares. This is very bad; we have to get our little one back as soon as possible.': - She said sadly.

Tim: - 'Don't worry dear, I will do everything to bring our little girl and her friends back, I promise!': - He said seriously.

John: - 'The war is upon us, and I really want to help fight, not just sit here on my bottom! I am a man; my place is in war!': - He stated firmly.

Menthis: - 'Yes, I know! But you also have to understand that this war is not like what you humans are used to, it will be completely different. Here you have to fight night monsters, which I will not be a walk in the park. These monsters are all born of the evil witch, and it will definitely take magic power to defeat them. As we know, if we go up there, even we don't have magic powers. But luckily for us, the little magic mushrooms will help us with this, but how can you help, since you can't even cast a spell, and you don't even have magic powers!!': - He said seriously.

John: - 'Yes, I'm aware of that, but it might mean something that I come from a family of wizards! It could also be that I have magical powers, I just need to reawaken them?': - He asked curiously.

Menthis: - 'Hmm! That's interesting what you say! If your descendants were wizards, then it must be in your veins, in your genes, it's there in you, you just have to wake up the sleeping fire.': - He answered thoughtfully.

John: - 'That's exactly what I'm saying!! Will you help me then??': - He asked excitedly.

Menthis: -'Come with me! Let's wake up the sleeping lion!': - He stated firmly.

John: - 'Happily! But where are we going?': - He asked curiously.

Menthis: - 'You will find out in time!': - He answered patiently. Menthis took John to a secret room in his palace, closed the door on behind them and went to one of the huge closets. He took a set of keys from his pocket and opened the closet door. In the cupboard there were books, different bottles with different liquids, but there were also different gadgets that were necessary for the magic. Menthis took out a very old book from the cupboard and placed it on the table. He opened the book and there was a knock at the door. Menthis went to the door and opened it. Standing in front of the door was Gorth.

Gorth: - 'I am here, sir, as we discussed!':- He said with a smile. John didn't understand how he got there since they were together the whole time, and he doesn't remember notifying anyone.

Menthis: - 'Come in my dear friend, I need your help! But close the door behind you!': - He said firmly.

Gorth: - 'Let me look at this young man!': - He stated seriously as he began to turn his face, looking at his ears, his hands, even his feet.

John: - 'What's all this? what are you doing to me? Do you really have to do this?': - He asked a little confused.

Gorth: - 'Oh, of course! I need to examine you well to find out if you really come from a wizarding family! Put your finger here, please!': - He said firmly. John held out his finger, Gorth took it and held it over a small bowl. He took out a large needle and pricked his finger with it, the blood that came out dripped into the bowl, which already had a certain magic potion prepared in it, to find out if there really is wizard blood flowing in his veins. After adding the right amount of blood, he started to mix it with the magic potion.

Menthis: - 'If your descendants were really wizards, then the potion will turn green, and if not, then the potion will turn purple.': - He said calmly. Gorth muttered something to himself as he mixed the drink with his blood. The potion began to change colour, all three watched the result with their eyes wide open. It didn't take him long to crow with it, the result was green.

John: - 'What did I say!! After all, the evil witch brought James to me for a reason, because she knew my family!': - He said happily.

Gorth: - 'Yes, you are indeed the descendants of wizards, but there is a little problem!': - He said.

John: - 'What's wrong?': - He asked in horror.

Gorth: - 'It's been a long time since you haven't used your magic, the potion turned green, but it's not the same green colour as when you're actively involved in the spell, this means that you should practice in order to rekindle the knowledge you have'.: - He reported confidently.

John: - 'I'm willing to do anything, just to free my son!': - He answered determinedly.

Menthis: - 'Alright then! While you study, you have to stay here in this room with Gorthal, he will help you, but be careful because we don't have much time left, the war is already upon us.': - He declared.

John: - 'That's right! I will stay as long as possible and study day and night if necessary.': - He answered firmly.

Gorth: - 'I have a feeling that he will learn quickly!': - He interrupted with a smile.

Menthis: - 'I'll leave you to yourselves, see you later!': - He said goodbye.

Evelin: - 'Hanna! Do you think they will win the war?': - She asked in despair.

Hanna: - 'I think so, they will win! They have to win, because if they don't, you'll never see your parents or your friends again! That's why you shouldn't think too much about it, rather trust them that they will win this war.': - She answered reassuringly.

Evelin: - 'And what if they still lose the war, because you know how much power the evil witch has now since she got that crystal?'

Hanna: - 'Yes, she really has a lot of power since she got that crystal, but that doesn't mean she can't be defeated!': - She answered.

Evelin: - 'What do you mean by that? You know something that you haven't told us yet?': - She asked hopefully.

Hanna: - 'I think so yes! There is a solution!': - She answered optimistically.

Evelin: - 'Is this serious? Why didn't you say this until now?': - She asked confused.

Hanna: - 'Listen! You know that I like to look up certain things, well I looked this up in the big library and it says that the crystal can be destroyed if it is broken. Then her power will not be as great as before, in fact her power will be equal to the power of an average witch.': - She answered.

Evelin: - 'But you can't just get the crystal that easily! Wait a second! After all, James is in the witch's palace, he could do it!': - She said excitedly.

Hanna: - 'It's possible that James is there, but don't forget that he's under a spell just like the others, so his chances are slim!

Unless! Someone releases him from the spell.': - She said.

Evelin: - 'You are a genius! We have to tell the head mage right away, let's see what they think about it.': - She stated firmly. Hanna and Evelin went to the head magician to tell them the good news. Mr. Tregas was talking to Menthis, it seemed that what they were talking about was very important, so they waited until they finished.

Evelin: - 'I wonder what they can talk about? It seems very important!': - She asked curiously.

Hanna: - 'It is not certain that we will find out!': - She answered with a smile. Menthis noticed that Hanna and Evelin were waiting for them, so they ended the conversation.

Mr. Tregas: - 'Hello girls! Do you want to say something?': - He asked them with a smile.

Hanna: - 'Yes, we want to say something very important!': - She stated firmly.

Mr. Tregas: - 'Well, I listening to you!': - He said with a smile.

Hanna: - 'The other day I read about the crystal in the library, how its power could be reduced so that it is no longer dangerous!..'

Mr. Tregas: - 'Oh, yes! We already know about that, Hanna! But it's very kind of you to look into this important thing! This is exactly what we talked about with Menthis earlier. We have already solved this important issue, only the execution awaits us. We will send one of the goblins to James's room when the attack happens, to help us with this, because if the power of the crystal is alive, we will not be able to defeat the evil witch.': - He answered with a smile.

Evelin: - 'What if this doesn't work and the evil witch finds out, then it's all over!': - She said worriedly.

Mr. Tregas: - 'We have already thought about this, believe me, what we have planned should work! Go home now because it's going to be dark soon.': - He said encouragingly.

The big day has come for the parents, they arrived in London. They were already very excited about what they were going to accomplish in terms of the children. They arrived at their accommodation, put down their suitcases and met in the lobby.

Tim: -'Well, we're finally here! I've already ordered a taxi for all of us, we'll go to the meeting place if you want, you can be there with us, because I don't think it's necessarily just me and Kev that have to be there!': - He said excitedly.

Amanda: - 'I would like to be there to hear what she has to say!': - She answered with a smile.

Jenifer: - 'I would like to be there too!': - She stated firmly.

Kev: - 'Alright, then we'll all be there since it's about our children, right?': - He asked firmly.

Receptionist: - 'Excuse me, sir, your taxi is here!': - He said kindly.

Tim: - 'Thank you!': - He answered.

Tim: - 'Can we go?': - He asked excitedly.

Jenifer: - 'Let's go, we will finally find out something about them!': - She said excitedly. They got into the taxi and headed to the Sky Garden. They were very impressed by the sight, since they had not been to London yet because they had no reason to, except Tim, of course, because he had already been everywhere as a secret agent. They arrived at the Sky Garden, the building was huge and beautiful. Their table was already reserved, since everything is provided by Naiara. They went to the reception and announced their arrival, the receptionist guided them and gave them a card to find their table. Of course, they had to go up to the top floor by elevator. When the elevator door opened, they all stopped breathing, Tim had been here more than once, so it was natural for him.

Amanda: - 'Wow! This is beautiful, I can't believe we had to come here! This is probably a very expensive place!': - She said in amazement.

Jennifer: - 'Oh my God! This is beautiful! Someone pinch me, maybe I'm just dreaming!': - She said dreamily.

Kev: - 'This is really beautiful! But today we are the bosses!': - He poked Tim on the shoulder. A waiter there stepped a few steps away from the elevator and welcomed them.

Waiter: - 'Welcome to Sky Garden! Can I have your card?': - He asked politely.

Tim: - 'Greetings! Of course, here it is!': - He handed over his card.

Waiter: - 'Thank you! Follow me this way, please!': - He invited them to their table. As they walked to their table, they couldn't help but stare, Tim was following the worker. While they were looking around, Kev bumped into one of the waiters, as he didn't notice because they were all looking the other way. Everything that was in the hands of the waiter fell to the ground.

Kev: - 'Oh my goodness! I'm really sorry! That wasn't intentional! I'm sorry!': - He blurted out and apologized in fright.

Waiter: - 'No problem, sir! Everything is fine, it happens here every day!': - He answered with a smile.

Jenifer: - 'You scared me, my love! Are you okay? Are you hurt?': - She asked frightened.

Kev: - 'Yes, everything is fine! I was staring so much that I didn't pay attention to where I was going, it was my fault, I'm sorry!': -

He answered with a little smile.

Jenifer: - 'Are you okay too? Is it okay?': - She asked the waiter politely.

Waiter: 'Everything is fine ma'am, nothing serious happened! Enjoy your stay here, have a nice day!' They continued while following the waiter who was escorting them to their table. Their table was set in a place where they were surrounded by tall plants and flowers, as if they had stepped into a fairy tale world, no one saw their table, only the worker who accompanied them there knew that they were sitting there, this is a special place where only secret guests reserve a table in such a place, only the particular waiter who will serve them can know about this. They give you a card for such a secret table because everything is already arranged in that card, which means that they only have to ask for what they want and in the end, they don't have to pay because it has already been paid for. Well, they took their seats, asked for their drinks and waited until noon, because then Naiara would arrive. It was only five minutes until noon, so they didn't have to wait long. They were pleasantly lost in that room, laughing, talking, drinking and having a good time. It seemed as if they had forgotten why they had gone there, so engrossed in that magical place. In the middle of the big conversation, a big black cloud suddenly darkened and surrounded their place, and Naiara arrived.

Naiara: - 'I welcome you! I see you had found your table, impressive!': - She greeted them.

Tim: - 'Greetings to you too, Naiara! We are glad that you were willing to meet us! I would like to introduce my wife......': - He tried to be nice and polite, but Naiara interrupted.

Naiara: - 'Yes, I know who they are, and I even know their names, very nice, but you don't have to bother with the details. Well, I also know why you are here, I think you really want to know what is going on with the children! Well, since we've all just arrived, I suggest that we rest, drink, eat and you'll find out everything at the end!': - She said firmly.

Jennifer: - 'Alright! I agree! And you guys?': - She interrupted, smiling a little. Everyone looked at Jenifer, who was immediately embarrassed by this, the smile faded from her face. They started eating, which took place in a rather tense atmosphere, but they had no other choice. They finished lunch and nobody really dared to speak, but Tim broke the silence.

Tim: - 'Ahhmm!!(He sharpened his voice) I think we can get into the middle of it now!': - He said firmly.

Naiara: - 'Yes, indeed, because that's why we're here, right? Well, first of all, don't make any sudden moves, I want you to pay attention! What will happen now, no one here will see or hear, and I made sure of that too, I protected our place with magic. The point is that I would like to request a strand of hair from Jenifer and Amanda, they will be important parts of the magic potion I will make. May i?': - She asked for the locks of hair firmly. As they were busy with their hair locks, the table was transformed according to Naiara's needs. Everyone just watched, but no one dared to say a word. When the hairs were added, Naiara had to add them to the prepared cauldron. She stood over the cauldron and began muttering an incantation.

Semeritum Showhum!

Persontum Active!

Imedium Placeitum!

At the moment when she recited these incantations, green smoke arose from the cauldron and it began to rotate until a visible place was formed in the middle where the children were down in the world of the goblins. You could see that they were fine, they were safely having lunch and talking at a huge, big table where several people were sitting, but they didn't see James, because he wasn't with them.

Naiara: - 'Well, you can see that everything is fine with the children, you don't have to worry, they are in good hands. Is there anything else I can do for you?': - She asked with a smile.

Tim: - 'Ahhmm! It's very kind of you to help us out again, but I hope you understand that it was very important for us to know if everything is okay with the children, since they have been missing in this world for quite a long time and we want to know when they will come back!': - He answered in despair.

Amanda: - 'The police are still investigating them, and we just can't tell them that they are in another world right now! Really, how can we find out when they will come home?': - She asked curiously.

Naiara: - 'It's okay! Listen carefully to what I'm saying now, you won't like what you hear, but since you are the children's parents, I think you have the right to know the truth!'

Evelin: - 'Hanna? Did you feel this too? I had a very strange feeling; a cold breeze ran over my face! But maybe I'm just imagining it! But I had the feeling that suddenly someone was watching me!': - She said confused.

Hanna: - 'Yes! I felt it too!': - She answered.

Oliver: - 'What did you feel? I want to feel it too!': - He interjected jokingly. This was overheard by the Menthis.

Menthis: - 'Ahhmm! Oliver! What did you feel?': - He asked him suddenly.

Oliver: - 'Nothing! The girls said that they felt something strange at the table earlier!':- He answered with a half-smile. In the meantime, Hanna poked Oliver in the side.

Hanna: - 'You don't have to tell everything that is being said here right away, you pushed me!': - She whispered in his ear.

Oliver: - 'Sorry! But suddenly I couldn't think of any excuses!': - He excused himself.

Menthis: - 'Girls! You don't want to say anything?': - He asked curiously, and of course he was also curious if they would answer honestly. Evelin wanted to answer, but Hanna poked her ankle.

Hanna: - 'Hmmm!! But we will tell you! Three minutes ago, when we were eating, a cold breeze hit our faces and...

Oliver: - 'Oh that!!! Oh yes, I felt that too, but I thought that Hanna was playing with me!': - He interrupted Hanna.

Menthis: - 'Alright then! I'm glad that you were honest, yes, what happened to you earlier was because someone from your world just happened to check on you to see if you were okay! With the help of a witch there, your parents asked for help from a witch to make sure everything is okay with you, that's all that happened.': - He answered with a smile.

Evelin: - 'Then our parents saw us, what we were doing?': - She asked excitedly.

Menthis: - 'Oh yes, they saw everyone here, not just you.': - He answered with a smile.

Oliver: - 'That's really cool! If I had known this, I would have waved to them! Are they still looking?': - He asked with a grin and started waving.

Menthis: - 'No, they're not watching anymore!': - He replied laughing.

John: - 'Damn it! I promised Tim that if I get here successfully, I will somehow send him a signal that everything is fine with the children. But so much has happened since then that I've completely forgotten!': - He whispered to Mr. Tregas.

Mr. Tregas: - 'No problem, John! Now they know that's all that matters, and I think they will soon find out the truth about what is really going on here.'

Menthis: - 'That's right, Mr. Tregas! The parents of the children will find out the truth about what is really going on here today, and I don't think they will really like it, so I am prepared for this eventuality. The messenger is already on his way, and he will mail them a letter, and in the letter I have included 4 special pills that they will have to take at the time that I have prescribed for them in detail. These pills are used so that when the war starts, they will see that the children are safe here and they can watch our war all the way through, of course they will decide whether they want to see it or not!': - He interrupted.

Mr. Tregas: - 'That's a good idea Menthis! Really impressive! I would like to ask you something!': - He said with interest.

Menthis: - 'Go ahead, Mr. Tregas!': - He said.

Mr. Tregas: - 'This will be a serious question! I would like you to honestly tell everyone here whether we will survive this war or not?': - He asked seriously.

Menthis: - 'Hmm! Well, according to the current situation, yes, we will win this war, we must win it, although if we lose it, those sitting at the table here will never see their family members or their friends again. A strategy has been developed for this as well, which should work! We trust that it will be like this, let's not lose our faith in it, because the faith to win this war makes us stronger, but last but not least, love, which is indestructible in this war.': - He answered seriously.

Oliver: - 'You said that very well, I'll give you that! If we're stuck here, I'll be just fine here too! I will only miss my parents, but I will skype with them!': - He said with a smile. The others laughed at what Oliver said.

Oliver: - 'What is it? You can Skype from down here too, can't you?': - He asked confused.

Hanna: - Hellooooo, idiot! Wakey wakey! There is no internet here if you hadn't already noticed!!!!: - She said laughing.

Oliver: - 'Oh yeah! Well then, I'll call them on Magic Skype, it's pretty much the same thing, right?': - He asked with a big grin.

Jessy: - 'That's why I love you, you little idiot!': - She said laughing.

Robnis: - 'Father, we need to talk, this is very important!': - He told his father at the table.

Koldvir: - 'All right, my son, if it's important, this cannot be left unheard!': - He answered.

Robnis: - 'Father! I say let's bring forward this whole marriage proposal because I have a very bad feeling. Send more letters and inform them to come a week earlier please!': - He requested his father.

Koldvir: - 'What do you base this bad feeling on? What's all the hurry? I don't see any problem!': - He asked curiously.

Robnis: - 'Father, you have to trust me! Now it won't take long to bring this all a week ahead, we can solve it since I'll help with this too, right? I will make arrangements in the palace so that everything is ready on time, just leave it to me.': - He said firmly.

Koldvir: - 'Well, if you insist on it so much, we will bring it forward, I don't think it will be an obstacle.': - He answered with a smile.

Robnis: - 'Thank you, father! Then I'll go and make arrangements.': - He answered excitedly.

Amanda: - 'What would we even have to say? What truth do we need to know?': - She asked in despair.

Naiara: - 'Good! The war will soon begin there, everyone will unite against the evil witch in order to defeat her and deprive her of her evil power. But the problem here is that if they don't succeed in winning this war, you will never see your children again, as the evil witch's heart will completely change to evil, there won't be a drop of love left in her, then everyone who is near her will die. However, your children will be alive because they are not near the evil witch, they are safe in the goblin world. What you could see first was the world of goblins. What you didn't see was James, because he is held captive in the palace by the evil witch under a strong spell, that's why you could only see John.': - She finally said.

Kev: - 'So does that mean that if they lose, we won't see Evelin again?': - He asked, horrified.

Jenifer: - 'But that's not going to happen, is it?': - She asked in despair.

Tim: - 'We can't leave it at that! We have to do something so they can win this war! We have to do something!!! I can't watch this passively like this, I have to rally Abby about this!': - He announced while walking back and forth.

Naiara: - 'Nobody does anything! Everyone calms down and then maybe we can talk about this further!': - She tried to calm them down.

Tim: - 'But still, how can we calm down when we think about the fact that we might lose our daughter and they might lose their boys! You can't settle for that!!!': - He answered angrily.

Naiara: - 'Tim!!! Please sit down and listen!': - She asked firmly.

Amanda: - 'Come back here dear and let's listen to Naiara, please!': - She said.

Naiara: - 'Well, the situation is that the goblins already have a plan that seems very likely to work. Their job will be to trust the goblins there and the other clans who have joined forces in this war. Even though they are not alone in what is being done there, those monks there all want to defeat the evil witch, because they can no longer bear her torment. The plan should work against her, I'm sure they will defeat her in some way, since I'll help them from here, because I'm in contact with the boss of the goblins, everything is planned, you don't have to worry. Oh yeah, one more thing! When you get home, a letter will be waiting for you, which you should read very carefully and act accordingly, I have nothing else to say.' They pretty much wanted to ask her one thing or another, but they didn't have the chance because she told them what was important, so she didn't waste any more time there.

Amanda: - 'That was fast! We couldn't even tell her thank you!': - She said suddenly.

Jenifer: - 'I think she heard that we thanked her, or at least she knows!': - She interrupted. Tim got up from the table and started pacing again and scratching his head, wondering what would come out of this.

Kev: - 'I wonder what might be in the letter waiting for us at home?': - He asked curiously.

Tim: - 'I don't know what could be in it, but it has to be good, because it's about the lives of our children.': - he said angrily.

Jenifer: - 'I say that everything will be fine because Nia ...'

Tim: - 'Why are you so sure? I wouldn't be so sure about that after what she said here, I don't have a moment's rest!!': - He interrupted her.

Amanda: - 'I think we should go back to the hotel and go home as soon as possible!': - She said firmly.

Jenifer: - 'I agree with Amanda! We have nothing left to do here, let 's find out what's in that letter.': - He said to her.

Kev: - 'So far, this is all well and good, but who knows what's in that letter! What if we don't like what we're going to read?': - He asked.

Tim: - 'Whatever is in it, I hope it will be good, because then I don't know if I'll be able to hold myself back in what I'm going to do!': - He said angrily. They left the restaurant and went back to the hotel, packed up and checked out to go home immediately. By the time they got home, it was already midnight because there was no return train at that time, so they still had to wait three hours before they could go back to where they lived. But in the end, they were home, which mattered a lot to them. Tim opened the front door, and the letter was floating in the air waiting for them to return home. They were surprised when they saw the flying letter. Kev when he opened the main entrance door, the letter was also waiting for them, which of course surprised them, but they were no longer shocked by it.

Tim: - 'Well, dear, are you ready to read the letter?': - He asked excitedly.

Amanda: - 'Of course!': - She answered excitedly. Tim finally opened the letter.

Letter: '

Dear parents!

My name is Menthis! Of course, you don't know me, but I know you.'

Tim: - 'Why am I not surprised by this.': - He murmured in a low voice.

First of all, I would like to ask you not to worry, because the children are in safe hands. I can assure you that they won't get hurt here with us. The war we are preparing for is more than likely going to be won, as our plan against the evil witch is perfect and a sure win. I have attached two more pills for you! Yes, I know that now you are asking what are these pills for? But this pill is special and can only be taken on April 12 at 12:00 p.m. This is important because that's when the great war will begin, and if you want to see what's going on, you have to take the pill at the exact time as described here. This tablet ensures that you can watch the fight here for exactly three hours. Of course, you don't have to do this, only if you want to, it's up to you.

Kind regards,

Menthis

Tim: - 'What the hell? We can watch the war! But how is it possible from this pill? Well, when the time comes, I will definitely take the pill!': - He said firmly.

Amanda: - 'Honey! I'll take the pill with you too! Whatever happens, happens!': - She said firmly.

Kev: - 'Honey, I'm sure I'll take the pill when the time comes! I have to see how this war goes!': - He said seriously.

Jenifer: - 'My love! I will also take the pill because I don't want to miss it. I need to know what the outcome of this will be.': -

She said firmly.

~   The secret key!   ~

Koldvir sent the letters with his messengers to the kings about the event being brought forward. The kings received the letters and informed their loved ones that there had been a change in the request for the marriage proposal.

Nyaritis: - 'Please call my daughter here!': - He told his butler.

Butler: - 'Yes, Your Majesty!': - He answered humbly. Nivita was in the family garden and was about to write a letter to her love.

Butler: - 'Princess! Your father wants to see you!': - He bowed respectfully.

Nivita: - 'Ohh! It must be something very important! Thank you!': - She answered the butler. Nivita very happily entered the palace to her father. The guards opened the door to the hall for the princess to enter.

Nivita: - 'Did you call me father? Is there something wrong?': - She asked.

Nyaritis: - 'My dear daughter! Come sit here next to me. Well, I have good news for you, King Koldvir has brought the event forward by a week. Don't ask me why, but I think this is extremely good news for you, since you were just saying why this whole thing can't be moved forward, so now it's happened. I think King Nyaritis is up to something, otherwise why would he bring this event forward.': - He said with a smile. He didn't even finish what he had to say properly, another courier arrived with another letter.

Courier: - 'My King! Another urgent letter arrived from King Koldvir!': - He handed it over with a bow.

Nyaritis: - 'Hmm, that's interesting! What is Koldvir up to?': - He asked curiously.

Nivita: - 'Read it aloud, father, it will surely be exciting!': - She interrupted.

Letter: - "I would like to inform all dear guests with this letter that the event will be cancelled but instead I would like a wedding for the young people. Knowing how much they're looking forward to this event, I decided that all this formality is unnecessary, let's cut into the middle, since we have nothing to lose. So, let's unite our families, let's seal our common future together."

With which respect

 King Koldvir.

Nivita: - 'Yoohooo! I felt! I knew this could only be good news! I have to get ready right away, father, I have no time to waste!': - With that she got up and ran out of the room.

Nyaritis: - 'Hahaha! Youngsters! But it's nice to see them so happy! Well then, let's get ready for the big event.': - He said aloud to himself. The king of the north also received the second letter and, of course, informed his daughter of the great event brought forward.

Karnita: - 'Estel, did you hear the big news? They moved the event forward; it won't be a proposal but a wedding! I'm very happy about that, so at least I don't have to wait any longer, we'll get over it and I can finally be with my love! Isn't it wonderful?': - She asked excitedly.

Estel: - 'Yes, your grace! This is truly amazing! Then we have nothing left but to prepare for the big event.': - She answered with a smile.

Karnita: - 'Yes! That's right, we shall get to it right away. Call the tailor here, please!': - She ordered.

Estel: - 'I'm not here anymore, your grace!': - She said with a smile. There was a lot of activity in the Koldvir's kingdom, everyone was getting ready for the big weddings, because they had a lot of work due to the king's sudden announcement.

Robnis: - 'Listen here, my little brother! The big wedding will be soon and then we will part ways, but one thing is for sure, no matter what happens in the future you can always count on me, do you understand?': - He said seriously.

Valtinus: - 'I understand! But I feel something is wrong! Tell me, why did our father bring the wedding forward? You told him something, didn't you? What did you tell him anyway?': - He asked curiously.

Robnis: - 'No way! I didn't tell him anything, only that what's the point of proposing if we can have a wedding right away. I think it's unnecessary, because you already proposed when we were little, didn't you? You don't have to worry; I assure you there is

400

no background to this.': - He answered with a slight smile.

Valtinus: - 'Well, that's true! There was indeed a proposal for a girl when we were little, because our parents had already decided who we were going to marry, but I can honestly say that I don't even mind that they decided that way, because I really like Karnita, for example. She's pretty, funny, and also smart. Well, it won't be long before we seal our future with the beautiful princesses i love with a huge party'.: - He answered calmly.

Robnis: - 'Well, right! That's what im talking about, let's go back to the palace and immediately tell the tailor to make us our most beautiful clothes! Are you in?': - He asked laughing.

Valtinus: - 'Come on!! Let's run a race!': - He replied laughing.

The goblins and the other clans have already prepared for the big fight, the only clan that refuses to join the war is the goblins with the power of water. The day came when all the clan chiefs gathered to discuss the strategy for the war. Everyone showed up for the big talk, only Watim was missing.

Menthis: - 'I warmly welcome everyone! Today is the most important meeting for all of us. The strategy, which we must discuss thoroughly, will be very important to everyone later on. What we are facing has such a power that it is beyond the reach of many of us. As you can see, the head of the magic mushrooms is among us to help us in the fight and of course we can also welcome the bosses of the fairies at our table, which is a great honour for us in these times. I regret to inform you that our fellow goblins with waterpower are not willing to join us, the reason has not been explained, but I secretly hope that they will change their minds. Well, I think let's get to the point! We must know that in the world above everything is covered with darkness. The evil witch has created the most terrifying monsters of darkness, which means that we will have a tough time against them. There will be monsters among them that will not be easy to defeat. Since we won't have magic power up there, we found a solution for this too, thanks to the magic mushrooms. As they can provide everyone with the right magic power when we go into battle, regardless of that, we will have to fight hard because this kind of magic power is not what we are used to. This magical power that the mushrooms will provide will be just enough to stand up for ourselves, one wrong step or one wrong move and then it's over. Of course, we also have to reckon with the fact that there will be people who will fall in the war, and there will certainly be many of us who will die. But war, as we know, comes with victims and the most important thing is to defeat the evil witch once and for all. If we all work together, we shall succeed, thank you!': - He finished his speech.

Casandra: - 'We forgot to mention an important factor, James! He is in the palace with the wicked witch. Well, in this case, we need to get James to rid his mind of the spell so that he can help us.': - She interrupted firmly.

Atlindia: - 'It's true! We just need to plan how to get James to clear his mind when the war starts.': - She interrupted.

Bathes: - 'I think magic mushrooms could help with this the most!': - He interrupted.

Menthis: - 'I think so, because the little magic mushrooms that were in James' ear climbed out and came through my ear.': - He answered firmly.

Mushrooms boss: - 'I apologize for interrupting, but there is a solution for this! Those mushrooms didn't leave James's ear because they couldn't help him, they left their master because they came to me for help. When the right time comes, I fill up James's magic mushrooms with new power so that they can do their job. There is no need to worry about this, James will be in good hands at the right time.': - He said convincingly.

Fyrra: - 'Well then, we don't have to worry about that, thanks for the clarification! But what if something goes wrong! We have to prepare for this too, don't we?': - She asked firmly.

Kleopatra: - 'That's right!! We must prepare for every possible eventuality, since we have gathered here to discuss everything.': - She interrupted firmly.

Menthis: - 'One of my plans will be that one of the fairies will sneak up on James in his room and carry out this task. She takes the little mushrooms, and they crawl back into James's ears. When this is done, the mushrooms will immediately activate their powers and remove the charm from James. I would like one of you to volunteer, I don't want to choose because it implies, I'm doing this on personal grounds. So, you have to make the decision in this matter.': - He finished what he had to say. The fairies whispered together and after some time their decision was made.

Kleopatra:- 'Well, we have made our decision! I will take on this task, there is no question that I am the only one who has access underground and above ground, since I am the guardian of the earth, so it will be easiest for me to get to James.': - She finished what she had to say.

Menthis: - 'Alright then! I think you made the right decision! There is something else here that will be very important. In the evil witch's room, there is a sphere in which she holds the rest of humanity. Well, they will also have to be freed somehow, since they cannot stay in that sphere. Does anyone have any ideas on how to accomplish this?': - He asked curiously.

Atlindia: - 'If I am not mistaken, then only James will be able to complete this task! We will not be able to free them from that sphere because they are under the power of the evil witch, we will need the help of James here.': - She finished her sentence.

Menthis: - 'Hmm! It's true!': - He agreed.

Mr. Tregas: - 'If you'll allow me to say a few words?': - He asked.

Menthis: - 'Go ahead Mr. Tregas! We need all good ideas now!': - He said with a smile.

Mr. Tregas: - 'If my memory serves me correctly, James has something up his sleeve with which can help us, the only question here is whether he still has that something!': - He finished what he had to say.

Kleopatra: - 'And what might that be Mr. Tregas?': - She asked curiously.

Mr. Tregas: - 'When James came to this world, one of the magicians gave him a bottle that he can only use when the time is right to fight the evil witch. This bottle contains a magic powder that, if you open it at the right time, you can defeat the evil witch. Hopefully he still has this bottle.': - He finished what he had to say.

Menthis: - 'Yes, this is only interesting information so far! Well, we can only trust that the bottle will be there, but even if it is not, we will still need James' help no matter what happens.': - He said firmly.

Evelin was alone in her room and looked out the window with tears in her eyes. The war was constantly on her mind just like her loved ones, she was very afraid of James getting hurt because then she would never see him again. She was standing by the window with tears streaming down her face, a small bird landed on the windowsill and started chirping beautifully, as if he wanted to tell Evelin something. When Evelin looked over there and listened to the beautiful chirping of the bird, she started to cry even more, knelt down by the windowsill and watched how enthusiastically the little bird chirped its note and did not give up. Then Evelin remembered something and went to her bed, lifted the mattress and pulled out her suitcase from under her bed. She opened it and began to take out her things, looking for an important object, a key. While searching, she found the key, it was in a box, which she had to store carefully so that it wouldn't get lost. When she held it in her hand, he sat down on the floor, leaned against the bed and started turning the key in his hand. As soon as she looked at the key and turned it, the little bird was still there on the windowsill and chirped beautifully. Evelin's memories of this key and how she got it down in the basement came back. Then she also remembered that this key actually belonged to the cupboard that was in the house where that kind and strange aunt had taken them in. In the end, they couldn't go back to find out what could have been in the cupboard that needed this key. When she remembered all this and already knew where this key belonged, the little bird flew away from the windowsill. She got up from the floor and went through Hanna's room to tell her the story of that key. She knocked on her door and waited for an answer.

Hanna: - 'Come in!': - She said loudly. Evelin opened her door and looked at Hanna with big pleading eyes. Hanna already knew that Evelin had found something again, since she doesn't usually knock for no reason.

Hanna: -'Come in Evelin! Come sit here and tell me what's wrong!': - She invited her into her room.

Evelin went into her room, closed the door and began to tell Hanna her story about the key. Oliver and Jessy were out in the forest again at the clearing where they could talk well, so they could speak freely, and they were surrounded by the chirping of the birds. The two lovers sat huddled together in the grass and talked quietly. Jessy lay down in the grass and looked at the towering trees and listened to the chirping of the birds and the rustling of the breeze, which calmed her down in this upset and stressful period. Oliver also lay next to her, took her hand and lifted it up, he started to turn it around, they put their hands

405

together and then Oliver said this.

Oliver: - 'Jessy! When this war is over and the evil witch finally falls, I want you to come home with me to our world. I will be seventeen next month, but I already know that I want to propose to you. Be my wife!': - He asked for her hand in marriage.

Jessy: - 'Oliver! I really want to be your wife, but I don't know if my parents will agree to me going to your world. I think we should talk to my parents first and then we can make a decision about our future more easily. What do you think about it?': - She asked with a smile.

Oliver: -'You're right! Let's talk to your parents first! But I will still marry you, no matter what your parents decide!!! Hihihihi!': - He said laughing.

Jessy: - 'You're beyond repair. Hihihih!': - She laughed. They hugged each other and continued to lie there in the grass scanning the sky. After Evelin told Hanna how they got the key, Hanna made a rather surprised face.

Hanna: - 'Evelin! May I ask why you haven't told anyone about this until now? This key is not just any key you know!! (Meanwhile, she turned it in her hand and took a good look at it.) We have to report this to the head magician immediately, come quickly!': - She said hurriedly.

Evelin: - 'But what makes this key so special? It's just a plain simple key! I don't see anything special in it!': - He said in surprise.

Hanna: - 'Listen! When you were there with that old aunt, didn't you notice that her house looked like a palace from the inside? But from the outside, it looked just like any other traditional house. Based on this, you could have thought that something was wrong with this house, the old lady was a sorceress who is already 300 years old. I guess she also brought up her loved ones for you too!': - She said.

Evelin: - 'How do you know this, what she told us? But anyway, she really talked about her loved ones, we even felt sorry for her. How is it possible that you know about this sorceress?': - She asked curiously.

Hanna: - 'we know everyone who has something to do with wizardry, so I know that witch as well. This sorceress is a kind old lady who does no harm to anyone , in fact she only wants good for those who come to her, she helps everyone, but the most interesting thing in all of this is that she does not explain specifically what her things purpose is or what its for, this means that you have to solve the mystery about it yourself which she just gives a hint about. She led you to find the key, but she didn't tell you what it was for. With this, she wanted you to unlock the secret. It has always been this way since she existed and I don't think it will change.': - She answered with a smile.

Evelin: - 'This is all fine and good so far, but how did you know that we were going to decipher this?': - She asked curiously.

Hanna: - (Looked at Evelin) 'Did you seriously ask that?': - She asked with a smile.

Evelin: - 'What?? Aaaah! Of course! She is a sorceress!! I get it now! Now I understand everything, why that beautiful singing bird landed on my windowsill and gave me the feeling that I must consciously look for this key, which I finally did. Hmm, that's interesting!': - She said in surprise.

Hanna: - 'Right! I told you! Now let's try to get there as soon as possible.': - She said firmly.

Evelin: - 'I'm trying !!': - She answered with a smile.

The main magician was heading towards them, he noticed that they were trying hard to get somewhere, and he was surprised.

Mr. Tregas: - 'Where, where in such a hurry ??': - He asked in surprise.

Hanna: - 'Mr. Tregas! It's great that we ran into each other! Evelin gave me a key that she has been carrying with her for some time. This is very important to pass this on to you sir!': - She said seriously. Mr. Tregas took the key and started examining it, as soon as he got a good look at it, he looked at the girls, smiled, turned around and hurried to Menthis. When Evelin saw this, she immediately tried to follow him, Hanna was not far behind either.

Evelin: - 'Mr. Tregas! Please wait for us! Just tell me why this key is so important?': - She asked in surprise.

Mr. Tregas: - 'My child, this key you gave me came at the right time, I can only say that much! Why is this key important? Well, this kind of key does not grow in every bush for sure, in fact there is only one of them in this world. It has a special power that can only be used when it is needed, if it is not needed then it is just an ordinary key, just like the others.': - He answered in a hurry.

Evelin: - 'What do you mean that it has a special power? What makes it special?': - She asked curiously.

Mr. Tregas: - 'Evelin! Do you remember the day you found this key?': - He asked.

Evelin: - 'Yes, I remember!': - She answered.

Mr. Tregas: - 'Do you also remember what the key looked like?': - He asked.

Evelin: - 'Hmmm! Yes, I remember! It was a grey rusty key just like any other ordinary key!': - She answered.

Mr. Tregas: - 'Great! Now look at the key, what it looks like!': - He showed it hastily.

Evelin: - 'That's interesting! Its appearance has really changed, it is no longer rusty, its beautiful silver colour, and the upper part has a gold-plated dragon pattern in it, and red colour runs along the dragon's outline in the pattern.': - She said in amazement.

Mr. Tregas: - 'Well, my little girl, this means that there is a big problem and now is the time to use this.': - He answered.

Evelin: - 'How long will it be in this condition?': - She asked curiously.

Mr. Tregas: - 'Well, as long as we use it for the purpose for which it is intended.': - He answered.

Evelin: - 'I understand...' She wanted to continue what she was saying, but in the meantime they arrived to Menthis.

Menthis: - 'Welcome my dear friend! Where in such a hurry?': - He asked in surprise.

Mr. Tregas: - 'Phew! We were just trying to get to you, we have to give you an important key.': - He said while breathing heavily. He handed the key to Menthis and when he took it in his hands, he immediately saw that this was the key that could help them now.

Menthis:- 'Mr Tregas! Where did you find this key, if I may ask?': - He asked in surprise.

Mr. Tregas: - 'Evelin gave me this key a few minutes ago .': - He answered panting.

Evelin: - 'Yes....'

Hanna: - 'The sorceress gave her this key!': - She interrupted.

Hanna: - 'Sorry Evelin!' (Whispered in his ear)

Menthis: - 'I understand! So, everything is clear, then the only thing left is to call the meeting once more to talk about the new strategy again.': - He said firmly. With this he gestured to his butler, and he took action.

Menthis: - 'Evelin, you made the right decision to give us this key, it means a lot to us now, thank you!': - He said gratefully.

Evelin: - 'I'm glad I could help!': - She answered with a little smile, even though she still didn't understand why that key was so important. Hanna and Evelin left the palace of the goblins and walked back to their accommodation.

Evelin: - As You know, Hanna, so far it's all well and good that they are so happy with that key, but actually I still don't know why that key is so important!': - She said curiously.

Hanna: - 'That's right! We haven't had a chance to tell you yet, sorry, but I'll tell you now, we'll get to it, won't we? Come, let's go home and over a coffee I'll tell you what that key is for.': - She answered with a smile.

Evelin: - 'That sounds good, a coffee will be good now!': - She answered with pleasure. They got home and sat down in the living room with a coffee and made themselves some biscuits.

Hanna: - 'Well, that key is important because when there is a big problem, as you saw, it changes in order to help those who need it. This means that the key will be used to get to James's room, so it will be easier to free him from the power of the spell. In fact, with this key you can get anywhere where there is a problem. Since James is in great need of help, the key indicated the need. The leaders will gather and discuss who will be sent to James's room with the help of this key.': - She explained patiently.

Evelin: - 'I understand now! Then we have no choice but to wait for the right moment for the action!': - She answered.

Hanna: - 'Yes! But this will also be decided by the leaders after this, that the key will come to their aid!': - She answered.

After a week, everything in the Koldvir palace was ready to

receive guests. Everything in the palace was beautifully decorated, from the ballroom to the end of the hallways, the view was amazing. All that was left was to receive the arrival of the guests. Robnis was getting more and more nervous because he felt that something bad was going to happen, so he walked around the palace while sending the soldiers out for safety. As soon as he got up in the palace, Elisa was just walking there.

Elisa: - 'Robnis! All is well. You look nervous! The guests will be here soon, don't worry, son! You will get married soon and everything will be fine!': - She encouraged him.

Robnis: - 'That's not why I'm worried, mother! I feel like something bad is going to happen here and I won't be there to stop it! I think it will be best if I also ride out and check the road!': - He said firmly.

Elisa: - 'Come on son! The soldiers are outside, there's nothing to worry about, you belong here!': - She replied in despair.

Robnis: - 'Mother! I have to go out, I can't just wait here and do nothing, forgive me, but it's my duty!': - He answered firmly. With that, he stormed off so that Elisa didn't even have a chance to say a word. They prepared the horse for Robnis, and he jumped on his horse and left the palace. Of course, he was accompanied by his horsemen in the forest, since Elisa had ordered that he could not go out alone. The soldiers barely catch up to Robnis because he stormed out of the palace at such speed. He quickly rode out into the forest to make sure everything was alright, there were soldiers everywhere securing the way for the guests arriving there. As he rode further into the forest, he felt more and more strongly that something was wrong here. The soldiers who accompanied him both in front and behind him watched out for anything. They went deeper and deeper when a deep silence fell on the forest, not even the birds sang, the breeze didn't blow, as if life had stopped. Robnis immediately stopped his horse and

411

motioned for the soldiers to stop. Everyone stopped and began to watch, but they saw nothing, no matter where they looked, they saw nothing. The horses started to get more and more nervous, they couldn't stay in one place, they started bucking as if something was in front of them, but the soldiers and the Robnis didn't see anything either. But the horses became even more nervous, so much so that they threw everyone off their backs and started galloping in the completely opposite direction, leaving their owners there. Robnis and the soldiers got up from the ground.

Robnis: - 'Whoo! Stop!': - He tried to hold back his horse, but it didn't work because it also galloped away.

Soldier: - 'Sir, I'm reporting that we can't see anything here!': - He reported firmly.

Robnis: - 'Yes! I can see that too! But be on the lookout because there is something here that we don't even know is here!': - He stated firmly.

Soldier: - 'Yes, sir!': - He obeyed. Everyone scanned the forest with slow steps, but they still saw nothing. As soon as they moved on, suddenly a cold breeze arose out of nowhere, sweeping between them at such a level that they could not see anything through the leaves that were stirred up by the wind. The rotating wind was blowing stronger and stronger, only the shouting could be heard.

Soldier: - 'Be careful!!'

2 Soldier: - 'It is behind me!!'

3 Soldier: - 'Aaaah!!! Help!!!'

Robnis: - 'Try to stay together!'

4 Soldier: - 'Watch out, it's here again!! Aaaah!'

Robnis couldn't see anything except flying leaves, and it really annoyed him that he couldn't see his soldiers either, he could only hear them.

Robnis: - 'Who is there?? Show yourself!! I'm here if you want me! What's going to happen?': - He shouted all at once.

5 Soldier: - 'Sir, be careful!!! It's on you! Aaaah!' Robnis suddenly looked around but again saw nothing. The shouting of the soldiers became less and less, Robnis became more and more angry.

Robnis: - 'We're going back!! Retreat immediately!!' Robnis started running somewhere but he didn't know where because he couldn't see anything. After a while, the soldiers quieted down, they could no longer be heard.

Robnis: - 'Come forward if you dare and fight me!!' As soon as he said this, a huge monster stood in front of Robnis, it was the size of a giant, it had four eyes, four hands and four legs. He attacked Robnis with the four different weapons he held in his hands, one with a spiked sword, the other with six blades, the third with an iron ball with spikes attached to a chain, and the fourth with a giant hammer. When Robnis saw this, he suddenly didn't know whether to resist or run away. He suddenly froze from the mere sight of it and of course dodged the blows. But that was not enough, twenty such giants appeared from the forest. Seeing this, Robnis thought it would be better if he started running, but the giants were faster than Robnis, so they soon caught up. Robnis tried to dodge their blows by taking advantage of the fact that the smaller than them and started to hide under them and tried to somehow avoid the wielding giants. He was able to keep up this pace for a while, but they were already on him so much that he didn't really know where to run. He fell to the ground and felt that now everything will be over, the wedding is gone, his love is gone, he won't be able to see his loved ones anymore. Just when hope seemed to be gone, a loud shout suddenly broke the voice of the giants. The giants turned and King Koldvir himself arrived with soldiers to free Robnis . The fight between the humans and the giants began, Robnis also gained strength and jumped up from the ground and started to fight against the giants. There were 25 giants, and the king came with one hundred and fifty soldiers. The fight against the giants was not easy because they were able to fight and injure more than half of the humans due to their many hands. The fight lasted for five hours, but during this time the guests also arrived in the forest and saw from afar what was going on there, so the accompanying soldiers joined the fight and the guests stayed at a safe distance.

The brides watched the events from their carriages and were very afraid.

Nivita: - 'Mom, that's Robnis there!! God, if something goes wrong, I will die with him, I don't want to live without him even for a minute!': - She said sobbing.

Martha: - 'My daughter!! Calm down, please! Robnis knows what he's doing, and he even has help, you don't have to worry.': - She tried to reassure her.

Nivita: - 'Well, it's easy to say that when I see the monsters they're fighting!!': - She replied sobbing.

Karnita: - 'Oh my goodness!! What kind of monsters are these?? I hope Valtinus doesn't get hurt, because then I won't survive that!!': - She said crying.

Julia: - 'Hopefully everything will be fine, we have to trust that nothing will happen to them!': - She tried to comfort the princesses. During this time, everyone in the palace was very anxious about what would happen to their husbands.

Elisa: - 'Dear God, grant that everything will be alright!!': - She begged standing at the window and her eyes were tearing up. The fight was still going on, many people fell, but there were only three giants that had to be defeated. The soldiers were tired but did not give up the fight, they rushed at the giants with Robnis and Valtinus against them. One of the giants wounded both Robnis and Valtinus, they both fell from the horse, and as they lay there on the ground, the giant who had wounded them was just about to finish them off when the king jumped up and stabbed the giant in the heart. The giant looked at the king and collapsed to the ground. The other two giants were also executed by the soldiers, each giant fell. They helped the two princes up and placed them next to the guests arriving in the carriages, so they were transported to the palace. Eighty of the one hundred and fifty soldiers returned and forty were wounded. When they arrived at the gate of the palace, they opened it and with immediate effect began to care for the wounded. Both Robnis and Valtinus were nursed in their own rooms. The giant stabbed Robnis in the shoulder and hit Valtinus in the stomach, but fortunately in a place where he can recover in a couple of days so that he can walk, of course, full recovery will take time. The young people were left alone in their room, Karnita and Nivita also sat next to their lover and rubbed their foreheads, gave them something to drink, took care of them all night, until they finally fell asleep on the edge of their beds. It was dawn and both Robnis and Valtinus woke up, they were past the critical point, they opened their eyes and looked to the side to see that their love was lying on the edge of their beds and the wet towel was in their hands.

Robnis: - 'Good morning my dear!': - He spoke in a slightly hoarse voice. When Nivita heard this, she immediately jumped up and fell on Robnis's neck with a big smile.

Nivita: - 'Oh my God, you're better! My sweet Love! It's good to see you again.': - She said with great joy.

Valtinus: - 'Good morning my dear!': - He spoke a bit softly and

415

hoarsely.

Karnita: - 'Good morning, dear!! I'm glad you're better, my love! I was very worried about you, I thought I would lose you and I wouldn't have survived that!': - She said sadly.

Valtinus: - 'I'm here my heart, I'm not dead, thanks to you !!': - He said smiling and moaning. Both Nivita and Karnita immediately told the maids to bring breakfast and fresh water to the room, although they still have to take care of their love while they recover. Elisa and King Koldvir visited their sons in their room, they wanted to make sure that they were all right.

Elisa: - 'Good morning son, I can see you're better this morning, I'm very happy about that!': - She said kindly.

Koldvir: - 'Good morning Robnis! You're such a strong man, you'll get better soon, then we'll have a huge party.': - He said firmly, but still gently.

Robnis: - 'Good morning to you too! I'm much more better so we can even celebrate. But before that, I'll check on Valtinus to see how he's doing!': - He answered in a somewhat hoarse voice, but still strongly.

Nivita: - 'You were very lucky my dear yesterday, but you should rest, you are not fully recovered yet, your wound is fresh.': - She warned him to be careful.

Robnis: - 'They carved me out of hard wood, my dear, you don't have to worry, especially while you're here by my side!': - He answered with a smile and kissed her cheek.

Koldvir: - 'Son, we'll let you change, and we will see you later.': - he said goodbye. The king and queen left Robnis ' room and went over to Valtinus in his room, which was two corridors away. They knocked on his room and opened the door.

Valtinus: - 'Good morning to you!': - He spoke somewhat

hoarsely, since he was more injured than Robnis.

Elisa: - 'Good morning my son! How are you feeling?': - She asked with a little smile as she was scared due to his condition.

Valtinus: - 'Much better, mother! There's nothing wrong with me.': - He coughed, and his wound hurt.

Elisa: - 'Yes, I see that there is nothing wrong with you! You need to rest until you fully recover!': - He said firmly.

Koldvir: - 'He will recover soon, my son is not soft, he is a real man!': - He spoke harshly but still gently.

Valtinus: - 'That's right father! I'll be joining you for breakfast in a little while, until then I'll stay here with my beloved for a little while!': - He spoke in a weak but manly voice.

Elisa: - 'Come dear, let's let them talk and they will join us later.': - She said kindly.

Koldvir: - 'Strengthen yourself up, my son!': - He said with a wink.

Valtinus: - 'Will do father!': - He answered with a smile. The king and queen went back into the great hall to receive the guests at breakfast. Almost everyone was already there, they only had to wait for Queen Julia, but not for long, because after a few minutes she also arrived. Everyone took their place at the table and started their breakfast.

Erminus: - 'Good morning, everyone! Yesterday was a big battle with those giants, it caught us quite unexpectedly. I have a guess as to how they got there.': - He said knowingly.

Koldvir: - 'Yes! You say that right Erminus, only one person could have messed us up!': - He agree.

Erminus: - 'How are your sons?': - He asked inquisitively.

Koldvir: - 'They are better, thank God, but if we didn't intervene,

417

it could have ended worse.': - He said breathlessly.

Erminus: - 'That's right! I hope that on our way back it won't be so bumpy!': - He said.

Koldvir: - 'I hope so too! But you're staying here until my sons are fully recovered, you don't have to rush back.': - He answered.

Erminus: - 'Thank you for your kind hospitality, Koldvir, and we will accept it.': - He said with a smile.

Nyaritis: - 'Your sons are strong; they will recover soon and then we will have a huge wedding. The evil witch once again exposed herself to cross us, I only hope that this will end soon, and we can live the rest of our days carefree.': - She said a little sadly.

Koldvir: - 'I trust that the time will finally come when we no longer have to fear the evil witch. I hope that something will happen soon because this is not life, we are locked in here and we don't really have peace.': - He answered.

Erminus: - 'You speak well! I'm also secretly hoping that something will happen!': - He agreed.

Zulante: - 'Something has to happen; this it cannot go on forever!': - He said.

Anna: - 'I hope that those who stay near the evil witch are fine and are not hurt!': - She said worriedly.

Julia: - 'I hope they are well!': - She answered worriedly.

Martha: - 'They have to be good, that's all we have to think about!': - She said encouragingly.

Elisa: - 'I wonder what is happening with them there now? It would be good to know this and somehow help them if they are in trouble!': - She added.

Erminus: - 'Unfortunately, we won't find out here because our magic doesn't work here, so we can only guess in the dark.': - He said a little sadly.

Days passed and everyone in the goblin world was ready for the big war. The kings living in the sphere were also ready for the big wedding that the princesses had been waiting for so long had already arrived. During this time, the evil witch looked at the people living in the sphere and saw that they had defeated the giants that she had unleashed on them. She put the sphere back in its place and didn't care about it anymore, it was like that they would be destroyed soon anyway, and she didn't care about them anymore. But she took out her crystal and touched it to absorb even more power. The crystal then emitted a huge light that covered the entire empire. The people who saw this noticed this huge light, they didn't know where this huge light was coming from, although no one knew about the crystal except James, but he too was under the power of the spell, so he was also amazed at this huge light. The goblins' attack on the night monsters of the world above was only three days away. One of the fairies paid a visit to James's room, as she had to make sure what time he usually went to bed. Since everything was already planned, all they had to do was wait for the right time and then the big attack would take place. James went to bed because it was already very late, he settled in his bed and soon fell asleep. The little fairy visited James again in his room, crept to his pillow and looked at the sleeping James. The little fairy leaned close to James's ear and whispered these lines into his ear.

Fairy: -

James! You will soon wake up from this dream!
They are holding you captive under a very strong spell!

You have to fight against it to accomplish what you are meant to do!

The world has been taken over by darkness, there is nothing out there anymore!

The magic mushrooms will help you!

You have to overcome the spell inside you!

You have to complete your mission, never forget!

The fairy whispered these lines in his ear every night, but there were only two days left, after which the great war would begin. These lines had some influence on James. James started to dream, and, in his dream, he saw the darkness outside that surrounds the palace and he also saw the monsters, it was like a nightmare. But he also saw Evelin in his dream, which filled him with happiness. James met Evelin in his dream, but in reality, this happened, of course, in their dreams, because Evelin had the same dream with James, this is thanks to the little fairy. Both of them were very happy for the shared dream.

James's dream: - 'Evelin! It's good to see you! We're finally together again, does that mean we've defeated the evil witch? Everything is so perfect here, could it be just a dream?'

Evelin's dream: - 'James! You're finally here with me, you don't have to be held captive by the evil witch anymore!'

James's dream: - 'In captivity? Why, have I been in captivity until now?'

Evelin's dream: - 'Yes, you little fool! You do not remember? The evil witch has held you captive under a very strong spell!'

James's dream: - 'That's impossible! I wasn't in captivity; I was just in the palace for a while!'

Evelin's dream: - 'No way! That's what she wants you to believe, as she's holding other people captive as well, be careful!'

James suddenly woke up from his sleep and sat up in his bed and started looking around, but because the charm was so strong, he immediately fell back under the charm and forgot his dream. Evelin also woke up from her sleep, sat up in bed and thought about everything she saw in her dream. She got up from her bed and walked to the window, pulled aside the curtain and started to look at the beautifully shining stars, the tears came out of her eyes again, the pain took over her heart again, knowing that she could not help her love, who had been held captive by the evil witch for so long.

Evelin's thought: - 'My dear James! When will I see you again? I miss you so much my dear, I can't take this anymore! There has to be some sort of solution to this, I need to see you, James!' She was standing by the window and her tears were flowing from sadness, but then she had a very good idea. She began to think about where she had last seen that key and realized that it was in the goblin palace. She got dressed and crept out of the house carefully through the palace of the goblins to get the key, when she got to the gate, she opened it very carefully and crept into the palace. She started walking straight into the great hall where she had last seen the key, but guards were guarding the door, as the key was very important for this war. She hid behind the wall and thought about how to distract the guards, and she thought of something, so she acted immediately. She took out four pieces of candy from her pocket and threw them in the opposite direction in order to distract the guards from there, which she succeeded in. She quickly ran to the door, opened it and entered the great hall, closing the door behind her, but it sounded a little louder than it should have, so the guards noticed it and went to check it out. Evelin quickly hid in the hall so that the guards wouldn't notice her. The door opened and the guards entered to check the room,

421

because they immediately noticed the door clicking.

1 Guard: - 'Let's look around because I heard the door click, sure. that someone entered it.': - He said in a low voice.

2 Guard: - 'I heard it too! You go in that direction; I'll look at it from this direction.': - He replied in a low voice. After discussing this, they went to both sides of the room to see what could have entered the door. Evelin hid under the table that was laid and the tablecloth reached the ground, so they can't even see her there. They slowly walked through the great hall but did not see anything.

1 Guard: - 'Then let's look under the table to see if it's hiding there!': - He said confidently.

2 Guard: - 'That's a good idea, let's take a look there, just to be sure!': - he agreed. When Evelin heard this, she suddenly didn't know where to go, but she thought of something very quickly. She went forward under the table and sneaked out from under it, then she hid behind a large pillar, because they had already looked there once, so they wouldn't look at the same place again, so it was safe to hide there. The guards looked under all the tables, and when they were almost at the end, a cat ran out from under one of the tables, which scared the guards.

1 Guard: - 'So you sneaked in here, now I've got you!': - He said with a smile.

2 Guard: - 'Hahaha! It's a cat let's go back to our place, there is no one here!': - He said laughing.

Evelin was lucky with the cat, so she got away with it now. She snuck over to the key and took it to take it to James. There was wardrobe in the large hall, of course she went to one of them and opened the door, went inside the wardrobe and closed the doors behind herself, when she was inside the wardrobe, she put the key in the lock and constantly thought about James that she needs to get to him at all costs. When she turned the key, the key took Evelin to James's room. She opened the wardrobe door, took out the key and put it in her pocket again. She went out of the wardrobe and found herself in James's room, when she saw James, she immediately ran there and knelt at the edge of his bed.

Evelin: - 'James! James! Wake up! James! Wake up!': - She woke him up loudly.

James woke up and saw dimly from drowsiness, but he rubbed his eyes and then everything cleared up for him, Evelin, whom he saw in his dreams, was kneeling in front of him.

James: - 'This is just a dream; this is not reality! How did you get here?': - He asked in surprise.

Evelin: - 'Shh! Quietly, someone will hear us talking and then I'll be found! It's good to see you again James, I missed you so much!': - She said enthusiastically.

James: - 'You are Evelin, right?': - He asked curiously.

Evelin: - 'Yes, it's me! Don't you know me?': - She asked in surprise.

James: - 'Yes, I know you! I just don't know where from suddenly because I saw you a couple of times in my dreams.': - He replied kindly.

Evelin: - 'Oh yes, the spell, of course! Listen, James, I came to you here because I missed you so much, but you should know that....' She couldn't continue what she was saying because the spell that reigned there completely overwhelmed her mind, so she already forgot why she went there and forgot how to go back.

James: - 'You really missed me? But I've never seen you, only in my dreams!': - He said, surprised.

Evelin: - 'That's true! But now you are here in front of me, how is this possible?': - She asked in surprise.

James: - 'I don't know! Let 's find out!': - He said excitedly.

Evelin: - 'Okay, let's go! But where are we going?': - She asked confused.

James: - 'Well to Miriam, she knows everything, so we'll ask her, okay?': - He asked.

Evelin: - 'Okay! Let's go and ask her!': - She agreed. With that, they both went to Miriam's room in the middle of the night to find out all this. But the way to Miriam's room was long, they had to cross many hallways. During this time, while the young people were on the hallways, Menthis went down to check the key in the goblin's palace, and when he saw that the key was not there, he immediately blew an alarm. All the goblins and fairies gathered at the alarm.

Menthis: - 'Attention everyone! The key has disappeared from its place, now we have to find the key immediately, otherwise we won't be able to carry out our plan.': - He said angrily.

Fairy: - 'I know where the key went!': - She said confidently.

Menthis: - 'Where is the key?': - He asked curiously.

Fairy: - 'Evelin took it and went over to James; they are halfway to the evil witch's room.': - She answered calmly.

Menthis: - 'They must be stopped now!': - He issued the order.

Fairy: - 'I'm going right away!': - She said immediately. She couldn't even finish what she was saying, she had already gone to bring both Evelin and the key back to the goblins before she got into big trouble. The action was successful, the little fairy got there in time and brought back Evelin and the key.

Menthis: - 'What does this mean Evelin??': - He asked angrily.

Evelin: - 'Where am I! Oh, my goodness! I'm very sorry for what I did, but I have to ....': - She begged.

Mr. Tregas: - 'What is going on here? What is all this?': - He asked curiously.

Menthis: - 'We just saved Evelin and the key from the evil witch.': - He said angrily.

Mr. Tregas: - 'What? Evelin, my child, where did you think, you were going to get with this? Over there, everything is overwhelmed by the spell, which you also fell into. You haven't thought this through, have you?': - He looked at her nervously.

Evelin: - 'I'm really sorry for what I did, I really didn't think about it until the end, I completely forgot about the spell, I could only think that I had to see James, which I actually managed to do, but after that I don't remember anything, only that I'm here with you. I'm sorry!': - She apologized.

Mr. Tregas:- 'Indeed, but it happened because the spell clouded your mind, so we shouldn't go there, do you understand now?': - He asked her.

Evelin: - 'Yes, I understand! It won't happen again, I promise!': - She replied regretfully.

Menthis: - 'Correct! Now everyone should go back to their rooms and tomorrow will be the last day that we can still be together and then the war will begin.': - He instructed everyone. Everyone went back to their rooms, Mr. Tregas and Evelin started walking back in their house, they were halfway there when Mr. Tregas broke the silence.

Mr. Tregas: - 'Evelin! I know you miss James, but you should have been aware of the risk before you did this.': - He explained kindly.

Evelin: - 'Yes, Mr. Tregas! I'm sorry, but I wanted to see him so much that I didn't think about the risk.': - She said regretfully.

Mr. Tregas: - 'The point is that they brought you back here and it didn't turn into a major problem. And now go and try to rest because there is not much left until the war, but after that you will see James again. Good night.': - he said goodbye.

Evelin: - 'Yes, Mr. Tregas, good night to you too.': - She said goodbye. While this all was happening, James didn't really notice anything, he only noticed that Evelin disappeared from his side, but then the little fairy cast a forgetting spell on him so that he wouldn't remember anything about it, because then he would tell the evil witch and then it would ruin the plan of bringing Evelin back.

James: - 'Hmm. What am I doing here in the hallway, how did I get here?? Well, while I'm here, then I'll go downstairs and eat something, I can't even sleep!': - He discussed it with himself. He went down to the kitchen to make himself some food and before he got there someone tapped him on the shoulder. James was scared because it caught him off guard, he turned around to see who it was, and it was Miriam.

Miriam: - 'Well James? What are you doing here so late? Why aren't you sleeping?': - She asked in surprise.

James: - 'Ohh! It's you! Well, I don't even know why I actually came out of my room, but if I was already outside, I came downstairs to eat something, I can't sleep anyway.': - He answered thoughtfully.

Miriam: - 'If I understood correctly, you said that you were on the hallway and you don't know how you got there?': - He asked curiously.

James: - 'Something along those lines! I think I'm a sleepwalker, it's happened to me before, you don't have to worry!': - He answered with a smile.

Miriam: - 'Can I join you too?': - She asked with a smile.

James: - 'Of course! Well, let's see what we can eat so late. - He

426

asked curiously.

Miriam: - 'Whatever we want!': - She said laughing.

James: 'That's right! How would you like if I made a delicious sandwich?': - He asked with a smile.

Miriam: - 'It sounds good, sandwich it is!': - She answered thoughtfully. The only thing on Miriam's mind was what James told her, she didn't let it rest, she had to follow it up. After eating the sandwich, they went back to their room and went to sleep, at least James thought that Miriam also went to sleep, but Miriam went to her secret room where she kept the crystal and the sphere. She closed the door behind herself and took out her crystal to see what really happened to James. The crystal rose into the air and began to spin. Miriam read a spell that showed her what happened to James. When the crystal showed her what actually happened, she was amazed at what she saw.

Miriam: - 'I can't believe this!! How did I not realise this is outrageous! To hell with these fairies!!!': - She yelled angrily. Miriam angrily went back to her room and went to bed, but of course she couldn't sleep, she just tossed and turned in her bed. Gilbert also woke up from how much Miriam was tossing and turning.

Gilbert: - 'Everything okay dear? Can't you sleep?': - He asked surprised.

Miriam: - 'I can't fall asleep!! I think it's because of the full moon.': - She answered with what suddenly came to her mind.

Gilbert: - 'Come here next to me dear, I'll hug you maybe you'll fall asleep easier.': - He said kindly. He hugged her, kissed her, caressed her, but Miriam just couldn't fall asleep, Gilbert fell asleep before Miriam. The night seemed very long as usual, this was because the great war was in preparation and not many people could sleep peacefully, they were too excited about the battle ahead. Everything was ready for the fight; they were just waiting for the time to finally get into it.

~ Fall of the Witch! ~

Morning finally arrived, which everyone was waiting for, they were excited about the war, of course no one knew for sure what the end would be, but the main thing was that the fighting spirit was there and the desire to win was not lost either. They persistently encouraged each other and what is important is that they concentrated on the strategy they had already planned against the evil witch. It was five o'clock in the morning when they were already preparing for the attack according to the planned out attacked. They had to follow the plan because that was the point of it all. The little fairy was entrusted with going to James's room with the key and the little mushrooms that should go back in James's ear and the fairy took the first step towards her goal. The little mushrooms went back into James' ear before he woke up, after all, that was the point, so that he wouldn't wake up until the mushrooms went back into his ear. As soon as the mushrooms went back into James's ear, they immediately began casting the spell so that when he woke up, he would no longer be under the spell. The little mushrooms did what they had to do; the plan has been successful so far. The fairy went back to the goblins and reported the successful operation.

Menthis: - 'I would like to draw everyone's attention to the fact that the little mushrooms have successfully completed their task, the rest is up to us and, of course, James. Well, when everyone is ready, I would like to ask the boss of the mushrooms to issue the instructions to the mushrooms. With that, he looked at the boss of the mushrooms and gestured with his head that the action could begin. The boss of the mushrooms gave the command to the mushrooms in an undead voice, and they crawled into the ears of the goblins like a procession. The goblins of the three different clans totalled one hundred and fifty thousand, the missing goblins clan who said they would not participate in the war still failed to show up, even though the Menthis secretly hoped that they would come too. There were two hundred thousand fairies in total and everyone was ready for battle. When the mushrooms had crawled into the last goblin, Menthis continued his speech.

'Dear friends! This day means a lot to all of us! The evil witch tormented us for years, but today we will put an end to it! We will get our freedom back so that we can live and raise our children in peaceful. There will be no more suffering, destruction, starvation and unexpected surprises, we will soon fight for this together, together we will defeat the evil witch! One of the fairies has already started the campaign, the little mushrooms are already in James' ears!!! Fight!! Fight!!': - He encouraged those going into battle.

Majority: - 'Fight!! Fight!!

Someone from among the goblins: - 'Victory shall be ours!! Victory!!'

Everyone at the same time: - 'Victory!! Victory!! Uraaaa!!! Uraaaaa!!'

Menthis: - 'Are you ready??': - He asked loudly.

Majority: - 'Yes!!!'

Menthis: - 'Then let the fight begin !!!' He waved the flag high above his head and everyone disappeared from there, they went up into the darkness where the monsters of darkness reigned. The parents also took the pills because they wanted to follow the fight. The parents were together with the Tims family in their apartment because they wanted to be together on this important day, they also want to know who the winner will be.

Tim: - 'Well, are you prepared?': - He asked impatiently.

Kev: - 'We are ready!': - He answered impatiently.

Tim: - 'Then we take the pills at three. One, two, Three! As soon as it reached three, they all took the pills at the same time.

So, the great battle began, monsters of darkness attacked from everywhere, swords, spears, spears and arrows, huge spiky hammers clattered. James woke up in the meantime and as soon as he looked around, he remembered that he actually went there to defeat the witch, he just didn't understand why he was in that room. But when these questions were circulating in his head, the little mushrooms immediately activated James's thoughts and refreshed his memories. James immediately knew what had happened, so he behaved as he always had, so as not to be noticed by Miriam.

A day before....

In the sphere, where the rest of the people were, the big wedding, which everyone had been waiting for, finally started for the people and kings.

Koldvir: - 'I warmly welcome everyone on this big day! I called the three kingdoms together in order to unite our children, thereby uniting the kingdoms as well. However, I regret to inform you that the king for the southern kingdom cannot be here with us, as everyone knows why they cannot be here with us today. In the last few days, there was a clash in the forest that we didn't expect. The evil witch really showed herself up today, but luckily, she didn't succeed, as we defeated her giants sent against us. Many people were wounded that day, including my sons, and unfortunately many lost their lives in the battle. But let today be about fun and love, my sons are getting married!! I want everyone to have a good time and have fun as much as possible! Let the fun begin!!!': - He shouted happily.

People: - 'Long live the princes!! Long live the princes!! Long live the princes!!' The rejoicing began, the people and the princes and the kings also had fun.

Robnis: - 'Nivita my love! We are finally together now no one can separate us from each other!': - He said calmly.

Nivita:- 'My dream came true today! Now I can be with you day and night without having to hide from someone!': - She answered with a smile.

Valtinus: - 'Karnita dear! Now there's no going back, your mine forever!! I won't let you go anymore!!': - He said mischievously.

Karnita: - 'You don't have to let me go; I'm not going anywhere without you!! I will stay by your side forever, until the end of time, my love.': - She replied mischievously. The young people were very happy, they danced and had fun, which is the most important thing for couples in love.

Erminus: - 'Just look, dear! It's a pleasure to watch them, they are so happy together!': - He said with a smile.

Julia: - 'Of course, dear! They are very happy, it's a pleasure to watch them!': - She answered with a smile.

Nyaritis: - 'Just tell me, Erminus, were we so happy at that time?': - He asked jokingly.

Erminus: - 'Hahaha! Nyaritis, don't joke, you old hag! I don't even remember anymore; it was a long time ago!!': - He replied laughing.

Martha: - 'Hahaha! You are incorrigible!': - She said with a laugh.

Julia: - 'Yes! The eternal masters of joking!': - He said laughing.

Martha: - 'Julia! Let's go out for a walk in the garden!': - She invited her.

Júlia: - 'Alright then, that's a good idea!': - She agreed.

Erminus: - 'Where did you two go?': - He was interested.

Martha: - 'We're just going for a walk; we won't be away for long long!!': - He answered with a smile.

Nyaritis: - 'Let them go!! We'll take the watch the party goers in the meantime!! Hahaha': - He said laughing.

Erminus: - 'Of course, of course! Until then, we'll have a great time here! Hahaha .': - He agree. Martha and Julia went out into the garden for a little walk and chat.

Martha: - 'You know Julia, I noticed that our daughters get along very well compared to when they were very young when they last saw each other. This fills me with great joy.': - She said with satisfaction.

Julia: - 'Yes, I noticed that too, but they're young, and besides, they're in love, there's a common topic they can talk about, that always brings people together quickly, doesn't it?': - She asked in agreement.

Martha: - 'Oh, yes indeed!': - He answered.

Julia: - 'But something tells me that that's not why you wanted to come out here, right?': - She asked curiously.

Martha: - 'I see, you know me well! That's really not the only reason I wanted you to come out here in the garden with me, there's something I've been wanting to share with you for weeks and I never got the chance to tell you.': - She answered a little breathlessly.

Julia: - 'Is there anything wrong?': - She asked inquisitively.

Martha: - 'No way!! In other words, I don't know if this is a problem!': - She answered uncertainly.

Julia: - 'Martha! Please don't scare me, tell me what's bothering you!': - She was interested.

Martha: - 'Even before we came here for this wedding, I had a vision, and it certainly wasn't good. By this I mean that in the world outside, where the evil witch is, darkness is everywhere and in the darkness terrible monsters rule the earth. But that's not the end of it, I also saw that a big war will start tomorrow, the goblins and fairies will fight against the monsters of darkness.': - She answered confidently.

Julia: - 'That sounds horrible! Couldn't you have just dreamed this?': - She asked in surprise.

Martha: - 'No! I saw it as clearly as if I had been there among them!': - She answered firmly.

Julia: - 'Hmm! That might mean something! Did you tell Erminus ??': - She asked curiously.

Martha: - 'I haven't told anyone but you!': - She answered honestly.

Julia: - 'What if this is really true! You should tell Erminus somehow!': - She warned.

433

Martha: - 'Yes, I already thought about it! Today after the wedding party I will tell Erminus, Nyaritis and Koldvir as well.': - She answered firmly. Meanwhile, Elisa also went out in the garden just by chance, she saw the two queens walking there, she sneaked over there and overheard their conversation, and finally pretended to stumble into them.

Elisa: - 'Ohh, are you here? Did you come out for a walk? I also came out to get some fresh air! What were you talking about, if I don't offend you by asking?': - She wondered.

Martha: - 'Oh, no way! Come, let's sit down here, it's such a cozy little place!': - She invited her next to them. They sat down in a small pagoda full of beautiful flowers and there Martha told Elisa what they were talking about.

Elisa: - 'What you say is really very interesting! Well, I'm curious how our husbands will react to this.': - He answered in surprise.

Martha: - 'I'm also curious about that.': - She answered firmly. They stayed outside the pagoda for a while and after which they went back to the guests. When they went back, it was a lot of fun, everyone danced, laughed, and had a good time. The kings and queens started dancing along with the guests. King Nyaritis noticed on the Martha that something was bothering her.

Nyaritis: - 'My dear, I can see that something is weighing on your heart! Tell me, what were you talking about out there?': - He asked curiously.

Martha: - 'Hmm! Yes, I want to talk to you about this, but the noise here is too loud, we should go to a quiet place and then I can tell you!': - She replied with a half-smile.

Nyaritis: - 'Alright then! Come now, we'll go to a place where we won't be disturbed!': - He answered firmly. As soon as he said this, they started to leave the ballroom, but both Julia and Eliza noticed this. They looked at each other and both whispered in their husband's ear to leave the ballroom immediately. So, the kings and queens left the ballroom, but of course the fun continued. They went out in the garden again, but it was already half past nine in the evening. They went to a large pagoda where they could all sit down and discuss all of this.

Nyaritis: - 'Well, dear, we're all here, I'd like you to tell us what's on your heart.': - He kindly asked. Martha told him again what kind of vision she had and that it must be some kind of sign, because she had never seen anything before like this so clearly.

Nyaritis: - 'Hmm! That's just interesting my dear! It's really not a dream, because you've never had a dream like this, to dream in advance what will happen! When did you have this vision?': - He asked curiously.

Martha: - 'Before we came to the wedding, it happened a week before.': - She answered thoughtfully.

Elisa: - 'This is very interesting! My son Robnis also started telling me at that time that something bad would happen to the guests coming here, but he couldn't explain it clearly.': - She interrupted.

Koldvir: - 'You didn't even tell me this until now, my dear!': - He said, surprised.

Elisa: - 'I didn't say because something always got in the way and It somehow left my mind, I'm sorry!'

Nyaritis: - 'Okay! This means something, the only question here is how can we track this down?': - He asked curiously.

Koldvir: - 'I have an idea!': - He interrupted firmly.

Erminus: - 'We are listening!': - He said curiously.

Koldvir: - 'Well then, join me, I'll take you to a place where even my own sons don't know about it, in fact no one but my advisor, so to speak.': - He said with a smile.

Erminus: - 'We will follow you, my friend, wherever you take us.': - He answered curiously. King Koldvir nodded, and the servant immediately spoke to the king's advisor.

Advisor: - 'Yes, my king, did you call me?': - He asked humbly.

Koldvir: - 'Yes, I called you, my friend! Now the time has come for what we have already discussed.': - He said firmly. Everyone looked at King Koldvir, but they didn't understand anything. Well, they started walking inside the palace, crossed many hallways until they reached a door that led them to the basement of the palace. When they set off on the hallway, they stopped again in front of a door, the advisor took out an interesting key and opened the door, they entered the great hall, which was perfectly decorated. Everyone looked around the room in surprise, there were lots of bookshelves lined up, it was equipped with small and large dividing walls where there were different laboratory rooms. They stopped at one of them, which was down the middle of the room, and walked in there. The advisor looked at King Koldvir and waited for him to give the signal, which the king did. The others didn't understand anything, they just watched what the outcome of this would be now. They didn't have to wait long, the advisor walked over to the table, carefully lifted the shroud and there in front of them was a glass structure connected to other glass tubes containing different liquids. There were six larger glass cups on the table that contained six different liquids, he lifted one of the greenish-yellow ones and poured it into a large cauldron. Everyone who was there stood around the table waited curiously to see what would happen. The advisor continued his work, after the liquid was in the cauldron, he then took out a dried frog's leg, a poisonous snake's tooth, an owl's eye, a rat's excrement and a raven's feather and threw them all into the cauldron and began to stir them, then he stirred it for a minute from which multicoloured smoke rose out of it, in which the world above appeared in front of them, where darkness reigned

436

everywhere and they could see the monsters of darkness, of course, the two palaces, which were completely protected against all of them. The next picture was that the goblins, fairies and magic mushrooms are preparing for war and how they clash with the monsters of the night. Then the colored smoke and the image disappeared.

Erminus: - 'This is incredible! I can't believe what you have been working on in secret down here!': - He said in awe.

Martha: - 'That's exactly what I saw in my vision, what you've all just witnessed here.': - She said bravely.

Koldvir: - 'Yes, it took a lot of work, but it's a useful little structure.': - He said with a smile.

Nyaritis: - 'What we saw here will happen tomorrow?': - He asked in amazement.

Koldvir: - 'Yes! This will happen tomorrow.': - He answered seriously.

Nyaritis: - 'Well, then we can only pray that nothing happens to the sphere we are in, because then we are all finished here.': - He said scared.

Koldvir:- 'You don't need to be afraid that we will be hurt, you should rather be afraid that the ones above won't get hurt!': - He interrupted.

Julia: - 'Wait a minute! What we saw here was magic, wasn't it?': - She asked her.

Koldvir: - 'Well yes, it was magic!': - He answered.

Julia: - 'Then I had an idea about how we could help them in the fight.': - She said firmly.

Koldvir: - 'How?': - He asked curiously.

Erminus: - 'Yes, how could we help from here?': - He asked

curiously.

Everyone focused their attention on Julia and waited curiously to see what she would come up with.

Julia: - 'Well, since you can create certain things with magic here in this room, I came up with the idea to create a lot of dragons here and now, because they can be useful in this kind of war and the goblins, fairies and mushrooms will also be grateful to us because of this.': - She explained the idea.

Koldvir: - 'Hmm! This is a really good idea, Julia! Cantos, did you hear what Juliet said, now you must see to it, that dragons are summoned!': - He ordered.

Counsellor's name Cantos: - 'I'm already on the task, Your Majesty!': - he answered with respect.

Koldvir: - 'Well, my friends, we have finished our work here, the rest of the tasks will be done by Cantos, which won't take long.': - He said firmly.

Elisa: - 'I have a question! If those dragons are ready, how will they get out to the evil witch's world, if we can't go out there either?': - She asked curiously.

Koldvir: - 'Well, I've been waiting for this question, that's why I have an answer! The dragons that Cantos summon are not assembled here but assembled there in the world of the evil witch, there is indeed a huge mountain where the dragons are born, the magic itself will take place in that cave and then the dragons can go to the aid of the fighters.

Elisa: - 'Ah! I understand now! I have no more questions.': - She answered with satisfaction.

Martha: - 'I have a question! How can you do magic, I thought you couldn't do it here?': - She asked curiously.

Koldvir: - 'Yes, I also thought that until we tried it with Cantos, and it worked, we just need to use the appropriate ancient magic items and that's it.': - He answered with a smile.

Nyaritis: - 'We are lucky that the evil witch doesn't look at us much, otherwise she would have already noticed this.': - He answered.

Koldvir: - 'That's right! She looked at us once and even then, she sent those giants to us. I was only able to go out to help because my courier immediately came to tell me that my two sons had gone into the forest to ensure the arrival of the guests, so we immediately came down here with Cantos and saw what would happen. to happen and when we saw this, I immediately went out with the army to help them. It's very lucky that we discovered it, otherwise we might have been dead by now.': - He replied dejectedly.

Erminus: - 'It's really good that you discovered this, my friend, I want to congratulate you, there's no doubt about it.': - He shook his hand enthusiastically.

Koldvir: - 'Thank you for the recognition, my friends, I also wanted the gathering here at my place because I wanted to show you this at all costs.': - He answered with a smile.

Nyaritis: - 'When will the dragons be ready?': - He asked curiously.

Koldvir: - 'Well, I think that while we were talking here, they are already ready, the only thing left is what is ready in any moment, so that they will attack tomorrow and also find out who needs to be exterminated.': - He answered consciously.

Nyaritis: - 'Well then, I think we can go back to the guests since they must have noticed that we are not there.': - He said laughing.

Koldvir: - 'That's right! Let's go back to have fun!': - He replied laughing.

With that, they went back to the fun, because the fun is not real without the kings. The big wedding lasted until almost five in the morning, by which time everyone was tired and sleepy, so everyone went back to their accommodation to rest from the fun.

A day Later....

Returning to the war, everyone fought as hard as they could. The magic mushrooms completely surrounded the evil witch's palace, because they were so small that the monsters didn't even notice them. When they had completely surrounded the palace, they began to murmur counter-spells to the people of the palace to release them from the spell.

The Magic of Magic Mushrooms:

Faciatum Escentus!

Hollars Spectium!

Accias Presitum!

Zeptis Vepius!

This is what the magic mushrooms kept muttering in the palace, it takes the mushrooms an hour to untie the charm, but in that one hour the witch was in action. James knew that he couldn't behave in front of the evil witch weirdly, which is why he held himself so that he wouldn't get caught. Before leaving his room, he took a deep breath and opened the door of the room, and finally went out. He saw that everyone was smiling, so he also started smiling non-stop, he played his part quite well. He arrived in the great hall where they used to have breakfast, but Miriam was not there.

He sat next to the Gilbert to find out where Miriam was.

James: - 'Good morning, Gilbert! We have a very nice day today! What good are we going to do today, have you figured it out yet?': - He asked with a smile.

Gilbert: - 'Good morning to you too James! I don't know yet, we'll discuss it after breakfast!': - He answered with a smile.

James: - 'Oh, that will be great, I can't wait!': - He tried to behave properly. They started eating their breakfast while the battle was in full swing outside the palace. John also took part in the fight because that was his request, but the goblins tried to somehow take care of him so that he wouldn't be killed.

John: - 'Ahh! Ahhh! I'm fine, you don't need to take care of me!': - He swung at the monsters with his sword.

Goblins: - 'We are not even looking after you!': - They shouted back.

John: - 'Watch out!!': - He warned one of the goblins and with that momentum he cut off the head of one of the monsters.

Goblin 1: - 'Thank you!!': - he thanked him.

John: -'You're welcome!' He replied with a smile.

Goblin 2: - 'This one is mine!': - He shouted.

John: - 'And this is mine!': - He shouted and quickly beheaded it. The fairies were trying to blind most of the monsters so they couldn't see anything, of course they didn't succeed in blinding all of them, but they did their job pretty well. They had already killed a lot of monsters, but somehow it seemed as if more and more were coming again and again, as if they didn't want to run out. When the situation seemed hopeless, the Goblins with waterpower suddenly appeared who did not want to participate in the fight. Everyone was surprised when they saw them and immediately, they were very happy. James and Gilbert finished

441

breakfast, they got up from the table and walked out into the garden.

James: - 'Gilbert! Where do you think Miriam is?': - He asked with a smile.

Gilbert: - 'I don't know where she is, but she must be busy as always!': - He answered with a smile.

James: - 'Gilbert, I'm going back to the palace because I forgot something in my room, go to that pagoda in the meantime, I'll come back with a surprise.': - He said smiling.

Gilbert: - 'Oh ! I like surprises, I'll wait for you there!': - He answered with a smile. James hurried back to the palace to find Miriam, he didn't have to search for a long time, because she was in the room where she kept the crystal and the sphere in which the rest of humanity was held captive. James crept up to the door and watched what Miriam was doing. Miriam had just raised the crystal and wanted everyone who fought outside to perish. When James saw this, he suddenly fell through the door and fell on Miriam, with that momentum the crystal fell out of Miriam's hand, but James somehow caught it and held the crystal in his hand.

Miriam: - 'James!! Give me back the crystal nicely!': - She asked carefully.

James: - 'Aaah! I will not give you this crystal again!': - He answered seriously.

Miriam: - 'Well, well! You're not under the spell!! What a surprise! May I know why you don't have the spell on you?': - She asked angrily. With that, she raised both hands and began to cast the spell on James once more, but to no avail.

James: - 'Hahah! This won't work anymore, you can't control me anymore, Miriam! The crystal is in my hands, and it will stay here, you will not get any more of it here and now, let all this suffering be enough.': - He said firmly.

442

Miriam: - 'This will only end if I say so!': - She replied angrily. With that, she raised her hand again and tried to take the crystal from James with her magic, which she almost succeeded, but James reached for it and the crystal finally fell to the ground and shattered into small pieces. As soon as this happened, the big light immediately went out and the many millions of small pieces rolled around and barely had any light.

Miriam: - 'What have you done, you stupid kid??': - She asked, looking at him angrily.

Meanwhile, the fight was not going very well, the monsters became more and more numerous, even though they were slaughtered, more simply came out of nowhere. Then dragons suddenly appeared in the sky and began to burn the monsters.

John: - 'Well, that's something!! Help has come, not just any kind of help!': - He shouted enthusiastically.

As long as the great battle was going on, the people living in the sphere did not notice any of this. After breakfast, the kings went back to their secret place again to see what was going on with the fight. Once again, everything was prepared in the cauldron to look into the current events and whether the dragons had successfully arrived.

Koldvir: - 'Well, as far as we can see, the dragons are there on the battlefield and they provide quite a lot of help to the fighters.': - He said excitedly.

Erminus: - 'Let's wait! Is that a person there?': - He asked in surprise.

Koldvir: - Yes! That man is James' father.': - He answered.

Erminus: - 'How is that possible? Where does he get his magic power from?': - He asked curiously.

Koldvir: - 'Well, the goblins helped him and the little magic mushrooms.': - He answered calmly.

Erminus: - 'I get it! But it seems quite dangerous for a human there, don't you guys think?': - He asked, surprised.

Koldvir: - 'Yes, it seems, but he is safe as you can see.': - He answered calmly. As soon as these lines were discussed, the kings, goblins, fairies and of course John fought very hard. They were in the middle of the fight when John was attacked by a monster twice as tall as John. The John was standing there in front of him, swinging his sword from one hand to the other, he took the attack position to protect himself from this huge monster, everyone else around him was busy killing monsters, so they couldn't pay attention to John at that very moment. The monster started walking towards John, he raised his big hand to strike John down. Miriam was very angry with James so much so that a black cloud appeared in the room. Miriam reached out and magically lifted James off the ground, holding him suspended in the air and guiding her hand to his neck. Gilbert couldn't imagine where James would stay for so long, so he went after him in the palace to look for him, he didn't have to look for long because the servants there immediately told Gilbert where to find James. Gilbert tried to get up in the room, as the charm was no longer affecting anyone, the little magic mushrooms took the spell off people, because of this everyone was terrified when they found out what the evil witch wanted to do with James. Gilbert reached Miriam's room very quickly and when he saw James suspended there in the air with his head bent back because Miriam was about to strangle her own son. He carefully entered the room and said:

Gilbert: - 'My love! Tell me, what are you doing? Why are you keeping James there?': - He asked the questions cautiously. Miriam was not herself, her eyes were bloodshot with hatred, and with a slow movement she turned her head towards Gilbert, looked him in the eyes and said in a changed voice:

Miriam: - 'You have nothing to do with this! You leave here right now, or I'll kill you too!': - She said in a deep distorted voice.

Gilbert: - 'Yes, I'm going! But don't forget, that there is our common child!': - He said cautiously. When he said this, she lifted James even higher and started squeezing his throat more. As James was suspended in the air, he still had enough strength to reach into his pocket and hold in his hands the little bottle he got from that blind old mage. When he had a good grip on the bottle, he said this to Miriam in a very raspy voice.

James: – 'My dear mother! I've already done everything to get here to you!'

I did my best to touch your soul!

I came to you to help you!

I am of your blood; you have looked after me and protected me!

You held me when I cried!

You kept me safe so I wouldn't get hurt!

I know that goodness and love lie deep in your heart!

I also know that you love me, because you wouldn't have accepted me in your house!

What you whispered in my ear when I was a baby, I'm telling you back now, mother!

You said that when the right time comes, the love in my heart will save you and I have to convince you of this at all costs!

That's why I tell you now my dear mother, if you kill me now, you will no longer have a successor, you will eradicate the fruit of your love forever, the light in your heart will go out and   you will lose everyone who has ever loved you.

Open your heart and let the light out because I love you very much!

I love the way you fought for me and my father, so that we could be together!

I will always love you my dear mother until my last breath!

I LOVE YOU MOTHER!

When James said these lines, tears flowed from his eyes and he opened the small bottle, at the end of his sentence he raised it and sprinkled the magic powder into her eyes. The light from the powder blinded Miriam so much so that she let James go, James fell to the ground and waited for its effect, he didn't have to wait long - his speech had an effect on her immediately, the magic dust was just an encore. The big black clouds disappeared, and Miriam rose into the air, both hands were spread out and a huge light came out of her heart, its light was so bright that it covered the whole country. The evil mushrooms that got into Miriam's ears died immediately, they couldn't escape, love was so powerful. When this happened, everything returned to its original place, the monsters of the night disappeared, the darkness disappeared, everything that was there before returned to its place.

Miriam: - 'My sweet son! Dear James! You really did it, I'm so proud of you James! I also really love you! I knew you would do it; you wouldn't leave it at that!': - She finally hugged and kissed her beloved son. Gilbert didn't go that far, so he quickly went back in the room to celebrate with his loved ones.

Gilbert: - 'Oh my God, James! I can't believe you finally made it! I'm very proud of you, you know that, right?': - Thank you.

Miriam: - 'I am very sorry that I strangled you so much, but I was not aware of what I was doing, please forgive me!': - She apologized while tears ran down her face.

James: - 'The point is that it's over and no one has to live in fear anymore.': - He said gratefully and in a rather hoarse voice.

James: - 'I think we should go and see how many wounded

people are out there.': - He said firmly.

Miriam: - 'That's a good idea my son!': - She held him by the shoulder, and they started walking out of the palace. When they got out of the palace, they walked around to see the wounded, unfortunately there were quite a lot of them. James specifically looked for his foster father among the wounded and dead. In the distance, he noticed a limping goblin who was walking towards James. James noticed it and started walking towards him, when he got there all he saw was that the goblin stopped and pointed to the east. James rushed there and his foster father lay on a pile of corpses.

James: - 'My father!! Come, let us help you enter the palace!': - He said in despair when he saw that he was wounded and covered with pure blood.

John: - 'Son!! But it's too late, you can't help me, I'm going to die! But I want you to always be as brave as you were today, never give up the fight no matter what!': - He said with a snort.

James: - 'No, no, no! This won't end here dad! Miriam do something, please? Use your magic power!': - He requested crying. Miriam couldn't do anything because it was too late. James knelt over John and watched him take his last breath and leave this world with tears streaming down his face. He put his arms around him and kissed his forehead and didn't let him go for a minute. Finally, the guards cleaned John in the palace and prepared him for the journey, although he had to be transported back to his world in England. Everyone was very happy that James finally reached his goal and defeated the evil mushrooms, there was a huge celebration. Evelin can finally marry her love, James.

Evelin: - 'You managed to break the crystal exactly as I dreamed, I am very proud of you!': - She said smiling.

James: - 'We finally managed to restore order, this is the most important thing, now we can go home, I'm sure they are already worried about us.': - He said with a smile.

Well, the big day came when everyone had to go back to their own homes in England, the big farewell took place and finally everyone returned home using a magic spell. James sat tightly next to John and did not him let go for a minute. When everyone was back at home, John and James were also home, James couldn't stop crying, he was very sad that his father died. But what James didn't know was that his father had actually only died in that world, in his own home, meaning England, there wasn't a scratch on him.

John: - 'Why are you crying so bitterly, my son?': - He asked with a smile.

James: - 'Because you died! What? You're alive? How?': - He asked in surprise.

John: - 'MAGIC!'

Everyone was really happy that they could finally return home, not so much for Oliver since he had to leave his love in the Boletus world. Back in the Boletus world, the people there were very grateful to James for giving them back their freedom and they can live their normal lives again without having to fear for a minute.

Gilbert: - 'Well my love!! Where did we leave off ??': - He asked with a mischievous smile.

Miriam: - 'Hmm! Let me think! I think we left off around here!!': - She jumped on her love with a big smile. For King Devilus the spell finally wore off and he began to behave and rule normally. The people were very grateful for this, to commemorate this day the stonemasons carved a monument for James so that everyone would remember this historic event.

Jessy regretted that Oliver had to go back, but she felt that if he

448

could come here once, he would be able to come back again. It really happened that way, Miriam made a passageway in their world so that they could visit each other at any time, so it was as if they had never left, everything remained the same, at least for them. The return of the children was also reported to the police, where everything was sorted out with a little white lie (the little white lie was James' magic). The headmistress of the school, Mrs. Hildred asked James to help her out with a little magic so that everyone would forget about this little absence with the students and teachers at the school, of course James agreed because that way no one had to explain to anyone where they went and why they were missing, so it was a win-win for everyone. The parents were very happy that they could finally be together again with their children, whom they had missed so much. They threw a big party together to celebrate their success.

On a beach in England, disappearances were being reported into the police which were also shown in the news.

James: - 'Evelin, come quickly and listen to what is being said on the news!........'

~

Written By L.M. Maya

Translated by Norbert Lengyel

Printed in Great Britain
by Amazon